WITHDRAWN

The Late Novels
of Eudora Welty

SANTA FE COMMUNITY COLLEGE
LIBRARY
3000 N. W. 83 STREET
GAINESVILLE, FL 32606

The Late Novels of Eudora Welty

Edited by Jan Nordby Gretlund
and Karl-Heinz Westarp

Foreword by
Reynolds Price

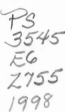
PS
3545
E6
Z755
1998

University of South Carolina Press

017000

All essays © 1998 by the University of South Carolina
Foreword © 1998 by Reynolds Price

Published in Columbia, South Carolina, by the
University of South Carolina Press
Manufactured in the United States of America
02 01 00 99 98 5 4 3 2 1

Library of Congress Cataloging-in-Publication Data

The late novels of Eudora Welty / edited by Jan Nordby Gretlund and
  Karl-Heinz Westarp ; foreword by Reynolds Price.
    p. cm.
  Includes bibliographical references (p.) and index.
  ISBN 1-57003-231-9
  1. Welty, Eudora, 1909–   —Criticism and interpretation.
  2. Women and literature–Southern States—History—20th century.
  I. Gretlund, Jan Nordby. II. Westarp, Karl-Heinz.
  PS3545.E6Z755 1998
  813'.52—dc21   97-33949

Contents

Foreword

A Useful Offer

Reynolds Price

Eudora Welty's blessedly long career has been regarded from many angles, some saner than others. This collection of studious looks at her late novels comes as a welcome—if overdue—aid to her readers, old and new, and to young writers in need of hope. What is perhaps not a salient fact to her academic critics, so formidably displayed here, may be useful to state—and to state in the voice of a fiction writer who has benefited from her work since his own adolescence some fifty years ago.

The happy result cannot have been a part of a plan that Welty conceived for her books as they came to her; but any contemporary discussion with three or more younger writers from the states of the Old Confederacy is likely to reveal that—far more than William Faulkner, the obsessively studied Male Heavy Ordnance of the region—Eudora Welty has served as an eminently useful transitional figure, a superbly excellent and benign guide, for the men and women who were reared like her in the South and whose special problem as apprentice writers has been the finding of true, yet authentically native, voices for the communication of their unique findings: findings which are nonetheless often variations upon or transformed echoes of the work of their Southern predecessors in narrative prose.

Faulkner, as a guide in narrative and emotional matters, can be followed nowhere but to Hell. His concerns are so intensely private, so fitfully illumined from within by a set of compulsions as tyrannical as Poe's, that he has proved to be of little use to another writer as currency (none of which denies his enormous gifts; it is only to state that he is not available as a surrogate parent). The same is true, if to a milder degree, of the novels of Warren and McCullers and the stories of O'Connor. Any young, or regrettably aging, writer who finds him- or herself employing any one of those writers' numerous angles or voices is sure to be arrested soon by a watchful reader in what amounts to virtual and lamentable impersonation.

Eudora Welty, though, and, to a lesser extent, her own predecessor Katherine Anne Porter are as distinct, as recognizable in every sentence, as their peers; yet through a so-far-undescribed clarity of language and vision, they have proven to be successful translators, virtual midwives for their successors. Their visions—especially the later Welty's in its withdrawn but unflinching yearning posture—have fertilized and encouraged a whole new generation of Southern-born novelists, novelists driven to speak their own fresh ancient news (which is, after all, the most that any writer achieves, at his or her height). And that rich service of Welty's shows no sign of abating in its power.

It was no idle remark, then, long years ago when the Texan William Goyen said to Frank Lyell, a friend of Miss Welty's and mine, that Welty was "the matrix of us all"; and in her deep and resounding late novels, above all else, that grave and courtly and generous hand—as potent as Virgil's—is still extended to reader and writer, a guide to both the threatening shades and the brilliant peaks of human life. Behind that hand lies a store of wisdom, a force of compassionate vision and memorable incantation, and a genius for craft that are second to none in American fiction. Its diffident offer can only be strengthened by these essays.

Abbreviations

Works cited in the text refer to the following editions:

C   Eudora Welty, *Conversations with Eudora Welty,* ed. Peggy W. Prenshaw (Jackson: University Press of Mississippi, 1984).

CS   Eudora Welty, *The Collected Stories of Eudora Welty* (New York: Harcourt Brace Jovanovich, 1980).

DW   Eudora Welty, *Delta Wedding* (New York: Harcourt Brace Jovanovich, 1946).

ES   Eudora Welty, *The Eye of the Story: Selected Essays and Reviews* (New York: Random House, 1978).

LB   Eudora Welty, *Losing Battles* (New York: Random House, 1970).

MC   Eudora Welty, *More Conversations with Eudora Welty,* ed. Peggy W. Prenshaw (Jackson: University Press of Mississippi, 1996).

O   Eudora Welty, *One Time, One Place: Mississippi in the Depression, A Snapshot Album* (New York: Random House, 1971).

OD   Eudora Welty, *The Optimist's Daughter* (New York: Random House, 1972).

OWB   Eudora Welty, *One Writer's Beginnings* (Cambridge, Mass.: Harvard University Press, 1984).

P   Eudora Welty, *Photographs* (Jackson: University Press of Mississippi, 1989).

PH   Eudora Welty, *The Ponder Heart* (New York: Harcourt, Brace, 1954).

RB   Eudora Welty, *The Robber Bridegroom* (Garden City, N.Y.: Doubleday, Doran, 1942).

Reading Eudora Welty's Late Novels

Jan Nordby Gretlund

Eudora Welty's reputation as an outstanding twentieth-century American writer is secure among professional critics and in the general public, both at home and abroad. It was no real surprise to anybody that President Clinton called Miss Welty on April 13, 1994, to congratulate her on her eighty-fifth birthday. The initial success of the Mississippi author was the result of her achievement in the genre of the short story, as demonstrated in the collections *A Curtain of Green, The Wide Net and Other Stories,* and *The Golden Apples,* published in the 1940s, and *The Bride of the Innisfallen* (1955), which were all gathered—with two new stories—as *Collected Stories* (1980). The majority of her short stories are set in the American South and reflect the language and culture of her region, but Welty's treatment of universal themes clearly transcends regional boundaries. While critics do not concur on all aspects of Welty's short stories, the preeminence of her work in this genre remains unquestioned.

Besides enjoying fame as a short story writer, Eudora Welty has also established her reputation as a critic. Her literary criticism has been collected in *The Eye of the Story: Selected Essays and Reviews* (1978) and in *A Writer's Eye: Collected Book Reviews* (1994). Welty is also a photographer. Since the 1930s she has taken photographs of her world, which resulted in several collections, e.g. *One Time, One Place* (1971; revised edition, 1996) and *Photographs* from 1989, with a selection of 226 prints. But Welty's greatest popular success came as a result of three mainly autobiographical lectures at Harvard University in 1983, which became the best-selling *One Writer's Beginnings.* It is a tribute to the author's superb style that the book stayed on the best-seller list for almost a full year. In short, her careers as a writer of short fiction, a critic and reviewer, a photographer, and an autobiographer have received much attention and deserved praise over the years, and Eudora Welty's name is still associated with these fields of interest. What is obviously missing from the enumeration of Welty's achievements is a mention of her career as a novelist!

Although Eudora Welty's novel-writing career started as early as 1942 with the publication of *The Robber Bridegroom,* her work in this area has not received the attention it merits from critics or the reading public. This is particularly true of her last two novels. Both *The Robber Bridegroom,* which brings together history and fairy tale, and her second novel, *Delta Wedding* (1946), which is in the tradition of the plantation novel, were upon publication compared negatively with her short fiction. But today the first novels are almost unanimously regarded as classics in their special genres. Similar recognition has not yet been given Welty's last two novels, which is the main motivating factor behind the publication of this volume. *Losing Battles* (1970) is an experiment in narrative technique that some readers could not finish and some critics found too episodic for a novel. *The Optimist's Daughter* (1972), though it won a Pulitzer Prize, was a disappointment in its apparent lack of action, and the novel has only recently begun to come into its own with the advent of the era of aggressive feminist criticism. For these reasons we invited eminent scholars to write new essays that focus on these two novels and encouraged them to contribute to the ongoing discussion of Welty's range and stature as a novelist.

As editors of *The Late Novels of Eudora Welty* we believe that the time has come to see Welty, the novelist, in international perspective. We see the late novels as her most exciting work both in innovative technique and postmodern existential statement. Not all Welty critics agree with us. Some consider Welty's late novels inferior to her short stories, and their opinions are reflected in the collection. The essays have been selected because they offer ideas that differ markedly from the traditional American, primarily Southern-based, criticism of Welty's work. We think, therefore, that these essays on the late novels are well suited to call attention to an often ignored aspect of Welty's genius.

The collection is framed by two essays. The first, by Michael Kreyling, appropriately sums up Welty's achievements as a novelist prior to the late novels. The last contribution to the collection is a forward-looking essay by Peggy Prenshaw. By focusing on gender issues and Welty's Southernness she gauges the state of Welty scholarship and indicates where it is heading.

Kreyling opens the collection by leading us into the subject with a historical approach to Welty's career as a novelist. First he places her in relation to the tradition of the Southern novel, as represented by Augusta Evans Wilson and Margaret Mitchell, and then he details the situation in Welty criticism today with an emphasis on Welty's novels. He considers the influence of Katherine Anne Porter on Welty as a novelist and ends by offering a reading of *Delta Wedding* that clearly shows how the novel in its modernism looks forward to Welty's late novels. It is with these novels that Welty becomes an international modernist writer. Under the influence of Virginia Woolf, she evades plot by "layering and juxtaposing frames of vision," uses autobiography as a shield, fragments the obligation to form and content, and writes an essentially symbolic narrative. In his wide-ranging opening essay Kreyling manages to introduce most of the topics in the collection.

In an encompassing effort Jane Hinton includes a consideration of the short novel *The Ponder Heart* (1954) in her broad essay on the late novels. She notes that Welty often writes of men who are seen lovingly through the consciousness of women. Welty's male characters tend to be optimistic and certain that the power of their love can save everybody. Her women tend to be more realistic. Surprisingly, Miss Julia's idea of progress in *Losing Battles* is seen as being fully compatible with Agrarian values and ideas, as it reflects the principle of realistic self-knowledge. In a final point Hinton emphasizes that the idea that life is to be celebrated, whatever our failures, is unflinchingly held to light by Welty. Her laughter of recognition and acceptance resounds throughout the novels. Hinton's essay looks forward to Sally Wolff's contribution to this collection.

The first part of the volume, which contains six essays on the often ignored *Losing Battles,* begins with an essay by Ruth Weston. She asks whether Welty ever was a true novelist, and in asking the question she contributes to the debate on the definition of the genre. She points out that Welty often merges the characteristics of the genres of the short story and the novel in a fruitful way, e.g. by the extensive use of lyricism and associative rhythms in her "epic novel" *Losing Battles.* In this way her novels are, on the one hand, "indelibly marked by elements of the short story" and deserve to be read closely. On the other hand, Weston concludes, the "novels" demonstrate enough essential, novelistic elements not to be short stories.

Richard Gray focuses on Welty's novels as novels and sees them as belonging in a great tradition. He argues that the Southernness of *Losing Battles* enables Welty to give us an understanding and "a more universally valid declaration of the extraordinary ways of words." In an extensive comparison with the novels of William Faulkner, especially with *Absalom,*

Absalom!, Gray points out that each tale belongs to a larger body of speech, "a continuum of storytelling." In an unending human debate, men and women struggle to weave an identity out of words, and the family re-union in *Losing Battles* fashions a web of words that constitutes the family identity. Gray emphasizes that both the literal and the metaphorical webs that compel our attention in that novel are expressions of communality and verifications of a sense of being and belonging.

What is the existential nature of the community that enjoys such a powerful sense of belonging in Welty's novel? By adducing a wealth of textual evidence from *Losing Battles* Karl-Heinz Westarp attempts to make us focus less on history and more on religion in Welty's late novels. He renders probable the assumption that it is "the business of fiction," in Flannery O'Connor's words, to "embody mystery through manners" and that this is true also of Welty's fiction. He argues that she is not only aware of the presence of holiness and mystery in the lives of the farmers, but also that evil and sin "loom large" in the novel. He finds that the English of the Bible permeates *Losing Battles* and that the biblical material seems to be second nature to Welty, and therefore should be considered carefully in any reading of the novel. He sees a move-ment toward harmony embedded in the very structure of the novel. The Vaughn-Beecham-Renfros' hope for a new beginning is a result of for-giveness. The movement in the novel is, it is argued, from evil and sin to forgiveness and good deeds. The essay concludes that Welty does allow us to sense mystery and peace beyond the experience of lost battles.

In his argument Westarp is in harmony with Bridget Smith Pieschel. In her essay she uses the parable of the Good Samaritan to show that Welty in *Losing Battles* ridicules the modern so-called "progressive" con-viction that salvation can be effected by a machine. Pieschel also brings in Flannery O'Connor's fiction by pointing out that this conviction was one of the Georgia writer's favorite targets for satirical comments. Miss Julia Mortimer, the schoolteacher, is the one who needs rescue, but her Good Samaritan arrives too late to do much good. The schoolteacher's flaw is that she puts all her love and faith in her own educational system. The biblical parable demands that the self be negated, but Welty's teacher can-not allow that and therefore must perish. Pieschel shows that the only real value of any machine in the novel resides in the humanity that can be projected onto it.

Sally Wolff continues Westarp's and Pieschel's discussions of Welty as a "religious" novelist. She argues that *Losing Battles* is a novel about "love of different kinds" and that the ambiguous, complex, and mysterious nature of love is at the heart of the novel, and indeed at the heart of all of Welty's fiction. Wolff believes that the novelist reaches deeper emotionally and philosophically in her late novels. In *Losing Battles* a young woman is judging the territorial boundaries of her private sphere within the family. The dispute between loyalty to the family and the need for privacy—the tension between private relations and societal obligations—is always a central concern in her fiction. Welty seems to say, it is maintained, that familial and social influence on love is essential in supporting a love relationship.

Darlene Unrue is curious about Katherine Anne Porter's importance for Welty's development as a novelist. *Losing Battles* and Porter's *Ship of Fools* seem to be very different novels, yet Unrue's comparison demonstrates that they have much in common. They both failed to fulfill current artistic expectations and insisted on art's freedom from prevailing definitions by introducing new ideas of what a novel can be. Both novelists focus on character rather than plot, introduce multiple episodes reminiscent of short fiction in a symphonic structure, and both consider dialogue an important tool. They write much about love, and its absence, but without sentimentality. Homer is seen as an influence on their modern renderings of age-old topics. Unrue points out that *Ship of Fools* is a modern *Odyssey*, whereas *Losing Battles* is an epic of kinship in the tradition of the *Iliad*. Both novels represent a quest and a confrontation with history. The epic-like figurative language startles and serves as an agent of comedy and satire. Unrue argues that Porter's and Welty's use of Homer by appropriation of themes, patterns, language, and techniques represents a modernist posture.

The second half of the volume is devoted to *The Optimist's Daughter*. In a continuation of the essays relating Eudora Welty's work in the novel to that of William Faulkner, Flannery O'Connor, and Katherine Anne Porter, Patrick Samway writes about the relationship between Eudora Welty and Walker Percy. Her appreciation of his novels is above all focused on his attention to the mysterious and comic in human nature. It is also possible to read Welty's comments on Percy's achievement as reflections on the creative writer's task and as comments on her own work. This is especially true of her comments on the concept of "home." The essay offers Percy's thoughts on Welty's relationship with her native town. Her fellow novelist was, it seems, fascinated with the plain, yet illusive, manner in which Welty can depict place and home. Samway applies Percy's insight to *The Optimist's Daughter*, where family- and place-names are clues "that something resembling sleight-of-hand" is happening.

Just how this novelistic "sleight-of-hand" came about is the subject of Hans H. Skei's essay. He considers *The Optimist's Daughter* a novel in the tradition of the well-made novel. He asks how the work achieves its meaning, and just what that meaning is. The novel is serious in "a self-conscious way that almost undermines its own seriousness and honesty," it is postulated. The whole narrative is informed by a juxtaposition of civilized, correct living and teeming, utterly shameless living. Ironies arise when we are forced to question the values and judgments of the narrator. The Norwegian critic points out that the monologic narrative is questioned by the implied author, who is not necessarily in agreement with the narrator. The narrator pretends to be more open than she is. Welty's narrative manages to create doubts about the very values it defends, which, according to Skei, is no mean achievement.

The idea of a juxtaposition between expected and unexpected behavior in *The Optimist's Daughter* is also brought up by Mary Ann Wimsatt, who writes about the main character's thoughts on the past and the present. Wimsatt sees Welty's preoccupation with the role of memory and an understanding of the past as an expression of one of the primary concerns of the Southern Renascence. In *The Optimist's Daughter* the poor-white stepmother attempts to deny a past objectified by a closely knit, class-conscious community, in which she is not accepted. The portrait of the town, with its gossipy insularity, is seen as gently ironic criticism. Mount Salus, with all its aspects of settled Southern town life, is defined through its counterpoint in the novel, which comprises characteristics associated with life in West Virginia, such as isolation, independence, self-reliance, and freedom. Welty portrays the small-town South deftly, it is argued, "more deftly, perhaps, than any other Southern Renascence author." At the end of the novel the central character attains an understanding of the past, the town, her family, and herself. As Wimsatt sees her, the optimist's daughter can leave her hometown and feel relieved of the painful burden of the past.

Marion Montgomery is, like Mary Ann Wimsatt, interested in Welty's thoughts on our use of memory. He points out that the novelist in her fiction explores the mystery of creating, or "making," and its relation to memory. He reflects on correspondences between Saint Augustine's, T. S. Eliot's, and Eudora Welty's ideas of personhood. The issue in *The Optimist's Daughter* is not really to remember a personal history, he writes, but the recovery of a personhood. Our past and present are inescapably entangled, and at any present moment the past is "an existential reality." How this happens is finally a mystery, hardly reducible to formulae, Montgomery claims, and in this argument we hear echoes of the essays by Westarp,

Pieschel, and Wolff. What begins to stir in the main character at the end of the novel, Montgomery says, is love and acceptance.

It is Welty's "existential reality," in fact and fiction, that is the subject of the essay "Component Parts: The Novelist as Autobiographer." Welty's greatest popular success, the autobiographical *One Writer's Beginnings,* is often read as a companion volume to *The Optimist's Daughter.* Is the successful autobiography a result of an extensive use of novelistic techniques? It is suggested that we see the fiction in a biography in which Welty becomes her own inventor and the emplotter of her own past. The component parts of the biography reflect those of the novels, and, it is argued, the imagination of the novelist fictionalizes, distorts, and compensates freely in her memoir. But whereas the biographical book is unreliable as information about Welty's life, it is a reliable guide to the art of the novelist.

In the concluding essay, which helps frame the collection, Peggy W. Prenshaw discusses recent developments in Welty criticism. She also argues the importance of *One Writer's Beginnings* for an understanding of the late novels because parents, home, town, and region went into the making of the novelist. She notes that what Welty ultimately means by "place" is the whole world of the experience that she brings to her art. As an artist she was created by this world, linked lovingly to it, embraced, and sheltered by it. In her fiction she first deconstructs her region and then reconstructs it. Her South was never the plantation South but, as the novels show, a region of matriarchs, teachers, and preachers. A confluence of imagined and formalized tensions between her place and the world becomes a central strain in the novels. In her cultural imagination authorship is attached not only to region but also to gender, for much stereotyping of gender roles was common during the author's childhood. Her Agrarian friends may not have noted, Prenshaw suggests, how "the South" is essentially a metaphor for "female" in her fiction. Her native land, as we see it in the late novels, is clearly a woman's world. Welty has been able to take the South of the Agrarians, Prenshaw demonstrates, and make it reflect her world of female experience.

As the history of Southern literature documents, it is, in order to apprehend the South and be nourished and sustained by it imaginatively, not enough to be able to see beyond the region. A journey of self-discovery is required in order to gain the necessary distance and vision, and Welty's two late novels triumphantly constitute such a journey from the discovery of her place to self-discovery and vision.

The editors of this volume are convinced that Welty's late novels have not yet received the acclaim they merit, and we have planned the collection of critical essays as one way of giving Welty's two late novels their due. The fourteen contributors include a group of well-established, experienced American critics, a few new names in Welty criticism, and four European South-watchers. We believe that our various readings of the novels, in a context of Southern literature and literature in general, substantiate our claim that Welty's late novels deserve broad critical and public attention. We hope that the foreword by Reynolds Price and these new essays will stimulate interest in her fiction and serve as a helpful tool in reading and teaching the late novels of Eudora Welty.

The Late Novels
of Eudora Welty

Introductory Essays

Eudora Welty as Novelist

A Historical Approach
Michael Kreyling

In the second interview in *Conversations with Eudora Welty* ("The Artist and the Critic: Millsaps College Symposium/1960"), Professor George Boyd utters the words "Edna Earle," the name of the garrulous heroine of *The Ponder Heart*. Like many Southerners, he had gone to school with a girl who bore that name, but he did not know where the name originated. His wife had to tell him Edna Earle is the name of the heroine of Augusta Evans Wilson's best-selling novel of 1866, *St. Elmo,* the *Gone with the Wind* of the previous century.

George Boyd hastens to add that he is not so old as to know the original. "It's before [my time] too," Welty answers. She continues: "Well, I had so many letters from people all over the country whose names *were* Edna Earle, and they said where in the world did you get hold of my unusual name? And so I wrote some of them back and said you were named after Edna Earle in *Saint Elmo,* which I never read, but I know she's supposed to be the epitome of virtue, and a whole generation of people were named after her" (C, 8).

Almost twenty-five years later, in *One Writer's Beginnings* (1984), Wilson's novel and her "epitome of virtue" reappear. In the first part of her memoir, "Listening," Welty remembers what she read and heard that seems to have pushed her onward to the life of the writer. There were books and poems and songs and storytelling; but, she insists, "*St. Elmo* was not in our house. . . ." After disavowing any first-hand knowledge of the novel, Welty then gives a thumbnail synopsis of the plot (C, 7): virtuous young woman overcomes notorious roué by the sheer stamina of her moral and intellectual character, then marries him. Like all synopses, Welty's is a little fast and loose. *St. Elmo* goes on and on for hundreds of pages, exhausting even the heroine, who does not so much capture the roué as collapse into his arms a few pages from the end. She is out cold for two hours before the sun sets in the west, and tears solemnly consecrate the union of the roué-turned-clergyman and the epitome of virtue. The original Edna Earle could have said with her namesake in *The Ponder Heart:* It took a lot out of me, being smart—and pure and proud and vigilant and resourceful.

It is not my intention to draw an itinerary of the tedious plot of Wilson's novel and map it upon *The Ponder Heart,* hoping to prove by circumstantial evidence that Welty did know *St. Elmo.* Wilson's novel, like *Gone with the Wind,* is one of those books one can "know" without ever having read it. Instead, I want to focus on how and why a modern novelist (so thoroughly "modernist," as you will see in the essays that follow, as to be unthinkable before Chekhov and Joyce and Woolf) would consistently disavow a precursor novel and its author, yet use their narrative "strategies" in her own work—not only consciously and satirically, as in *The Ponder Heart,* but surreptitiously and guardedly, as in her first published novel, *Delta Wedding.* I am aimed, like Ruth Weston in her essay on Welty as "lyric novelist," at the issue of genre: What did Eudora think when she thought "novel" or "me-as-novelist?" She is cagey in her own comments. Recently, in an interview with Sally Wolff (1988), Welty shades the distinction between novel and "long short story" in the case of *The Optimist's Daughter* (MC, 164). Deflecting the direct question is not atypical of Welty. She similarly deflects *St. Elmo,* yet seems to know all that is significant about it. I think it worthwhile to be interested in the kind of novel *St. Elmo* is, in the kind of literary precursor we can understand it to have been for a white Southern woman writer of modernist leanings in the twentieth century, and in how its specific and generic literary qualities (direct rather than oblique, preachy rather than suggestive, prolix rather than deftly balanced) are nevertheless fused to Welty's novels like the albatross around the neck of the ancient mariner.

As firmly ensconced in the canon of Southern literature as Welty is (and Mary Ann Wimsatt makes the case persuasively in her essay on *The Optimist's Daughter*), her reputation is most often rendered ahistorically. A case in point is Richard Gray's essay on *Losing Battles,* an essay arguing that universal elements thought to be embedded in words and storytelling constitute Welty's "Southernness." These universals raise her above mere history and establish her credentials as artist and Southerner. Often a related argument is made on the basis of thematics; Sally Wolff argues in her essay that the universal "love" identifies Welty in her work. Arguments in this direction are difficult to resist. Welty has written only a few "historical" pieces. Some of the Natchez Trace stories in *The Wide Net* are intentional "Mississippi" stories. "The Burning" is an exercise in the Faulknerian South. *The Robber Bridegroom* is, frankly, more akin to an animated Disney feature (Welty and her friend John Robinson, in fact, tried to sell an adaptation to Disney in the 1940s) than to the actual history of the Natchez Trace. Calling it "not a *historical* historical novel" (in her essay "Fairy Tale of the Natchez Trace"), Welty admits that simple history is not enough for any of her work and deflects yet again demands that her fiction answer to empirical corroboration. Those of us who have written about her work have had a devil of a time tracing the outlines, latent or manifest, of history in anything she has written.

Most of the critical work is thematically based, like Gail Mortimer's *Daughter of the Swan: Love and Knowledge in Eudora Welty's Fiction* (1994) and Rebecca Mark's *The Dragon's Blood: Feminist Intertextuality in Eudora Welty's* The Golden Apples (1994). Both recent studies take motives from *The Golden Apples* and build upon them toward a summary statement about what Welty's fiction teaches. Studies of her literary technique (my own *Eudora Welty's Achievement of Order*, 1979, is as useful an example as any) also seem to abound.

Jan Nordby Gretlund's *Eudora Welty's Aesthetics of Place* (1997) attempts to describe the poetics that knit Welty's fiction to Southern "place," viewed through the lens ground by the Agrarians. "Place," though, can sometimes be the opposite of history, especially in the hands of the Agrarians: a set of immaculate and unchanging conditions, often synonymous with "The South" but not necessarily so. I confess I do not expect any of us to have much luck with a Southern novelist who looked upon Sherman's burning of Jackson, Mississippi, her own hometown, as a wonderful opportunity for "a fresh start."[1] If Welty is a Southern novelist, then the two identifying labels (Southern and novelist) sometimes mesh and sometimes grate.

We are impoverished in not having a critical mass of work that attempts to tell us what kind of novel (understood as an evolving genre encountered in a specific moment) Welty thought she was writing, where it came from, and how it occupies literary history. Albert Devlin's work *Eudora Welty's Chronicle: A Story of Mississippi Life* (1983) attempts to trace the lineaments of a distinctive Welty vision in the historical genre of "the plantation novel," begun in the antebellum South and picked up by Welty a little over a century later. Devlin sees the historical genre as the key to Welty's "Southern Aesthetic." Welty, he argues, tackles the social and cultural changes of the early twentieth century with the form of the nineteenth, thus energizing both. To arrive at this claim, though, Devlin must—for example—trim important significance from the character of Ellen Fairchild, seeing her only in the company of predecessor plantation mistresses. No doubt she can be taken this way, but the single direction of Devlin's comparison cannot account for important aspects of her meaning in the novel. In short, the reference point of historical subject matter alone does not seem to me to provide enough room for this exploration. What is needed is a kind of historicized understanding of novel-as-genre.

Let me attempt to historicize the novel as genre in Welty's case. In "Introduction to Part II" of *The History of Southern Literature* (1985), Rayburn S. Moore succinctly states that in spite of the devastation of the Civil War, Southern literature survived in a recognizable form: "Interest in the community, the land and the people in it—the poor white and the black man as well as the planter—and the language of all levels not only characterizes the writing of the period [1861–1920] but suggests ties with the past of Simms and Longstreet and also looks forward to the work of Faulkner, Wolfe, Warren, and Welty." Moore has no room for details, but his suggestion that Welty is at one extreme of a long historical reach deserves more exploration. Later in Part II of *The History* a historical exploration with more credibility does appear. Guess whose name comes along with it? In "Varieties of Local Color," Merrill Maguire Skaggs rounds up the usual suspects, thrice-named authors—male and female—of this or that Southern backwater. It is a less-than-memorable roll call, with one exception. Skaggs sees Augusta Evans Wilson as the rare local colorist who "generated surprises." And Wilson, Skaggs argues, surprises us in novels such as *St. Elmo, Macaria,* and *Beulah* because of her heroines: independent women with "ambitions and capabilities" who often express their "extreme bitterness at society's habit of judging women strictly by the beauty of their faces." "Dependence" is a fighting word to Wilson's Edna Earle and her sisters; they struggle through long plots—predictable and tedious to the last comma—not toward "love" (although they have to win it on the last page to sell the story at all—a lesson no more vividly illustrated than in Louisa May Alcott's *Little Women*) but toward "emotional, intellectual, and economic independence." Novels such as *St. Elmo* "say" less about historical circumstances—in a Southern context—than they do about the cultural and psychological conditions of being female in unconventional ways, and wanting to write about it.

Perhaps Welty disavows *St. Elmo* and Wilson as precursors, not because she does not know the works and the buried tensions they dramatize, but because she knows them only too well. Just as Wilson's novels balance precariously between the historical/social matter of the American South and the subject matter of gender self-representation and cultural power, so do Welty's. Welty has repeatedly deflected any and all attempts to be drawn into political and ideological discussions. Read, for one example among many, her responses to Barbara Diamondstein's questionnaire reprinted in Peggy Prenshaw's *Conversations*. Welty's personal predisposition to steer away from the politics of literature might serve as a paradoxical indicator that, on the level of imagination, she knows full well that literature is political and that the novel is the most political form of all.

Many writers protect themselves and their work by such disavowals, but that does not stop ideology from seeping into aesthetic productions. The politics and ideology Welty did not "want" were carried by precursor novels in the narrative form Wilson used. Welty eventually came to burlesque that form in *The Ponder Heart*, but that does not mean that she had not found other uses for it in earlier work.

Nina Baym, in *Woman's Fiction: A Guide to Novels by and about Women in America, 1820–1870,* is a reliable eye to the interweaving of ideology and form in the kind of novel Welty insists she did not have in the house: Women's fiction works are "written by women, [are] addressed to women, and tell one particular story about women. They chronicle the 'trials and triumph' (as the subtitle of one example reads) of a heroine who, beset with hardships, finds within herself the qualities of intelligence, will, resourcefulness, and courage sufficient to overcome them." This fiction has been undervalued, Baym argues, because most reviewers and scholars were not of the community to whom it was addressed. Such novels as *St. Elmo,* therefore, were relegated to "a subliterary or quasi-literary genre": women's fiction, the sentimental novel, etc.[2] Contemporary critics might have been sharp enough to gather in the "manners" and fabric of social history, but they were deaf to the "significance" the stories repeated in and through structured form. They were not (or could not risk being) literate in the ideological implications of form.

That is not the case in the 1990s. Elizabeth Fox-Genovese, in her introduction to Wilson's novel *Beulah* (1859; reprinted, 1992), extends Baym's view by giving us a more detailed outline of the form of the typical woman's novel and a glimpse at its ideological "significance." You start with a "not-too-pretty child about ten years old," preferably a girl. Then you kill off the mother, kindly, if she is not already in the hereafter. You should dispose of the father too, either by death or irretrievable absence. If you allow daddy to stay, he is almost always "married to a shallow, fashionable woman." A good surrogate mother is hampered by tuberculosis or some other set of negative circumstances that leave the way open for a wicked stepmother—a Mrs. Danvers. As the good stepmother wanes in influence, a brooding Byronic man enters to menace the heroine. Initially she refuses him; he sulks. His attentions are accelerated; she still refuses. He departs; she proves herself independent, self-reliant, correct in trusting her own virtue and talent. He returns; she sees that NOW a marriage is possible. She submits. End of novel.[3]

This plot has a long life and great popularity. After such a synopsis one can easily see that an actual word-by-word reading of a specific novel is not necessary. One can "know" *St. Elmo* by reading *Rebecca* or *Jane Eyre* or *Little Women* or *Gone with the Wind.* As Fox-Genovese points out in her analysis of the character Beulah, the plot (as aesthetic "device" or form) is not as important as such particular issues as woman's proper intellectual sphere, her social place, her work—in short, gender—which are presented embedded in form.

It is interesting to consider how closely this standard formula describes in general terms the plots of *The Optimist's Daughter* and *The Ponder Heart,* and in more distanced terms the plot of *Delta Wedding.* The similarity suggests as well that the author has/had a stake in the issues embedded in novelistic plot. It would have been creative death, though, for a literary modernist (which is what Eudora Welty is) to embrace this plot without deflection. We know how the modernist foremother Virginia Woolf coped with the complex ideological and aesthetic claims of the English novel as she confronted it; using Joseph Frank's work in *The Idea of Spatial Form* (1991), we can see how Woolf "spatialized" plot that had been "naturally" linear and logical, how she fragmented the narrative consciousness that had been seen as "naturally" unified. How did issues of plot, literary influence, Southern identity, and literary modernism shape the ways Eudora Welty became a novelist?

The story of Eudora Welty's getting started in the literary life is relevant to these questions; her preference for the short story and resistance to the novel touches them as well. Having short stories accepted in non-paying quarterlies and university-based journals was apparently not much of a problem for the young writer. Having collections of her short stories published as books was another matter. When an unknown Eudora Welty sent and personally took her stories to the offices of publishers in New York, she was greeted with polite but recurrent rejection. The refrain was: your stories are very accomplished, BUT do you have a novel we might read? Welty had entered the empirical economics of publishing—not the same as "literature." As one editor explained to the young writer, readers were willing to pay two or three dollars for a novel but expected to get their short fiction in magazines for much less. No publisher, then, was willing to invest in a product for which there was little chance of return.

Welty also sensed the politics of her situation. The novel was the grown-up, masculine form; short stories were for lesser talents. She had identified with the short story. For her it had, as form, a "logic" and organic process that the novel foreclosed. The correspondence between Welty and her friend and literary agent Diarmuid Russell is filled with discussion of the ideal form of the short story. Russell tended to prefer an Aristotelian form, a form that could be logically analyzed and explained. Welty was otherwise inclined. Their differences became acute over the story "The Winds." In writing this story Welty had gone further than ever before beyond the logically clean and well-lighted processes of earlier work. Russell was puzzled by "The Winds," and Welty tried to explain as much of her technique as she understood at the moment: "It occurs to me that you write stories by one of two methods, just as you can think by one of the two, inductive and deductive—you sum up or conclude your story from all that you find and are able to relate of it, or you start out with a generality and it fills itself in—and this is the first time I have ever tried the inductive" (March 21, 1941).[4] As subsequent stories, including "The Delta Cousins"—from which *Delta Wedding* grew—became longer, the discrepancies between "summing up" and letting the story fill itself in became more and more problematic. A broker was needed to get Welty from what she could do to what she must do in order to become a novelist.

The novel had plot, dealt with issues, required summing up and concluding, and demanded that the author know the destination before embarking. There was politics *in* the novel as well as the politics *of* the novel. The latter meant overcoming conventional plot of the proportionless, relentless type that *St. Elmo* represented. The former meant satisfying the conventional need for issues and themes. Wilson had solved the problem simply: by having her characters talk about issues on every page; there is never a doubt as to what *St. Elmo* is about. A modernist could not operate by that set of rules.

Welty had seen this tangle frustrate and block her friend and mentor, Katherine Anne Porter, when the two were at Yaddo together in the summer of 1941. Porter had begun what was to be published, twenty years later, as *Ship of Fools*. At the writers' colony Welty could see firsthand how the political atmosphere had taken over from Porter's creative imagination. Welty saw her own work being searched for latent political content. She wrote to her agent:

> Do you realize that it ["First Love"] might be interpreted as profascist, poor Aaron Burr's unexplained little dream, that I meant to be only a symbol of what everyone has—some mar-

velous sway and magnetism that it can give—It is stupid and wild, but that is the way people seem to be thinking, every-thing is dynamite, suspicious. Even KAP, who wants us to enter the war instantly, sees fascism in everything she doesn't like, and while it may be a very intricate insight into deep relation-ships, I still hate that fever to creep into what we think of books or music, because eventually it will leave nothing to be itself . . . (June 26, 1941; Kreyling, *Author and Agent,* 76).

The younger Welty had great admiration for Porter's dedication to the form of the short story; indeed, Porter was the model of the artist who resisted a market clamoring for "the novel" and stuck to art. When, how-ever, Porter did dedicate herself to the novel, Welty implies, political contagion necessarily came along, forcing the author into political con-texts that were, to say the least, uncomfortable.

Ironically, the pupil was to finish and publish a novel before the teacher. *Delta Wedding* was published in 1946, while Porter was still drifting with *Ship of Fools.* The psychological politics of this situation also contributed to Welty's unease with the novel as a genre and with herself as novelist. When Welty was leaving San Francisco (1947) for home, she floated out to Porter, who was then in Hollywood, the possibility of a visit on her way east. Ambiguous signals came back, and Diarmuid Russell put his finger on a possible explanation:

> I think KAP is a little miffed. Her own novel has been talked about so much and there you are, in a sense her protégé she feels probably, who has had the impudence to bring out a novel first, almost going behind her back (January 31, 1947; Kreyling, *Author and Agent,* 124).

Novels, it seems, caused nothing but misery—personal and political.

The cornerstone of her relationship with her agent was that he would not take part in the political rally in favor of the novel. This relationship had always personalized and intensified the question of the novel for Welty. In one of her earliest letters to Russell, she pleaded: "Please do not tell me that I will have to write a novel. I do not see why if you enjoy writing short stories and cannot even think in the form of a novel you should be driven away from it and made to slave at something you do not like and do badly" (June 10, 1940; Kreyling, *Author and Agent,* 34). The pressure must have been considerably intense to cause a Mississippi writer to use the analogy of slavery to convey her resistance to "the form of a novel." On one side she faced psychological and cultural barriers; she had to find ways to negotiate around her trusted agent, friend, and mentor. On the other side was the problem of reconciling a personal, "inductive" creative process with the inescapable claims of the long prose form to be about something.

Welty has been, by consensus, identified as one of the first modernists of American literature, a writer whose distinctive imagination has produced works in intricate ways distinctly feminist. Darlene Unrue, in this collection, routes this thesis through the "influence" of Porter on Welty. Louise Westling, in *Sacred Groves and Ravaged Gardens* (1985), positions Virginia Woolf at the crossroads of Welty's growth as a novelist. In Westling's view, this case of influence has much to do with feminist ideology, but comparatively little to do with history: "Virginia Woolf's feminism in particular is so central to her entire creative life that it is difficult to imagine Welty's failing to respond to it. As we explore the elements of *To the Lighthouse* which reappear in *Delta Wedding*, we shall begin to see how only another woman could have helped Welty develop the celebration of distinctly feminine fertility and community which existed merely as germs in 'The Delta Cousins' [the earlier version of *Delta Wedding*]."[5]

I also think Woolf is significantly responsible for the breakthrough to the novel in Welty's writing career. She was the broker Welty needed for *Delta Wedding*. But I do not think that Woolf was the only "other woman" or that the answer to the problem of the novel lay in finding feminine utopia as subject matter. Welty already had another woman breathing down her neck with feminist material, but it was embedded in the "antiquated" Wilsonian plot that she could not use. What she needed was a form, a new poetics of plot; she was less in need of a myth of female community.

When Welty approached the writing that became *Delta Wedding*, she had already decided that traditional plot was a burden she would not carry. She chose the year 1923 for the time frame of her novel, not because the paucity of events of historical significance in that year made it easier for her to accomplish the "pastoral" end of the project (the "celebration of distinctly feminine fertility and community"), although no doubt the uneventfulness of that year helped to that end. She chose a comparatively uneventful year because that time frame would excuse her from the obligations of plot—of accounting for the whereabouts of her characters with respect to a flood, a war, an election, etc. It was not historical representation she was after, although there was a compulsory minimum she had to achieve. The historical realism of *Delta Wedding* comes in large, inert blocks: catalog descriptions of rooms, stores, garden plots. The action and interaction come not in linear or sequential accumulation (concluding and summing up), but in spatialized association (filling in).

Welty found in reviewing Woolf's *A Haunted House and Other Stories* (1944) that chronological plot was not essential to the completion of a novel. Reading Woolf's short story "An Unwritten Novel" for the *New York Times Book Review,* Welty found the guidance she needed. It came in the spring of 1944, just as she was deeply into the process of turning the Delta "stuff" into *Delta Wedding.* She wrote of Woolf's prose: "In the experience of observing, the observer is herself observed, her deft plunges into another's obscure background become reachings into her own hidden future, error makes and cancels error, until identification between the characters examined and the writer examining seems fluid, electric, passing back and forth" (*NYTBR,* 16 April 1944, 3). This is not an enabling insight into ways of moving action along a line, of completing a block of dialogue so as to do justice to an "issue." It is a way of arranging a mass of associations within a frame.

Welty-as-novelist presents to us, as she did to the reviewers who tried to place her in some current novelistic context, a problem in disentangling—if that is possible or desirable—elements from two very different ways of seeing and telling. The *St. Elmo* way of telling submits to history, as Edna Earle herself eventually submits to the inevitable St. Elmo Murray. Woolf's example provided a way out of the inevitability of plot, enslavement to the novel as it was conventionally seen. Although Welty-as-novelist was interested in Wilsonian issues, the form was off-limits. What Woolf provided was a "fluidity" to counter Wilson's inert construction, a poetics of seeing rather than of saying, and a way to break down the unification of point of view that enforced separation between character and character, character and narrator. How would we begin to unwrap the historical from the aesthetic in *Delta Wedding,* Wilson from Woolf?

Let us revisit the boiled-down plot summary that Fox-Genovese extracts from earlier sources. The cast of *Delta Wedding* is headed by an orphan, Laura McRaven, whose own living father is kept in the shadowy background of Jackson while his daughter attends the wedding of his deceased wife's niece. There is a kindly surrogate mother, Ellen Fairchild; if she is not clinically sickly, she is nevertheless preoccupied with her health. She is pregnant for the tenth time as the action of the novel progresses. There is no obvious wicked stepmother, although Aunt Tempe sometimes seems to fit the bill. The chorus of maiden aunts also seems apt for the function.

The Byronic George Fairchild is not targeted on Laura (although she has a strong and quasi-sexual attraction to him) but rather at several of the women in the novel who are attracted to him. Ellen, mother of nine and George's sister-in-law, is nevertheless powerfully moved by his erotic presence. As she watches him nap, she indulges in a kind of fantasy: "In the darkened room his hair and all looked dark—turbulent and dark, almost Spanish. Spanish! She looked at him tenderly to have thought of such a far-fetched thing, and went out" (*DW*, 50–51). "Far-fetched" such a momentary fantasy might seem to a woman who is a little swamped by the events swirling around her, and by her near-total submersion in fertility. Ellen's voyeuristic moment, however, fulfills the demands of the pattern of George's attractive Byronism. George himself plays upon his "image" as sexual predator. When Ellen tells him she had surprisingly met a strange white girl in the woods, George replies that he had encountered her as well: "Yes, and I took her over to old Argyle gin and slept with her, Ellen . . ." (*DW*, 79). This is alleged to be what heroines of Edna Earle's type both desire and fear. Through such camouflaged departures from the typical, Welty acknowledges the presence of the Wilsonian hero. She could not, except in parody, have gotten away with Wilson's high-octane St. Elmo Murray: "A stranger looking upon St. Elmo Murray for the first time, as he paced the floor, would have found it difficult to realize that only thirty-four years had ploughed those deep, rugged lines in his swarthy and colourless but still handsome face, where midnight orgies and habitual excesses had left their unmistakable plague-spot, and Mephistopheles had stamped his signet."[6]

St. Elmo does account for more of *Delta Wedding* than the author might want to admit. St. Elmo is twice the age of Edna Earle: he is nearly twenty-seven when twelve-year-old Edna Earle first sees him. The age rupture between woman and man adds spicy taboo to the familiar plot—Rhett is twice Scarlett's age; Maxim de Winter is at least twice the age of the second Mrs. de Winter; and Troy Flavin is exactly twice Dabney's age (*DW*, 31). Welty "borrows" the plot units but distributes them spatially among several of her many characters so as to break down the monolithic "novel" bearing down on her from Wilson and her "tradition."

St. Elmo first erupts into the orphaned Edna Earle's life through a duel; the young girl sees his bloody victim. The ideological significance in this plot unit is that male presence means violence. That violence might be randomly directed as part of conventional male character; or, it might be symbolically directed at the woman. Wilson's Edna Earle, for example, fears the latent power of St. Elmo; the suspense of *Rebecca* is that the second Mrs. de Winter comes to fear that she might be a target for murder; Scarlett is deliciously attracted to the powerful shoulders and brutal ways of Rhett Butler. The linking of violence and the conventionally heterosexual male is one of the repeated motives in the patterned narrative structure of *Delta Wedding*, often relegated critically to neglect behind the more celebrated formal functions of the trestle incident. Early in the novel, through Ellen's eyes, we are shown a scene in which George rescues Robbie Reid from the bayou. With great Leda-and-Swan-like splashing, George strips Robbie of her dress and petticoat and carries her to the bank "screaming in her very teddies, her lost ribbon in his teeth, and the shining water running down her kicking legs and flying off her heels as she screamed and buried her face in his chest, laughing too, proud too" (*DW*, 25). Ellen is not unmoved; from her vantage—as perhaps both voyeur and clairvoyant—she senses something threatening as well as "boldly happy" in this vicarious ravishing. Edna Earle does not succumb until she swoons (probably from intellectual overwork) into St. Elmo's clerical arms at the end of the novel. Rhett's abduction of Scarlett up the gaudy staircase of the Atlanta house is legendary. The obligatory scene acts out the "issue" of the ambiguity of heterosexual love for the heroine: is surrender also submission and erasure? Welty's Edna Earle waits for a Mr. Springer who never shows up.

Ellen seems happy in her dissolution into "Fairchild" commonality, giving up to her symbolically named husband, Battle. Robbie Reid, however, seems less anxious to capitulate. She wants George to love her, to be physically honed on her, body to body—Ellen's alternative of personal love through the mediation of kin is not acceptable. Nor is the argument that Ellen triumphs through fertility influential with Robbie. She is not prepared to allow "the old bugaboo of pregnancy" to count as decisive (*DW*, 144).

Ellen clearly has done so, and Dabney, too, wants to have a baby as soon as possible. Shelley, on the other hand, "the Hipless Wonder," is not inclined to see her fate biologically. Late in the novel, when she gets the news of her mother's pregnancy, she charges Battle, her father, with blame for putting her mother in this "predicament" (*DW*, 229). Battle pretends not to know what his daughter means. Westling's view of triumphant fertility must, it seems, be remodeled to make room for the female characters of *Delta Wedding* who carry the Wilsonian distrust of conventional, phallocentric constructions of female sexuality as solely fertility. Wilson offers readers one character, Edna Earle, who moves successively through stages of confusion, awareness, denial, and submission. Welty provides separate characters for each "stage" coexisting in the novel spatially rather than developmentally.

In oblivious, patriarchal reaction, Battle serves as the key to another, issue-oriented point of convergence between *Delta Wedding* and the type of novel it supposedly is not. Critics concur that "woman's fiction" sets out to examine the issue of the proper spheres of the sexes. So many of the heroines in the genre are, for this reason, writers: Jo March, Wilson's Edna Earle, Shelley Fairchild. Welty has not omitted this issue from *Delta Wedding*, although in paying a little too much attention to the pastoral leanings of the work we tend to overlook or underestimate Shelley's importance. If there is a feminine space in *Delta Wedding* it is probably not the grove or garden (for the men are shown as owning these female spaces as real estate), but rather the private space of the writer's room. Shelley's room, tribute to Woolf's "room of one's own," is cluttered with memorabilia. The most significant article is "a photograph of Shelley in a Spanish comb and a great deal of piled hair" (*DW*, 83). Shelley is not only the woman-as-writer in *Delta Wedding* but also Welty's self-acknowledged and authorized delegate. Welty's Jackson friend Lehman Engel had captured her in a similar snapshot in which the author as a young woman poses in Spanish get-up perched in the fork of a tree.[7]

Shelley's room is not the only space in which patriarchal power is undermined. Early in the novel she has Dabney reflect on her father's possessiveness: of her, of his plantation, of his power. Her urge to marry Troy is in some ways the urge to free herself from the name of the father: "It would kill her father—of course for her to be a Fairchild was an inescapable thing, to him. And she would not take anything for the relentless way he was acting, not wanting to let her go. The caprices of his restraining power over his daughters filled her with delight now that she had declared what she could do" (*DW*, 33). It is not as if Dabney, only seventeen, does not know both the father's "restraining power" and her "delight" in subverting it. If her marriage to Troy would kill him, so be it.

The passage just quoted is followed closely by one in which Dabney, having just ordered Man-Son back to work chopping cotton, remembers a moment in her youth when her two uncles, George and Denis, emerge nude from a bayou to break up a knife fight between two black youths. George is cut, or is smeared with the two fighters' blood, when Dabney envisions him: "When George turned around on the bayou, his face looked white and his sunburn a mask, and he stood there still and attentive. There was blood on his hands and both legs. . . . She almost ran away. He seemed to meditate—to refuse to smile. She gave a loud scream and he saw her there in the field, and caught her when she ran at him. He hugged her tight against his chest, where sweat and bayou water pressed her mouth, and tickled her a minute, and told her how sorry he was to have scared her like that. Everything was all right then" (*DW*, 36). This moment in Dabney's life and recollections is redolent of sexual power and fantasized indulgence in it. In a later work, "Moon Lake," Loch Morrison's nudity, sunburn, and "little tickling thing" are signifiers as well of his male sexuality and power. Nina and Jinny Love, who spy on his demonstration, attempt to dismiss all that the pose represents. In *Delta Wedding* Dabney runs forward to embrace the significations as inevitable.

This episode is repeated, as another element in the spatial narrative, much later in the novel when Shelley ventures to Troy's office to fetch him to the wedding rehearsal. Blood on the doorsill spooks Shelley (*DW*, 195–96). Everything is not all right with her. Rather than embrace the looming phallic power as inevitable, Shelley opts for literature. She is reading Fitzgerald's *The Beautiful and Damned* as *Delta Wedding* goes on, and she is preparing to travel to Europe with her Aunt Tempe on a ship called the *Berengaria*. Not coincidentally, *Berengaria* is the name of the ship that takes Gloria and Anthony Patch to Europe in Fitzgerald's novel. Shelley's room, or world, or system of significations is filled with representations. Welty cleverly pushes empirical and self-reflexive registers upon each other; *Delta Wedding* is, therefore, both a novel and a novel about "the novel." Shelley's own experiences (the borrowing of the ship's name suggests as much) are vicarious but, because of that, multidimensional. She achieves what Welty the reviewer considered Woolf the author to have achieved: the fluid, electric, passing back and forth between writer and the thing the writer makes.

Whereas a novel in the mainstream of a genre, such as *St. Elmo*, would have foregrounded such issues in the outright conversations of the characters, in the direct address of the author, or in the clear progression (development) of the heroine from earlier to latter stage, Welty-as-modernist fragments the monolithic obligation to form and content, and distributes it spatially among several characters, embedding it in an essentially modernist, symbolic narrative. The genre represented by *St. Elmo* was necessary to Welty because at her time and place this novel represented what could not be repeated. Issues of the unrepeatable appear in Welty's works with undeniable frequency, but they are mediated by self-conscious deflection: modernist fragmenting in *Delta Wedding*, sly parody in *The Ponder Heart*, the shield of autobiography in *The Optimist's*

Daughter. This is the point for which Welty "found" Virginia Woolf, the Woolf who showed her how to beat plot by evading it—to evade it by layering and juxtaposing frames of vision, acts of seeing rather than acts of acting.

Assuming two strong historical influences on Welty-as-novelist (the historical character of the genre and her precursors, which she has deliberately summoned to attention only to renounce; and the modernist, Woolf, whom she has credited with her breakthrough at every opportunity), one sees mixed and sometimes mutually interfering currents in *Delta Wedding* and the later novels. As Peggy Prenshaw argues so eloquently in her concluding essay in this collection, Welty was never as far removed from time and place (her particular historical moment) as we critics have sometimes seemed to think.

Notes

1. David Streitfeld, "Eudora Welty, In Her Own Words," *Washington Post,* 4 December 1992, Section D, p. 3.

2. Nina Baym, *Woman's Fiction: A Guide to Novels by and about Women in America, 1820–1870* (Ithaca, N.Y.: Cornell University Press, 1978), pp. 22–23.

3. Elizabeth Fox-Genovese, "Introduction," in *Beulah,* by Augusta Jane Evans Wilson (Baton Rouge: Louisiana State University Press, 1992), p. xvii. Fox-Genovese paraphrases and amplifies Alexander Cowie's synopsis in his *The Rise of the American Novel* (1948).

4. Michael Kreyling, *Author and Agent: Eudora Welty and Diarmuid Russell* (New York: Farrar, Straus & Giroux, 1991), p. 70.

5. Louise Westling, *Sacred Groves and Ravaged Gardens: The Fiction of Eudora Welty, Carson McCullers, and Flannery O'Connor* (Athens: University of Georgia Press, 1985), p. 68.

6. Augusta Jane Evans Wilson, *St. Elmo* (1866; rpt., Tuscaloosa: University of Alabama Press, 1992), p. 51.

7. Lehman Engel, *This Bright Day: An Autobiography* (New York: Macmillan, 1974), p. 41.

"Good as Gold"

The Role of the Optimist in Three Novels by Eudora Welty
Jane Hinton

In *One Writer's Beginnings* Eudora Welty comments on her own need to be "invisible" in her work, stating that "perspective, the line of vision, the frame of vision—these set at a distance" (*OWB*, 87). The perspective, or line of vision, stretching from the airy comedy *The Ponder Heart,* through the rich dramatizations of *Losing Battles,* to the mature vision of *The Optimist's Daughter* frames in each novel an optimist, a male character seen with both love and detachment through the consciousness of one or more of the women characters in the novel. The interaction between these optimistic males and often more realistic females reveals a theme interpreted differently in each novel: the paradoxical view that life is to be celebrated even as its dark sorrows and failures are unflinchingly held to light.

Daniel Ponder from *The Ponder Heart,* Judge Oscar Moody from *Losing Battles,* and Judge Clint McKelva from *The Optimist's Daughter* are manifestly different and from very different types of works, yet they share some common elements. All three are from prominent families in their respective small towns; all three are subjects of community gossip and storytelling; and all three are to some extent fools of love. All three men are also optimists, although only Judge McKelva is explicitly described as such. Welty's optimists are men who believe that the power of their love or will can save or change people or their circumstances. They also believe in the power of institutions to right the balance of human lives, or at least, in the case of Daniel Ponder, believe that institutions can do no harm. In Uncle Daniel's comic world law, medicine, and education cannot touch the truly innocent; one imperturbable individual can topple the whole edifice. The two judges are firmly entrenched in the law, although Judge Moody is forced to dole out justice tempered with mercy in a way that the legal code would never recognize.

As a number of critics have noted, these men, powerful in the eyes of their communities, are seen differently by the women who know them best. Louise Westling comments that "Welty pictures the masculine hero from outside. Repeatedly she presents a beloved male observed and indulged by a whole family, especially by its women."[1] The phrase "good as gold," often used in Southern idiom to describe well-behaved children, is used by Edna Earle to describe Daniel Ponder, by Judge McKelva's nurse to describe him on his sickbed, and by implication by Maud Eva Moody to describe her husband Oscar Moody on his "mercy errand" in Boone County. They are good men in their absence of notable sins or crimes, good in their social roles and reputations, good in the love that they give and get back from others. None of them, however (like Welty's own father) can bear pain very well. Their dependence on outside codes of institutional or social behaviors is seen by women in these works as embodying an incomplete view of life. For their "good as goldness" in conduct and generosity these men are loved, but in their frequent blindness and their tendency to shy away from the tragic, the women often feel a need to protect or pity them, powerful and influential though they may be in the community. Throughout these works the women variously protect and champion, in the case of Edna Earl and Daniel, or interpret and bear pain, as Laurel does for her father Judge McKelva, or serve as a shrewd counterpoint to emotions that were previously hidden, as in the interchanges between Maud Eva and Judge Oscar Moody. Of course, the women also bear some of the irony because they are perfectly capable of their own illusions. Edna Earle skirts the fact of Daniel's basic incompetence. Julia Mortimer believes that she can awaken others to self-knowledge and is taught her own lesson. Laurel initially wants her dead parents to stay fixed in her memory without adding the reality of Fay to it.

The first of these three optimists is Daniel Ponder, the fool for love who triumphs in his own way. True, he loses his young wife, Bonnie Dee Peacock, but he defeats the forces arrayed against him. The mental institution of Whitfield cannot hold him; in fact he delights in it as a place of interesting society and fascinating stories. Tried for murder after his wife's death, he cannot be held by the legal institution as the jury acquits him. Not even the Ponder reputation and money can hold him as he leaves the courtroom after his dismissal, handing out the family fortune to all in his path.

The only point of view given of Uncle Daniel is that of his family-worshipping niece Edna Earle. She is the one who ordains that Daniel is irresistible and universally loved. Of course, her words are full of dramatic irony at every point. She has a high opinion of her own intelligence—"It's always taken a lot out of me, being smart" (PH, 10)—of her shrewdness as a judge of character, and of her commercial sense. To save the deserted Ponder place, she is of the opinion that "a chinchilla farm may be the answer" (PH, 44). In order to soothe herself, one of her favorite recreations is to "read a good quiet set of directions through" (PH, 73). With her literal mind and her perceptions, keen within their narrow range of distinctions and prejudices, Edna Earle is a foil to her Uncle Daniel. A child who has never had to grow up and go "into the world," he is never initiated into evil and remains always the fool of love, devoted to company, conversation, good manners, and good food. Edna Earle sees him as he is but protects and nurtures him at every turn. He marries the little country-come-to-town Bonnie Dee in order to have someone to give to on a permanent basis, or as permanently as the sweetly vague Uncle Daniel can comprehend. Bonnie Dee herself refers to their union as a "trial marriage." After his wife dies, Edna Earle comments that Uncle Daniel has "still got that love banked up somewhere" (PH, 70). In the interplay between the eternal optimism of Uncle Daniel, the uncritical, protective acceptance of him by his niece, and events of the materialistic world the full range of the humor unfolds.

Behind the comedy lies the implication that the Ponders—their money given away by Daniel, the big house abandoned, and the hotel unprofitable—are on the way down the social scale. Edna Earle realizes with surprise and perhaps some unease at Bonnie Dee's funeral that "the Peacocks at one time used to amount to something . . ." (PH, 78) and have "gone down" just as other families have in the community. Uncle Daniel's eternal optimism leaves him unaware of this fact. Edna Earle is much more aware of what might happen to the Ponders, but she counters such thoughts with family pride. Part of Welty's comic art in each of these three works is to show that decline is inevitable for each of these families. The Renfro-Beecham-Vaughn clan is hanging on to survival by a thread; the McKelvas are almost gone. With the Judge dead and Laurel gone back to Chicago, Fay's Snopsian mother speaks of turning the family home into a boardinghouse for transients (the "wrong element" that Edna Earle alludes to as those who pass through knowing nothing of the importance of family).

In contrast to the tour-de-force monologue that gives a vivid, deliciously biased picture of Uncle Daniel Ponder, Welty's use of varied points of view paints a rich portrait of Judge McKelva. The effect is to deepen the insight into the mystery of "a single, entire human being, who will never be confined in any frame" (OWB, 90). He is seen by his daughter Laurel in his old age and death and as she remembers him over the years of her lifetime. The family's longtime domestic servant, Missouri, whom he took in as a protected witness in a murder trial, recalls him. Their close neighbor, Miss Adele Courtland, knows him well, as do other friends and neighbors who recall his memory with stories that trouble Laurel because they do not match her memories of his character. As in the other novels, the Judge's thoughts are unknown to the reader; he is seen at a remove through the perceptions of family, friends, and community.

Superficially Daniel Ponder and Judge McKelva seem an unlikely comparison, but there are strong similarities. Uncle Daniel is the thoughtless, purely childlike giver; Judge McKelva is a man of thought and considered action, but his basic emotional nature is the same as that of Daniel Ponder. Both men have proper middle-class first wives, then "marry down" the second time.[2] Bonnie Dee and Fay are of the same mold; their interests are seen as superficial and materialistic; they have neither culture nor taste. Edna Earle details the inappropriate clothes that Bonnie Dee Peacock wears as a sign of her class difference from the Ponders; for example, on a warm summer day she wears a hunter green velveteen suit to watch the man bring electricity to Ponder Hill. Fay's taste is critiqued with miniature but telling strokes, as when Laurel notices that Fay wears green shoes with stiletto heels. Her bearing and her actions are clearly portrayed as what Laurel is too well bred to call her: tacky. The country births and lack of advantages shared by these two women are not noted for any snobbish reasons, but rather as outward and visible signs of their emotional failings. Neither woman can summon an emotional response to match the ardent generosity of their husbands. The optimistic giving of Daniel and that of the Judge lead to chains of events that result in deaths. Bonnie Dee, in the farcically spun out series of tales, actually dies laughing as Daniel tickles her to distract her from the electrical storm that she fears. In The Optimist's Daughter it is the Judge who dies suddenly after Fay screams in his face while he is recovering from eye surgery.

The families from the lower social orders profit financially from these deaths. Fay's family, the Chisoms, are what the Peacocks have become twenty years later, as they drive onto the scene in their pick-up truck with the "Do Unto Others Before They Do Unto You" bumper sticker. Even their names hint at their qualities: the Peacocks are vain but empty-headed and harmless; the Chisoms are grasping, ignorant chiselers who will inherit what comes from the Judge and destroy it—they have, after all, a "wrecking concern" in Texas. Only the grandfather and young Wendell retain the dignity of the folk culture that they all sprang from. The Peacocks profit from their daughter's death in the most comically literal way. When Uncle Daniel leaves the stand at his trial for murder, he hands out great handfuls of the Ponder money. The Peacocks hold out for a few moments but then join the greedy throng. Their childish cry might have been echoed by the later Chisoms: "'Finders Keepers'!" (PH, 105). Edna Earle's response to the demands of her uncle's nature is typically generous. She refuses to stop him from giving away what is also her inheritance: "And I don't give a whoop for your approval! You don't think I betrayed him by not letting him betray himself, do you?" (PH, 148). She knows that giving away money is the worst thing that you can do because "You can't go on after it and still be you and them" (PH, 149). The irony of these optimistic, blindly loving natures is that generosity only serves to induce human greed and indifference.

Edna Earle's view of Daniel is clear, but after Judge McKelva's death, Laurel must assess the meaning of his life out of her confusion. Laurel feels that his life as a public servant has been overlooked. He has served his time as town mayor and worked hard on civic projects, such as flood control. He never made much money until he came into "a little oil money" (OD, 120) from the McKelva land that he held on to after the "Big Flood" wiped out the house. He had written Laurel after his modest windfall, "There was never anything wrong with keeping up a little optimism over the Flood" (OD, 121). She had not known until after his death that her father had helped send the young Courtland to medical school and provided instruments for the high school band, which assembles at his funeral.

By recalling the past, Laurel is forced to recognize that the public successes of her father's life were not always matched by private happiness—as seen in his wife Becky's tormented last years of dying, marked by her bitter accusations. Her daughter remembers him as a man of great "delicacy" of family feeling, but even so she recalls her anger at his seeming acceptance of her mother's blindness and coming death: "he seemed so particularly helpless to do anything for his wife. He was not passionately enough grieved at the changes in her! He seemed to give the changes his same, kind recognition—to accept them because they had to be only of the time being, even to love them, even to laugh sometimes at their absurdity. . . . he apparently needed guidance in order to see the tragic" (OD, 145). His optimism takes the form of "his belief that all his wife's troubles would turn out all right because there was nothing he would not have given her" (OD, 146). When he reaches an impasse with this situation at home, he reacts much as Daniel Ponder does: he puts on his hat and goes out. Daniel goes looking for company, and the Judge goes to his office for work, but the goal of distraction is the same.

Laurel is impatient at hearing his old friends describe him before his funeral as "goodness itself" (OD, 86), "humorist. . . . crusader. . . . And an angel on the face of the earth" (OD, 82). It is the painfully mixed portrait of the man that she wants to do justice to in her memory. When her father's promise to take his dying wife back to her mountain home is seen as false by Becky, "That was when he started, of course, being what he scowlingly called an optimist. . . . Whatever she was driven to say was all right. But it was *not* all right!" (OD, 150). He could neither save her nor despair of saving her—an intolerable situation for someone who refuses to see the tragic. His second marriage, so inexplicable to his old friends, seems more understandable when Fay is seen as a relief from trying to cure the incurable or turn back time itself. Coarse, vital, and caught up in the moment, Fay is so easy to give to. All she seems to want are green shoes, a peach satin bedroom, and Sunday dinners at the hotel. Fay can no more cure Clint than he could cure Becky. Neither can she entertain the thought of tragedy. At his death she screams in eternal child's rage: "Why did this have to happen to me!"

A question that is left suspended, unanswered by any of the characters, is why Clint McKelva dies. It is made clear that the cause is not his eye surgery. Yet Clint dies after Fay screams "I tell you enough is enough!" and, according to his nurse, grabs him as though "to pull him out of that bed" (OD, 32). Laurel feels that Fay's violence shocks him into death. Critic Gail Mortimer echoes the prevailing view that he has "seen" too much—Fay's cruelty and his mistake in believing she is like his first, gentler wife Becky—and that in his despair at seeing, he has just given up. Clint surely had seen long before that Fay is the opposite of Becky in every way. Perhaps the reason he chooses to give in is that in his death he can be a giver, an optimist still. He gives Fay what she wants: permission to be free, to be part of the Carnival, to cut loose from the past that oppresses and surrounds her in Mount Salus. His death, oddly enough, does not seem despairing but rather a loving offering up of what he could do; his own death is a quiet, delicate act. His expression after death suggests both this secret and his childlike emotional nature: he has "the smile of a child who is hiding in the dark while the others hunt him, waiting to be found" (OD, 34). Miss Adele Courtland hints that his death was a chosen thing: "People live their own way, and to a certain extent I almost believe they may die their own way . . ." (OD, 56).

After her father's funeral, Laurel spends a long night weaving the threads of memory from her grandmother, parents, late husband, and herself into a coherent whole. She is, after all, a fabric designer. In the climactic final scene of the novel, she finds that she can leave Fay unpunished and her own family possessions untouched. She leaves the optimism of her father and her own illusions about the past.

Judge Oscar Moody of *Losing Battles* stands between Daniel Ponder and Judge McKelva on the scale of humor: he is less broadly comic than the former, but more a figure of fun than the latter. The point of view in this novel is, of course, dramatic as countless inventive stories and actions swirl about these characters during a family reunion. A son breaks out of the penitentiary for his grandmother's birthday; the judge who sentenced him shows up at the reunion; and a legendary schoolteacher dies and is buried. Judge Moody lives for the institution of the law and its life and death power, but while he is trapped as his Buick is stuck on the ridge, the law cannot help him.

Oscar Moody is the optimistic twentieth-century traveler who, like the reader, is confidently dependent on machinery, on institutions, and on his position in the community for his reality. Deprived of his car in a rural maze, taken away from the legal system and his sense of self-importance, he is helplessly thrown back on the human family to have some of his illusions stripped away. He, like the other male characters discussed, does not bear pain well. Throughout the stories of the reunion, especially those about Miss Julia Mortimer's tormented invalidism as she was thwarted by the sadistic Lexie, he moans in sympathy, covers his face, and stands and tries to leave when the stress gets to be too much.

Oscar Moody was Miss Julia Percival Mortimer's first protégé. She was ten years older, his neighbor, his inspiration, and the force that launched his successful career. He comments that his career could have gone further if he had not taken Miss Julia's advice to stay close to home where he was needed, advice, as he says, he "took and cherished against her" (*LB*, 307). He has been on his way to find Miss Julia in response to her deathbed letters when he ends up at the reunion, to be offered the school chair and to learn lessons about family-life and the ineffectuality of the law. Miss Julia still teaches him from her deathbed and most of all through her death. It is clear from his memories of Miss Julia, and of those who "aspired" to her hand in her youth, that he has long loved the dedicated teacher. When he says that he has no secrets about Miss Julia, his sometimes shrewd wife Maud Eva remarks, "Your real secrets are the ones you don't know you've got" (*LB*, 306).

In the course of the letter that Judge Moody reads to the reunion, Miss Julia warns him not to be tempted by innocence to "conspire with the ignorant" (*LB, 300*). Later during the reunion he does just that as he rules that Jack and Gloria have committed no crime by marrying, even though they may be first cousins. He is moved by the couple and their child. He sees this action as one more betrayal of Miss Julia, yet it marks a step in his movement away from optimism into self-knowledge.

In a sense he, like the other two men, married down in marrying Maud Eva Moody. Maud Eva has a firm grip on her social position as the wife of an important man, on her Presbyterian rightness, and on the consciousness that in her purse is a spotless pair of white gloves. She is a former schoolteacher herself, but the longer the couple stays at the reunion, the more she sounds like the sharp-tongued country women gathered around them. She has an indulgent, sometimes impatient attitude toward her husband. For all of her awareness of her propriety, she is clearly no Julia Mortimer, who was a woman of formidable intellect and class.

Critics of *Losing Battles* continue to debate whether the clan at the reunion is being celebrated for its family-centered agrarian solidarity or satirized for its refusal to enter the modern world. Similarly, the schoolteacher Miss Julia Mortimer is viewed by some as the heroine who would drag this benighted group into the twentieth century and by others as a rigid, though heroic, academician who would change the group identity and way of life. To the sympathetic, listening reader, the truth seems to lie somewhere in the middle. Both sides, as Miss Julia writes in a letter, use the same tactics to survive. Miss Julia may represent progress, but contrary to the prevailing view, her progress is not incompatible with Agrarian values. True, she finds no harm in birth certificates and documents, but she urges all of her pupils to return home so all that is needed can come from the community. She espouses no New South crassness or commercialism. She lives off the land, selling milk to keep the school going, but freely giving away peach cuttings from her trees to share with others (cuttings which the recipients generally let die through negligence). The struggle against self-worship that she would like to root out of the country families shows her belief in the classic "Know Thyself" doctrine of agrarianism. She is not even an outsider, but a member of a longtime Ludlow family, one of missionary stock. What she chiefly stands for in *Losing Battles* is the principle of self-knowledge. In appreciating the irony of her life and death Judge Moody sheds the attributes of optimism. He sums up her life by saying, "She knew exactly who she was. And what she was. What she didn't know till she got to it was what would *happen* to what she was. Any more than any of us here know . . ." (*LB*, 306).

Each of these three novels ends with a paradox: though the optimist is defeated to some extent, the narratives end with a positive movement. At the conclusion of *The Ponder Heart,* Daniel is summoned downstairs by a pleased Edna Earl who can offer him his favorite things, a good meal and a new listener to hear his stories. In *The Optimist's Daughter* Laurel is "freed" from optimism and "gains a new sense of the continuity of self. . . ."[3] She starts her journey toward life over again, sped on her way by the waving hands of schoolchildren. As *Losing Battles* draws to a close, Oscar Moody has been through a series of outlandish experiences, has been forced to be dependent on a man he sentenced to jail, and has been made to face the limits of the law. Yet, as he leaves the funeral of Miss Julia Mortimer, the woman he has virtually worshipped, he is laughing. His is the laughter of recognition and acceptance, the same laughter that resounds through these three novels.

Notes

1. Louise Westling, *Eudora Welty* (Totowa, N.J.: Barnes & Noble, 1989), p. 32.

2. For an interesting discussion on this topic, see John Edward Hardy, "Marrying Down in Eudora Welty's Novels," in *Eudora Welty: Critical Essays,* ed. Peggy Prenshaw (Jackson: University Press of Mississippi, 1979), pp. 93–119.

3. Jan Nordby Gretlund, *Eudora Welty's Aesthetics of Place* (Columbia: University of South Carolina Press, 1997), p. 22.

Part I

Losing Battles

Eudora Welty as Lyric Novelist

The Long and the Short of It
Ruth D. Weston

A recent check of Eudora Welty scholarship recorded in the *Publications of the Modern Language Association* (PMLA) Bibliography (CD-ROM) revealed 202 separate listings between 1988 and early 1994, including books, articles, and doctoral dissertations, most of which were studies of theme or narrative techniques and no more than ten of which could be considered even partial genre studies. However, an emphasis on Welty as novelist, especially in light of the oft-expressed opinion that the novels are inferior to the short stories, provides an opportunity to discuss Welty's unique approach to these genres.

Critics often have trouble settling questions of genre in Welty because, while her fiction is clearly marked by the experimentalism of her modernist forbears, its significant differences from their work have led some critics to call her a postmodernist.[1] Several scholars have recently argued in favor of Welty's classification as postmodernist because of her modification of, and thus interrogation of, specific texts of the Western literary tradition in terms of theme, technique, and, briefly, genre. Harriet Pollack, for example, shows how Welty merges and alters existing genres, "experimenting with readers' expectations," to force a contrast between "a literary memory and the fiction-at-hand," creating "not . . . correspondence so much as transformation . . . , [the contrast of which causes] the reader to revise initial predictions" based on received knowledge of the genre.[2] Rebecca Mark asserts that Welty deconstructs "patriarchal myths and masculinist texts," transforming in particular the "heroic narrative of masculine domination."[3] Thomas McHaney suggests that, as a postmodernist work that defies the traditional novel genre, *The Golden Apples* be called simply "a text." McHaney presents a many-layered argument for the cyclic nature of *The Golden Apples* and finally judges it neither a collection of stories nor a novel but, rather, a genre "too ineffable to have a name." Welty has refused to call it a novel, but most critics recognize that it is more than a collection of stories. McHaney cites T. S. Eliot's remark that if Joyce's *Ulysses* is not a novel then perhaps "the novel is a form that will no longer serve"; and he cites Tzvetan Todorov's argument that "the study of genres must be undertaken on the basis of structural characteristics, not on the basis of names [of genres]."[4]

Welty has made no secret of her reluctance to write novels, and she generally characterizes herself as a "story writer." It is also true that each of her longer narratives has a close connection with short stories. Is she, then, a novelist; or is she a short story writer who occasionally writes on a little longer? An obvious first response is that Welty is at least as deserving of the title of "novelist" as is James Joyce, another short story writer who occasionally wrote on at some length. A second is that the "ineffable" *Golden Apples* is as much a novel as is another famous short story cycle, Sherwood Anderson's *Winesburg, Ohio*. Although *Winesburg, Ohio* is usually called a novel, genre theorist Ian Reid says that "the tight continuous structure of a novel is deliberately avoided . . . [because] Anderson said he wanted 'a new looseness' of form to suit the particular quality of his material. His people are lonely, restless, cranky . . . [and the 'looseness' afforded by the short story cycle] can convey with precision and pathos the duality that results: a superficial appearance . . . of communal wholeness, and an underlying actual separateness."[5] Reid could have been describing Welty's *The Golden Apples* or even William Faulkner's *Go Down, Moses*.

The decision to write on the topic of Welty as novelist suggests the question of whether the title "novelist" is more prestigious than that of "short story writer." It *is*, according to theorists such as Robert Scholes, Robert Kellogg, and Mary Louise Pratt, who defend the primacy of the novel, asserting that it is, in Pratt's words, the "dominant, normative genre of prose fiction."[6] Pratt argues that the novel "tells life," or narrates "a full-length life," while the short story tells "only a fragment" of life; that the novel deals with many things, while a short story deals with one; and that the novel is a "whole text," meaning a separately published book.[7] Although Charles E. May, another genre theorist, says that in America the short story was "in the shadow of the novel only until Sherwood Anderson,"[8] Pratt, in an article entitled "The Short Story: The Long and the Short of It," asserts that, nevertheless, "the short story has developed along lines in part determined by the novel." For example, she says that "by novelistic standards, the moment of truth is an especially good fragment of a life to narrate because it projects itself by implication backward and forward across the whole life."[9] As Frank O'Connor puts it, the novel "creates a sense of continuing life while the short story . . . merely suggests continuing life."[10]

If we agree that the title of "novelist" is desirable, and that it seems deserved if Joyce is any standard, can we then get beyond "ineffable text" in the case of *The Golden Apples* and beyond "a short story that goes on longer" in the case of Welty's other fiction? Can we, in other words, define some of Welty's fiction as bona fide novels, supporting the assertion by genre theory? Although there has never been consensus about what makes a novel, recent theories about recognizable attributes of short stories and novels are helpful in discussing genre in Welty's fiction. To speak only of Pratt's criterion of the telling of a character's whole life, I find the narrative of Virgie Rainey's life in *The Golden Apples* as novelistic an attribute as that of Julia Mortimer's in *Losing Battles*.[11]

Todorov distinguishes between theoretical determinants of the short story and novel genres, which are established deductively by observing characteristics derived from a system of criteria such as length, and determinants of historical genres, which are discovered through induction from individual works.[12] Since Welty freely combines existing forms, the deductive method does not do so well as the inductive in calculating the genre of her works. Two categories of attributes apply: (1) those associated with the classical genres that influenced or developed into the modern novel; and (2) those associated with the short story, as defined by contemporary short story theory.

Theorists who write on the novel as genre usually do so not in comparison with the short story but, rather, in comparison with the classical Greek forms, the central principle of which seems to be what Northrop Frye called the "radical of presentation": that is, the relationship between "the poet and the public." For example, to use Frye's terms, the lyric is the lone voice of the author, in song or meditation, which is "overheard" by an unseen audience; the drama presents actors who address the audience directly while it conceals the author; and the epic, regardless of length, is recited by the author while it conceals the characters. Of these genres, it is the epic, in a written mimesis of the direct address of drama, and thus a mixed genre to begin with, that became what we know as narrative fiction, or the novel.[13]

If, after Todorov, we define a genre as a cluster of characteristics instead of a category of works, then any work can be said to partake of certain characteristics of genre; and genre, then, is seen as only one ingredient of a work.[14] By this means of generic identification, we can say that Eudora Welty's fiction partakes of either novelistic or short story characteristics, length being only one determinant, and on a broader scale that a work can partake of lyric, epic, and/or dramatic characteristics.

Welty saw every work as a new puzzle to be solved, and she solved each with a new structure, often beginning as a short story a narrative that later developed into a longer form. After publishing her first two collections of stories, Welty was urged to write a novel, but she resisted. Her adult fairy tale, *The Robber Bridegroom,* is within short-story length; but its separate publication, its classic plot structure with rising and falling action, and its treatment of two generations of the Musgrove family are three significant novelistic traits. When Welty's agent sent out "The Delta Cousins," first to *Harper's Bazaar* and then to *The Atlantic Monthly,* both magazines asked for substantial cuts in the story. Yet every time she tried to cut it, as Michael Kreyling reveals in his *Author and Agent,* the story "continued to expand, like the contents of the 'jinxed pot,'" as she discovered new connections to other "Delta stuff," including new materials from the diaries in John Robinson's family attic. In time, of course, the story became *Delta Wedding,* first as four installments of a serial for *Atlantic Monthly* and finally as her first full-length novel.[15] Before Harcourt published *The Ponder Heart* as a novel, Welty always thought of it as a story that needed the context of other stories. As she told Diarmuid Russell, "publishing Uncle Daniel as a separate book . . . is against some story-writer instinct of mine."[16] Like *Delta Wedding, The Optimist's Daughter* and *Losing Battles* also began as short stories. And even though *Losing Battles* is so long and so episodic that it has been called an epic,[17] its brief time span gives it the feel of a slice-of-life short story, albeit one with deeper and more tangible soundings.

One aspect of the classical genres that seems particularly relevant to Welty's novels is what Northrop Frye calls a work's "rhythm." For example, to continue in Frye's terms, epic poetry is marked by the "rhythm of recurrence," but when the epic storytelling method developed into prose fiction, it came to exhibit the "rhythm of continuity," the "semantic rhythm of sense." The lyric, though, partakes of the "rhythm of association," which is noncontinuous and mostly below the level of consciousness, including "sound links," "ambiguous sense-links," and "memory-links."[18] Also relevant to Welty, as a writer influenced by the full spectrum of artistic genres, are several connections between each classic genre and other modes of communication and understanding. For example, drama grew out of ritual, the epic is closely related to Bible stories and other traditional tales, and the lyric has an intimate connection with dream or vision. The genres have never been pure, and they became even less so with modernist experimenters such as Ezra Pound, who lyricized the epic poem in his *Cantos*.[19]

Eudora Welty also merges characteristics of the three genres the Greeks thought of as separate. In fact, she has lyricized her own epic in *Losing Battles* with passages such as that which opens the novel:

> When the rooster crowed, the moon had still not left the world but was going down on flushed cheek, one day short of the full. A long thin cloud crossed it slowly, drawing itself out like a name being called. The air changed, as if a mile or so away a wooden door had swung open, and a smell, more of warmth than wet, from a river at low stage, moved upward into the clay hills that stood in darkness. . . .

> A dog leaped up from where he'd lain like a stone and began barking. . . .

> Then a baby bolted naked out of the house. She monkey-climbed down the steps and ran open-armed into the yard . . . [and] used all her strength to push over a crate that let a stream of white Plymouth Rocks loose on the world. . . .

> The distant point of the ridge, like the tongue of a calf, put its red lick on the sky. Mists, voids, patches of woods and naked clay, flickered like live ashes, pink and blue. (*LB,* 3–4)

This is a celebration of the birth of the day as if it were the beginning of time, and as if the dog and the naked "monkey-climbing" baby were brave, newly evolved creatures in it. The passage suggests the lyric aubade; but as an ironic mixture of positive images of the dawn on Banner Top and negative images of the surrounding hills that are still "in darkness" and full of "mists, voids, and ashes," it suggests the classical or Shakespearean dramatic prologue, which might include both exhortation and disclaimers about a play's limitations.[20]

Mary Anne Ferguson has rightly called *Losing Battles* "a comic epic in prose,"[21] because the novel evinces both aspects of the epos: (1) its many storytellers give it the character of individual recitations; and (2) their many stories make it episodic. Yet because it is written almost entirely in dialogue, with infrequent and brief choruslike narrative passages, it also approximates the objectivity of a drama, as Welty intended it should (*C,* 181). In fact, Welty has said that she "wanted to try something completely vocal and dramatized" (*C*, 31), and that she realized that *Losing Battles* might be "a transition toward writing a play" (*C*, 77). Some will remember that, in an early review of the novel, Reynolds Price compared it to Shakespeare's *The Tempest*.[22] The most recent work showing that Welty's fiction is closely related to drama is Peggy Prenshaw's article on *Bye-Bye Brevoort* in the *Southern Quarterly*.[23]

Dramatic ritual is employed in two major ways in Welty: in theme and narrative style. Marriages, funerals, and other ritual gatherings are the subject matter for much of her fiction; and the narratives often suggest choreographed motions. One of the most striking uses of choreography is in the short story "Lily Daw and the Three Ladies," in which the three ladies circle around Lily, conjuring the girl in a parody of the witches from Shakespeare's *Macbeth*. But ritual choreography is basic also to Welty's narrative technique in the novels, in the stylized motions of, for example, the mock duel between Jack and Vaughn and the funeral procession over Banner Bridge in *Losing Battles*.

Ritual movements in the novels are often complemented by, or even upstaged by, stylized dialogues. In *Losing Battles* they include the stories that usually come out by means of question-and-answer conversations characterized by echolike repetitions. A striking example is the antiphon in which the subtext of Gloria and Lexie's indirect responses to each other constitute a record of Julia Mortimer's primary losing battle, metaphorically portraying their dead mentor through the roses she had "trained up," as a civilizing force giving way before the recovering wilderness:[24]

> "It was the last time I went across to see Miss Julia," said Gloria. . . . "The Silver Moon rose was already out, there at the windows—"
> "It's about to pull the house down now," said Miss Lexie.
> "The red rose too, that's trained up at the end of the porch—"
> "That big west rose? It's taken over," nodded Miss Lexie.
> "She'd filled the cut-glass bowl on the table," said Gloria. "With red and white."
> "She didn't cut 'em any longer," Miss Lexie said. . . . (*LB*, 247)

Such verbal patterns, as well as the numerous recitations in the novel about Julia Mortimer's life and legacy, achieve the epic rhythm of recurrence in *Losing Battles*. Analogous rhythms of recurrence in *The Robber Bridegroom* appear in its formulaic fairy-tale diction, including the repeated warnings of (1) a raven: "Turn back, my bonny, / Turn away home"; and (2) a locket: "If your mother could see you now, her heart would break" (*RB*, 13, 31). In *The Ponder Heart* they are apparent in redundant hyperbole such as the several variations on the refrain "I'm going to kill you dead, Miss Bonnie Dee" (*PH*, 66).

Associative rhythms are those more subtle links between the level of language and the level of major themes and images in the fiction. *Losing Battles* is about the eternal human battles against ignorance, poverty, and change, including what Julia would certainly have viewed as the scandal of mortality, as well as against the universal forces of nature. It is also about individual battles: fistfights between Jack and Curly; the "human chain" tug-of-war to keep the judge's Buick from falling off the mountain (*LB*, 385); the watermelon battle over Gloria's family ties; and Gloria's inner struggle between teaching and love. Supporting this major structural pattern are analogous minor images such as those of the "two wooden churches . . . [on] opposite sides of the road, as if each stood there to outwait the other and see which would fall first," and "Banner School and Stovall's Store sat facing each other . . . as if in the course of continuing battle" (*LB*, 406, 410). Also contributing to the associative logic is diction that suggests the larger losing battles: for example, in Miss Beulah's warning to Lexie, "You've got coming night to contend with now"; and in the many mentions of crossroads and "blind crossing[s]," which suggest movements at cross purposes (*LB*, 281, 407).

Rhythms of association may seem more characteristic of short stories than of novels: one thinks instinctively of the internal landscapes of stories such as "The Winds" and "Going to Naples." And certainly short story technique is fundamental to Welty's writing practice. In fact, because the short story form seems so natural to Welty's practice, it should be no surprise that some of the most helpful theoretical approaches to Welty's fiction come from contemporary short story theory. One of the most basic of these theories concerns the two major types of stories—the mimetic and the lyric. As Eileen Baldeshwiler explains, the mimetic narrative exhibits "external action developed 'syllogistically' through characters fabricated mainly to forward plot, culminating in a decisive ending that sometimes affords a universal insight, and expressed in the serviceably inconspicuous language of prose realism"; while the lyric is marked by "internal changes, moods, and feelings, utilizing a variety of structural patterns depending on the shape of the emotion itself. It relies for the most part on the open ending, and is expressed in the condensed, evocative, often figured language of the poem."[25] The lyric short story, then, is a direct descendant of the classical lyric genre.

But it is not only Welty's short stories that partake of the rhythm of association and other lyric qualities; these are also important to novels such as *Delta Wedding* and *The Optimist's Daughter,* which take place to such a great extent in the minds of their protagonists. One example is the passage in *Delta Wedding* in which Ellen, during the wedding dance, momentarily loses sight of her daughters among the dancers who "all looked alike" and is somehow reminded that she does not really know them. Her mind shifts from the people to the place that produced them: from the indistinguishable dancers to the present "season of changeless weather, of the changeless world, in a land without hill or valley." The contrast between her daughters and herself, accomplished here through the contrast between the Mississippi Delta and Ellen's native Virginia, with its wild mountains and changeable weather, makes her wonder how she could "ever know anything of her own daughters, how find them, like this" (*DW,* 221). In *The Optimist's Daughter* the logic of association is seen in the ambiguous sense links between optics and optimists, between retinal cataracts and the rushing waters of the "Cataract of Lodore," and (as Marion Montgomery reminds us in another chapter in this work) between optical spectacles and the spectacle as subgenre. Certainly, memory links are vital to Laurel McKelva's climactic epiphany in *The Optimist's Daughter.*

The associative rhythm, however, is employed not only in the novels characterized by internal monologues but also in the more dramatically dialogic fiction. In *Losing Battles,* to speak only of two passages previously quoted, this largely subconscious rhythm is achieved by subtle sound and sense links. In the antiphon of the roses, the sonorous *o* and *r* sounds in *Gloria, moon, too, rose, over, bowl, longer,* and *porch* combine with the complementary assonances and sight links of other *o* words, such as *across, nodded, now, out,* and *down,* to conjure a mournful tone appropriate to the unspoken but clearly felt elegy that neither Gloria nor Lexie can articulate. These sound links are, of course, based on the original English; some will remain in French, but perhaps will be lost in other translations (*LB,* 247).

In the opening passage of *Losing Battles,* similar sonorous sounds join with negative diction to undercut the surface celebration. But, in addition, ambiguous correspondences between the images of the naked baby, the dog that is likened to a stone, and the Plymouth Rock chickens constitute subtle links to the naked clay of the hills. It is a technique that reifies the animate objects, while the moon with "flushed cheek" and the ridge top with a calf's "tongue" animate the inanimate. The result is an unusual means of identifying humanity with the rest of the created world: the naked human clay, contributing its own "open-armed" chaos to the world. All of these associative links contribute to a text of multiple poetic resonances rarely achieved, or even sought, by novelists intent on advancing plot.

Rhythms of recurrence and association are common to Welty's short stories and novels, but only in the longer fiction does she also employ the novelistic rhythm of continuity—Northrop Frye's "semantic rhythm of sense"[26]—in solving the mysteries of each plot while maintaining the sense of life's mystery. In *The Optimist's Daughter* both associative and recurrent rhythms result from the storytellers and their respondents, from the interplay of memory and present event as they revise each other, and from verbal and visual identifications between Fay and Laurel. The recurrent rhythms of some paired passages suggest that Laurel and her stepmother function in the novel as alter egos: When Fay complains that Judge McKelva's death has left her "no one to call on but me, myself and I," her rhetoric is echoed by her mother, when Mrs. Chisom announces Laurel's similar status, without "father, mother, brother, sister, husband, chick nor child. Not a soul to call on . . ." (*OD*, 69). But it is the more logical rhythm of continuity, of conscious reasoning through analogy, that Laurel follows to an understanding that she has not been so different from Fay in her grandstanding insistence on her own interpretation of the lives of her beloved dead.

One distinction that has been alleged between novel and short story is that of theme: for example, that the short story often deals with an outsider in isolation.[27] It is to that end that Frank O'Connor argues in *The Lonely Voice* that the short story, not the novel, depicts "an intense awareness of human loneliness."[28] Certainly the short stories of Eudora Welty emphasize loneliness, yet her novels may emphasize it even more by placing the lonely character in a multitudinous family or community intent on ignoring uniqueness, as the Fairchilds ignore Laura's grief in *Delta Wedding*.

On the question of technique, the manner of closure is significant for genre. Charles May notes that the short story "is esthetically patterned in such a way that only the end makes the rest of the story meaningful."[29] Russian formalist B. M. Ejxenbaum says that while in a novel the ending involves "a point of let-up," the short story "amasses its whole weight toward the ending."[30] Welty often manages both let-up and epiphanic weight at the ending of a novel. In *The Ponder Heart*, for example, as Uncle Daniel is acquitted, readers experience not only comic relief but also the realization that nothing will change for Edna Earle, except perhaps that she may become even lonelier, the same fate that the reader comes to understand awaits Maria in James Joyce's story "Clay." The same technique is employed in *Losing Battles,* as the end of the novel brings closure in one sense after the end of the reunion, the cessation of the frantic activity to rescue the Buick, and the funeral for Miss Julia; yet the novel also achieves the sense of continuing possibility that accompanies the open-ended short story. The reader knows, as Gloria and Jack Jordan Renfro do not, that love will not be enough to protect from future battles two young people with very different expectations about life.

In the final scene, as they walk home together from the funeral, Gloria confidently predicts, "some day yet, we'll move to ourselves. And there'll be just you and me and Lady May"; but Jack, with "one of his eyes still imperfectly opened, and the new lump blossoming on his forehead for his mother's kiss," answers, "And a string of other little chaps. . . . You just can't have too many, is the way I look at it" (*LB,* 435–36).

It may be, as Mary Louise Pratt claims, that the short story has developed in ways determined by the demands of the novel. But in Eudora Welty's fiction, the dynamic of generic determination is reversed. Her novels are not simply long short stories; they demonstrate important novelistic elements. Yet they are indelibly marked by elements of the short story, especially by lyric techniques such as associative rhythms. John Edward Hardy was right when he told us long ago that *Delta Wedding* must be read "close, like a poem."[31] In fact, the closer we read all the novels, the more we understand that Welty is a lyric novelist.

Notes

1. Mary Louise Pratt, "The Short Story: The Long and the Short of It," *Poetics* 10 (1981): 187.

2. Harriet Pollack, "On Welty's Use of Allusion: Expectations and Their Revision in 'The Wide Net,' *The Robber Bridegroom,* and 'At the Landing,'" *Southern Quarterly* 29 (1990): 5, 31.

3. Rebecca Mark, *The Dragon's Blood: Feminist Intertextuality in Eudora Welty's* The Golden Apples (Jackson: University Press of Mississippi, 1994), pp. 3, 21.

4. Thomas McHaney, "Falling into Cycles: *The Golden Apples,*" in *Eudora Welty: Eye of the Storyteller,* ed. Dawn Trouard (Kent, Ohio: Kent State University Press, 1989), pp. 173–74, 189.

5. Ian Reid, *The Short Story,* Vol. 37, The Critical Idiom Series (London: Methuen, 1977), pp. 47–48.

6. Mary Louise Pratt, qtd. in Mary Rohrberger, "Between Shadow and Act: Where Do We Go From Here?," in *Short Story Theory at a Crossroads,* ed. Susan Lohafer and Jo Ellyn Clarey (Baton Rouge: Louisiana State University Press, 1989), p. 36. See also Robert Scholes and Robert Kellogg, *The Nature of Narrative* (New York: Oxford University Press, 1966), p. 3.

7. Pratt, "The Short Story," p. 183.

8. Charles E. May, *The Short Story: The Reality of Artifice* (New York: Twayne, 1995), p. 10.

9. Pratt, "The Short Story," pp. 184, 183.

10. Frank O'Connor, qtd. in Pratt, "The Short Story," p. 184.

11. Although not a novelistic attribute, what Pratt calls a "conspicuous tradition in the novel" is its tendency to focus on "writing and bookishness." See "The Short Story," p. 189.

12. Tzvetan Todorov, qtd. in Austin M. Wright, "On Defining the Short Story: The Genre Question," in *Short Story Theory at a Crossroads,* ed. Lohafer and Clarey, pp. 47–49. Contemporary theory defines the short story as any prose narrative that is not drama and (1) that is between five hundred words and the length of James Joyce's "The Dead" or Joseph Conrad's "Heart of Darkness," (2) that deals with character and action, (3) that has only a few episodes and no subplots, (4) that has a minimum of waste, (5) that favors the epiphanic ending or the moment of truth, and (6) that "leaves significant things to inference" (Wright, pp. 51–52).

13. Northrop Frye, *Anatomy of Criticism: Four Essays* (1957; rpt., Princeton, N.J.: Princeton University Press, 1971), p. 249.

14. Wright, "On Defining the Short Story," p. 48.

15. Michael Kreyling, *Author and Agent: Eudora Welty and Diarmuid Russell* (New York: Farrar, Straus & Giroux, 1991), pp. 107, 112.

16. Welty, qtd. in Kreyling, *Author and Agent,* pp. 162–63.

17. See Mary Anne Ferguson, "*Losing Battles* as a Comic Epic in Prose," in *Eudora Welty: Critical Essays,* ed. Peggy Whitman Prenshaw (Jackson: University Press of Mississippi, 1979).

18. Frye, *Anatomy of Criticism,* pp. 271–72.

19. Frye, *Anatomy of Criticism,* p. 272.

20. It should be no surprise that other elements of drama as well are incorporated throughout her fiction, since Welty was fascinated by the theater and tried her hand at play writing.

21. Ferguson, "*Losing Battles* as a Comic Epic," p. 305.

22. Reynolds Price, qtd. in Henry Mitchell, "Eudora Welty: Rose Garden Realist, Storyteller of the South." [1972] (*C,* 71).

23. Peggy Whitman Prenshaw, "Sex and Wreckage in the Parlor: Welty's 'Bye-Bye Brevoort,'" *Southern Quarterly* 33 (1995): 107–16.

24. See Ruth D. Weston, *Gothic Traditions and Narrative Techniques in the Fiction of Eudora Welty* (Baton Rouge: Louisiana State University Press, 1994), p. 148.

25. Eileen Baldeshwiler, qtd. in Rohrberger, "Between Shadow and Act," pp. 39–40.

26. Frye, *Anatomy of Criticism,* p. 272.

27. Wendell Harris, qtd. in May, *The Short Story,* p. 13.

28. Frank O'Connor, qtd. in May, *The Short Story,* p. 30.

29. May, *The Short Story,* p. 59.

30. B. M. Ejxenbaum, qtd. in May, *The Short Story,* p. 116.

31. John Edward Hardy, "*Delta Wedding* as Region and Symbol," *Sewanee Review* 60 (1952): 406.

Needing to Talk

Language and Being in *Losing Battles*
Richard Gray

"Maybe nothing ever happens once and is finished," observes Quentin Compson famously in *Absalom, Absalom!*

> *Maybe happen is never once but like ripples maybe on water after the pebble sinks, the ripples moving on, spreading, the pool attached by a narrow umbilical water-cord to the next pool which the first pool feeds, has fed, did feed, let this second pool contain a different temperature of water, a different molecularity of having seen, felt, remembered, reflect in a different tone the infinite unchanging sky, it doesn't matter: that pebble's watery echo whose fall it did not even see moves across its surface too at the original ripple-space, to the old ineradicable rhythm.*[1]

It may seem perverse to begin talking about *Losing Battles* by quoting *Absalom, Absalom!* After all, *Absalom, Absalom!* is arguably William Faulkner's most Gothic novel, in which the abiding Southern presence seems to be Edgar Allan Poe. It is melodramatic, even tragic, whereas *Losing Battles* is comic; it deals with the ghost-haunted gentry, while *Losing Battles* invites us into the lives of hill people fallen upon hard times. Faulkner's narrative weaves backward and forward over centuries, between Virginia, Haiti, Mississippi, New Orleans, and Harvard. In contrast, Welty's focuses on just a day and a half during the Depression and a family reunion; while not quite observing a classical unity of time and place, it seems to be quietly edging in that direction. However, quite apart from the Faulknerian resonance of the title (which reminds us that Welty shares with her fellow Mississippian a quite un-American interest in the romance of failure, and a typically Southern sense of the reality of defeat), there is in *Losing Battles* a deeply Faulknerian sense of the way many lives are woven into one life: repetition and revision are seen here as the norms of consciousness and narrative—so that "*maybe nothing ever happens once and is finished.*" "I wanted," Welty has said, when talking about how she came to write this novel, "to get a year in which I could show people at the rock bottom of their lives." But the year—more specifically, the day—that supplies the centerpiece of the story becomes a tapestry into which Welty can then weave the story of other days in other years. The family reunion, celebrating the ninetieth birthday of the oldest member of the clan, "Granny" Elvira Jordan Vaughn, becomes "*attached by a narrow umbilical water-cord*" to pools of memory, the "*old ineradicable rhythm*" of life as it has been lived by the Renfros and the Beechams for four generations along with the lives of various neighbours. "I wanted," Welty has also said in connection with this book, "to see if I could do something that was new for me: translating every thought and feeling into speech . . . I felt that I'd been writing too much by way of description, of introspection on the part of my characters."[2] The statement suggests exactly how Welty weaves the connections between past and present here, connecting one pool, one moment in space and time to another, which is just as Faulkner does, through the human voice debating, recollecting, revising, reinventing, each character constructing his or her own version of place and past. With sympathy and humor *Losing Battles* describes people waging a disgracefully unequal struggle against circumstances, but who remain hopeful despite everything—and who remain so, above all, because they use old tales and talking as a stay against confusion, as some kind of temporary defense.

"We need to talk, to tell," said Faulkner of Southerners once, "since oratory is our heritage." He might have been referring to the characters in *Losing Battles*. "Can't conversation ever cease?" asks one character, an outsider, toward the end of the novel; and any reader can easily see what he means. The Beechams and the Renfros, who make up the majority at this family reunion, never seem to stop talking. There are tall tales, family legends, personal memories, folk humor, religious myth, stories of magic and mystery; and everyone seems to possess his or her own storytelling technique. People comment on one another's storytelling abilities: when Uncle Percy Beecham, for example, begins to imitate the characters he is describing, his sister-in-law Birdie Beecham comments appreciatively, "He gets 'em all down pat . . . I wish I was married to him. . . . He'd keep me entertained." The dead, too, along with the living, are praised for their verbal gifts. Grandpa Vaughn, for instance, is chiefly remembered for his eloquence as a preacher, which his replacement as the local Baptist leader, the unfortunate Brother Bethune, can never match. "The prayer he made alone was the fullest you ever heard," recalls one of his grandsons, Uncle

Noah. "The advice he handed down *by itself* was a mile long!" Sometimes advice is offered to a novice speaker while he or she is speaking. "What's Normal?" asks Lexie Renfro when Jack Renfro's wife Gloria refers to her time at Normal School. "Don't skip it! Tell it!" Lexie receives advice in turn when she is about to embark on one of her more heartless tales about her experiences as a nurse: "Let's not be served with any of your stories today, Lexie," Beulah Renfro warns her.

Accompanying the main text, the talk requiring the reunion's attention, there is a subtext of comment, criticism, and anecdote, like that background of anonymous voices, inherited folk speech and wisdom, that gives resonance to traditional ballads and epic. There is the constant sense that each tale and conversation, however trivial, belongs to a larger body of speech, a continuum of storytelling; stories knit into one another, one anecdote recalls another in the series, and tales are told that we learn have been told many times before: "I wish I'd had a penny for every time I've listened to this one" (*LB*, 215),[3] murmurs Ralph Renfro as his wife Beulah begins to recall the story of her parents' mysterious drowning. Weaving backward and forward in time, repeating and embroidering, the family reunion fashions a rich tapestry of folk speech: a web of words that constitutes their identity, their moment in space and time.

The figure of weaving is chosen advisedly here, not least because the dearest gift that "Granny" Elvira Jordan Vaughn receives on her birthday is a quilt: "'Believe I'll like the next present better. I know what *this* is,' Granny told them, as she took a box covered in yellowing holly paper. . . . She took out the new-piece quilt. A hum of pleasure rose from every man's and woman's throat. When the mire of the roads had permitted, the aunts and girl cousins had visited two and three together and pieced it on winter afternoons. It was in the pattern of 'The Delectable Mountains' and measured eight feet square . . ." (*LB*, 222).

It is not difficult to catch the connection between the literal and metaphorical webs that compel our attention in *Losing Battles*. Both are expressions of communality: the strenuous effort to weave a pattern out of—and, in the end, against—the difficulties, discontinuities, and downright mess that constitute the basic fabric of these lives. Despite the "mire," the women of the family have struggled to make something that gives them a sense of identity, personal and communal: a feeling of being connected with their neighbors, their family, and their ancestors—other women who have woven something substantial in which to live and, eventually, to die ("'She'll be buried under that,' said Aunt Beck softly. 'I'm going to be buried under "Seek No Further,"' said Granny, 'I've got more than one quilt to my name that'll bear close inspection'"). And despite the mess, the battles constantly lost that define their material existences, both women and men also fight to weave an identity out of their words: to use language not only to give themselves a local habitation and a name, but to make them feel a part of that habitation—its present, its past, and its possible futures. It is entirely appropriate that, immediately following the presentation of the quilt to Granny, all the voices at the reunion rise "as one" in song:

> *Gathering home! Gathering home!*
> Never to sorrow more, never to roam!
> Gathering home! Gathering home!
> *God's children are gathering home.* (LB, 223)

In form and message, the song alerts us to that need for "home," for being and being a part of something that finds its expression in family gatherings, folk art, and folk speech. It is also entirely appropriate that the narrative should add this comment—this bass note, as it were—to that song: "As they sang, the tree over them, Billy Vaughn's Switch, with its ever-spinning leaves all light-points at this hour, looked bright as a river, and the tables might have been a little train of barges it was carrying with it, moving slowly downstream. Brother Bethune's gun, still resting against the trunk, was traveling too, and nothing at all was unmovable, or empowered to hold the scene still fixed or stake the reunion there" (*LB*, 223). "Nothing at all was unmovable": the metamorphoses of nature continue, despite our elaborate patternings, our attempts to tame and subdue things. The song, or speech, takes place within a world of flux, constant transformation; it can only give the temporary sense—or, rather, illusion—of stability and control.

There is another reason why the figure of the web seems so appropriate here, when talking about the evident need of the characters in *Losing Battles* to talk and to tell. Faulkner once suggested that *The Brothers Karamazov* would have been a much shorter and much better book if Dostoyevsky had "let the characters tell their own stories instead of filling page after page with exposition." He was joking, of course, in his own typically deadpan way, but the joke contained a serious point. Like Lexie Renfro, Faulkner believed that people need to "Tell it!": that all people, not just Southerners, need to speak themselves into being. And, unlike Lexie, Faulkner clearly felt that this was not just a moral imperative but an existential one: not just something that human beings *should do,* in other words, but *had to do* if they were to function as fully human. The key text here is, again, *Absalom, Absalom!,* and the key passage is one embroidering an image with which any reader of *Losing Battles* would be broadly familiar: "you are born at the same time with a lot of other people, all mixed up with them . . . all trying to make a rug on the same loom, only each one wants to weave his own pattern into the rug and it can't matter, you know that, or the ones that set up the loom would have arranged things a little better, and yet it must matter because you keep on trying or having to keep on trying."[4]

The sense of struggle is more to the foreground here than it is in Welty's use of the practice and figure of quilting. Even here, though, we should remember the mire through which the women struggle to make the quilt—and, of course, the darker shadows cast upon that practice by all those circumstances to which Welty's chosen title for the book alerts us. Battle is never very far from either Welty's or Faulkner's mind when they talk about talking. In both *Absalom, Absalom!* and *Losing Battles* human experience is seen as a kind of feverish debate in which each participant, eagerly or otherwise, struggles to make himself heard, fights to weave his own pattern into the complex web of voices that constitute his life. Both books—each, of course, in its own way—allow or rather compel the characters to tell their own stories, not for economy's sake, of course, so as to save "page after page of exposition," but so as to make the simple, fundamental point that this is how we make our lives.

Voices, talking: the entire process of a life assumes for Welty, as it does for Faulkner, the character of a seamless pattern of dialogue. The individual human being—be he or she a Quentin Compson or a "Granny" Vaughn—is seen entering a web of relations that constitute human history. To this extent, both writers produced works that are genuinely dialogic, works in which, as Mikhail Bakhtin suggests, "a character's word about himself and his world is just as fully weighted as the author's word usually is." "Language, discourse," Bakhtin insists, "is almost the totality of human life." The preceding statement could almost stand as an epigraph for either *Absalom, Absalom!* or *Losing Battles*. So, for that matter, could this longer observation of Bakhtin's, which returns us to a familiar image and an abiding obsession: "The living utterance, having taken its meaning and shape at a particular historical moment in a socially specific environment, cannot fail to brush up against thousands of living dialogic threads . . . it cannot fail to become an active participant in social dialogue."[5] Welty would almost certainly resist the terms Bakhtin uses here. She belongs, after all, to "a verbal community"—to use Bakhtin's phrase—

that was and is quite different from the one Bakhtin knew. However, that should not blind us to the fact that for both of them, as for Faulkner, communication implies community. What Welty's characters do is what Bakhtin argues the human subject *must* do and therefore the fictional character *should* do: engage in "the *social* dynamics of speech," as *part of* and yet also *apart* from a common verbal culture.

As social beings and yet autonomous individuals, Welty's people participate in what Bakhtin would have called a great dialogue or open dialogue, in which "the object is precisely *the passing of a theme through many and various voices.*" It is, of course, the passing that matters, the process of dialogue. For Welty, as for Bakhtin, language (speech) is an open system, a "mobile medium" (as Bakhtin puts it) that resists closure. "Each individual utterance," Bakhtin observes, "is a link in the chain of speech communication"; and since, by its very nature, that chain is of indefinite length or duration, it can have no beginning or end. The possibility of a final, finalizing discourse is consequently excluded, along with the claims of an authoritative one. Each talker is involved for a while in what Bakhtin calls "a continuous and open-ended . . . dialogue" that went on long before they began talking and will continue long after. We are reminded of this, the potentially unending nature of the human debate, the web of words we weave, when, toward the end of *Losing Battles,* Uncle Noah Webster says to Gloria, his niece: "Gloria, this has been a story on us that never will be allowed to be forgotten. Long after you're an old lady without much further stretch to go, sitting back in the same rocking-chair Granny's got her little self in now, you'll be hearing it told to Lady May [Gloria's baby daughter] and all her hovering brood . . . I call this a reunion to remember . . ." (*LB,* 354). Even the reunion that supplies the setting for most of the novel is to be given substance and weight, it seems, a sense of authenticity, by the feeling that it will one day be the subject of, rather than the occasion for, talk. What happens here and now will become part of a story by being woven into the fabric of speech.

Part of this story that Uncle Noah refers to is the suspicion, entertained at least for a while, that Gloria may in fact be a Beecham, entitled by blood rather than marriage to be a part of the reunion. Clearly, the possibility of incest that this raises is of little interest to the family. What excites them is the bright hope that they can press this apparent outsider into the group and so close the magic circle around themselves even tighter. "Say Beecham!" the women chant at Gloria. "Can't you say Beecham? What's wrong with being Beecham?" This is a Southern family romance with a vengeance, in which, as in so many romances from the region, the family tries to enforce relationship, to press the unwilling into member-ship. For a moment we are invited to consider a darker side to the reunion, the more coercive element implicit in the talk. After all, the way the family members bear down on Gloria is almost like a rape:

> the aunts came circling in to Gloria . . . all the aunts and some of the girl cousins . . . a trap of arms came down over Gloria's head and brought her to the ground. Behind her came a crack like a firecracker—they had split open a melon. She struggled wildly at first as she tried to push away the red hulk shoved down into her face, as big as a man's clayed shoe, swarming with seeds, warm with rain-thin juice.

> They were all laughing. "Say Beecham!" they ordered her, close to her ear. They rolled her by the shoulders, pinned her flat, then buried her face under the flesh of the melon with its blood heat, its smell of evening flowers. Ribbons of juice crawled on her neck and circled it, as hands robbed of sex spread her jaws open. (*LB*, 268–69)

A watermelon rather than a corncob, on this occasion, but it serves a similar purpose to that of the notorious instrument of violence in Faulkner's *Sanctuary*. It enables those "robbed of sex" to force themselves and their will, for a while, upon an unwilling victim; it becomes part of a strategy of violence, to make "one of them" become "one of us." The other part of that strategy is, of course, the chant that accompanies and reinforces the action, turning a violent series of impulses into an equally violent ritual. The chant—"Say Beecham!" "Can't you say Beecham?"—reminds us that what these women are trying to do is drown Gloria's voice and being in their own. "I don't want to be a Beecham!" Gloria cries, just before she is forced to the ground. But the aunts and cousins want her to change her speech, to "say" the name that articulates a new identity. "I achieve con-sciousness," Bakhtin argues, "I am conscious of myself and become myself only while revealing myself for another, through another, and with the help of another. . . . To be means to be for another, and through the other, for oneself."[6] However, neither Welty nor her characters need any help—from Bakhtin or anyone else—to realize that, in human terms, to say is to be: that it is through speech that people enter into consciousness of self and community, and so into the possibility of deliberate, moral action. The women who try to force Gloria to "Say Beecham!" understand, only too well, how words enable identity. Through their incantation they register their own innate sense of the power, and the human inevitability, of language; they also offer us a measure of just how much that power can be for good *or* ill.

"A reunion," Welty once said in an interview, "is everybody remembering together—remembering and relating when their people were born and what happened in their lives, what that made happen to their children, and how it was they died. There's someone to remember a man's whole life, every bit of the way along. I think that's a marvelous thing."[7] That statement also explains clearly why the Beechams and Renfros need to talk: the way talk enables them to escape from their loneliness into a sense of being and belonging. To put it simply, they feel they are there because they say they are and other people say so too. Yet all the while they are saying so, there are warnings about the other side of things. Quite apart from those elements and moments in the narrative, such as the attack on Gloria, that recollect the darker possibilities of language, there are reminders all the time of the mystery of personality, the secret phases of experience, the accidents in life—all those things that no dictionary, no web of words can ever quite accommodate.

Gloria Renfro is important here too because, despite all the pressure that is put upon her, she continues to insist that she is different—not a Beecham or a Renfro but an orphan, alone and apart. "I'm here to be nobody but myself," she declares at one point; and elsewhere, "I'm one to myself, and nobody's kin, and my own boss, and nobody knows the one I am or where I came from." Sometimes she comes close to feeling defeated. "Oh, if we just had a little house to ourselves. . . . And nobody could ever find us," she exclaims to her husband, and then adds hopelessly, "But everybody finds us. Living or dead." At the end of the book, however, she has not given up. She is still insisting on her separateness, her and other people's essential privacy ("people," she declares, "don't want to be read like books")—still standing out against the family and what she, at least, sees as the imprisoning web of its stories.

And then there is Judge Oscar Moody: a rather different matter from Gloria, but still a reminder that the story told at the family reunion is a partial one. He is a comic ghost at the feast, brought there by chance, cut off by education and social position from the easygoing manners of his hosts, and slightly embarrassed by the recollection that it was he who put Jack Renfro in jail. The event that brings him and his wife to the reunion is a car accident: swerving to avoid Gloria and her baby, the Judge drives his Buick off the road, and it ends up balanced uncertainly on the edge of a precipice called Banner Top. There it provides a grotesque reminder of the way things happen to spoil even our best-laid plans: the accident, in short, calls our attention to the accidental. It seems elephantine, or at least less than sensitive to Welty's light touch, to add that it also offers a comic emblem of the precarious nature of things, the abyss that hovers beneath us and our chattering. Still, the emblem is there, however delicately or allusively it may be sketched in; and it is pointed by such nice touches as the fact that the hickory sign on which the Buick rests, as it sticks out over Banner Top, asks the question "Where Will YOU Spend Eternity?" The question is never answered, of course, just as the plaintive demands made by the Judge's wife to be returned immediately to "civilisation" never meet with a satisfactory response. But the reader is reminded by such things that there are other dimensions of experience, different vocabularies standing on the edge of this particular verbal world. The sign warns us that *any* sign merely marks out a boundary.

As far as warnings of this kind are concerned, however, one character stands head and shoulders above the rest: Miss Julia Mortimer. During the course of the reunion, the news is brought that Julia Mortimer has died. Many of those present were taught by her and remember her, not necessarily with affection, as a magisterial presence. Now they rehearse her story and try to recollect what sort of impression she made on them; and this impression is summed up, really, by their response to her own words in a letter that Judge Moody, another of her former pupils, reads out to them. The letter, written by Julia Mortimer not long before her death, is a sort of apologia, an explanation or defense of the aims that sustained her throughout her career. "All my life," she confesses defiantly, "I've fought a hard war with ignorance. Except in those cases that you can count off on your fingers, I lost every battle." And the reactions of the Beechams and Renfros, as they listen, are notable for three things above all: uneasiness, incomprehension, and amusement. "Don't read it to us!" several of them cry before the Judge begins; then, when he has begun, "I can't understand it when he reads it to us. Can't he just tell it?" "I don't know what those long words are talking about," complains Aunt Birdie Beecham; while Beulah Renfro appears to speak for most of the Judge's audience when she concludes, "Now I know she's crazy. We're getting it right out of her own mouth, by listening long enough" (*LB*, 299).

Julia Mortimer, it is clear, spoke in another idiom, a language foreign to most of those assembled at the reunion. She believed in enlightenment, progress, making something of oneself. "She had designs on everybody," Uncle Percy Beecham recollects; "she wanted a doctor and a lawyer and all else we might have to holler for some day." She also believed in traveling beyond the horizons of one's local community and culture: for instance, she told one Beecham, Uncle Nathan, to see the world. "He took her exactly at her word," comments Beulah Renfro, Nathan's sister. "He's seen the world. And I'm not so sure it was good for him." All her life, in fact, she was committed to a vocabulary and vision that demoted the Beechams, the Renfros, and all that their reunion represents to the level of the provincial, the backward, and the ignorant ("you need to give a little mind to the *family* you're getting tangled up with," she apparently told Gloria just before her marriage). The Beechams and Renfros, in turn, hardly began to understand her when she was alive, nor even want to now that she is dead; as they see it, she was domineering, eccentric, or, more simply, crazy. Welty's point is not, of course, that either side is right in this debate (although, by setting her book well back from the time of writing it, she may just possibly have been working from the assumption that the forces of progress, represented by Miss Julia, have been losing less of this particular battle recently than those forces embodied in the family reunion). What she is doing, rather, is giving a further edge, another accent to the talk of the family reunion. She is throwing the "remembering and relating" of these hill folk into sharper relief by reminding us of other forms of intelligence, other ways of turning the world into words, that for good *and* ill the reunion dialogue happens to leave out.

And then there is the simple, brute fact of Julia Mortimer's dying. Lexie Renfro was Miss Julia's nurse, and the news of her death prompts Lexie to recall what Julia was like during the final stages of her life. "All her callers fell off, little at a time, then thick and fast," Lexie remembers, put off by her abrasive manner, her unwillingness to suffer fools gladly; and Miss Julia was left waiting, sitting in her front yard, for people who never came. "I used to say," Lexie declares, "Miss Julia, you come on back inside the house. You hear? People . . . aren't coming visiting. Nobody's coming." But evidently Miss Julia took no notice. So for her own good, Lexie insists, with that bland authoritarianism characteristic of so many nurses, she tied her charge to the bed. "I didn't want to, but anybody you'd ask would tell you the same: you may have to."

Miss Julia was reduced to writing letters, incessantly and feverishly, with her tongue hanging out, Lexie recalls with amazement, "Like words, just words, was getting to be something good enough to eat." Lexie mailed them, she admits, because she "couldn't think . . . what else to do with 'em." It is, of course, one of those letters that Judge Moody reads out to the bewilderment of the family. Eventually, though, even this resource was taken away from her. Miss Julia's pencil was snatched from her hands by her ever-solicitous keeper ("I could pull harder than she could," says Lexie triumphantly), and she was then reduced to the mere gesture of shaping words with her finger on the bedsheet or her palm. Then Lexie left her—"I had the reunion to come to, didn't I?" she asks her audience plaintively (*LB*, 284)—and it was while she was by herself that Julia Mortimer died: virtually imprisoned, it seems, and without close friends, visitors, or even sympathy.

The final picture Julia Mortimer presents is a pathetic one, certainly, but pathos is not Welty's primary aim. What she is alerting us to here is something else: a series of subtle variations on the theme of old tales and talking, the need to tell that all her characters share. Miss Julia, the former schoolteacher, betrays the same compulsion as the men and women whom she once taught: to communicate and so substantiate, to create a feeling of being someone somewhere rather than just anyone anywhere via the use of language. In her case, the language is more a written than a spoken one; but that perhaps is less significant than the fact that, for her, the compulsion becomes exactly and simply that—a compulsion. She continues to write herself into life even when the instruments of writing are denied her. Her hands trace out an identity—or, to be more accurate, the need for an identity—far more starkly and finally than even the voices of the Beechams and Renfros ever can. Nobody receives the message since nothing is even written; but Miss Julia still continues to resist death through her compulsive and constant gesture.

Faulkner once claimed that everything ever written ultimately carries one message, "*I was here.*"[8] And Miss Julia seems to be repeating that message, with a change of tense—more "I *am* here" than "I *was* here"— as she runs her fingers over her palm or the bedsheet; as long as she writes, she senses, she still *is*. If Miss Julia's writing herself— that is, her writing from, about, and finally *of* herself—is a shadowy transcription of the speaking themselves, talking themselves into being, favored by her former pupils, then the isolation from which she writes during her final days acts in turn as a memento mori: a haunting reminder of the vacuum over which any bridge of words is built. The letters, visible and invisible, are another sign like the one on Banner Top, "Where Will YOU Spend Eternity?" They offer the chilling message that, whatever communication and community we may enjoy during our lives—and, in particular, on occasions such as a reunion—we must all eventually die alone.

Of course, Julia Mortimer is not the only person writing herself into life; Eudora Welty is doing the same, or something similar. Behind the tellers of the tales in *Losing Battles* lies the teller of the tale *Losing Battles*: the web of words is one that also speaks the message "*I was here*" for Welty. It is a web of words that begins to establish itself as just that—a web of words, an elaborate verbal construct—right from these opening sentences on the first page:

> When the rooster crowed, the moon had still not left the world but was going down on flushed cheek, one day short of full. A long thin cloud crossed it slowly, drawing itself out like a name being called. The air changed, as if a mile or so away a wooden door had swung open, and a smell, more of warmth than wet, from a river at low stage, moved upward into the clay hills that stood in darkness.

> Then a house appeared on its ridge, like an old man's silver watch pulled once more out of its pocket. A dog leaped up from where he'd lain like a stone and began barking for today as if he meant never to stop. (*LB*, 3)

A portrait like this is a triumph of specificity and containment: Welty presents us here with a shifting, evanescent place which nevertheless seems to have been caught for a while and composed. We are in that shifting, metamorphic, and yet somehow briefly harmonized environment where, after the gift of the quilt to "Granny" Vaughn, the members of the family reunion sing their song. Something of the Mississippi hill country at a particular moment on a particular summer morning has been grasped, snatched from the dream of time passing, and framed; and in catching it, Welty matches up to her own description of the ideal photographer or story writer who knows, she says, just "when to click the shutter," the precise instant at which people or things "reveal themselves." Yet for all that, something, it is intimated, has been squeezed out and remains elusive: some quality of the moment remains uncaught and seems to slip through the artist's fingers, eluding every one of her traps and snares. The way this is intimated to the reader is subtle but inescapable.

The prose never stops emphasizing its own fragility and artfulness. It is compulsively metaphorical, insistently figurative, and even sportive, as though the author were trying to point out that this is, after all, an artifact, a pattern made out of words. Within the space of three sentences, for instance, a cloud is compared to a name; the air is said to change "as if . . . a wooden door had swung open"; and a house suddenly appears in the dawn light like a watch pulled out of a pocket (and not just *any* watch or *any* pocket: here as elsewhere, the figurative reference assumes a dramatic life of its own). The very insistence of this by the constant use of "like" or "as if," little touches such as the metaphor of naming, or portraying the dog as believing he is barking/voicing the day into life all help to remind us that the writer's language, like every other means used to alleviate our separateness, is an imprecise and not entirely trustworthy medium. Even when fought with this weapon, it seems, all battles must be losing battles, although they are never irretrievably lost.

For Faulkner, writing was a quest for failure; for Welty, evidently, it is a losing battle—but a battle that has constantly to be fought. And, for both writers, there is clearly a link between their own art and the broader human project that their characters dramatize—of trying to spin a sense of reality out of language. "The mystery lies," Welty has said, "in the use of language to express human life." All her work is concerned with that mystery: the aboriginal impulse that, as she sees it, we all share to render life comprehensible through the use of the spoken and written word. It is, perhaps, wrong to place too much emphasis ultimately on the role the Southern love of talk played in her life. It *was* important, certainly, for Welty just as it was for Faulkner; but it was important in that it allowed her, just as it did her fellow Mississippian, to learn very early about the power and possibilities of speech—and then led her from this quickly to understand the vital part that language plays in *all* our lives, regardless of whether we are Southern or not. Quite simply, she came to know through the Southern "need to talk" that we all need to talk in order fully to live. It is hardly an accident, after all, that two of the three sections into which Welty's book about her beginnings as a writer is divided place the major emphasis on voice: "Listening" and "Finding a Voice." Nor is it by chance that one crucial moment in what Welty calls her "sensory education" is described in this way:

> At around six, perhaps, I was standing by myself in our front yard waiting for supper, just at that hour in a late summer day when the sun is already below the horizon and the risen full moon in the visible sky stops being chalky and begins to take on light. There comes a moment, and I saw it then, when the moon goes from flat to round. For the first time it met my eyes as a globe. The word "moon" came into my mouth as though fed to me out of a silver spoon. Held in my mouth the moon became a word. It had the roundness of a Concord grape

> Grandpa took off his vine and gave me to suck out of its skin
> and swallow whole, in Ohio. (*OWB*, 10)

The beauty of a passage such as this, like the intricate beauty—on a larger canvas—of her novels, is that Welty manages to convince the reader simultaneously that words are everything *and* nothing. They are everything because they constitute all the world we make for ourselves. Issuing out of our fundamental, definitively human rage for order—not only to see, but to know—they are as vital to us as breath. They register for us the irresistible otherness of things in terms that are, at their best, vivid and sensory. Another American writer, William Carlos Williams, suggested that a thing known passes from the outer world to the inner, from the air around us into the muscles within us. And the word "moon" seems to achieve the same vital transit: as Welty recalls it, "moon" is not just an abstract, arbitrary sign; it has the "roundness" of a sensory object—it generates the sense that contact between the namer and the named has taken place. This is a gift, offered with "a silver spoon," that we are all offered—although very few of us can take as much advantage of that gift as Welty does. And it can fill us with a sense of presence, as it does the six-year-old girl recalled here: we, like her, can feel that we know and can participate in the world through the word. It is everything, then. It is, however, also quite literally nothing. The word "moon," despite the way it assumes shape and fullness in the mouth, is "no thing": it is, at best, a powerful, sense-laden sign for the mysterious, distant object that shimmers in the evening sky.

Caught in this moment, in effect, as it is caught at length in the novel *Losing Battles,* is the sense that the world must remain irreducibly other—set apart from all our attempts at naming. Just below the web of words that we are continually spinning, in order to tell ourselves that we live, is the "something" that must always remain ungrasped and unknown: the "something" that is intimated, for example, in a shifting, metamorphic natural scene, in the loneliness of an outsider, or in rumors of the abyss and death. *Losing Battles* is a comic novel, certainly, and as definitively Southern in its own way as *Absalom, Absalom!* But its comedy offers a serious revelation of the human impulse that, above all, makes us human; and its Southernness enables a clearer general understanding, a more vivid and universally valid declaration, of the extraordinary ways of words. At least one question is answered, then, by the time the novel draws to a conclusion: "Can't conversation ever cease?" The answer is no, not while there are people like the Beechams and Renfros around—which means, finally, any people at all.

Notes

1. William Faulkner, *Absalom, Absalom!* (New York, 1936), p. 261. An earlier version of this essay appeared in the *Southern Literary Journal,* to which due acknowledgment is made.

2. Linda Kuehl, "The Art of Fiction XLVII: Eudora Welty," *Paris Review 55* (Fall 1972): 77. See also p. 85.

3. See also William Faulkner, "An Introduction to *The Sound and the Fury,*" *Mississippi Quarterly* 26 (Summer 1973): 412.

4. Faulkner, *Absalom, Absalom!,* p. 127. See also *Lion in the Garden: Interviews with William Faulkner 1926–1962,* ed. James B. Meriwether and Michael Millgate (New York: Random House, 1968), p. 18.

5. Mikhail Bakhtin, *The Dialogic Imagination,* ed. and trans. Caryl Emerson and Michael Holquist (Austin: University of Texas Press, 1981), p. 276, see also 332; *Problems of Dostoevsky's Poetics,* ed. and trans. Caryl Emerson (Manchester, 1984), pp. 7, 131, 265; *Marxism and the Philosophy of Language,* trans. Ladislav Matejka and I. R. Titunik (Cambridge, Mass.: Harvard University Press, 1986), p. 96; *Speech Genres and Other Late Essays,* trans. Vern W. McGee (Austin: University of Texas Press, 1986). For the sake of convenience, I have attributed the works usually associated with Bakhtin's name to him. However, I am aware of the problems of attribution involved here and, in particular, of the probability that Medvedev and Volosinov were at least partly responsible for some of these works.

6. Bakhtin, *Problems of Dostoevsky's Poetics,* p. 287.

7. Kuehl, "Art of Fiction," p. 80.

8. *Essays, Speeches, and Public Letters,* ed. James B. Meriwether (New York: Random House, 1966), p. 114.

Beyond Loss

Eudora Welty's *Losing Battles*
Karl-Heinz Westarp

> It is the business of fiction to embody mystery through man-
> ners. . . . The mystery [h.s. James] was talking about is the
> mystery of our position on earth, and the manners are those
> conventions which, in the hands of the artist, reveal that cen-
> tral mystery. [The fiction writer is] concerned with ultimate
> mystery as we find it embodied in the concrete world of sense
> experience.[1]

Does Flannery O'Connor's characterization of fiction and the fiction writer
hold true also of the Eudora Welty of *Losing Battles*? Or does Welty in
this novel only describe "manners" with little concern for any "ultimate
mystery"? In other words, are the characters in the novel left with the
experience of their battles and their losses, or is there any "beyond" that
gives depth to their life pilgrimage? It is the prime aim of this essay to
discuss the feasibility of an anagogical or spiritual reading of *Losing Battles*.
After comments on other readings of the novel I will offer some examples
of the overwhelming presence of biblical material in the text, which to me
seem to legitimize an interpretation of the novel as the depiction of a
painful pilgrims' progress through numerous lost battles to the peace and
hope of forgiveness.

Losing Battles has been interpreted in many different ways as the
clash between the agrarian Southern past of the Beecham-Renfro families
and the future as taught by Julia Mortimer. Michael Kreyling[2] and Jan
Nordby Gretlund[3] have given us helpful critical surveys of first reviews
and later interpretations, and Peggy Whitman Prenshaw[4] collected five
substantial essays on *Losing Battles,* including three in which Douglas
Messerli, Louise Y. Gossett, and Robert B. Heilman discuss possible religious overtones in the novel. Both Gossett and Heilman place central
importance on Jack as a figure with biblical character traits. "For his
family, Jack is a radiant innocent, a 'blessed mortal,' and a good Samari-

tan [Luke 10.30–37]. He is an incorruptible Prodigal Son [Luke 15.11–32] prodigally received with a feast and rejoicing and forgiving."[5] Welty uses the image of the prodigal son as an epithet for Jack several times (*LB*, 80, 82, 84, 126, 149, 163), yet the comparison halts, since Jack is not—as in the biblical parable—the alien "saving" Moody's Buick; rather, he is one of the family. In characteristic Welty fashion the image is satirized when Mrs. Moody, herself a Presbyterian, comments on a group of hungry Methodists coming from Sunday service, "headed home for dinner," who pass the site of the accident without offering help (*LB*, 133). "I'd just like to see a bunch of Presbyterians try to get by me that fast!" she says (*LB*, 134). Yet unlike his model, Jack did not leave his family on his own account, as did the youngest son in the New Testament story. After all, he carried off Curly's safe in an attempt to defend and restore his family's honor. Nevertheless, I think Welty uses the narrative elements from the stories of the Good Samaritan and the Prodigal Son so convincingly that they become an integral part of our understanding of Jack.

Jan Nordby Gretlund has correctly pointed out that Welty "at times indulges in caustic satire on religious topics," directed in *Losing Battles* mainly against the religious denominations of Methodists, Baptists, and Presbyterians. She enjoys leveling acid comments at religious hypocrisy, but I do not agree with Gretlund's conclusion that "Welty's own religious inclinations are singularly undramatic. In her fiction she does not offer religious hope."[6] In support of this rather dogmatic statement Gretlund adduces Welty's comment in *One Writer's Beginnings:* "I painlessly came to realize that the reverence I felt for the holiness of life is not ever likely to be entirely at home in organized religion" (*OWB*, 33). Gretlund overlooks Welty's rather cautious formulation that her reverence for the holy is "not ever *likely* to be *entirely* [my emphases] at home in organized religion." Into the bargain he leaves out the direct continuation, in which Welty moderates her statement: "It was later . . . that the presence of holiness and mystery seemed, as far as my vision was able to see, to descend into the windows of Chartres, the stone peasant figures in the capitals of Autun . . . in the shell of a church wall in Ireland still standing on a floor of sheep-cropped grass with no ceiling other than the changing sky." That is, she is certainly aware of the presence of holiness and mystery and that they actually could reside in places of "organized religion." I consider Welty's sentence immediately after this remark even more revealing: "I'm grateful that, from my mother's example, I had found the base for this worship—that I had found a love of sitting and reading the Bible for myself and looking up things in it" (*OWB*, 33). Welty's answer to John

Griffin Jones in a 1981 interview corroborates this: "I love to read the Old Testament. The Old Testament has the best stories. The King James Version stays with you forever, rings and rings in your ears" (*C,* 324). Little surprise, therefore, that a close reading of *Losing Battles* proves that Welty's language is permeated with the English of the Bible.

The family Bible is of pivotal importance for the life and history of the "God-fearing" (*LB,* 344) Vaughn-Beecham-Renfro families. Apart from the births, marriages, and deaths recorded in it, it contained Ellen's now fatally lost gold ring (*LB,* 24, 266), Ellen's hair in Chronicles, Grandpa's spectacles "deep in the crease of First Thessalonians," and close to it Sam Dale's card to Rachel (*LB,* 266). More important than this physical existence of the Bible is its spiritual presence in the different layers of language and narrative. I already mentioned the New Testament parables of the Good Samaritan and the Prodigal Son. Welty's love of Old Testament stories can be seen in her use of story elements and names. The information about Julia Mortimer's death makes Gloria cry, "as if she had been struck in the forehead by a stone out of a slingshot," as Goliath was struck down by a stone from David's slingshot (*LB,* 157 [1 Sam. 17.49]). In the morning after the reunion Miss Beulah compares Jack to Samson, "Reminds me of Samson exactly" (*LB,* 394 [h.s. Judg.16.29–30]); in turning over Moody's car he proves to be even better than Samson because he shows judgment and afterward "still got strength" (*LB,* 435, 434), whereas Samson got killed in the act.

Robert B. Heilman has drawn attention to a number of casual allusions to the Bible,[7] and his list can be extended considerably.[8] Kreyling has observed the eponymous overtones in Moody's and Mortimer's names.[9] He says, for example, that Mortimer suggests death for the "primitive men" of Banner.

Most striking is, I think, Welty's ample use of biblical names and the significance they obtain once the names are transferred into English. The farm was built by Jacob Jordan, grandfather to Granny. "Jacob" means "supplanter"—i.e., for Esau (Gen. 25.25–26)—and "Jordan" is the Hebrew for "flowing down," since he is the oldest source of the "family river," which continues through Granny (Miss Thurzah Elvira Jordan; *LB,* 179), the last of her generation, and Jack, who also bears the name of Jordan. Another Old Testament name, "Nathan," means "gift." It was a gift—though also a sin—that Nathan stood up for the family against the exploitations of Dearman and killed him. Through repenting and cutting off his hand Nathan reminds the family that "Destruction Is At Hand" (*LB,* 115 [Luke 21.20]) with Welty's wonderful sense of the absurd contrast between the figurative meaning of "at hand" and the preacher's amputated stump. The warnings on his other posters show the same message of warning and admonition: "Where Will YOU Spend Eternity?" (*LB,* 404) and "Live For Him" (*LB,* 431). As already mentioned, Jack's last name, Jordan, links him to the old family, but his first name, "Jack" or John, which means "gracious," indicates that he also belongs to the "new dispensation," as did John the Baptist through his double link with the Old and New Testaments. In drawing attention to those names I am not suggesting that Eudora Welty was aware of all their overtones, but they certainly are a further indication of the fact that biblical material is almost second nature to her and must be considered carefully in any spiritual reading of the novel.

At this point Gretlund and others might object that Welty uses biblical materials only as elements of the narrative without further spiritual significance. After all, Welty is a storyteller, and as such she loves the biblical stories, not as a preacher or a philosopher. To her, "fiction isn't the place for philosophy," at least not "when put in as philosophy" (*C,* 60). As Shelby Foote said in a conversation with Welty, "I've never known Southerners do anything but tell stories";[10] they have—and these are Welty's own words—"inherited, a narrative sense of human destiny" (*C,* 78). Particularly in connection with *Losing Battles,* which Welty wanted to be "novel-as-drama," with some 90 percent dialogue,[11] in which all should "be shown forth, brought forth, the way things are in a play . . . the thought, the feeling that is *internal* is *shown* as external" (*C,* 46). I cannot interpret this in any other way than as a clear authorial statement that the surface, the story, "manners" are not all, that we have to look for something "beyond"; in other words, *Losing Battles* is not only the story or the stories of a family's "multifront" battles but that the stories have deeper dimensions as well. This is precisely what the Greek word *mystærion* indicates, namely that which is not seen or said.

In 1972 Welty told Charles T. Bunting, "The sense of mystery in life, we do well to be aware of. And, of course, I think we do try to suggest that mystery in writing a story, not through any direct or cheap way but by simply presenting the way things happen" (*C,* 57). The detailed description of place and setting is never an end in itself; it leads the reader on to a deeper "beyond." In *The Eye of the Story* Welty states that all the arts are connected with place and "all of them celebrate its mystery" (*ES,* 119). "From the dawn of man's imagination, place has enshrined the spirit" (*ES,* 123). Against this background Cleo's teasing question in connection with Gloria's wedding gains greater depth: "Do you all worship off in the

woods somewhere?" (*LB*, 49). Welty also comments on mystery in relation to her characters: "They know something else is out there. It's just an
awareness of spaciousness and mystery of—really, of living, and that was
just a kind of symbol of it, a disguise. I do feel that there are very mysterious things in life, and I would like just to suggest their presence—an
awareness of them" (*C*, 307).

Flannery O'Connor described the depth dimension of character as
the novelist's central concern: "A story always involves, in a dramatic
way, the mystery of personality," and characters lean "toward mystery
and the unexpected."[12] Welty seems to be in full agreement with her fellow Southern writer, who acknowledges the need to see through
appearances and look for a deeper meaning: "If the writer believes that
our life is and will remain essentially mysterious, if he looks upon us as
beings existing in a created order to whose laws we freely respond, then
what he sees on the surface will be of interest to him only as he can go
through it into an experience of mystery itself."[13] Kreyling has summed
up Welty's presentation of deeper dimensions in her fiction: She "displays
in the time- and place-bound particulars of Banner, Mississippi, the timeless combatants of a larger battle, one that can genuinely be termed cosmic.
. . . Welty views her people and their condition with the depth and breadth
of the philosopher who sees the universal in each moment."[14]

One of the striking features of *Losing Battles* is the great number of
family quarrels, told repeatedly from different angles to show how they
affect and hurt the single family members dead and alive. The characters
have a growing awareness of the consequent guilt that lies heavily on
them. Therefore, one of the essential battles they fight is the recognition
of evil. Everybody in the Banner community knows that the individual
who loses this battle with evil will sin, and that the only way back to
fellowship and understanding is forgiveness. Forgiveness means a rees-
tablishing of the ties of friendship and affection that were broken through
conflicts, enmities, or even crimes. Forgiveness means a change of people's
relationships with each other, where animosity is replaced by peace and
understanding replaces hate. Yet forgiveness—on a different level—also is
a form of losing. In her fiction Welty accepts the presence of evil, but she
does not seem to acknowledge "sin." In his first interview with Eudora
Welty (1980) Gretlund suggested: "You do not seem to be interested in
the concept of 'sin' or in the idea of 'evil,'" to which Welty answered: "I
am, though. Not in 'sin'—not from a Roman Catholic point of view like
Flannery O'Connor, because I am ignorant of that religion. But I do believe that there is 'evil.' I believe in the existence of 'evil,' or else your

reaching for 'good' could not mean anything. I do feel there is 'evil' in the world and in people, very really and truly. I recognize its power and value. I do!" (*C*, 227). Therefore, Gretlund concludes that Welty "makes no attempt to hide the fact that inexplicable evil exists among the Mississippi farmers" and that "there is no attempt to explain away the tale of Miss Lexie's premeditated evil," which is later atoned for because Miss Lexie is "converted" to helping Jonas Hugg (*LB*, 377). Yet Gretlund is not willing to accept, as some critics do, "that only the presence of unexplained evil will give Welty's fiction its full depth."[15]

The following examples will show that evil and sin loom large in *Losing Battles*. Jack was sent to Parchman because he had "stolen" the safe, but Uncle Noah defends his innocence, saying that Jack did not sin because his upbringing taught him what it means to steal: "If a boy's brought up in Grandpa Vaughn's house, and knows drinking, dancing, and spot-card playing is a sin, you don't need to rub it into his hide to make him know there's something a little bit the matter with stealing" (*LB*, 44). Awareness of sin is even present in little Elvie's skipping song: "*Yield not to temptation for yielding is sin* . . ." (*LB*, 137–38). Welty lets Judge Moody define "sin" as follows: "I suppose it just aggravates whatever's already there, in human nature—the best and the worst, the strength and the weakness. . . . And of course human nature is dynamite to start with" (*LB*, 319). In that sense almost all members of the reunion sense the presence of sin. Uncle Curtis remembers Grandpa's last sermon in connection with the previous reunion: "Oh, he thundered! He preached at us from Romans and sent us all home still quaking for our sins" (*LB*, 183). It is Uncle Nathan's mission, as his posters show, to raise consciousness of sin, which is a necessary presupposition for a growing understanding of forgiveness. As "the car is salvaged only after it has fallen; similarly, the family must accept its fall, its doom of death, before its members can be saved."[16]

Forgiveness is the central theme of Brother Bethune's sermon, and it is of paramount importance to notice the progression from Grandpa's last threatening sermon, based on Saint Paul's letter to the Romans, to Bethune's admonition, based on John the Baptist, whose central message to his fellow Jews was to "repent, for the kingdom of heaven is at hand" (Matt. 3.2). Brother Bethune says, "Forgiveness would suit us all better than anything in this lonesome old world" (*LB*, 209, 321, 372, 427 [Luke 24.47]). Forgiveness is so much in the air that Judge Moody can come up with the curiously contradictory statement "Forgiving seems the besetting sin of this house" (*LB*, 319). Even Nathan's homicide can be forgiven.

When he had confessed to Julia, she told him—says Beulah, who was present and heard it: "Nathan, even when there's nothing left to hope for, you can start again from there, and go your way and be good" (*LB*, 344 [Isa. 1.18; John 8.11]). Nathan obeyed this consoling piece of advice and changed to a life of atonement. Jack is aware of the capital crime that Nathan committed, and he is willing to take on vicarious suffering for Nathan in that he considers himself a stand-in for Uncle Nathan in going to the pen: "As long as I went and took my turn, maybe it's evened up, and now the poor old man [i.e., Dearman] can rest" (*LB*, 431 [Matt. 25.40]).

In spite of all the sufferings the family has to endure and the seemingly hopeless situation, there is hope for a new beginning, and this as a result of forgiveness. Welty told Bunting, "I wanted to show indomitability there. I don't feel it's a novel of despair at all. I feel it's more a novel of admiration for the human being, who can cope with any condition . . ." (*C*, 48). "I wanted to take away everything and show them naked as human beings" (*C*, 50). Danièle Pitavy-Souques concludes about Welty's description of the human condition that there is a "depth of the tragedy of human relations behind the brilliant surface. . . . Man's dignity and heroism is this endless fight against death and all forms of evil, which are forms of death."[17] "Ultimately what Welty shows us is that man has within him the capabilities of being both godly and sinful."[18] But there is in *Losing Battles* an unmistakable movement from evil and sin to forgiveness and being good. One of the most striking images of this is the "procession" of helpfulness and forgiveness between former combatants that Jack has arranged, with the school bus pulling the Buick and the van assisting with its brakes on their united way toward Banner (*LB*, 407). Seymour Gross comes to the conclusion that the novel's "spiritual ebullience is the result of Welty's grand understanding of the joys and griefs of her large cast of characters who, do what they will to tip the world, cannot upset its balance. There is something in the world which does not like a fall—call it the life force or the natural order or whatever."[19]

Apart from Jack, Gloria, "more sinned against than sinning," is the most prominent representative of innovation and life force. Again and again (*LB*, 111, 171, 314, 359, 361, 429, 431, 434) she underlines that she wants a life of independence for Jack, Lady May, and herself: "Oh, if we just had a little house to ourselves . . ." (*LB*, 271). Though she is forced to pronounce herself a Beecham (*LB*, 269)—or even may have Beecham blood in her veins—she is "standing her ground" in a family against which Julia Mortimer had warned her (*LB*, 250). As Kreyling has pointed out, "Gloria's fixation upon the future runs smack into the reunion's indifference to time."[20] Her last sentences in the novel are full of hope for a life "beyond" the quarrels of the reunion: "And some day, some day yet, we'll move to ourselves. And there'll be just you and me and Lady May" (LB, 435).

What kind of future can there be for Jack, Gloria, and Lady May after the reunion and Julia's funeral? A feasible answer to this question I see in Welty's extended use in Losing Battles of central images from Bunyan's Pilgrim's Progress. In Bunyan's allegorical narrative the central character Christian leaves the City of Destruction, is refreshed on the Delectable Mountains, and travels through the country of Beulah on his way to the Celestial City. His wife Christiana follows after, accompanied by her neighbor Mercy. They are escorted by Great-heart, who overcomes Giant Despair before they reach the Gates of the Celestial City. In Losing Battles Miss Beulah, the hostess of the family reunion, holds a central position. And I mentioned Welty's idea that this novel is not a narrative of despair. Three times reference is made to the design on Granny's quilt as "The Delectable Mountains" (LB, 222, 287, 347), which could be seen as an image of the mountains of Banner country. Gloria uses the term "The Gates of Beyond" (LB, 110) both about Lady May's sleep and also about Jack's being beyond the borders of Mississippi and behind the bars of Parchman. But in the context of Bunyan's allegory the term is also a hint at life after death.

In an essay on Welty's "Angelic Ingenuity" of balance, Seymour Gross[21] has stated that Julia's last words, "What was the trip for?" (LB, 241), level Lady May's first words ever: "What you huntin', man?" (LB, 368), which in their turn possibly are a remembrance of Aunt Nanny's earlier words to Lady May: "Who you hunting?" (LB, 64). Both these quest formulations are in line with the Homo viator theme of Pilgrim's Progress. Mrs. Moody has a simple answer to the question of meaning in life: "All I know is we're all put into this world to serve a purpose" (LB, 306). Julia Mortimer understood her purpose here on earth as a vocation to bring knowledge, which was her "Heaven" (LB, 299). She "was ready to teach herself to death for you" (LB, 240 [John 15.13]), says Uncle Curtis. But her altruism was not accepted; on the contrary, Uncle Dolphus says, "Julia was our cross to bear" (LB, 240, [Matt. 16.24]). Julia's final instruction to the Banner community is given in her "post-mortem" letter: "And then, you fools [i.e., you, who did not want to learn]—mourn me" (LB, 292), upon which Brother Bethune quotes from the Bible, "Whosoever shall say, Thou fool, shall be in danger of hell fire"! (Matt. 5.22). Julia lost her battle as a teacher, as many critics have observed, but she was fully aware of the spiritual dimension of losing a battle: "The side that gets licked gets to the truth first" (*LB*, 298), she says in her letter to Moody, with clear overtones of the blessings of the fall.[22]

After having attended Julia's funeral Jack and Gloria notice Sam Dale's and Rachel's graves. The narrator comments on Rachel's sliding grave that it is "ready to go over the edge of the bank, like a disobedient child. The small lamb on its headstone had turned dark as a blackened lamp chimney"; whereas Sam Dale's rubbed name "shone out in the wet" (*LB*, 427–28). Maybe Rachel, whose name means "ewe" (Gen. 29.6), really was the black sheep of the family. Her mystery (*LB*, 251, 253, 259, 265) was linked to Sam Dale, as his card to her, which was so carefully kept in Granny's Bible, reveals (*LB*, 266–67). Gloria reports what Julia, who also knew about Rachel's secret, had told her: "She said every mystery had its right answer—we just had to find it. That's what mysteries were given to us for" (*LB*, 252). And Beulah observes that Gloria "might have been Rachel's secret" (*LB*, 256). Maybe the rather different state of the graves hints at Rachel's and Sam Dale's chances in a "beyond" after having fulfilled their life pilgrimages.

At this point I think it is important to note that Eudora Welty carefully embedded a movement toward harmony into the very structure of *Losing Battles*. She arranged a similarity of tone at the end of Part III, which after Brother Bethune's sermon ends in forgiveness, and at the end of Part VI, where forgiveness is actually lived out by all parties involved and which can therefore be described as the final climax of the novel. At the end of Part III the members of the family sing:

> *Gathering home! Gathering home!*
> Never to sorrow more, never to roam!
> Gathering home! Gathering home!
> *God's children are gathering home.*

There can be no doubt about the eschatological overtones of this hymn.[23] Similarly, at the very end of the novel Jack sings:

> *Bringing in the sheaves,*
> Bringing in the sheaves!
> We shall come rejoicing,
> *Bringing in the sheaves!*

Both songs have the joyful overtones of returning home with a good harvest, but also returning home with life's harvest through "The Gates of Beyond."

I hope to have shown that Welty is not only a writer who vividly describes external manners, but that she also allows us to sense mystery "beyond" manners. For her, too, fiction deepens the mind's "sense of mystery . . . by contact with reality, and its sense of reality . . . by contact with mystery." The interplay between internal and external, between mystery and manners defines fiction as "incarnational art" since it deals "with all those concrete details of life that make actual the mystery of our position on earth."[24] Similarly in the teaching of the church, the outward sign—say of water in connection with baptism—is indicative of the inward and spiritual reality of grace, as much as Jesus is the physical sign of the spiritual godhead—"and the word became flesh" (John 1.14), i.e., became incarnated. Saint Paul calls this a "mystery," and it is characteristic of any mystery that the spiritual or internal reality is hidden behind or "beyond" the visible or the external, as Welty calls them. In Flannery O'Connor's terminology, "The fiction writer presents mystery through manners, grace through nature, but when he finishes there always has to be left over that sense of Mystery which cannot be accounted for by any human formula."[25] The thrust of Welty's *Losing Battles* indicates that "beyond" the experience of ever so many lost battles in the Banner community, there is the peace of forgiveness on almost every single step of its inhabitants' life pilgrimages.

Notes

1. Flannery O'Connor, *Mystery and Manners* (New York: Farrar, Straus & Giroux, 1979), pp. 124, 125.
2. Michael Kreyling, *Eudora Welty's Achievement of Order* (Baton Rouge & London: Louisiana State University Press, 1980), pp. 140–42 (hereafter: *Achievement*).
3. Jan Nordby Gretlund, *Eudora Welty's Aesthetics of Place* (Columbia: University of South Carolina Press, 1997), pp. 177–78.
4. Peggy Prenshaw, ed., *Eudora Welty Critical Essays* (Jackson: University Press of Mississippi, 1979), pp. 269–366 (hereafter: *Essays*).
5. Louise Y. Gossett, "*Losing Battles*: Festival and Celebration," in *Essays*, p. 345 (cf. Robert B. Heilman, "Losing Battles and Winning the War," in *Essays*, p. 292).
6. Jan Nordby Gretlund, pp. 98–99.
7. "To Lucifer *(LB,* 81), the Crack of Doom *(LB,* 129), the book of Romans *(LB,* 183), the Flood *(LB,* 250), Job *(LB,* 404, also p. 293), the parting of the Red Sea *(LB,* 406) [as the road between Ora Stovall's Methodist and Brother Bethune Baptist churches in Banner], Solomon" (whose wisdom Jack senses in Gloria [*LB,*

432]). Heilman, "Losing Battles and Winning the War," p. 292, n. 3.

8. Other references are to "Noah's Ark" for the school bus (*LB*, 4 [Gen. 6, 14]) and for the Buick (*LB*, 135); the "Walls of Jericho" (*LB*, 5 [Josh. 6, 2–5]); "the cherubs of Heaven" (*LB*, 9); "Damascus" (*LB*, 49), the city of Saul's conversion (Acts 9, 1–19); the "Creation" (*LB*, 62, 250); and "The Day of Judgment" (*LB*, 83, 212, [John 5, 25–29]).

9. Kreyling, *Achievement,* pp. 149–50.

10. Louis D. Rubin, "Growing up in the Deep South: A Conversation," in *The American South,* ed. Rubin (Washington, D.C.: United States Information Agency, 1991), p. 60.

11. Heilman, "Losing Battles and Winning the War," p. 273.

12. O'Connor, *Mystery and Manners,* pp. 90, 40.

13. O'Connor, *Mystery and Manners,* p. 41.

14. Kreyling, *Achievement,* pp. 143–44.

15. Gretlund, *Aesthetics,* pp. 7, 182, 185.

16. Douglas Messerli, "'A Battle with Both Sides Using the Same Tactics': The Language of Time in *Losing Battles,*" in *Essays,* p. 361.

17. Danièle Pitavy-Souques, "Technique as Myth: The Structure of *The Golden Apples,*" in *Essays,* p. 267.

18. Messerli, "'A Battle with Both Sides,'" p. 366.

19. Seymour Gross, "A Long Day's Living: The Angelic Ingenuities of *Losing Battles,*" in *Essays,* p. 327.

20. Kreyling, *Achievement,* p. 148.

21. Gross, "A Long Day's Living," p. 329.

22. Welty's formulation is reminiscent of O'Connor's story "The Lame Shall Enter First" and of the biblical promise "The last shall be the first" (Matt. 19, 30).

23. Notice the similarity to O'Connor's "Judgement Day" story, which in the 1963 version had the title "Getting Home."

24. O'Connor, *Mystery and Manners,* pp. 79, 68.

25. O'Connor, *Mystery and Manners,* p. 153.

From Jerusalem to Jericho

Good Samaritans in *Losing Battles*
Bridget Smith Pieschel

But he, willing to justify himself, said unto Jesus,
"And who is my neighbor?"

(Luke 10.29, KJV)

"Nobody with a good car needs to be justified."
Flannery O'Connor, *Wise Blood*

Eudora Welty has made her place in modern fiction with, among other things, her ability to take an old story and retell it so that ancient truth is made new, even commonplace. Both her claiming of classical mythology in *The Golden Apples* and her sly reworking of the Brothers Grimm in *The Robber Bridegroom* illustrate her versatility with this method. And many have noted that Welty's use of myth is complex and layered. Rebecca Mark, for example, asserts that readers "only understand her meaning when we hear the interplay between the moment, the physical detail, and the echo, the metaphoric and symbolic resonance, what Welty calls 'the double—doubling back,' the process of dispersal and return."[1] In *Losing Battles* Welty uses the Parable of the Good Samaritan to ridicule the modern progressive conviction that salvation is by machine, rather than by love and compassion. At one level or another, many of the characters in this novel initially make the error of placing inordinate value and trust in some kind of machine, to the neglect of the living. In the largest sense Welty's theme in *Losing Battles* is Agrarian, in that it rejects the city and the outside world, and embraces the family. But the cultivation of the land is not the primary focus of the novel. In fact, the land is worn out, depleted. As Jan Nordby Gretlund emphasizes, Welty's "fiction has come out of a particular landscape and is based on her long familiarity with its people. . . . It is the human life lived there that gives place its emotional impact in her fiction."[2] The type of Agrarianism *Losing Battles* most clearly reflects is the family life Andrew Lytle describes in "The Hind Tit," close and self-sufficient until the father, convinced by his children (corrupted by "the state normals") that the old farm life is backward, "buys a truck," the first step downward into economic disaster.[3] The devaluation of the machine is seen most clearly in the actions of Jack Renfro, who in the course of the novel moves from a childlike, desperate love for his decrepit truck to choosing a companionable stroll with his wife over an offered back-seat ride on the velvet cushions of the Moodys' Buick. Thus Welty's treatment of the inner workings of a humanly flawed hero, Jack, produces a work which, as Albert Devlin says, "lacks the stiffness of agrarian ideology" but "takes the agrarian ideals as its text, warming them with humor and hope."[4]

In her reworking of the Good Samaritan story, Welty teases the reader with the association of Jack Jordan Renfro with both the danger to and the rescue itself of the Judge's car. In the parable, "A man went down from Jerusalem to Jericho and fell among thieves" (Luke 10.30), to be rescued later by a man from Samaria. In *Losing Battles,* Jack Renfro is both the thief (that is, he is just out of the pen for stealing Curly Stovall's safe) who causes the Buick's precarious balance on the ledge, and the means for the later rescue. As Gloria says, "For the sake of the reunion you were willing to run Judge Moody into the ditch. Now for his sake you are just as willing to break your neck" (*LB,* 126).

Jack, grateful for the fact that the Judge turned his car away from Gloria and Lady May in the road, labels himself as clearly as one of Uncle Nathan's signs. The Judge, who like everyone else assumes it is the car that needs saving, says, "A good garageman had better be sent for now, to bring that car down before something more happens to it" (125). When Jack asks for the privilege, saying "You got a Good Samaritan right here!" the Judge rejects his human compassion and gratitude for something else: "I'm not asking for a Good Samaritan. I'm asking for a man with some know-how . . . and a good piece of road equipment" (125). In his eyes Jack alone is insufficient—the good piece of equipment has to come first.

Like the original Samaritan, who personally treats the injured man's wounds and pays for his lodging, Jack wants to treat the Judge like kin because he "can't let some stranger shove his way in and help" rescue the car. All of the characters in this scene focus initially on the car as the most valuable thing, and Jack especially assumes his mission is rescuing the car, not the Judge, who is really the one in need of help.

Aycock Comfort provides the transitional image in the modern version of the parable. It is hard not to see Welty's joke here. Aycock comforts as the Holy Comforter, the Holy Spirit, especially when, later in the scene, Elvie begins singing the old Baptist hymn "Yield Not to Temptation." Some of the lines Elvie does not sing are from the chorus:

> *Ask the Savior to help you,*
> Comfort, strengthen and keep you
> He is willing to aid you
> *He'll carry you through.*[5]

Jack, the savior whom Gloria is going to "let . . . be a Good Samaritan one last time," is joined by "Comfort," who actually chose to go with Jack to prison, who has been his constant companion laboring in the Parchman fields, who parks himself in the Buick, and who gives it, for the first time, a benevolent human spirit. Aycock is modest, mentioning once to Gloria that he is "not the one they generally calls on" (38), but he is the most faithful of companions. So what if the car is now balanced on "Destruction is at Hand"; Aycock Comfort will not leave: ["And I will pray the Father and he shall give you another Comforter, that he may abide with you forever. (John 14.16)]. He has found his place in "a seat in a pleasure car" (130).

The story moves forward comically, with the Judge learning that he is stranded mainly because of the rigid keeping of the Sabbath; everyone is in church and every business is shut tight. In the original parable, first a priest and then a student of the law, a Levite, passed by the beaten man without a glance. Welty alludes to organized religion and to the law—both of which ignore the Judge's predicament. She uses more hymns, the folk poetry of the red clay hills, to introduce her version of the indifferent priest. Jack explains to Mrs. Moody that when the wind is right, the Methodists can be heard. On cue, they sing, "Throw out the life line! Throw out the life line! . . . Someone is sinking today!" (128) This sentiment falls short, however, when Uncle Homer Champion's van, marked with a "pilgrim father's" ax, careens by and flings out a "life line," that is, "a length of chain, a little shorter than the length of Jack's arm" (133). The life line has been thrown, but no one is holding on to the other end, and it will be up to Jack later to form his human chain far superior to the broken link Uncle Homer offers. Mrs. Moody, however, still wants to place her hope in "church people who'll stop and help" her, "a fellow worshipper," but Preacher Dollarhide's Ford coupe does not even slow down to look, rushing on toward Sunday dinner, oblivious to the Moodys' need (133). Jack is temporarily encouraged when Elvie drives the Banner school bus down the hill, hoping to "be the help," but everyone knows the bus is no good without Jack, and it ends up in the ditch, helpless as the Buick. Disgusted, Mrs. Moody deplores the lack of modern conveniences in Banner. Jack replies, "We got people . . . the best thing in the world" (141). The Judge, still convinced that the machine is superior, says, "I don't need anything but a single piece of machinery in good working order and a tow line." "And a driver," Jack reminds him.

As the tires start to explode, crippling the Buick, the Judge nervously asks his wife, "How much longer do you think Providence is prepared to go on operating on our behalf?" (142). Mrs. Moody is still putting her hope in Curly Stovall's telephone, and the Judge prays for "a good solid truck," still not recognizing that his savior is standing in front of him. Shortly afterward Curly appears, sent by "Providence," according to Mrs. Moody. Curly, of course, is the Levite, the law, the holder of the rule book who says first, "You're trespassing" (145). He disparages the "pleasure car," warning in a "deacony voice" that Banner Top is "full of temptations of all kinds" (146). Greeting Jack, he tells him that he is trying to formalize his legal position by running for justice of the peace, assuming that his (formerly Jack's) truck will help him be elected: "This truck is my answer to Homer. A solid-built, all around, A-one, do-all truck. . . . It's ready for anything and everything, you name it—from hauling in their hay for 'em to pulling 'em out when they get stuck. . . . Any act of neighborly kindness a justice of the peace can offer will be furnished cheap at the price" (147).

However, Curly's key interest here is "the price," when Jack, as the true Good Samaritan, never intends to charge a fee for any of his help. The biblical parable is the answer to the question "Who is my neighbor?," a question Curly Stovall cannot answer since he thinks being neighborly has a price. He also assumes—saying "This is the law!"—that he can order Aycock Comfort to drive the car to safety. Finally, after going up a dollar in price, he proclaims, "I don't do Sunday business! Tain't the law and tain't Christian" (151). Jack, who has always privileged love and compassion over the law, seems to see the car as more and more human: he jumps into the truck to "save" the "suffering Buick"; but Curly keeps control and finally deserts them for his campaigning at the fish fry. Jack has to begin accepting the fact that a machine is only as good as the one who is driving it, that the "great big truck" Mrs. Moody had such high expectations for was still only a machine driven by the imperfect law.

As Willy Trimble warns her, after delivering the Judge back to them, "Told him better to stay put with who he's with. . . . Stand still: your answer always comes along" (154). It is no accident that Willy Trimble is driving mules, not a car.

It is at this point in Welty's retelling of the parable that she expands the role of the lawyer, the Levite, to include the rigidly idealistic system of education represented by Miss Julia Mortimer, the system which could not save Miss Julia, or Jack, or Gloria (who never really wanted to be saved). Valuing knowledge even over love, Miss Julia "wanted people to spread out their minds and their hearts to other people, so they could be read like books," as artifacts, not as living beings. As Gloria later points out, "People don't want to be read like books" (432). The bus full of teachers, headed to Miss Julia's funeral, represents education's inability to rescue anyone or anything, no matter how good the intent. Speaking of Aycock, still patiently waiting in the Buick's backseat, one of the teachers says, "He's about to go off over the edge of doom, and there's not much you and I can do about it, Mrs. Grierson. We're only teachers" (156). Significantly, though, she is speaking of Aycock, not the car. She recognizes that the Buick's inhabitant is more important than the now nearly useless "pleasure car," but she still cannot offer any hope for rescue. They drive off, hurrying to witness Miss Julia's funeral.

Welty, for all of her sympathy for Julia Mortimer, presents her as a failure, incomplete, unable to ask for love instead of a book whose title she cannot remember. Uncle Noah Webster tries to explain her flaw: "Her voice! She had a might of sweetness and power locked up in her voice. To waste it on teaching was a sin" (295). She is as rigidly bound as Curly is by his "no business on Sunday" rule, and in the end she loses her battle without really admitting why. It is with Miss Julia that Welty begins to make the original parable most clearly her own story. She takes the wounded victim, left "half dead" in the road to Jericho, and looks at him through a prism or perhaps through the "spotted mirror" Jack shaves in on his first morning home. The one needing rescue—part Judge and Mrs. Moody, part Aycock Comfort, part "suffering Buick"—is finally Miss Julia Mortimer, but her Good Samaritan, the Judge, arrives too late.

Jack, still confident in his role as Samaritan, using his mule, a wagon, and Vaughn, takes the Moodys home to the bosom of the reunion. When the little group arrives back at the gathering, however, Welty shifts the myth and redirects it significantly away from Jack, still innocently confident in his Samaritan role, to the Judge and to Miss Julia, both fallen from that innocence. The role-shifting does not suggest an ambivalence about her theme, but, as Warren French poses, it illustrates Welty's assumption that "people are two things at once and that their 'identity' at any given moment is determined by the context in which they are discovered."[6] It is time now in the story for Jack to be taken care of. He will give up his Samaritan role for a time, while his own wounds are tended, and the Judge and Miss Julia will take the stage.

Willy Trimble found Miss Julia fallen down in the road, but she died before he could get her back to shelter. Her journey was incomplete, as was her rescue, because her call for her Samaritan was not answered soon enough. By the time the Judge hears of Miss Julia's last weeks from Lexie, he is fully aware of his failure, that he "passed by on the other side" (Luke 10.30) when he should have stopped and given comfort. What is worse is that Miss Julia called out in particular to him in a letter he carries in his pocket, a letter he reads aloud to his protesting listeners. His wife points out that because he has read the confidential letter aloud, he seems "unlawyerlike," but his relinquishing of "the highways and byways of Mississippi law" (319) comes too late for Miss Julia. The Judge confesses that he "suffered an attack of cowardice, there on the road" (305). The biblical parable never tells why the traveler set out to walk from Jerusalem to Jericho—we only know he intended to go and that he never got there, even after his rescue. It is Welty who remembers the omission, this incomplete journey and its apparent futility. Maybe the traveler should have just stayed home, for as Miss Julia says finally, "What was the trip for?" (241). Jack Renfro, desperate to get back home and stay there, would not have begun the journey to start with, seeming to echo Huck Finn's simple analysis of *Pilgrim's Progress* "about a man that left his family it didn't say why."[7] Or perhaps the trip was *for* being rescued, or to be the rescuer, and Miss Julia, in the end, was neither.

Welty's reflection of the parable is darkest when it focuses on Miss Julia as the wounded journeyer. Noel Polk touches on the importance of Miss Julia as traveler but misses the mark in explaining her journey's significance. He says that in *Losing Battles* "most characters in one place want desperately to be in another place and expend a good deal of energy trying to get there, even if they do not necessarily know where 'there' is or what they hope to find when they get there. I need not remind you that Miss Julia Mortimer actually dies in the road."[8] Welty is not emphasizing Miss Julia's death "in the road" as the main thrust of this scene, but rather that her Good Samaritan, who is supposed to be traveling the same road as Julia, does not rescue her. She dies "of neglect" and not because she wanted "desperately to be in another place."

In an astute reading, but one which actually makes Welty's characterization of Julia Mortimer more pointedly esoteric than it warrants, Douglas Messerli stresses that the journey metaphor Welty associates with Miss Julia is symbolic of Julia's "historicism, her view of life as a journey through time."[9] In a larger sense, Messerli's reading is sound, but the most obvious pattern Welty is repeating is the controlling metaphor of the Good Samaritan parable. Unlike Jack, who plays his part nearly effortlessly, the Judge as Samaritan is not "Good" enough. There is no rescue, no beast, no inn with a bed for Miss Julia. In a sense, Miss Julia, like the Moodys with their Buick, is putting her love and faith in a product—the product of her own educational system. The Moodys value the "pleasure car" over people (at least in the beginning); Miss Julia values books and the polished, educated person, the Judge, over a diamond in the rough like Jack Renfro.

Her rescue a failure, Miss Julia speaks through the Judge as he reads her letter at the reunion. Her point of view—lacking in the original parable—is that of the victim. Did the original traveler ever regret setting out for Jericho? Miss Julia considers the question herself and decides, "even if Providence allowed us the second chance, doubling back on my tracks has never been my principle." In her fallen state she asserts the rightness of her journey and its difficulty:

> Things like this are put in your path to teach you. You can make use of them, they'll bring you one stage, one milestone, further along your road. . . . There's a lesson in it. You can profit from knowing that. You needn't be ashamed to crawl— to keep on crawling. . . . Then you can find yourself lying flat on your back—look what's carried you another mile. From flat on your back you may not be able to lick the world, but at least you can keep the world from licking you. (299)

Miss Julia is deceiving herself. She has not kept the world from licking her. Her bravado—her assumption that she is not completely "beaten and robbed"—allows her to give the Judge the instructions that delay his rescue journey. First she says, come to Alliance "at your earliest convenience," and then she adds, "Bring your Mississippi law with you" (300). The Judge's role is set: he will not be the Good Samaritan unconcerned about his own time, or what is convenient to him; he is labeled by Miss Julia herself as the Levite, the lawyer, who "when he was at the place, came and looked on and passed by on the other side" (Luke 10.32). Although she wrote her plea on the "flyleaf out of her Testament," and although the

Judge had said "Anything for Miss Julia," he held her letter for a month (301). Yes, he started out the moment he received her map/"maze" in the mail, and he became "unlawyerlike" in reading her letter to the reunion, but he realized he "was already too late when he started," that "when at last she sent for" him, "he failed to get there" (306–7). Mary Anne Ferguson understands only part of Welty's point when she says that the stranded journeyers in *Losing Battles* "can depend only on themselves, though the passers-by have made some contribution to the rescue."[10] Miss Julia's tragic error is, although she tries to call for aid, that she only truly trusts herself to save herself. The parable demands that self be negated—Miss Julia cannot allow that, and perishes. Her system of life, her controlling passion, has been the construct, the machine, of education, and it has failed her. Even though, as Seymour Gross notices, "Beck, with 'awe and compassion' in her voice, says that Julia . . . went at it [education] just as hard as a steam engine," the machine breaks down—it cannot rescue her; it cannot pull her from the ditch.[11] The law, the machine, the Judge, will not get there on time because she depends on an artifact instead of on humanity.

Welty uses the drawn-out final "rescue" of the Buick as the triumphant fulfillment of her Samaritan theme. Jack comes back into clear focus as the true Samaritan, capable of unselfish compassion and willing to value the person over any machine or rule of law. In Part V Granny's comment that "'The Wayfarer's Bell . . . brought [everyone] running'" returns the plot to the stranded Buick (336). Judge Moody has to face his own failure and humble himself to ask for help. First Uncle Nathan reminds him, "I believe in the old method of traveling," that is, he privileges walking over the machine, the "pleasure car." As Judge Moody digests this information, his wife comments, "Judge Moody's ready to drop" (350). The Judge has admitted to himself that he could not save Miss Julia, that the law is foolish that would prevent probable cousins Jack and Gloria from marrying, that he cannot do anything but accept being "stranded" at the reunion as his due, that even the rescue of his own car is out of his hands. Stripped of all of his preconceived notions of right and wrong, he accepts the offer of the guest room, where Jack and Gloria would have slept and from where Lady May has to be removed. Here his healing can begin, and the tale can blur and refocus on the true Good Samaritan, Jack Jordan Renfro. Jack will rescue not only the Buick, but Judge Moody and, symbolically, Miss Julia Mortimer, all on his second day back in Banner.

The dreamlike sequence of Vaughn's nocturnal epiphany leads into the climax of the tale. Using the mirroring that has characterized the allusion from the beginning, Vaughn contemplates Jack, not as the Samaritan, but as the journeyer, the one who falls "among thieves" and is beaten and deserted: "had Jack all in secret fallen down—taken the whole day to fall, but falling. . . . Could Jack take a fall from highest place. . . . another part of people's getting tangled up with each other, another danger to walk up on without warning—like finding them lying deep in the woods together . . . ?" (363). But, Vaughn ponders, who can rescue Jack? Should he? Is he worthy? Is he able? He notices the Buick, focusing his attention on the stranded car that "looked like a big shadowy box mysteriously deposited . . . not to be opened [that is, by Jack] till morning." Forgetting the Buick, he comforts himself by gazing at the school bus (Vaughn is guiltily enamored of learning) "peacefully stranded in the ditch." Foreshadowing the scene to come in the morning, Vaughn "with the chain he'd brought . . . hitched her [Bet the mule] to the bus . . . and led her; and without the slightest fuss . . . the bus creaked once . . . and surfaced to the road" (364).

Vaughn has completed his own version of the parable, but the object he has rescued (even though he has brought it home using his own "beast") is still only a bus, not a human being. Thinking of the difference, Vaughn's satisfaction is muted, qualified. He grudgingly concludes, "without Jack, nothing would be no trouble at all." He tries fiercely to endow the school bus with humanity, conscious of how warm the radiator is, how the steering wheel is "warm and sticky as his own hands." Vaughn, "gritting his teeth . . . backed the bus up again . . . accomplishing the drop and hurdle of the ditch. . . . The bus, as long as he held the wheel . . . he could feel that bus on its own wheels rolling on his tongue . . . going down, inside and outside . . . the sky he could see went on performing . . . like a breaking chain" (365). Vaughn's chain will not hold, though he pours all of his desire and his force into it. He naively assumes as he passes the Wayfarer's Bell on his way to the house that "no one was lost any more." Jack may not be book smart, but he knows better than Vaughn that nearly everybody is lost.

Welty said once about Isak Dinesen's stories that the old "tales" on which those stories are based are a colorful "procession" within the text: "Sometimes they can be felt to be passing, like a procession not more than one street over; sometime we see their old rich banners and colors, catch their songs, and sight their retinues of seraphic or diabolic origin; and sometimes that procession and the procession of [Dinesen's] story cross and mingle . . ." (ES, 262). Welty could be speaking of herself here and of the "cross and mingle" of her own tale with the biblical parable, what

Michael Kreyling has called "the muted story which runs within the relatively 'real' story."[12] The funeral procession to Miss Julia's graveside service is a concrete representation of Welty's own procession metaphor. Flannery O'Connor's half-crazed evangelist might have said, "Nobody with a good car needs to be justified," but like O'Connor, Welty is suggesting that *everybody* needs to be "justified," because *nobody* has a good car, not even Jack, especially not Jack Renfro.

The morning of the funeral dawns rainwashed, and before the rescuer arises, the Moodys have set forth on their journey back to reconnect with the "suffering Buick," not even bothering to eat a "company breakfast." At breakfast Mr. Renfro tells Jack about his nighttime attempt to use dynamite to liberate the car, while being careful to keep Aycock safe. Mr. Renfro would not "harm a neighbor," recalling the question which prompted the Samaritan parable. And he reminds Jack of what he has learned of "neighbors," that they nearly always need looking after: "I've learned by my time of life you've got to go a little slower than you would be inclined, because wherever you put your foot down there's a fool like Aycock that don't know enough not to keep out of your way" (373). In the following scene Aycock is reinvested with the metaphor of the Holy Spirit, the Comforter, the "living Comfort inside the Buick," but as Miss Beulah points out when they head toward the trapped car, "Comforts generally act by contraries." The thematic point here is no less than a form of the eternal debate between what is God's will and what is human will. The Comforter is contrary; God's blessing is unpredictable, inexplicable. It requires humility and faith to recognize its worth. Is Aycock still inside the Buick? Only a foolish and childlike faith would assume so: Jack replies: "Sure he's in there, Mama . . . asleep on all fours, like a bird dog" (378). As Jack leaves, cheerfully headed for Banner Top, his mother concludes that the battle he is riding toward is not completely human: "Stovall and Moody are about to come to grips with their two machines" (375). However, the battle is not really between the two machines, but between the machine and the human spirit.

On Banner Top the actors gather for their final improvisational performance of the parable. First Curly backs his and Jack's truck partially up the hill, and although Curly is more concerned about his two dollars than anything else, Jack wants him as a partner (Curly "sticking to the wheel and [h.s. Jack] doing the engineering"). Then Jack stands at the top of the hill, arms open, embracing the scene, personifying the truck, calling it "her" and telling his mother that a driver has to "pamper" it. Welty teases us with a description of the truck: "With the spots and circles of oil

... it was iridescent as butterfly wings. .... On the brow of its cab the original wording had emerged, 'Delicious and Refreshing,' [though the windshield was] stuck up with adhesive like a cut face" (381). This description of the truck is significant because it alludes to the original parable and also because it emphasizes that the only real value in the machine is in the humanity Jack projects onto it. The "oil" whose spots make the "finish" as beautiful as a natural creation, the butterfly, is reminiscent of the medicinal oil and wine the Good Samaritan uses to treat the victim's wounds. "Delicious and refreshing," while literally referring to a soft drink, also recalls the wine and the meals the Samaritan bought when they reached the inn. And the mention of the adhesive and the "cuts" remind the reader of the bandages the Samaritan uses to cover the beaten man's injuries.

As the climax of the rescue nears, Curly tries to back out, but Jack has already tied him to the Buick and he cannot escape, even when he says he "ain't playing" anymore (383). That Jack is the hero of the rescue is now clear to his audience and to the reader. Mesmerized, the Judge concludes that "what chance we have depends on Jack," and Miss Beulah agrees, saying "Don't count on either one of those two machines," contrasting the "grab bag" mishmash of the truck's replaced parts with Jack's human wholeness.

The Buick, resisting rescue, slides over the ledge, its wheels turning "innocently in free air" (384). Jack refuses to let go, forcing the crowd to embrace him in a "human chain"—first Gloria, then the Judge, then Mrs. Moody, then Miss Beulah. As they hang suspended, Jack's urging to "hold things like they are so they don't get no worse" reflects Welty's theme as the iridescent circles of oil on the truck reflect the light. Holding, embracing is Jack's purpose. Those he loves seem to be sliding over the edge into darkness, deprivation, and death. Making the world better is perhaps impossible, but hanging on to what they have—each other—might keep things from getting any worse. He has forced them all into one embrace. Are they embracing and rescuing the Buick or Jack himself? Gloria still resents being a part of the "human chain" since they are "still where [they] were yesterday. In the balance," but when the rope snaps, she hangs on and follows Jack over the edge (390).

Jack, "like Samson," then pushes the perpendicular Buick back into driving position, and all begin the journey back onto the road. "We're all going to the same place," Jack cries (397) as Vaughn and the school bus join the procession, the final "human chain" moving toward Banner cemetery, "gathering" up schoolchildren from the "edge of nowhere" at Jack's urging (399). As they slowly pass the place from which Jack began his

Samaritan good deed, the Judge says, "that's my ditch," and all notice a new Uncle Nathan sign, paint still damp: "Where Will YOU Spend Eternity?" Continuing the journey metaphor, Mrs. Moody resigns herself to the difficulty of the path toward eternity, or the graveyard: "Well, just keep on twisting and winding. . . . I suppose we've got to get past everything there is before we're there" (404). "There" draws closer as the journeyers notice gourd birdhouses painted "skull-white" hanging above Preacher Bethune's house. Foreshadowing the democracy of the graveyard, the procession passes "election posters for races past and still to come . . . faces of losers and winners, the forgotten and the remembered, still there together and looking like members of the same family," Uncle Homer's poster listing his virtues "like a poem on a tombstone." This procession only pauses briefly to deposit the children at the schoolhouse, but it cannot stop long for Death, only for a short pause for Jack's scuffle with Curly and the Judge's futile effort at a phone call. Frustrated, the Judge forgets how far he has come: "We're stranded. Worse than yesterday. Stranded. . . . Completely stranded" (413–14). But then the dejected party spies the long line of vehicles they are soon to join heading toward the cemetery. The elusive Comfort senior stops by long enough to tow Jack's truck into oblivion, just before Jack regains consciousness. He is distracted from his worry about his beloved machine when he hears the Judge: "*Stranded?* . . . Who's stranded?" Jack pulls himself back into his role. He assures the Judge, "You ain't going to miss the burying in Banner! . . . No sir. I made you a promise to get you *back on your road*, and I'm going to keep it yet. . . . I'm going to *patch you up* in time to join in with the parade to the cemetery" (419, some italics added). Then he miraculously cranks the Buick with "some of [his] spit." Humbled and grateful, the Judge "put[s] out his rope-burned hand" and shakes Jack's "bloody one" (421). The Judge knows who has saved him, and Jack knows it too. Even Gloria, "in spite of herself," comments, "The one you'd been happy to see in the ditch, you saved and shook hands with."

The final movement toward the burial begins. The scene transcends the moment, and is the true center of the book, where "the procession" of the stories "cross and mingle" like a prismed kaleidoscope or a stained glass window:

> As the slow-moving procession followed the line of the bank and then turned to pour down its road toward the bridge, downfloating wands of light and rain tapped it here and there. . . . Behind the hearse the line seemed to narrow itself, grow thinner and longer, as if now it had to pass through the eye of

a needle. . . . Yet a moment came when the procession stretched and covered the full length of the bridge. . . . Cars with headlights burning on dim followed close one behind the other, and now and then would come a wagon all alike filled with hatted passengers. . . . The church bus . . . crawled past Jack and Gloria windows packed with returning faces. . . . Mr. Willy Trimble came last off the bridge and brought silence. . . . "Now or never!" cried Mrs. Moody, grabbing the wheel along with her husband. . . . The Buick moved slowly and edged into place behind Mr. Willy at the end of the line. (422–23)

In this passage the journey, the journeyers, the rescued, the rescuers, the living, and the dead process from Jerusalem toward Jericho to their rest, their grave, owned by both Death (Mortimer) and the Comforter, for we must remember that Mr. Comfort gives up his plot for Miss Julia. Jack's "human chain" is obviously re-created in the funeral procession, and practical Gloria emphasizes the superiority of humanity over construction when she labels Jack's lost truck as a mere "play pretty." She concludes, resigning herself and Jack to the loss of the machine: "It was never going to carry *us* anywhere. We'd always have to be carrying *it*. . . . I didn't feel all that sorry to see it go" (425).

Together they move past the family graves and greet the dead, an "army of tablets" as they make "the short-cut to the little road" back to the tamed and passive Buick. It is joined by "the cars and wagons, horses and buses . . . postman's pony and cart," Uncle Homer's van, "the school buses . . . the church bus, Mr. Willy Trimble's mules . . . docile, cement gray, like monuments themselves" (427–28). The artificial means of transportation are paused, sternly stopped, calmly subordinated to the human drama unfolded. No one is going anywhere except Miss Julia, and now she is *there*, the place where they will all arrive, even Jack, the prototypical savior.

Gloria does not completely understand that her desire for an isolated life with Jack would be the life of the grave. In the cemetery she says, "I've got you all by myself, Jack Renfro. Nobody talking, nobody listening, nobody coming—nobody about to call you or walk in on us—there's nobody but you and me, and nothing to be in our way" (431). But for Jack the Samaritan, someone will always be in his way, until he is dead and resting beside Gloria in Banner cemetery. And he will not be able to depend for aid on anything—rope, book, or car—only himself, and maybe old Bet who apparently is the only reliable transportation he has. Just at the end of this scene Welty hints at another rescue Jack is making, that of

Gloria from her rootlessness: "some day," she says, "we'll move to ourselves and there'll be just you and me and Lady May." But Jack gently
reminds her that life is never static when he adds, "and a string of other
little chaps to come along behind her" (435). In the parable, after the
Samaritan tended the injured man's wounds, he "set him on his own beast
and brought him to an inn" (Luke 10.34). As Jack urges Gloria toward
home, supper, and welcoming family, "Bet came down into the road. . . .
He lifted [Gloria] and set her up on Bet's waiting back, and took Bet by
the bridle and led her" (435).

Some might take Welty's final lines in the novel as comic, or at
least as gentle irony, when Jack, penniless and not likely to get the hay
in, sings "Bringing in the Sheaves." But this hymn merely uses harvest
as a metaphor; it is not about abundant crops, but about the fruits of
the spirit, the rewards of compassion. The first verse describes "Sowing in the morning, sowing seeds of, *kindness* / Sowing in the noontide
and the dewy eve."[13] Jack's harvest, probably the only one he will see,
is the sheaves bound by love and mercy. In his song we hear the echoes of the voices from the reunion the evening before, "Bless be the tie
that binds . . .," reminding us that in Welty's view it is not really the
land that nurtures, not even love of place, but love of human beings.
And Jack is the true agrarian, sowing the right sort of crop, confident
in his harvest. Jane Hinton is right in pointing out that by the end of
Losing Battles "all the wanderers and outsiders are in the process of being
gathered into the family."[14] Jack is the gatherer and Gloria is gathered in,
whether she realizes it or not.

Jack's story, of course, is not merely the retelling of a parable, not
even in the sense that *The Robber Bridegroom* is a retelling of Grimm,
but the parable is the tune upon which Welty improvises and harmo-
nizes. It is the fugue melody which swells and rises, sometimes in this
character, sometimes in another, sometimes in counterpoint to a minor variation. Just at the point we are distracted by a new melody, the
tenor line picks up the tune again, and it reaches its musical climax in
Jack's song when "All Banner" and all of us can "hear him" and "know
who he [is]" (436). Who is our neighbor? Why, he is *Jack;* we know
him well. On one hand, perhaps the novel can be labeled "agrarian"
in the broadest sense, since it elevates rural life over the prison of the
city; perhaps it "takes the agrarian ideals as its text," as Albert Devlin
asserts. On the other hand, Welty does not rank cultivation over machinery, but rather people over machines, whether they can grow
anything in the earth or not. The Banner graveyard, planted with

Renfros, Vaughns, and Beechams, seems to be the most fully worked field in the county, and Jack expects cheerfully to be a part of that sowing when he reaches the end of his journey. But until then, as Peggy Prenshaw reminds us, "the truth is that the good life is right in Banner with . . . the whole extended human chain of family and friends."[15]

Jack is the rescued and the rescuer, the beaten and broken one and the one who tends the wounds. For, as the parable originally implies, only the rejected, cast-out man from Samaria could see himself mirrored in the man by the side of the road. Only the Samaritan had compassion because he knew what it felt like to lie in that ditch. Although Miss Julia Mortimer "went at it [life and teaching] like a steam engine," she cannot rescue her flock from anything because she cannot see herself in them, cannot stand "face to face and . . . merge into mysterious accord"[16] as Jack can with the Judge, and, to a certain extent, the Judge with Jack. She wanted to "read people like books" but not to bind their wounds; she wanted to journey by herself and did not accept the possibility of her own rescue until it was too late. She wanted the school bus to relinquish its load of children to her care, but she would not rescue them unconditionally when they fell among thieves. Emotionally warped Lexie, who "fell down on Virgil" and was left to lie there by Miss Julia, cannot feel compassion and will not even join the "human chain" when Jack begs her.

It is not, as Messerli asserts, Miss Julia's "view of life as a journey through time" which dooms her, but her refusal to stop a moment on that journey to look at the wounded on the side of the road. Welty says we are all journeyers, that the man who journeyed toward Jericho, the priest, the Levite, and the Samaritan were all traveling the same road. But only the victim and the Samaritan stopped. Only these two are remembered, while the priest and the Levite (and the robbers) journeyed on into oblivion: "'Which now of these three, thinkest thou, was neighbor unto him that fell among thieves?' And he said, 'He that shewed mercy on him.' Then said Jesus unto him: 'Go and do thou likewise'" (Luke 10.36–38).[17]

Notes

1. Rebecca Mark, *The Dragon's Blood: Feminist Intertextuality in Eudora Welty's* The Golden Apples (Jackson: University Press of Mississippi, 1994), p. 12.

2. Jan Nordby Gretlund, *Eudora Welty's Aesthetics of Place* (Columbia: University of South Carolina Press, 1997), pp. x

3. Andrew Lytle, "The Hind Tit," in *I'll Take My Stand: The South and the Agrarian Tradition* (Baton Rouge: Louisiana State University Press, 1977), pp. 201–45, 232, 246.

4. Albert Devlin, "Eudora Welty's Mississippi," in *Eudora Welty: Critical Essays,* ed. Peggy W. Prenshaw (Jackson: University Press of Mississippi, 1979), pp. 157–78, 163.

5. *Baptist Hymnal* (Nashville: Convention Press, 1956), p. 364.

6. Warren French, "'All Things Are Double': Eudora Welty as a Civilized Writer," in *Critical Essays,* pp. 179–88, 180.

7. Mark Twain, *The Adventures of Huckleberry Finn* (Berkeley: University of California Press, 1985), p. 137.

8. Noel Polk, "Going to Naples and Other Places in Eudora Welty's Fiction," in *Eudora Welty: The Eye of the Storyteller,* ed. Dawn Trouard (Kent, Ohio: Kent State University Press, 1989), p. 158.

9. Douglas Messerli, "'A Battle with Both Sides Using the Same Tactics': The Language of Time in *Losing Battles,*" in *Critical Essays,* pp. 351–66, 362.

10. Mary Anne Ferguson. "*Losing Battles* as a Comic Epic in Prose," in *Critical Essays,* p. 316.

11. Seymour Gross, "A Long Day's Living: The Angelic Ingenuities of *Losing Battles,*" in *Critical Essays,* p. 334.

12. Michael Kreyling, "A Pathway of Love: The Natchez Trace in the Works of Eudora Welty," a lecture presented at The Natchez Literary Celebration: 300 Years of Influence. Natchez, Miss., May 30, 1996.

13. *Baptist Hymnal,* p. 432.

14. Jane L. Hinton, "The Role of Family in *Delta Wedding, Losing Battles,* and *The Optimist's Daughter,*" in *Critical Essays,* pp. 120–31, 128.

15. Peggy W. Prenshaw, "Woman's World, Man's Place," in *Eudora Welty: A Form of Thanks,* eds. Louis Dollarhide and Ann Abadie (Jackson: University of Mississippi Press, 1979), pp. 46–77, 67.

16. John A. Allen, "Eudora Welty: The Three Moments," in *The Critical Response to Eudora Welty's Fiction,* ed. Laurie Champion (Westport, Conn.: Greenwood Press, 1994), pp. 254–71, 268.

17. Some, such as Chester E. Eisinger ("Traditionalism and Modernism," in *Critical Essays,* p. 22), prefer to see Jack as a "folk hero" or as a "perfect knight," avoiding any discussion of Welty's deliberate allusions to New Testament literature. I agree that Jack, like Jamie Lockhart, has many characteristics of the folk hero, including supernatural abilities, but I am startled at Robert Heilman's ("Losing Battles and Winning the War," in *Critical Essays*) statement that "the Bible behind the churches enters the story in only a few casual allusions and that (a colossal understatement) Welty "provides several perspectives on the myth" of the Good Samaritan (293, 295). Welty's use of biblical myth is anything but casual, and a discussion of her use of other allusions is still needed for (among others) the references to the Prodigal Son (105, 107), to Jack's miraculous use of "spit" to crank the Buick and its connection to Jesus' healing of the blind man by anointing his

eyes with clay and "spittle" in John 9, and for the allusion to the "eye of the needle" (Matt. 19) in the procession of cars to Miss Julia's funeral.

"Foes well matched or sweethearts come together"

The Love Story in *Losing Battles*
Sally Wolff

Returning on foot through a hot, dusty field to her estranged husband, Robbie Fairchild muses in *Delta Wedding* about the upcoming reunion with her spouse and wonders to herself, "What do you ask for when you love?" (*DW*, 146). The omniscient narration then adds: "So much did Robbie love George, that much the less did she know the right answer." Such a statement about the ambiguous, complex, and mysterious nature of love is the revelation at the heart of Eudora Welty's best fiction. From the lonely salesman in her earliest story to the infidels of *The Golden Apples* and the heartrending widow of *The Optimist's Daughter*, characters throughout Welty's works reach for love and answers to their "hearts' pull." The Natchez Trace, a boat landing, or a post office—and always the woods—provide settings for Welty's love stories.

From her first story of human relationships, "Death of a Traveling Salesman," Welty has written of the "pervading and changing mystery" people discover in responding to others. The mysterious quality of a relationship has been Welty's subject from her earliest days as a writer. The secret may simply lie in deserving to know the indecipherable identity of the lover; the search for a lover may prove elusive and mysterious; or the attempt—as in "Circe"—merely to fathom the indefinable idea of love may be futile. Love in Welty's stories is as mysterious and incomprehensible to those who experience it as for those who do not. "What do you ask for when you love?" becomes a keynote for Welty's long-held exploration of the ambiguous and infinitely complex fabric of relationships. Her characters who are willing to confront the mystery—and who are curious to know more of it—are those characters who often find the fulfillment they seek. William Wallace, in "The Wide Net," for instance, strains tirelessly for the entire story to understand secrets of human nature that seem withheld from him, especially regarding his wife's personality. In the last scenes of the story, he looks out from the porch, in the same direction of his wife's gaze, and at last he can see where she sees and know more of her perspective. Such characters usually grow in love and knowledge.

Welty's description of *Losing Battles* applies to much of her love literature: "I wanted to show that relationships run the whole gamut of love and oppression. Just like any human relationship has the possibilities of so many gradations of affection, feeling, passion, resistance, and hatred" (*C*, 221–22). These infinite "gradations" form the bases for most of her stories. From her early stories of searching through her first comic novels, later more meditative stories, and last novels of domesticity, Welty considers the many "alternatives and eventualities" in the world of relationships. Some couples know the "ancient communication" between two people, or the deep and time-tested commitment of Ellen and Battle Fairchild or Becky and Judge McKelva. She also depicts the harsh consequences that loss and death force people to confront. Paul Binding has observed that in fact "*Losing Battles* is dedicated to Welty's brothers—as *The Optimist's Daughter* was to be to Chestina Andrews Welty. These losses—in complex ways—stand behind both novels, giving them not just their darkness but their overall depth, their immensity of understanding. There are qualities of the heart in *Losing Battles* that were not even present in *The Golden Apples*."[1] Those who know and then lose or relinquish love are among Welty's most heartrending depictions. Laurel Hand is one such compelling figure, who has known and lost a marriage that was near-perfect in its wholeness, enriching and educating for both partners, as it was simultaneously one of challenge and security in providing mature life and love.

Welty's late novel *Losing Battles* returns to tested themes and narrative techniques from earlier works. She writes of a love that resembles those in *The Robber Bridegroom,* the early stories, and *Delta Wedding* in the focus on romance, domesticity, familial orientation, and happiness. She returns in *Losing Battles* to the "by ear" storytelling strategy, in which dialogue and dialect become almost as important to the story as the tale which it tells. Binding has seen this novel as "her largest scale tribute to the richness of Southern vernacular. . . ."[2] Dialogue and dialect weave the tale in *Losing Battles,* as Welty considers here, and in *The Optimist's Daughter,* serious questions about love. She reaches deeper, emotionally and philosophically, in these late novels than in some of her earlier works, such as *Delta Wedding.*

On the whole, *Losing Battles* is about love of different kinds. Joyce Carol Oates has termed it "a book about domestic love" in which "we hear about the young hero, Jack; we hear about his exploits, his courage, his foolishness, his falling in love with the young girl who is his teacher; we hear about the bride herself and about her infant girl; gradually . . . understanding how the hero and his bride came to be separated and how they will be joined again." In a larger sense, she adds, the book concerns the importance of family life: "What is important is love—the bonds of blood and memory that hold people together, eccentric and argumentative and ignorant though these people are. The basic unit of humanity is the *family*, the expanded family and not the selfish little family of modern day."[3]

A great degree of loyalty, allegiance, and commitment to the family, even at the expense of community involvement, is not a new topic for Welty. In *Delta Wedding* Robbie Fairchild's feelings of rivalry with the Fairchild clan for her husband's love is the most extensive treatment of the topic, although the issue of community intervention in familial relations occurs in "Lily Daw and the Three Ladies," "Petrified Man," "Asphodel," and other early stories. In *Losing Battles* the dispute between loyalty to the family and the need for privacy reaches the most clamorous levels ever in Welty's fiction, and she answers her own question with characteristic ambiguity.[4] The tension between private relations and societal obligations and needs remains a central concern for Welty.

Perhaps more than any other pair in Welty's canon, Jack and Gloria Renfro grapple with the difficult questions of marital allegiance, insularity and privacy, and the proper balance of familial obligations with communal and social roles. Besides their financial worries, this dichotomy between private affairs and community is the crucial problem in the marriage between Jack and Gloria. Symbolized by Judge Moody's car, balanced precariously on a tree limb, hanging from a cliff, this tension keeps both husband and wife shifting a balance toward equilibrium in their marriage—and not always achieving it.

More than many characters, Jack and Gloria adapt to the necessity for living "most privately when things are most crowded," for they must renew their love, passion, and commitment in the midst of a family reunion. They have their intimate moments, and some naturally are "in front of the whole family": "First kiss of their lives in public, I bet a hundred dollars" (73), Aunt Cleo announces upon Jack's initial embrace of his wife. Other moments find them quite blissfully alone. Nonetheless, their predominant dilemma is the need for privacy and intimacy—only heightened by Jack's long absence in jail—juxtaposed with the equally demanding necessity of developing a viable social context. Jack hopes for a lasting reconciliation between his family and Gloria, and she hopes for private time apart from the "clannishness" of his family.[5]

The value of privacy understandably becomes skewed in Gloria's mind, since her lot is cast amid a family of new in-laws, whom she does not seem to like, for the duration of Jack's jail term. Early in the novel in-laws criticize Gloria's characteristic insistence upon her privacy: "'Mind out, Sister Cleo, Gloria don't like to tell her business,' Miss Beulah called" (48). Later when Aunt Birdie assumes the entire family will tell Jack about his new baby, born since he went to prison, Gloria brings the whole family up short with a reassertion of her sense of marital and familial intimacy: "She's my surprise to bring" (69). Even later when the family begs her for the surprise, Gloria stays inside the house and calls out the window that she is "tending to some of my business." Trespassing further into Gloria's territory, "the crowd" of this family becomes increasingly intent upon telling the secret of the baby: "'Gloria! What have you got for Jack? Ain't it just about time to show him?' The crowd caught up with her in the kitchen, clamoring to her. 'I'll be the judge,' said Gloria from the stove" (74). What Gloria is judging is the width of her territorial boundary of the private sphere within the larger family.

The first intimate moment Gloria shares with Jack is a precious one, given the intrusive and insistent family: "Chewing softly, he kept his eyes on Gloria, and now in a wreath of steam she came toward him. She bent to his ear and whispered her first private word. 'Jack, there's precious little water in this house, but I saved you back some and I've got it boiling'" (75). When Gloria finally does show Jack their baby, the family realizes that by confidential, epistolary means, Gloria has already revealed to Jack, during his jail term, the secret of the baby. The surprise is now the family's—to find that Jack knows all: "'Gloria told him what she had. That baby's no more a surprise than I am,' cried Aunt Nanny. 'I'm not afraid of pencil and paper,' said Gloria" (94). After this pronouncement on this subject, Gloria firmly establishes not only her literacy, but also her views about the private sphere of her relationship with Jack: "'Lady May all along was supposed to be his surprise. *Now* what is she?' cried Aunt Birdie." Disappointment may reign in the ranks, but Gloria differentiates and sharply monitors the distinction between the public and the private domain, especially regarding the intimate subject of the birth of this child: "she was my surprise to tell" (92).

Conversely, Jack Renfro feels strong familial and social obligations. Reminiscent of George's conflict with Robbie (in *Delta Wedding*) about his loyalty to his family in maintaining large social context, Jack's entreaty to Gloria is to share with him in embracing his family: "'Say now you'll love 'em a little bit. Say you'll love them too. You can. Try and you can. . . . Honey, won't you change your mind about my family?' 'Not for all the tea in China,' she declared" (360). Jack wants Gloria to become his family in the broadest sense; his vision, like George's, is flexible and all-inclusive: "'Be my cousin,' he begged. 'I want you for my cousin. My wife, and my children's mother, and my cousin and everything. . . . Don't give anybody up. . . . Or leave anybody out. . . . There's room for everything, and time for everybody . . .'" (361–62).

Typically, however, Gloria takes the opposite view: she wants to devote herself to the marriage and her core family. She keeps her mind on "the future" (434) and romantically dreams of a day when she, Jack, and the baby can move to a "two-room house, where nobody in the world could find us" (412): "'Oh, this is the way it could always be. It's what I've dreamed of,' Gloria said, reaching both arms around Jack's neck. 'I've got you all by myself, Jack Renfro. Nobody talking, nobody listening, nobody coming—nobody about to call you or walk in on us—there's nobody left but you and me, and nothing to be in our way'" (431). Jack feels "sudden danger" at these ideas, which are, as Michael Kreyling suggests, "very real to a man of Jack Renfro's mind, in which family means safety, companionship, defense against chaos."[6] John Hardy has also pointed out that "Even more fiercely than Robbie Reid, Gloria believes that it is possible to marry a man without marrying his whole kin. She has not quite succeeded in convincing Jack. . . . In her own mind, she is still a long way from being taken captive by the tribe."[7] Louise Gossett adds that "Welty doesn't promise escape, for as Gloria looks away from the house to the future, beyond the bright porch she couldn't see anything."[8] So the battle lines are drawn and set.

At the end of the novel the argument remains unresolved—the battle is neither won nor lost. Gloria wants her privacy from family, and Jack still maintains, "You just can't have too many, is the way I look at it" (435). Welty commented in an interview that "every instinct" in Gloria wants them to "go and live by themselves," and "Jack, of course, is just oblivious to the fact that there could be anything wrong with staying there and having the best of both" (C, 305). Welty takes sides only to show the rationale for each character: "Jack is really a good person, even though he is all the other things. . . . he allows himself to be used by everybody. . . . [But that] comes out of his goodness. . . . Yes, I really like Jack. He's a much better person than Gloria" (*C,* 306). The struggle characterizes their relationship, and the tension remains high.

Jack and Gloria face a dilemma—not of goodness versus evil, or right versus wrong, but of the forces of togetherness and opposition in the marriage—and in other relationships—which draw together and push apart the individuals who wish to share their feelings of love. Both positions in the argument have merit, and Welty indicates that to balance privacy and community, passion and society does prevent Jack and Gloria from slipping into isolation or clannishness. To preserve the integrity of their most intimate relationships, Welty's lovers in these stories dodge intrusion to maintain their private relations. At the same time the familial and social influence on the couple seems essential in supporting a love relationship. Indeed, such a communal context may be the vital thread without which characters such as Livvie, Robbie, and especially Gloria risk unraveling the fabric of which their marital lives are woven.

Despite the concerns of social and familial roles, the relationship of Jack and Gloria Renfro flourishes as one of Welty's most romantic unions. Three full decades after *Delta Wedding,* Welty again writes of a happy love in a domestic setting. The marriage of Jack and Gloria depends for inspiration not upon exotic travels away from home, scandalous infidelity, or fairy-tale fantasy, but upon love generated between the two people in a realistic setting within traditional marital boundaries. Like so many other Welty love stories, this one resembles in structure the Shakespearian separation of lovers and their eventual, sweet reunion. The seventy-five-page prelude to Jack's arrival is a masterful narrative that anticipates the entrance of the newlywed husband, the recent bride, their quickly begotten child, and Gloria's reaction to her husband's homecoming. As in preparation for a wedding, the "girl cousins" march ceremoniously around Gloria like flower girls, chanting what might easily be a wedding song: "Down on the carpet you must kneel / Sure as the grass grows in this field" (29). Time seems suspended until the lovers reunite. The throng of people parts in Biblical splendor for the intensely dramatic moment when Jack greets his wife:

> They divided and there stood Gloria. Her hair came down in a big puff as far as her shoulders, where it broke into curls all of which would move when she did, smelling of Fairy soap. Across her forehead it hung in fine hooks, cinnamon-colored, like the stamens in a Dainty Bess rose. As though small bells had been hung, without her permission, on her shoulders, hips, breasts, even elbows, tinkling only just out of her ears' range, she

> stepped the length of the porch to meet him . . . Jack cocked
> his hands in front of his narrow-set hips as she came. Their
> young necks stretched, their lips tilted up, like a pair of rabbits
> yearning toward the same head of grass, and Jack snapped his
> vise around her waist with thumbs met. (73)

Like India in *Delta Wedding,* the onlookers can try to see "what there
was about a kiss." Welty even describes the cactus as the color of "mistle-
toe" (24), providing Jack with ample excuses for kissing in public. Poised
as they are amid the throngs of family, rejoined, the romantic couple now
takes center stage and full dramatic sympathy as Welty continues exploring her theme of *Delta Wedding*: "What do you ask for when you love?"
(*DW,* 146).

The omniscient narration Welty chooses begins the unveiling of this
story of love, as she reveals the first private conversations between a man
and wife. Gloria presents her husband with the gift of a new shirt that she
has saved relentlessly to buy for him. In the first of many intimate moments between them, she helps Jack dress in a scene deeply suggestive of
their sexual attraction and need.

> Without ever taking his eyes from her, and without moving to
> get the old shirt off till she peeled it from his back, he punched
> one arm down the stiffened sleeve. She helped him. He drove
> in the other fist. It seemed to require their double strength to
> crack the starch she'd ironed into it, to get his wet body inside.
> She began to button him down, as his arms cracked down to a
> resting place and cocked themselves there. . . .
>
> By the time she stood with her back against the door to get the
> last button through the buttonhole, he was leaning like the
> side of a house against her. His cheek came down against her
> like a hoarse voice speaking too loud. . . . She straightened him
> up and led him back into the midst of them. (78)

Their deep need cannot go unmet, and much like Jamie and Rosamund
(in *The Robber Bridegroom*) and George and Robbie Fairchild (in *Delta
Wedding*), Jack and Gloria leave for an afternoon alone together in the
woods. Miss Beulah Renfro, Jack's mother, articulates what is almost always true for Welty's lovers as they reunite: "this minute is all in the
world she's been waiting on" (94). Welty adorns the edenic couch for
them with detail of a Southern Paradise: bees crawl "like babies into the
florets" (98); and the birds move like "one patch quilt." The setting for

love is the woods, much as it is for Milton's Adam and Eve or for Shakespeare's midsummer night's lovers.

> They walked through waist-high spires of cypress weed, green as strong poison, where the smell of weed and the heat of sun made equal forces, like foes well matched or sweethearts come together. Jack unbuttoned his new shirt. He wore it like a preacher's frock-tailed coat, flying loose. . . . Then side by side, with the baby rolled next to Jack's naked chest, they ran and slid down the claybank, which had washed away until it felt like all the elbows, knees and shoulder, cinder-hot. . . . Keeping time with each other they stepped fast without missing a tie. . . . Jack reached for her. . . . (98)

The couch to which these two retire is not garlanded with Miltonic petals, however. Like Jamie and Rosamund's, the pallet has the Southern color of pine needles: "The big old pine over them had shed years of needles into one deep bed." The squirrels playing and courting over the lovers' heads reenact the playful romance in the human world below: "a pack of courting squirrels electrified a pine tree in front of them, poured down it, ripped on through bushes, trees, anything, tossing the branches, sobbing and gulping like breasted doves." Jack approaches Gloria with equal earnestness: his face rushes "like an engine toward hers" (99).

In two other love scenes during the novel's span of one day, Jack and Gloria plumb their passion, romance, and love. After accidentally bumping her head on a log, "Without stopping to be sorry for her head," Jack "crammed kisses in her mouth, and she wound her arms around his own drenched head and returned him kiss for kiss" (113). Jack comforts her as she explains the trauma of confronting Julia Mortimer in her opposition to the marriage: "He drew her near, stroking her forehead, pushing her dampening hair behind her ears. . . . He went on stroking her. . . . Gloria's tears ran down the face he was kissing" (168). And they reaffirm their vows to each other: "I ain't ever going to laugh at you, and you ain't ever going to feel sorry for me. We're safe." They agree that "being married" means "we're a family" (171).

Emotions run high, but the "deep bed" of pine holds them gently. Jack "held her in his arms and rocked her, baby and all, while she spent her tears. When the baby began to roll out of her failing arm, he caught her and tucked her into the pillow of the school satchel. Then he picked up Gloria and carried her the remaining few steps to that waiting bed of pinestraw" (171). Gloria returns from this brief, second honeymoon looking "like all the brides that ever were," and Jack confirms that she is still looking "just like a bride" (361) (even after the watermelon fight). In the ensuing discussion of Miss Julia's accusations of incest, Gloria reveals that her worst fears are all symbolized in three words: "null and void" (321). What she wants most is the marriage to Jack.

The moon, always a powerful romantic force in Welty's stories, intervenes "now at full power" (333) as Jack assuages Gloria's fears with his caring ways. The night-blooming cereus—that magical flower which lifts its blossoms triumphantly and nocturnally—joins the moon, too, as the natural world celebrates the reunion of the human lovers in a mid-summer night's dream. This scene, typically depicting the lovers in their most intimate moments in the privacy of their bedroom, is complex in its illustration of the sacredness of the love communion and of the truths about the importance of privacy and sharing. Under the magical "white trumpets" of the night-blooming cereus, the moonstruck Gloria and Jack entreat one another in their third love scene of the day to protect the boundaries of their love and let no one intrude:

> She put her mouth quickly on his, and then she slid her hand and seized hold of him right at the root. And so she convinced him that there is only one way of depriving the ones you love— taking your living presence away from theirs; that no one alive has ever deserved such punishment . . . and that no one alive can ever in honor forgive that wrong, which outshines shame, and is not to be forgiven until it has been righted. (362)

Like Shelley, the love observer in *Delta Wedding*, the young boy Vaughn in *Losing Battles*, still lying awake nearby, ponders the mysteries of love as he watches Jack and Gloria. He found them earlier in the day "lying deep in the woods together, like one creature" (363). The image of the lovers thus conjoined is reminiscent of that in Loch Morrison's mind in *The Golden Apples* as he gazes in half-innocence at the lovers in the abandoned house next door. Loch thinks they look "like a big grasshopper lighting, all their legs and arms drew in to one small body, deadlike, with protective coloring" (*CS, 282*). Vaughn may see the physical manifestation of love—two people joined as one creature—but he cannot comprehend the fuller meaning of love or the sexual and emotional ways of people "getting tangled up with each other." To this "moonlit little boy," who seems a young version of Jamie Lockhart, this mysterious phenomenon is a "danger"—and something for later and farther away. But Jack and Gloria have found the end of waiting. Love is in the here and now—not to be postponed an instant longer. As they drift to sleep by the light of the silvery moon, Jack and Gloria take their place among Welty's most joyful lovers, yet they have many battles ahead of them to be lost and won.

Notes

1. Paul Binding, *The Still Moment Eudora Welty: The Portrait of a Writer* (London: Virago Press, 1994), p. 233.

2. Binding, *The Still Moment,* p. 229.

3. Joyce Carol Oates, "Eudora's Web," *Atlantic* 225 (1970): 118–19.

4. See Gail L. Mortimer, *Daughter of the Swan: Love and Knowledge in Eudora Welty's Fiction* (Athens & London: University of Georgia Press, 1994) for discussion.

5. Michael Kreyling, *Eudora Welty's Achievement of Order* (Baton Rouge & London: Louisiana State University Press, 1980), p. 35.

6. Kreyling, *Eudora Welty's Achievement,* p. 149.

7. John Edward Hardy, "Marrying Down in Eudora Welty's Novels," in *Eudora Welty: Critical Essays,* ed. Peggy W. Prenshaw, (Jackson: University Press of Mississippi, 1979), p. 105.

8. Louise Gossett, "Eudora Welty's New Novel: The Comedy of Loss," *Southern Literary Journal* 3 (Fall 1970): 128.

Losing Battles *and Katherine Anne Porter's* Ship of Fools

The Commonality of Modernist Vision and Homeric Analogue
Darlene Unrue

Eudora Welty and Katherine Anne Porter are frequently mentioned in the same breath: both highly acclaimed writers more consistently praised for their short fiction than their novels, both writers speaking from a per-spective identifiably Southern American and within a set of moral and literary values admittedly modernist. They were mutual admirers of one another's art; they were devoted friends in spite of the nearly twenty years that separated their ages.[1]

On the surface *Ship of Fools* and *Losing Battles* seem decidedly dif-ferent from one another. *Ship of Fools*, aside from framing scenes in Mexico and Germany, is set aboard a ship at sea during a period of about a month, and many of the more than nine hundred contentious and alienated char-acters of seven nationalities are neither admirable nor likable. Porter enters her characters' minds easily, counterpointing their interior thoughts with exterior dialogue in dramatic scenes. Subsuming both the rendering of conscious thoughts and the presentation of dialogue is a strong narrative voice that establishes an all-wise standard against which the limitations of the characters' awareness are measured. *Losing Battles,* in contrast, is set in a fictional Southern hill community; the events take place during little more than twenty-four hours; and the characters are generally likable members of three related families and other community members who touch their lives. Very little interior thought is presented in the narrative, which is mostly dialogue; the primary focus is on the group rather than on individual characters; and broad comedy contains any dark themes that lie beneath the surface.

However, there are some immediately discernible similarities. The action of each novel is prefaced with a cast of characters; and each work is broken into numbered parts, three in *Ship of Fools* and six in *Losing*

Battles. In addition, a close analysis reveals deeper similarities: in each novel there is a focus on character rather than plot; each work encompasses multiple episodes reminiscent of its author's methods apparent in her short fiction; powerful irony is present in both works; in each work dialogue moves the novel's so-called action forward; and some names in each novel have apparently symbolic meanings.[2]

Reviewers and critics of each novel have identified implicitly many of these similarities as well as others. Howard Moss reviewed both *Ship of Fools* and *Losing Battles* at the time of each novel's publication. In 1962 he wrote that Porter in *Ship of Fools* "manipulates one microcosm after another of her huge cast in short, swift scenes. Observed from the outside, analyzed from within, her characters are handled episodically."[3] Eight years later he described *Losing Battles* also as episodic, "one tale made up of many, layer upon layer, the novel . . . [advancing] in a series of rural comedy scenes."[4] Moss pointed out the absence of plot and the presence in differing kinds, degrees, and proportions of both violence and comedy in each novel. He identified in each work the subject of love among the major themes and praised the absence of sentimentality. He said that Porter in *Ship of Fools* "commits herself to nothing but . . . the novel's top layer and yet allows for plunges into all sorts of undercurrents." He said that Welty in *Losing Battles* "transcends the narrow range of . . . the novel's focus," for "under the comic surface of the novel the vapors of the dungeon rise." Moss compared *Ship of Fools* in its intellectuality to Thomas Mann's *Magic Mountain* and in its epic grandeur to *Moby-Dick*. He called *Losing Battles* an "epic of kin rather than a family chronicle, specifically American in its speech but universal in its poetry, as if Mark Twain and the Shakespeare of 'A Midsummer Night's Dream' had collaborated."

Other reviewers and critics reinforced Moss's general assessment of *Ship of Fools* and *Losing Battles* while indirectly indicating still other similarities.[5] But not every reviewer or reader admired *Ship of Fools* and *Losing Battles,* and even some of the points on which each novel was found wanting place them in a common category. Moss, in his otherwise laudatory review of *Ship of Fools,* concluded that during the protracted composition of her only long novel Porter had sacrificed "the peculiar magic of her shorter pieces," magic which he defines as "impulse" and "suspense." In a similar spirit, Robert Cayton in *The Library Journal* summarized his assessment of *Losing Battles* by charging that Welty in her longest novel had "sacrificed too much of the lyricism, the color, and the delicacy of style that stamp her previous work."[6]

95

The substance of the common criticism against *Ship of Fools* and *Losing Battles* was twofold: on the one hand that Porter and Welty had written works different from—and inferior to—their short fiction; and on the other, that each had failed to fulfill a current concept of what a novel should be. In the face of reviewers' criticism, Porter and Welty each spoke to the differences between her short fiction and her novel, and each described her concept of a novel. Porter explained to Barbara Thompson in an interview published in the *Paris Review* in 1963 that

> a novel . . . is really like a symphony . . . where instrument after instrument has to come in at its own time, and no other. I tried to write it as a short novel, you know, but it just wouldn't confine itself. I wrote notes and sketches. And finally I gave in. . . . It needed a book to contain its full movement: of the sea, and the ship on the sea, and the people going around the deck, and into the ship, and up from it. That whole movement, felt as one forward motion: I can feel it while I'm reading it. I didn't "intend" it, but it took hold of me.[7]

Welty told Charles Bunting that her novels always began as short stories, and she explained the composition of *Losing Battles* as much the same process Porter described. "As it grew," she told Frank Hains, "the parts grew." She explained that she worked in "scenes," which she had to revise and expand. "I originally saw . . . *Losing Battles* as a long story," she told Walter Clemons in another interview, "but as people became dearer to me—it changed. When I got Jack home to the reunion, I realized I'd just begun." Welty also explained to Bunting her view of the novel form:

> A novel's different from the very first sentence. It's as if you were going to run a race. If you just had to go two hundred yards, you would rely on a different takeoff and drive and intention, a different wind, than if you were going to run three miles. . . . But it is a sort of a different girding up that you have to do. It's a different pace, a different timing. . . . In a novel you have time to shade a character, allow him his growth . . . you have time for subordinate characters, gradations of mood, subsidiary plots, other things that complement the story or oppose it. The difference is much more than a matter of length—it's a matter of organization and intention and in final effect.[8]

In addition to writing novels that were different from their short stories, Porter and Welty also wrote novels that were outside their age's dominating formalist concepts of what a novel ought to be. Wayne Booth, writing in the *Yale Review* the summer after *Ship of Fools* was published, declared the novel "disappointing" because it had "no steady center of interest except the progressively more intense exemplification of its central truth: men are pitifully, foolishly self-alienated." He admitted that Porter's long novel ran afoul of his own notions of what a novel should be.[9] And while *Losing Battles* did not generate a debate on its genre as did *Ship of Fools* or Welty's *The Golden Apples*, for some critics and readers it clearly failed to fulfill one or another current artistic expectation. One might argue, however, that both Porter and Welty, classical stylists who rejected for themselves—while at the same time admiring—the linguistic experimentation of Stein[10] and the dislocations of syntax and time of Joyce, Virginia Woolf, and Faulkner, are nevertheless writing in the spirit of modernism. They insisted on art's freedom from prevailing definitions of realism and genre and also on the artist's necessary role as the creator of new perceptions of order, the illuminator of meaning—what Porter called "the business of setting human events to rights and giving them meanings that in fact, they do not possess, or not obviously," and what Welty called "the fiction writer's feeling of being able to confront an experience and resolve it as art, however imperfectly and briefly."[11]

Porter's and Welty's theories reflect those of E. M. Forster, whom they expressly admired.[12] In *Aspects of the Novel* (1927) Forster sets forth his modernist vision by arguing that story, separate from plot, is the "simple and fundamental aspect" of a novel, and that a story may unfold in a variety of constructs of time, essential but not so artistically useful as place. He divided characters into flat and round classes, both of which he considered important in a novel. Distinguishing between history, which develops in chronological time, and art, which stands still, he saw all novelists, regardless of period, in a great room writing, the surface differences among their works reflecting their different places and times, the essential meanings of their works timeless. He placed great emphasis on pattern and rhythm within the novel and on the significance of tradition. He agreed with T. S. Eliot, who said that part of the business of the critic is "to see literature steadily and to see it whole . . . to see it not as consecrated by time, but to see it beyond time."[13] By way of example throughout *Aspects of the Novel,* Forster draws upon writers Porter and Welty admired: Austen, the Brontës, Sterne, Proust, Hardy, Henry James, Virginia Woolf, T. S. Eliot, Gide, and Tolstoy, among others.

At the heart of such modernism are two concepts: the sense of—and expression of—disorder with a replacing, new or different, order; and a movement toward a degree of knowledge, however slight, in the form of a reconciliation, however tenuous. For an important group of influential critics and artists such as Forster, modernism also included simply and primarily a new use of traditional materials. For these artists, to break with tradition was not to repudiate it altogether, but rather to reshape its usable elements. Such a posture rests on an aesthetic philosophy that crosses boundaries of literary genre and also boundaries of artistic expression. It explains why Porter and Welty could claim modernist identification with poets as well as fiction writers, with painters, sculptors, and musicians as well as writers. If the avant-garde and the cultural upheavals of the twentieth century are expressed by Joyce, Virginia Woolf, and Faulkner largely in style, form, and the treatment of time; by poets such as Pound and Eliot in a self-consciously new and intellectual poetic; and by painters such as Picasso and Degas in revolutionary attitudes toward space and time, then cultural crises and the avant-garde are expressed by Welty and Porter in social content, represented by setting in *Ship of Fools* and *Losing Battles*— in both instances Western civilization between the world wars and during the worldwide economic depression. The modernism of Porter and Welty aligns them not only with Joyce, Virginia Woolf, and Faulkner but also with Picasso, Degas, Pound, Eliot, and especially Rainer Maria Rilke.[14]

In addition to the uniquely personal, imaginative elements in *Ship of Fools* and *Losing Battles*, Porter and Welty are presenting anew certain traditional materials. *Ship of Fools* reveals analogies to *The Divine Comedy*, More's *Utopia*, Saint Augustine's *Confessions*, Brant's *Das Narrenschiff*, Erasmus's *The Praise of Folly*, Voltaire's *Candide*, and especially the *Odyssey*. It is not immaterial that critics and reviewers could not agree on which tragedy or comedy or epic poem, or on whether Homer or Shakespeare or Twain or Cervantes, *Losing Battles* evokes. Beyond the obvious conclusion that it is Homer who is a common influence on both *Ship of Fools* and *Losing Battles*, it also becomes apparent that the great differences in texture and flavor of *Ship of Fools* and *Losing Battles* can be accounted for not only by the artistic integrity and unique artistry of Porter and Welty but also by their different Homeric models. *Ship of Fools* is a modern *Odyssey* just as surely as was Joyce's *Ulysses*, while *Losing Battles* may be Welty's version of the *Iliad*.

Porter and Welty expressed and on occasion discussed their mutual admiration for Homer's works. In naming the great works of western civilization, Porter always placed at the top of the list the *Odyssey*. In

1956 Porter wrote to Welty to express her pleasure in Welty's *Place in Fiction*. "Bless you," she told Welty, "for writing it in the first place, and bless you for sending it. I hope sometime you will make a collection of these pieces: next to the Odyssey, perhaps it is about my favorite reading matter now." Porter had finished a long essay on Circe two years earlier, and she was reminded of Welty's story titled "Circe," completed in 1951. Porter added to her letter, "I think our pieces about Circe so near together a strange coincidence—after thinking about it for some fifteen years I finally got to it in March 1954."[15] Fifteen years earlier would have placed her thinking about Circe near the time she put down the first words of the novel that became *Ship of Fools,* first words she shared with Welty when they were together at Yaddo in 1941.[16]

Welty was no more restrained than Porter in her praise of Homer. Henry Mitchell in his 1972 essay based on his interview with Welty, comments on an unnamed reviewer who objected to Reynolds Price's comparison of *Losing Battles* with Shakespeare's *The Tempest* and then himself compared it to the *Iliad* and *Don Quixote*. When told that the reviewer had said, "*Losing Battles* reminds me of the *Iliad,*" Welty replied noncommittally, "Everything reminds me of The Iliad." Mitchell elaborates: "The speech of the narrative, the plainness and elegance of the language, the stripped quality of the action, the intense quality of the personal relationships and the occasional heightening of the dialogue for emotional effect—even to the extent of introducing an archaic note—all reflect the general method of Homer more than Shakespeare" (C, 68).

The two major works of Homer, the *Iliad* and the *Odyssey,* have been central to modernist literature that incorporates either a quest or a confrontation with history. Porter's use of the quest, the search for truth, is the foundation of her fictional canon,[17] and some critics have argued that it is Welty's confrontation with history that marks her canon.[18] Porter claimed to have loosely modeled *Ship of Fools* on Sebastian Brant's fifteenth-century allegory *Das Narrenschiff*. Little more than the title and the symbol of life's voyage are drawn from Brant, however, and as a universal source the *Odyssey* is more relevant. The richness of Porter's cast of characters, the depth and breadth of cultural history and human experience the characters collectively represent, and their single-minded desire and long struggle to return "home" parallel Odysseus's ten-year voyage home to Ithaca. And Odysseus's struggle to establish his identity provided Porter with one of the major themes of her novel. Just as Joyce was intellectually committed to re-producing his model, Porter was very much aware of the relationship between her novel and the *Odyssey*. The source is much deeper for Welty.[19]

Losing Battles, as Mitchell notes, broadly suggests the *Iliad,* the action of which encompasses a few weeks, with a single day's action given detailed account in books 11 through 18, one-third of the twenty-four books that make up the work. The first ten books describe the quarrel (with the complications of intervening gods) that leads to the war, two days of fighting, and the futile attempts to assuage the angry Achilles. As books 19 through 24 unfold, the tragic consequences of anger, pride, and excess ultimately give way to the resolution: the burial of Hector by the defeated Trojans. *Losing Battles* shares with the *Iliad* concentrated action and a relative unity of place and time, with relevant events brought into the arena of the work's central action by the process of recollection and the techniques of recitation. The process is achieved in the *Iliad* by the effects of formulaic repetition, and in *Losing Battles* largely by dialogue that re-creates events of the past.

In adapting the spirit and structures of the *Odyssey* and the *Iliad,* respectively, to *Ship of Fools* and *Losing Battles,* Porter and Welty appropriated the Homeric simile, essential ingredients of which are uniqueness and comparisons based on nature and homely images. In the *Odyssey,* for example, Athena rushes to Nausicaa's bed "like a blast of the wind" (VI.20), and Odysseus, whose hair flows "like the hyacinth flower" (VI.231), emerges from the bushes "like a mountain-bed lion, who, relying / On his strength goes rained on and blown on, but his eyes within / Are burning, and he chases after oxen or sheep / Or after the wild deer" (VI.127–33).[20]

In the opening frame of *Ship of Fools,* set in Vera Cruz, before the ship sets sail for Bremerhaven, an unreasonably fat woman has "legs like tree trunks"; a tall, thin young woman—a leggy "girl" with "a tiny, close cropped head waving on her long neck, a limp green frock flapping about her calves"—strides in "screaming like a peahen in German at her companion, a little dumpling of a man, pink and pig-snouted . . ."; four pretty Spanish girls, dark-skinned, long-necked, with an air of professional impudence" rush "in and out of shops . . . their urgent Spanish chatter going on noisy as a flock of quarreling birds. . . ."[21] In dialogue and narrative description throughout the novel Porter sustains such comparisons to the natural world.

In the *Iliad* similes are both simple and elaborate. Aias's shield is "like a wall"; men attack like wolves or lions and fight like fire; the island of the Phaeacians lies "like a shield" in the sea.[22] As in the *Odyssey*, elaborate similes are extended with explanations of the historical significance of the referent, but some similes are complete in themselves. Consider a simile in book IV, in a scene in which the goddess Athena is described brushing an arrow away from its mark: "She brushed it away from his skin as lightly as when a mother / brushes a fly away from her child who is lying in sweet sleep."[23]

In *Losing Battles* the Homeric similes are abundant. In the opening paragraphs "a long thin cloud" slowly crosses the moon, "drawing itself out like a name being called"; a house appears on a ridge "like an old man's silver watch pulled once more out of its pocket"; a dog leaps up "from where he'd lain like a stone"; "a wide circle of curl-papers, paler than the streak of dawn, bounds around" a girl's head; a baby's little legs run "like a windmill"; Miss Beulah keeps behind Granny, "not touching her, as though the little pair of shoulders going low and trembling ahead of her might be fragile as butterfly wings"; the Mississippi air is "still soft as milk"; Elvie's hair is "pale as wax-beans"; Uncle Percy's string of fish twist "like a kite-tail"; Gloria's dress of four yards of organdy sounds "like frolicking mice."[24] And so on, relentlessly and artfully.

In both *Ship of Fools* and *Losing Battles* the epic-like figurative language is intended to startle. In fact, the similes are in great measure the agents of the satire and comedy in both *Ship of Fools* and *Losing Battles*. Porter sets up her ironic comparisons in *Ship of Fools* largely by simile and metaphor and allusions embodied in characters' names, and Welty often creates comedy and social satire by the explicit comparisons in the similes and in names of characters and places that establish a standard of epic grandeur the characters, singly or collectively, ludicrously fail to meet.

The Homeric material in *Ship of Fools* and *Losing Battles* is useful in defining the modernist postures of Porter and Welty. In their common admiration for Homer and their appropriation of elements of his epic poems, they are illustrating the theories of Eliot and Forster, among other modernists, on the function of tradition in modernist art in general and in the novel genre in particular. In Porter's and Welty's individual uses of Homer's themes, patterns, and techniques, they reveal the differences in their artistic visions and lead us toward a better understanding of the creative process through which evolved their longest imaginative works.

017000

Notes

1. For their personal accounts of their friendship, see Katherine Anne Porter, "Introduction," in *A Curtain of Green and Other Stories,* by Eudora Welty(New York: Harcourt, Brace & World, 1941), pp. xi–xxiii; and Welty, "My Introduction to Katherine Anne Porter," *Georgia Review* 44 (Spring/Summer 1990): 13–27.

2. Both Porter and Welty commented on the unintentional use of symbols in their fiction. See "Recent Southern Fiction: A Panel Discussion (Panelists: Katherine Anne Porter, Flannery O'Connor, Caroline Gordon, Madison Jones, and Louis D. Rubin Jr., Moderator)," *Bulletin of Wesleyan College* [Macon, Georgia] 41 (January 1961): 1–16; rpt. in *Katherine Anne Porter: Conversations,* ed. Joan Givner (Jackson: University Press of Mississippi, 1987) pp. 42–60. Charles T. Bunting, "The Interior World: An Interview with Eudora Welty" (C, 40–63).

3. Howard Moss, "No Safe Harbor," *New Yorker* 38 (28 April 1962): 165–66, 169–70, 172–73.

4. Howard Moss, "The Lonesomeness and Hilarity of Survival," *New Yorker* (4 July 1970), pp. 73–75.

5. On *Ship of Fools* see, e.g., Carroll Arimond, "Books," *Extension* 57 (August 1962): 25; Louis Auchincloss, "Bound for Bremerhaven—and Eternity," *New York Herald Tribune Books,* 1 April 1962, pp. 3, 11. On *Losing Battles* see, e.g., James Boatwright, *"Losing Battles," New York Times Book Review,* 12 April 1970, pp. 32–34; John W. Aldridge, "Eudora Welty: Metamorphosis of a Southern Lady Writer," *Saturday Review,* 11 April 1970, pp. 21–23, 35; Jonathan Yardley, "The Last Good One?," *New Republic* 162 (9 May 1970): 33–36.

6. Robert Cayton, review of *Losing Battles, Library Journal* 95 (15 March 1970): 1050. Negative criticism of *Losing Battles* was generally mild. *Ship of Fools,* on the other hand, generated a heated controversy that still rages today among critics. See Mark Schorer, "We're All on the Passenger List," *New York Times Book Review,* 1 April 1962, pp. 1, 5; and Theodore Solotaroff, *"Ship of Fools* and the Critics," *Commentary,* October 1962, pp. 277–86.

7. Barbara Thompson, "The Art of Fiction XXIX—Katherine Anne Porter: An Interview," *Paris Review,* 29 (1963): 87–114; rpt. in Givner, *Katherine Anne Porter: Conversations,* pp. 78–98.

8. Bunting, "The Interior World," pp. 43, 45–46. Frank Hains in C, pp. 26–29. Walter Clemons in C, pp. 30–34.

9. Wayne C. Booth, "Yes, But Are They Really Novels?," *Yale Review* 51 (Summer 1962): 632–34.

10. Porter's criticism of Gertrude Stein, with which Welty agreed, predated her being rebuffed by Stein, an event that has been erroneously described as the source of Porter's enmity toward Stein. See Joan Givner, *Katherine Anne Porter: A Life,* rev. ed. (Athens: University of Georgia Press, 1991), pp. 353–55, 374. Although Porter had admired Stein until the late 1920s, she expressed distaste in a letter to Lincoln Kirstein, 19 October 1933, nearly fifteen years before the event Givner discusses. See *The Hound and Horn Letters,* ed. Mitzi Berger Hamovitch

(Athens: University of Georgia Press, 1982), p. 34. Welty in a letter to Porter dated 25 June 1948 (Katherine Anne Porter Papers, The University of Maryland at College Park) praises Porter's satiric piece on Stein, "The Wooden Umbrella," originally published as "Gertrude Stein: A Self Portrait," *Harper's* 195 (December 1947): 519–28.

11. Katherine Anne Porter, "St. Augustine and the Bullfight," in *The Collected Essays and Occasional Writings,* (1970; rpt. Boston: Houghton Mifflin/Seymour Lawrence, 1990) p. 94. And Welty in *C,* pp. 74–91.

12. Both Porter and Welty met Forster, and each wrote essays on his works. See Katherine Anne Porter, "E. M. Forster," in *The Collected Essays and Occasional Writings,* pp. 72–74; and Eudora Welty, "E. M. Forster's *Marianne Thornton*" and "E. M. Forster's *The Life to Come and Other Stories,* in *ES,* pp. 221–34.

13. E. M. Forster, *Aspects of the Novel* (New York: Harcourt, Brace & Company, 1927). Forster quotes from Eliot's introduction to *The Sacred Wood* (1920). Welty's philosophy of *place* is clearly related to Forster's critical theories. See Welty, "Place in Fiction," *ES,* pp. 116–33.

14. Both Porter and Welty claimed attachment to Yeats. Porter acknowledged a debt to Pound. Welty granted Eliot's importance but seemed not to appreciate him to the degree Porter did. See Givner, *Katherine Anne Porter: Conversations,* pp. 62, 65, 95, 104, 141, 147, 151–52, 170; and *C,* pp. 12, 13, 25, 70, 133, 331. Aside from Yeats, Rilke was the poet most beloved by Porter and Welty. Their correspondence contains references to their common admiration, and Porter chose a quotation from Rilke's *The Journal of My Other Self* to conclude her introduction to Welty's *A Curtain of Green and Other Stories.* See Jan Nordby Gretlund, *Eudora Welty's Aesthetics of Place* (Newark: University of Delaware Press, 1994), pp. 4, 12, 17, 23, 24–28, 37, 401.

15. Katherine Anne Porter to Eudora Welty, 20 February 1956, in *Letters of Katherine Anne Porter,* ed. Isabel Bayley (New York: Atlantic Monthly Press, 1990), pp. 498–99.

16. Porter's novel in progress was called "No Safe Harbor" at this point. See Welty, "My Introduction to Katherine Anne Porter," p. 21.

17. I develop this point throughout *Truth and Vision in Katherine Anne Porter's Fiction* (Athens: University of Georgia Press, 1985).

18. See Welty, "Place in Fiction," in *ES,* pp. 116–33; and Gretlund, *Eudora Welty's Aesthetics of Place,* pp. 219–20, 227–28, 288.

19. Welty explained to Bunting, "When you're writing, your influences are by way of imagination only. That doesn't mean that there couldn't be many unconscious forces at play" (*C,* p. 58).

20. Albert Cook, trans., Homer, *Odyssey* (New York: Norton, 1974).

21. Katherine Anne Porter, *Ship of Fools* (Boston: Atlantic-Little, Brown, 1962), pp. 15–25.

22. Richmond Lattimore, trans., *Iliad of Homer* (Chicago: University of Chicago Press, 1951), p. 41.

23. Lines 130–31. Lattimore's translation of Homer's *Iliad*, 116.

24. *LB*, pp. 3–15. Welty discusses her use of similes in an interview with Jean Todd Freeman (*C*, pp. 181–82).

Part II

The Optimist's Daughter

Eudora Welty's Indirect Critique of The Optimist's Daughter

Patrick Samway, S.J.

La mort du Père enlèvera à la littérature beaucoup de
ses plaisirs.

S'il n'y a plus de Père, à quoi bon raconter des
histoires?

Roland Barthes

On October 24, 1990, Eudora Welty participated in a memorial service for Walker Percy at St. Ignatius Church in Manhattan, one of two
public tributes she would give in honor of her deceased friend.[1] At St.
Ignatius, Welty, as the published version of her tribute indicates, imagined
Percy simultaneously as a doctor about to retire and as a writer about to
begin. The doctor-within-Percy encourages the infant writer-within-Percy,
a writer with no experience, to prove that he has talent. And Percy soon
writes *The Moviegoer,* a text that shows that Percy already knew the
world—he already knew the literature of the world, he knew himself, and
he had some compelling thoughts about the rest of us. "I suspect," Miss
Welty said, "that he had prepared for being a novelist for as long as he
had lived." And after reading one of his novels, we, along with Welty, are
likely to ask ourselves: "Where are we? Where in the world is he taking
us? . . . There was some real, everyday, but mysterious happening going
on in the country around us—right up our road, in fact." And what Percy
does, according to Welty, is to take his reader back home. "Home lies
before us in a different light, and its face is turned toward a new perspective, but it's still where we live. Only *we* have been altered." Welty had
been impressed not only by Walker Percy's sense of home in his fiction,
but also previously by the poetic reference to home in the fifth part of
William Alexander Percy's poem "In New York," entitled "Home," as
found in *In April Once,* the first book that Welty bought as a college
student (*OWB,* 78–79).

Welty noted that though Percy eventually elected not to practice medicine, he still was a brilliant diagnostician, who could read the signs and portents of despair. "He could detect how easily a spiritual disorder can overtake a fellow human being, a familiar society, or the nation that we live in, and normally take for granted." In her tribute Welty pursued this notion of medical, social, and literary diagnosis: "The physician's ear and the writer's ear are pressed alike in the human chest, listening for the same signs of life, and with the same hope and with a like involvement in the outcome. Each of us listens for the heartbeat with his own heart, scans the brain of his fellow man with his own brain, to find out whether mankind is living or dying at the moment." For Percy, what is worse than being deprived of life is being deprived of life and not knowing it. "The poet and the novelist," Percy once wrote elsewhere, as Welty noted, "cannot bestow life, but they can point to instances of this loss, name and record them." Above all, whether he was writing an essay or a novel, Percy sought to tell the truth. "I think that only a judicious portion of this truth is the factual kind," Welty reminded those at St. Ignatius; "much of it is the truth of human nature, and more of it is spiritual." Percy's reader "catches sight of a novel's truth through the movement of his characters (sometimes in opposition to their protestations), overhears it in what they say or do to one another or in what they fail to say or omit to do. In a work of fiction, truth has to be not told, or explained, but shown." Welty felt, finally, that Percy shared with Dean Swift a hatred of human folly and a concern for human souls. And what is more, his novels are filled with mystery. "The fact is that *they,* the novels, are clear, *they* are consistently lucid—and the *subject* is mysterious—eternally so; *we,* human beings, are the subject, and able to read his novels with an enchantment of discovery and recognition."

Three salient points are worth noting about Welty's tribute to Percy. First, the tribute delivered at St. Ignatius differs from the written version. Miss Welty orally presented one version and then several weeks later submitted to Robert Giroux, the unacknowledged editor of the collection of tributes, a slightly different version. In the spoken version, there is a more expansive emphasis on the motif of "home": "Actually, of course, home is the same place it always was when we started," Welty originally said. "But we may be different. We have been treated to a fresh recognition of suspicion of ourselves as not alone but as connected human beings. And we have reached the intuition of what our world and our time is on its way to become." Second, when Welty thanked Percy for his talk at the inaugural ceremonies, on March 15, 1982, in honor of the founding of the Eudora Welty Chair of Southern Studies at Millsaps College in Jackson, she likewise referred to Percy as a writer and diagnostician.[2] Her spoken tribute about Percy in St. Ignatius incorporated a good portion of what she had written for the celebration at Millsaps, though it was toned down and modified when included in the commemorative booklet of tributes. Third, in another tribute to her deceased friend, presented to the American Academy and Institute of Arts and Letters in New York City and written a few weeks after the one delivered at St. Ignatius, Welty reiterates her belief that Percy's fiction embodies a concern for mystery, one that is also attuned to the comic in human nature. "He was really 'up to' exactly what we see before us. It comes to whatever could make him best able to confront our common riddle, to encompass the subject before us, always clear to his gaze." In this second tribute, Welty did not radically alter her appreciation of Percy or his fiction, though she included biographical information mentioned by Percy in his introduction to William Alexander Percy's *Lanterns on the Levee.*

There can be no doubt that Eudora Welty and Walker Percy were good friends. I had the honor of sitting between them at a table during the Ninth Annual Awards Banquet of the Mississippi Institute of Arts and Letters, on May 26, 1988, held at the Mississippi Museum of Art in Jackson. Clearly Welty and Percy enjoyed one another's company that evening as they talked about a host of topics, ranging from music that was popular during the 1920s and 30s to Shelby Foote's Civil War narrative. The friendship between Welty and Percy dates from May 1967, when they first met by chance on a train speeding northward to New York City so they could attend the joint ceremony of the American Academy of Arts and Letters and the National Institute of Arts and Letters.[3] They remained friends, though not the closest of friends, throughout Percy's life. In interviewing Miss Welty before Percy's death, I sensed her tremendous reverence and affection for Percy. At the same time, she had difficulty remembering the specifics of his novels. Both her comments about Percy at the time of the inauguration of the Welty Chair in 1982 and her subsequent use of those same remarks in 1990, especially the fact that none of his novels was mentioned on either occasion, might lead one to believe further that her various tributes to Percy are really self-reflective exercises about the nature of the creative writer's task—as related to her own works, especially *The Optimist's Daughter.*

What causes me to make such a hypothesis? Five of Percy's novels were published by the time of the inauguration of the Welty Chair; yet in each, other motifs, such as developing a love relationship and searching for the divine, seem more important to Percy as novelist than the task of establishing a home. In *The Moviegoer* Binx Bolling lives fairly content-edly in a room in Mrs. Schnexnadyre's boardinghouse; in *The Last Gentleman* Will Barrett visits Ithaca, but since his former home is associ-ated with loss and death because his father committed suicide there, he willingly moves on to Santa Fe, the city of holy faith; in *Love in the Ruins* the Howard Johnson Motel replaces Dr. Thomas More's home in Para-dise Estates, though at the end—and hastily, it seems to me—he makes a new home with his second wife, Ellen, in refurbished slave quarters; in *Lancelot* Lance Lamar blows up his house, murders his wife, and winds up in a clinic for the mentally disturbed; and in *The Second Coming* Will's home now seems to be Allison's greenhouse and St. Mark's Convalescent Home as much as any other place. In short, except for *The Last Gentle-man,* in which Will does go through a process of recognition and transformation when visiting the old homestead, Welty's comments about the significance of home in Percy's fiction ring truer for her fiction than they do for his. While it could be argued that home, especially his home in Covington, Louisiana, meant everything to Percy, and that his novels rep-resent an unconscious quest to locate his family roots and to explore those locales that were significant in his personal development, he had little desire to return to his original home and rediscover this particular place from new perspectives.[4]

Percy, in fact, hinted that Welty was more interested in the motif of home than he was. In the Spring 1969 Welty issue of *Shenandoah,* Percy singled out the notion of place, of home, as being characteristic of Welty both as a person and as a writer of fiction. What Percy found remarkable about Welty is that she wrote most of her adult life while living in the same house:

> Being a writer in a place is not the same as being a banker in a place. But it is not as different as it is generally put forward as being. It is of more than passing interest that Eudora Welty has always lived in Jackson and that the experience has been better than endurable. . . . For Eudora Welty to be alive and well in Jackson should be a matter of considerable interest to other American writers. The interest derives from the coming need of the fiction writer, the self-possessed alien, to come to some terms with a community, to send out emissaries, to strike an entente. The question is: how can a writer live in a place without either succumbing to angelism and haunting it like a ghost or being "on," playing himself or somebody else and

watching to see how it comes out? The answer is that it is at least theoretically possible to live as one imagines Eudora Welty lives in Jackson, practice letters—differently from a banker banking but not altogether differently—and sustain a relation with one's town and fellow townsmen which is as complex as you please, even ambivalent, but in the end life-giving.[5]

In dealing specifically with the question of whether or not a novelist should write about home, Welty maintains in her essay "Place in Fiction" that it is "both natural and sensible that the place where we have our roots should become the setting, the first and primary proving ground, of our fiction. Location, however, is not simply to be used by the writer—it is to be discovered, as each novel itself, in the act of writing, is discovery. Discovery does not imply that the place is new, only that we are" (ES, 128). For Welty, place is seen as a frame, not an empty one but a brimming one, and the writer always sees two pictures at once in his frame—the writer's and the world's. "Place absorbs our earliest notice and attention, it bestows on us our original awareness; and our critical powers spring up from the study of it and the growth of experience inside it. It perseveres in bringing us back to earth when we fly too high. It never really stops informing us, for it is forever astir, alive, changing, reflecting, like the mind of man itself" (ES, 128). A writer might have a special place, closer to the writer than the writer's original home, but "the home tie is the blood tie. And had it meant nothing to us, any other place thereafter would have meant less, and we would carry no compass inside ourselves to find home ever, anywhere at all. We would not even guess what we had missed" (ES, 131). What characterizes Welty as a modern writer is not so much that she feels the pang and tether of home or place—other contemporary writers such as Reynolds Price and Mary Lee Settle are not without similar concerns—but rather the apparently plain, yet intricately illusive manner in which she depicts place and home.

No doubt, seeing the Impressionist paintings in the Chicago Art Institute, when traveling back and forth from Jackson to the University of Wisconsin in the late 1920s, gave Welty a chance to reflect on the use of space and form in works of art, especially to appreciate the tendency in the viewer's mind to find linear cause and effect in cubistic works of art. Because the viewer tends to restructure the forms in such paintings, he or she mentally disfigures the works of art and, in effect, cocreates with the artist to mediate something that makes good human sense, even though it finally remains beyond the reach of the viewer. Two of Welty's literary heroines, Katherine Anne Porter, as shown in her essay "No Plot, My

Dear, No Story," and Virginia Woolf, as shown in *To the Lighthouse,* were likewise acutely sensitive to the liberating dimensions of modernism. When Welty first read *To the Lighthouse,* she felt that the connection between the novel and autobiography seemed "meteorological in nature."[6] The reader is transformed, not so much by a sense of recollection, but "under" the heavenly signs of this novel—here, too, an oblique pointer as how to read Welty's own fiction.

In *The Optimist's Daughter* Welty's family names and place names should give a clue to this illusive quality in her writing, that something resembling sleight of hand is happening. New Orleans is named after a city in France; Madrid, Texas, after a city in Spain; Missouri is a woman who works for the McKelvas; Mount Salus is not built on a mount, nor, as the site of a funeral, does it live up to the Latin root of its name; and the first names of both Judge McKelva and his daughter are the same as two cities in Mississippi; a boardinghouse is called Hibiscus; Laurel is named after a flowering bush; a rose is called a Mermaid; a hotel is called Iona; the name of Wanda Fay suggests a host of possibilities associated with the King Arthur legend; the family name of Chisom (a family that travels a good deal in this novel) is probably a corruption of Jesse Chisholm's last name, which itself became the name of an important cattle trail in the mid-1880s; Mrs. Chisom's husband is buried in Bigbee, Mississippi, which is neither big nor a bee; and Miss Tennyson Bullock, Laurel's mother's closest friend, has a name—the height of bombastic nomenclature—that points in directions that are so opposite that only the human imagination could ever link them together. The undertaker, Mr. Pitts, though, has a totally appropriate name, as does the Judge's former secretary Dorothy Daggett, called "Dot." Thus in this novel, names become polyvalent signs that open out to other signs in an endless series of possibilities, suggesting that, though the basis of a good novel might be a plausible plot with plausible characters, it is, in the last analysis, a semiotic sign system of tremendous proportions.

As they begin to depart, Mrs. Chisom, suggesting the expansive nature of this novel, says to her daughter: "Tell you one thing, there's room for the whole nation of *us* here" (*OD,* 96). The evening after they take Mr. Dalzell to the operating room, Laurel notes a "strange milky radiance" in the corridor. "The whitened floor, the whitened walls and ceiling, were set with narrow bands of black receding into the distance, along which the spaced-out doors, graduated from large to small, were all closed. Laurel had never noticed the design in the tiling before, like some clue she would need to follow to get to the right place" (*OD,* 31). One of Laurel's tasks is to go through a process of discernment that will, if possible, give her an understanding of what it means to live in the future more maturely. "Father, beginning to lose his sight, followed Mother, but who am I at the point of following but Fay? Laurel thought" (*OD,* 132). Perhaps the only constant is change and the only mystery is that there is more of it.

In *The Optimist's Daughter* the McKelva house in Mount Salus is clearly the central locus of the novel, though the locales of Baltimore, Bigbee, Chicago, New Orleans, Madrid, and especially "up home" in West Virginia each claim a rightful independence that at times is juxtaposed with one or more of the other locales and at other times fuses with them to form remarkable confluences (a favorite Welty word) or literary palimpsests (*OWB,* 102). Both the Judge and his father had gone to the University of Virginia, and both Becky's mother and father were Virginians. In addition, Becky's father had been a lawyer too. Becky, like the Chisoms, comes from a large family. It is almost as if the novel created a series of constellations that appear, from a distance, to exist on the same plane, whereas, in fact, they are on differing planes, reflecting the time periods when they were created. And as the reader moves through the text, these constellations move and rotate, so that the stories they represent modify themselves in time and space. As Michelson and Morley knew in the scientific experiments they conducted concerning the Earth's motion in relation to surrounding space, the presence and position of the observer cannot be excluded from any interpretation of what is happening in the "real" world; *mutatis mutandis,* the reader cannot be excluded from any discussion of a work of fiction.

Upstairs in the McKelva house, the bed serves as one of the focal points of the novel. Here Becky and Clinton slept as husband and wife, as did Wanda Fay and Clinton; here Laurel was born and years later Becky died; and here in the present is where Wanda Fay sleeps when she is not visiting her kin in Madrid. This particular bed serves as an object to unite all four of the novel's protagonists; yet it is not the hospital bed that either the Judge or Laurel's grandfather died in, nor the bed that Mr. Dalzell left empty when he disappeared from his hospital room. Yet of all the objects in the novel, the bed in the McKelva home has witnessed acts of love, birth, death, and especially companionship between husband and wife; yet this bed is not unique in this regard, as other beds, at varying times and in other places, hold dying people or are vacated when no longer considered useful. Welty seems to be suggesting, in an asymptotical way, that one bed, though important in the lives of people who are related to one another, does not exhaust its symbolic effect; there have been, are, and will be so many beds in the world that the imagination can barely begin to discover how human beings either singly or with others have used these particular objects. Furthermore, after death, no one seems to have claim to his or her particular bed; others will use it until the time comes when it will be discarded and perhaps replaced by another.

For some, such as Philip Hand, who was lost at sea, there is no final physical bed to lie in. For the dead, who obviously undergo a transformation, their new home, their new bed, is the coffin. Mrs. Chisom's son Roscoe committed suicide in Orange, Texas, by stuffing the windows and door and turning on the stove. In his coffin Roscoe is said to have looked as pretty as a girl. And at the Judge's wake, Wendell is not even sure of the identity of the corpse. When Laurel insists that what is happening is not real, Miss Adele says, "The ending of a man's life on earth is very real indeed" (*OD*, 82). Jan Nordby Gretlund sees the novel partly as "a social comedy satirizing small-town prejudices and human weaknesses," and maintains that the poor white comedy of manners shocks the genteel sensibility, but this does not mean that the emotions of the Chisoms at the Judge's wake are less genuine or more faked than the emotions expressed by genteel Mount Salus.[7]

"Fatherlessness," as André Bleikasten has explained about the father figure in literature, "is not so much the absence of a relationship as the relationship to absence."[8] Ironically, pecan-loving Grandpa Chisom becomes the new patriarch of the clan. Though Laurel greets neighbors and her extended family while standing at the head of her father's coffin enveloped by foolish pink satin, the same color that smothers the windows and spills over the upstairs bed, she lacks the authority both to have the casket lid remain closed during the wake and to decide the location of the burial site, which in this case abuts the new interstate highway, where the windshields of the passing automobiles tend to blind her, a situation as curious in its own way as when Dr. Bolt uses the same blessing at Judge McKelva's funeral as he used at the table. When Mr. Pitts inquires whether the wake should be held at the funeral parlor or at the McKelva "residence," Laurel decrees it will be at her father's "home," which Mr. Pitts continues to call a "residence" (*OD*, 50), thus putting funeral parlor, home, and residence in juxtaposition with one another as they vie for their own place in the Welty cosmography, or, as Becky Thurston preferred, Milton's Universe. It is appropriate that when Laurel listens for the striking of the mantel clock downstairs in the parlor as she is about to fall asleep, it never comes.

Another object of great significance in the McKelva house, the Judge's desk, made in Edinburgh and originally owned by his great-grandfather, had been emptied except for the Judge's cigar box. Where were the letters Laurel's mother and father had written to one another? "He'd never kept them: Laurel knew it and should have known it to start with. He had dispatched all his correspondence promptly, and dropped letters as he answered them straight into the wastebasket; Laurel had seen him do it" (OD, 122–23). The only traces of the past that remained were drops of nail varnish, presumably left by Wanda Fay as she polished her nails and threw out the correspondence she desperately avoided reading. Yet, before her departure, Laurel discovers in the sewing room the old plantation secretary, a second desk, which contains the very letters she thought had been discarded, plus an old family scrapbook. With this discovery, part of her properly mapped universe implodes; it needs to seek a new trajectory and attitude. These letters and pictures transport her to the past, to the time when her mother accompanied her own desperately sick father on a raft, until both reached a juncture where they could catch a train to Baltimore. In reliving this particular episode in her family's history, one that has definite resonances with Welty's own family history as told in *One Writer's Beginnings* (OWB, 51), Laurel has an opportunity to appreciate once again her mother's courage and physical strength in coping with the final illness and death of her father. Her father's and grandfather's deaths are in alignment as they comment through her to one another. In the hospital in Baltimore, Becky's father, suffering from a ruptured appendix, said, "If you let them tie me down, I'll die" (OD, 143). Though he never articulated the same words, most likely because no one thought he was in imminent danger of dying, the Judge, in fact, died while the hospital staff kept him as immobilized as possible. Just as Becky contacted no one in Baltimore to help her, neither did Laurel in New Orleans. Both brought the coffins of their fathers back to their hometowns. Ironically, yet fittingly, Laurel took the same train bearing her father's corpse to Jackson that she had taken with her fiancé, Philip Hand, in order to be married in the Mount Salus Presbyterian Church. And both times she was greeted by her bridesmaids. The Judge had insisted on a big wedding for his daughter, just like Wanda Fay wanted a big funeral. "Neither of us saved our fathers, Laurel thought. But Becky was the brave one. I stood in the hall, too, but I did not any longer believe that anyone could be saved, anyone at all. Not from others" (OD, 144). Laurel drew strength from realizing that her mother had to rely on her own inner strength: "But Becky had known herself," Laurel reflects (OD, 144).

Becky had undergone a cataract operation performed by Dr. Nate Courtland (obliquely juxtaposed to the poem "The Cataract of Lodore"— itself an image of the torrent of water that carried Becky and her father to the train station—which Laurel reads in *McGuffey's Fifth Reader*). Before the Judge's retina had slipped, Dr. Courtland had discovered a cataract in his other eye. The Judge seemed helpless to do anything for his wife during the last five years of her life when she was confined to bed, and because of this Laurel, recently widowed, turned against her father:

> Her father in his domestic gentleness had a horror of any sort of private clash, of divergence from the affectionate and the real and the explainable and the recognizable. He was a man of great delicacy; what he had not been born with he had learned in reaching toward his wife. He grimaced with delicacy. What he could not control was his belief that all his wife's troubles would turn out all right because there was nothing he would not have given her. When he reached a loss he simply put on his hat and went speechless out of the house to his office and worked for an hour or so getting up a brief for somebody. (*OD*, 146)

When Laurel's father did come home, her mother questioned why she had married a coward, and then she held his hand to help him bear it—which is one of the most poignant scenes in the entire novel.

Though the Judge promised to take Becky back to the house on the mountain, Laurel knew it was an empty promise because by then it had probably burned. After a stroke had crippled her further, Becky thought that she had been placed with strangers. She died without speaking a word, keeping everything inside herself in anger and humiliation. Earlier, in her last words, Becky had told Laurel, "You could have saved your mother's life. But you stood by and wouldn't intervene. I despair for you" (*OD*, 151). Like Becky in Baltimore, Laurel felt that she had been left abandoned in Mount Salus. Can she find her way home with some degree of flexibility and grace, knowing that houses, too, have fates—some burn down and others are divided up into apartments. Becky was buried in Mount Salus, a long way from West Virginia, as one of her brothers said. Phil Hand died even further away from home. Though we tend to see Becky, the Judge, and Laurel as forming a tight-knit family, the reality is slightly different as they adjust, however awkwardly, to changing situations.

Welty's bird imagery seems to point invariably to the darker aspects of life; in depicting a cardinal dipping into the fig tree and brushing his wing with a bird-frightener, she notes that others follow, thereby creating frenzied interaction. "Those thin shimmering discs were polished, rain-bright, and the redbirds, all rival cocks, were flying at their tantalizing reflections. At the tiny crash the birds would cut a figure in the air and tilt in again, then again" (OD, 117). Miss Adele considered it nothing but a game, but games are not what birds perform; people do. Surprisingly, Wanda Fay, whose behavior is outlandish at times, adjusts remarkably well to her new life with Clinton, though not always in ways appreciated and approved by the Mount Salus community. What this community, whose memory of the past drives their social engines, must learn to recognize as they talk and interact with one another is that Wanda Fay and the Judge were most likely a happy couple who loved one another. Once they accept the truth that is before them, once they open themselves up to love and its revelatory nature, they, too, might be liberated. Tish Bullock, now divorced, must confront an analogous (and awkward) situation as she witnesses young women creep through her son's bedroom window to spend the night with him.

One of the voices that emerges from the letters that Laurel reads is that of her own husband, thus giving this story a quality that transcends time and place. As Laurel weeps for love and for the dead, she imagines Phil's voice: "I wanted it!" (OD, 155). Like Wanda Fay, Phil's background breaks any predictable pattern; Phil studied architecture at Georgia Tech, far from his native Ohio. Welty enjoys playing with Phil's last name; when he talked to the Judge about the Japanese kamikazes who attacked the American minesweepers in the Pacific, he said they came so close that you could shake hands with them. Phil set up his work space in the kitchen of their South Side apartment in Chicago. Miss Adele Courtland says "'Here in the kitchen it will all start over so soon' . . . as if asking for forgiveness" (OD, 56). And perhaps it was here in the Chicago kitchen that he made a breadboard that he gave to Becky as a gift, one that Fay had cracked walnuts on with a hammer and defaced with cigarette burns. In a final defiant gesture, Laurel raises the board as if to hit Fay. "Laurel held the board tightly. She supported it, above her head, but for a moment it seemed to be what supported her, a raft in the waters, to keep her from slipping down deep, where the others had gone before her" (OD, 177). Philip, Becky, the Judge, Chicago, Mount Salus, Madrid, West Virginia, Baltimore, the McKelva house, the past, the present, the future—all align themselves at this moment in this new constellation. The moment of revelation is at hand. "'The past,'" Wanda Fay says to Laurel, "'isn't a thing to me. I belong to the future, didn't you know that?'" Wanda Fay offers Laurel the breadboard, but Laurel says she can get along without it. "Memory lived not in initial possession but in the freed hands, pardoned and freed, and in the heart that can empty but fill again, in the patterns restored by dreams" (*OD,* 179). Like the bird she frees, Laurel herself is liberated; she burns not only the letters she has found, but also the diagram of Milton's Universe. What she saves, at Miss Adele's insistence, is a little soapstone boat, an object that points to a raft, which, in turn, points to a breadboard.

The novel's end is also a beginning. Curiously, Wanda Fay celebrates her birthday on the very day that the Judge dies. And when Laurel passes the first-graders at recess on her way to the airport, she sees the "twinkling" of small hands, "unknown hands, wishing her goodbye" (*OD,* 180). The death of her husband, her beloved handyman, now opens out to the hands of the children waving goodbye, or perhaps waving welcome. The myriad images that we have seen now configure themselves to this final one: that of a daughter of an optimist both leaving the past and taking it with her as she returns to a home in Chicago that we as readers have, at best, just glimpsed. In not relating Laurel's life in Chicago, it would seem that Welty has deliberately left a void in the text, as if Laurel, on her return, would need to give it depth and character. From one perspective, Chicago, as a place where Laurel designs, represents an invitation to an artistic person (was Welty subconsciously thinking of herself?) to create a future and thus fill the void.

Too much undiscerning love can be as devastating as too little. As Welty said about Laurel in an interview with Jan Nordby Gretlund, "She was enormously enriched by all she had gone through, and it was her understanding she had gotten. She did not abandon anything. She took it with her, but in a form of accepting it and understanding it for what it was."[9] People are not beautiful statues, like Becky in Laurel's mind, but do become, alas, crazies, as Fay saw Becky; it is bizarre, as Faulkner dramatized in "A Rose for Emily," to preserve exquisite corpses in one's house. Wanda Fay sees her husband as he is, even in the coffin where the bags under his eyes have disappeared and the eye bandage has been removed. "Laurel closed her eyes, in the recognition of what had made the Chisoms seem familiar to her. They might have come out of that night in the hospital waiting room—out of all times of trouble, past or future—the great, interrelated family of those who never know the meaning of what has happened to them" (*OD,* 84). Yes, Dr. Courtland pressed his physician's ear and Miss Welty her writer's ear to the human chest, listening for the same signs of life, and with the same hope and with a like involvement in the outcome. "Each of us listens for the heartbeat with his own heart, scans the brain of his fellow man with his own brain, to find out whether mankind is living or dying at the moment" (OD,84). When asked by her mother how long she intends to stay in her new home, Wanda Fay said "Just long enough" (OD, 97). "'Once you leave after this, you'll always come back as a visitor,' Mrs. Pease warned Laurel. 'Feel free, of course—but it was always my opinion that people don't really want visitors'" (OD, 112).

In this novel Welty has figured and refigured diffused psychological space, which has been architecturally orchestrated like a rite of passage. Laurel must realize that life refuses to remain merely the beautiful but passive object of a naive tourist's romantic longings. Instead life has willed itself to become an acting subject with its own drive and power and beauty, which constantly startles and informs us, like the simple charm of small children waving at a passing stranger during recess time. Will Laurel back home in Chicago, where she has lived for twenty years, continue to design theater curtains for repertory companies or undertake a new task? As with all open-ended sign systems, ultimate meaning in this novel is thus put off and deferred to the future.

Did Walker Percy approve of what Welty had accomplished in this novel? Certainly, he would have approved of the novel beginning in New Orleans, the site of The Moviegoer, and he must have been pleasantly surprised that Welty named her protagonist Laurel Hand; he had named one of the characters in a version of The Moviegoer Grantland Lanson Hand, but changed it because Lanny Hand might be confused with another character, Lonnie Smith. I know that Walker Percy liked The Optimist's Daughter very much. He told me so once point-blank. Along with Evan S. Connell Jr., Leslie Fiedler, Jonathan Yardley, and William H. Gass, Percy was a member of the 1973 National Book Committee for the National Book Awards, and among the books Percy recommended was Welty's The Optimist's Daughter.[10] He was most upset when it did not win this award, though rejoiced that it did win the Pulitzer Prize.

Notes

1. Eudora Welty's tribute, published in Walker Percy: 1916–1990 (New York: Farrar, Straus & Giroux, 1991), unpaginated, was also taped at St. Ignatius Church. The second tribute was delivered at the American Academy and Institute of Arts and Letters in New York City on 5 November 1990.

2. Eudora Welty, "Afterword," in *Novel Writing in an Apocalyptic Time,* by Walker Percy (New Orleans: Faust Publishing Company, 1986), pp. 25–28.

3. Interview: Mrs. Mary Bernice Percy. Welty had received a bound proof of Percy's *The Last Gentleman* in 1966 and thus was familiar with this novel by the time they met on the train. She had also read *The Moviegoer,* as she told me in an interview, and was extremely taken by it. Miss Welty would later discuss her reaction to Percy's novel *Lancelot.* (See Jean Todd Freeman's interview with Welty in C, pp. 193–94.) Welty and Percy were together in May 1972 when Welty was inducted into the Academy of Arts and Letters and Percy into the Institute of Arts and Letters. On 12 December 1972 Welty and Percy were both guests of William F. Buckley, Jr. on *Firing Line,* taped at WMAA in Jackson. (See C, pp. 92–114. The transcript of this *Firing Line* show is available from the Southern Educational Communications Association of Columbia, South Carolina; a videotape of this show can be seen at the Museum of Television and Radio in New York City.) Percy attended the Eudora Welty Day in Jackson in August 1973. (See letter of Reynolds Price to Walker Percy, 15 August 1973, in the Percy Family archives.) Percy and Welty were together at a Conference on Southern Literature in Chattanooga in late April 1981 and were again in the same city in early April 1989 for the Fifth Biennial Conference on Southern Literature sponsored by the Fellowship of Southern Writers. Percy delivered, on 15 March 1982, an address at the inaugural ceremonies in honor of the founding of the Eudora Welty Chair of Southern Studies at Millsaps College in Jackson. When Percy's nephew, LeRoy Percy, taught at Millsaps, Welty would join the Percys, sometimes including the Covington Percys, for dinner. Both Welty (1983) and Percy (1985) received the St. Louis Literary Award presented by St. Louis University; both were also recipients of the Compostella Award (Welty, 1984; Percy, 1985) presented by the Cathedral of St. James in Brooklyn. They were also the honored guests (along with C. Vann Woodward) on 17 May 1983 for the Fifth Frank Doubleday Lecture in the Flag Hall of the National Museum of American History in Washington, D.C. They were both present in mid-October 1985 when the last gathering of the great Southern literary eagles assembled at Louisiana State University in Baton Rouge for the 50th anniversary of the founding of *The Southern Review.*

4. See Patrick Samway, S.J., "Walker Percy's Homeward Journey," *America* 170 (14 May 1994): 16–19.

5. Walker Percy, "Eudora Welty in Jackson," *Shenandoah* 20 (Spring 1969): 37.

6. Eudora Welty, "Foreword" in *To the Lighthouse,* by Virginia Woolf (New York: Harcourt Brace Jovanovich, 1981), p. vii.

7. Jan Nordby Gretlund, *Eudora Welty's Aesthetics of Place,* (Columbia: University of South Carolina Press, 1997), p. 95.

8. André Bleikasten, "Fathers in Faulkner," in *The Fictional Father: Lacanian Readings of the Text,* ed. Robert Con Davis (Amherst: University of Massachusetts Press, 1981), p. 117.

9. Gretlund, *Eudora Welty's Aesthetics of Place,* p. 242.

10. See Jonathan Yardley, "The Verdict of Walker Percy," *Washington Post,* 14 May 1990. See also the letter of Walker Percy to Shelby Foote, 1 May 1975, in *The Correspondence of Shelby Foote and Walker Percy,* ed. Jay Tolson (New York: Norton, 1997), p. 208.

The Last Rose of Mount Salus

A Study of Narrative Strategies in
The Optimist's Daughter
Hans H. Skei

Eudora Welty's reputation will forever rest on her short story achievement. She is a wonderful short story writer, and although she has written successful novels, her major talent is not a novelist's. Two or three of her novels are really long short narratives, which leaves us with only *Delta Wedding* and *Losing Battles* as novels in a real and meaningful sense. *The Optimist's Daughter* was, of course, designed and executed as a long short story and was published in its original form in *The New Yorker*. William Maxwell read the story early in 1967, then titled "Poor Eyes," and, "thought it so good that it would swamp any collection in which it might appear."[1] So the good story became a novel because of separate publication, which Welty did not really like, thinking "that a story so closely grounded in autobiographical events would get undue attention unless it was camouflaged by other stories."[2]

Nevertheless, it is useless to haggle over borderlines between related genres, and my discussion of *The Optimist's Daughter* does not rely on clear-cut divisions between story and novel. In generic terms, I think it only fair to treat this extended narrative, with very limited action, as a novel, since it incorporates many types of narration, moves easily from outside description to internal reflections, and includes capsule stories which mirror the longer story of the narrative as a whole. Only the novel is flexible and inclusive enough as a genre to do this, but at the same time Welty's narrative in *The Optimist's Daughter* is so tight and to the point, aimed at one single purpose, that it most certainly is not the kind of polyphonic, dialogic novel described by Mikhail Bakhtin.[3] It is rather this glorious and joyful thing of our past, the well-made novel, which, at its best, is also the one bright book of life. Unfortunately, it goes on for a long time but tells a very limited story. The text seems to be uncertain about what to include or exclude. It is brilliant and very, very serious, but in a kind of self-conscious way that almost undermines its own seriousness and honesty.

When I first read *The Optimist's Daughter* back in the mid-1970s, I found the book to be very typical of a certain way of looking at life which I had come to associate with sincere and serious, but actually very boring, Southern books. Those are books in which nothing happens, in which few if any desires are awakened, and in which the world hinges on whether someone says the right word at the right time, and acts within debilitating rules of conduct and morality. Conversation may be good in such books, however, and the basic values presented and defended appear to be so vital that a decent life in a society of and with your fellowmen is all but impossible without them. Whether these values are inherited from the stoic Romans of old or from the British ancestors, who peopled certain regions of the South, is unimportant. The significance lies in the validity of them, even in the modern world. A sense of belonging, of family roots and place, and a keen understanding of what is permissible and what is not—in private as well as public life—contribute to this value system, which, all traits combined successfully, gives a person his or her character. Laurel McKelva Hand has no doubt about her values. We may find that they are questioned and redistributed at the end of the narrative about her, if we take the narrator's attempts at being sophisticated or profound at face value. The Laurel we get acquainted with as the optimist's daughter is, as far as we are being informed, a living dead, bloodless, tame, nostalgic, given to easy and superficial emotions (which she keeps to herself), and her new understanding changes very little. Dead is of course also Mount Salus, and so are even the ways of the old world, although most of the friends of the Judge whom we listen to cling to the past in order to be protected from the problems and challenges of the living present.

In a sense we thus have the decent, controlled, civilized, correct way of life, opposed to the teeming, busting, bewildering, and utterly shameless, shallow life of the poor white characters in the book—represented by Fay, by her family at the funeral, and by the family we meet in the waiting room at the New Orleans hospital. This juxtaposition may not appear to be very central, but it really informs the whole narrative, and there is no doubt, despite the text's attempts to look at Laurel from more than one side and even letting one of the ladies talk in favor of Fay, as to the narrator's understanding of human behavior. The reader's sympathy is directed to stay with Laurel, and even those narrative strategies that try to invalidate her understanding of herself and her past really serve to reinforce her position in the text. And, obviously, the narrative dares not mention those aspects of her life and of her choices that would reveal how extraordinarily *literary* a character she is. This distribution of sympathy and antipathy cannot be corrected or shown to be different by claims such as the obvious one that Laurel is not reliable as the central intelligence of the novel. *The Optimist's Daughter* is only minimally a dialogic novel, ruled and governed by its third-person narrator who is not manifest but who nevertheless reveals himself to the readers. He stubbornly believes so strongly in his understanding that the narrative voice lies above and subdues all other voices.[4] Yet in our final interpretation of the novel, we may be strongly tempted to look for possible levels of irony in the text, and perhaps the monologic narrative is modified and finally questioned by the implied author we can establish in this text, and who is not necessarily in agreement with the narrator.

Dialogue is nonetheless used to comic effect in some chapters of the novel, but as far as I can see, this only supports and strengthens my claim that the narrator is in full control. The new perspectives on Laurel as well as on the Judge and on Fay, given by some people in Mount Salus, may be seen as a deliberate narrative strategy. We nearly come to think that the narrator loosens his tight grip on the narrative, almost to the point where contesting opinions are given priority. But this is deceptive. Thus the novel as such pretends to be more open than it is, the narrator more profoundly in search of the truth than he is, and the central character more honest and serious about who she is—especially when she reaches a final understanding of her past and of the forces that molded and shaped her. It succeeds in doing all this, which is no mean achievement, in particular when the novel by implication also creates doubts about the very values it defends.

The Optimist's Daughter is one of those books in which no deviation is *really* permitted, but which opens up for minor disturbances in its monologic narrative and its one-sided understanding of character and life—this to such an extent that critics have been tempted to find that Laurel has serious doubts about herself, or to find that even Fay's behavior can be excused. On one hand, within the limitations laid down by the narrative, I cannot see that this is possible. On the other hand, having analyzed all formal aspects of the book, one may go on to an interpretation of the text in which one relates it to some kind of extra text, e.g., real life in the world by real people, and speculate about what it says or means in this respect. The particular narrative method in this book clearly sets some of the premises for our contextualization. One is therefore forced to read the text's potential meaning against questions about the past and the function it has in the present: questions of coming home and of being exiled; the deterioration of old values and their replacement by something new and different. But to enable us to discuss such problems brought forth by the text, we must study the text's handling of them, in scenes and fragments, in images and kernel stories, and assess their relative significance in the overall structure and thematic interest of the novel, *before* we begin to speculate and naturalize the text so that it, finally, means something serious, beautiful, and true. We may not get to this point, however.

Let me, then, proceed to a more specific analysis of the text, commenting on a number of aspects that I find important and that all point in the direction I have indicated earlier: viz. that *The Optimist's Daughter* is a strongly controlled and willed narrative, in which even the apparent modifications or complications of character and behavior only serve to strengthen the control, since these tempt readers into believing even more firmly in the narrator's deceptively honest voice. My second point is that there is, indeed, very little narrative desire or any other desire in the novel.[5] It is being told slowly, unwillingly but deliberately, with no desire for the end, with a plot amounting to nothing, in order to brood and speculate and remember. The minimal narrative seems to be there to allow the narrator, mostly through the central focus, Laurel, to reformulate her past on the basis of fragmented and scattered recollections she never seems to have paid much heed to and, more than anything else, to allow the text as a whole to become a lamentation, a eulogy, and an elegy. Jan Nordby Gretlund has, in the title of the chapter discussing this book in his Welty study, found a fitting expression: "Old Mount Salus Blues."[6] *The Optimist's Daughter* is indeed just that, although Gretlund claims, as have numerous other critics, that it is something much more and different. Any analysis of this text must investigate the intricacies of the narrative strategies and the clever manipulations of the reader. It is easy to overlook the obvious and ubiquitous lacunae in the text—especially when it consists of quoted or narrated monologues, sometimes not even spoken at all, by Laurel McKelva Hand.

Laurel's mind is deliberately set for the kind of memories she has, and she appears utterly unaware of the distortions and adjustments made by time itself and by our subconscious wishes to forget certain unpleasant experiences. Her memories are of the open, daylight kind, brought forth by similarities with the past in the present situation, and the language in which they are transferred to us is very much in the symbolic, not the semiotic, code. To see, for instance, in the breadboard incident elements of her subconscious surfacing to disturb her and lead her on to new and better understanding of her past and of herself is to some extent to be deceived by the narrator into accepting Laurel's changes as fundamental and significant. They change nothing. There is, indeed, little if anything to disturb the traditional understanding traded down by the McKelva ancestors and anachronistic Mount Salus. Laurel can return to Chicago and her designer's and widow's life, knowing that she is taking good care of her heritage, blood and all, by ending it. But then, according to Laurel McKelva Hand, we are probably all terminal cases.

The story in *The Optimist's Daughter* unfolds over a period not much longer than a month's time. Opening with Judge McKelva, his daughter, and his young wife's visit to Dr. Courtland in a New Orleans hospital, the story remains as static as the patient in his bed for a period of more than three weeks. A little later, patiently and stubbornly refusing to recover, the Judge dies—even though the eye which had undergone surgery seems to have improved. This story is told with heavy emphasis on the critical points—the examination by the doctor, the surgery, and the dying of the patient—whereas the rest of the discourse is devoted to a description of time passing. Laurel and Fay take turns sitting with the Judge, but since Laurel is the focal intelligence—the point of view, even if the voice is the narrator's—we get to know little except from Laurel's time with her father and from her first thoughts about her father's past life and her own.

Part 1 of the novel's four parts has four chapters and is placed in New Orleans during Carnival time. It is only fitting that there is a heavy-handed parallel between the hospital scenes and the Carnival setting. It underlines the passing of the old and its subsequent renewal. And the laughter and mirth from the streets might have reminded Laurel that we owe more to the living than to the dead. The section ends with the body of Laurel's father being brought back to Mount Salus, Mississippi, on the New Orleans–Chicago train, and Laurel is coming home, in many and troubling senses of this impossible phrase.

Part 2, also in four chapters, takes us through the arrival in Mount Salus, the reception in the Judge's house, and his burial. The mourning and all the small talk, including the serious and well-intended remarks and speeches about what the Judge had been in life, are broken up by the arrival of the Chisoms. The descriptions of this family from Madrid, Texas, and the conversation that goes on between the family members are hilariously grotesque and at the same time full of life, zest, stupidity, and optimism. The suicide story about the son who beat the fire truck to make it to Heaven, where he, same as the Judge, is at peace now, is wonderful.

But the story is out of place and told at the wrong time, and telling it shows a total lack of delicacy of feeling or respect for the deceased and the bereaved daughter. As a part of the text the Chisom story contributes some of the same slightly disturbing juxtaposition as the Carnival did in the New Orleans part.

In part 1 the Judge was taken ill and died; in part 2 he is buried, and so the good ladies of Mount Salus are allowed their small talk and gossip in the first chapter of part 3, whose discourse is quoted dialogue, introduced by the narrator's naming of the speaker and comments on who they are and what they represent. Basically, however, the dialogue runs uninterrupted, even by Laurel, until the question of coming back to *live* in Mount Salus is introduced.

From this point, with the discussion of whether Laurel's memory in Chicago of Mount Salus is comparable to the real thing, Laurel comes do dominate the text almost completely. With the exception of chapter 3 of the third part, containing the gossip of the so-called "bridesmaids," the rest of the narrative deals with story elements of little importance. There are strong symbolic overtones, however, in the discursive pattern which the author has given these elements through her narrator, and the narrator positions Laurel at the center of everything. The story moves straight forward, and there are no serious discrepancies between story and discourse in the sequence of events. Laurel's associations, started by minor clues in the house, the sewing room, and her mother's letters and diary, tend to go back to when she was a child and then move on to the memories of her mother's struggle before she died. The West Virginia parts of the narrative may, of course, be described as retrospective, a story of the past told after events in the present; but since everything of the past is presented as thoughts, reflections, dreams, or memories, we might as well think of it as part of the normal narrative, dealing with a story line that unfolds slowly but smoothly from arrival to departure. The story events in this part of the narrative are minor, but they contribute significantly to the textual meaning we shall later return to, so at least these minor episodes and facts should be mentioned: the library scene—beloved books and drops of nail varnish; the bird in the house and the chase to get it out; the West Virginia material; Laurel's mother's struggle for five years before dying; Laurel's memory of Phil and herself on the train; the incident of the soapstone boat; and the breadboard and the final encounter with Fay.

The narrative of *The Optimist's Daughter* is a simple structure. It tells the tale of Judge McKelva's death and burial and sings a few lines of Mount Salus blues. Since it turns to the past only through an effort of remembering, with no explicit intention of telling stories of the past except as a natural reaction in Laurel's mind upon the death of her second parent, it runs chronologically and in a well-regulated shift between scenes, summaries, and pauses. The third-person narrator is in control of it all, and the narrator's diction, choice of phrases, imagery, comparisons, qualifiers, and intensifiers demonstrate strongly how much the mediator of the story determines the final interpretation of it through the discourse in which the simple story is told. I find no flaws in the narrative pattern; it is and does exactly what the text intends to do. The main point about it is still its monologic character and its unwillingness to let contending narrative voices—or even competing narratives by characters within the master narrative—tell themselves.

The lack of narrative desire is in this text understandable and excusable, because the story material is so brief and the discourse dwells so extensively on what might have been and of coming to terms with the past. Laurel's desire may have been spent once and for all in her short time with Phil, and after he is killed in the war, she only has her memories. "Love was sealed away into its perfection and had remained there" (154). Story-telling, narrative desire cannot rely on what might have been. The novel can, however marginally, incorporate such an element, but what it loses is its drive forward, its desire for the end, its vitality and flow.

Formal aspects as well as the story elements contribute to a whole series of thematic concerns in *The Optimist's Daughter,* and they cannot be subsumed under one final "interpretation" of the text. I do think that this narrative is more stable and less prone to incessant play than many, and it does not have an endless potential for new meanings whenever it is approached once more. It is nevertheless futile to search for the final meaning. My point is simply that to ask what this text means is as valid as to ask how it achieves its meaning, which is basically what I have speculated about so far. My thematic discussion opens with an elaboration on the book's title.

Laurel is an only child, and knows it. "The Only Child" was the title of an early version of the story; this is a fact that does not add much to our understanding, since the perspective it indicates is kept in the title of the published version. It does, of course, emphasize the exceptional thing of being an only child, compared to most other children she knows, and the precarious situation she early finds herself in between her father and mother. Also, later in life, hers is the responsibility and duty to see both parents die. Particularly painful are the years of serious illness before her mother dies. Perhaps this early title can also remind us that the author placed much stress on Laurel's being an only child as a very important formative factor in her life.

Another discarded title, "Poor Eyes," seems to shift the perspective from Laurel's absolute centrality to an emphasis on the death of mother as well as father, but obviously most on the father. Looking more closely at the text, one may notice the descriptions of blindness and vision, of having one's eyesight and still not seeing what goes on, whereas the blind—Becky for one—see and feel and understand more than the seeing. Laurel is also described as losing her sight, albeit by Fay in the hospital, when she had fallen asleep sitting up: "Putting your eyes out, too?" (25). Fay also has the popular misunderstanding that Judge McKelva's eye trouble is a result of the time he has spent over dusty old books, thus contesting (although we are led to see how stupid it is) the value of books and reading as compared to the kind of life which she hears outside in the street and refers to right after her bit of thinking about book reading. In the country of the blind, we know how easy it is to be king, but we should also remember how reduced and limited a view this offers. Perhaps Laurel McKelva Hand should be understood in this perspective—those closest to her lose their sight and die, and she lives on, with a dimmed vision of reasons and motives and people's reactions—until the text tells us that she finally discovers something, by looking into herself and becoming aware of her blindness. But the awareness is a general feeling of loss, and a universal grief, kept at bay for a long time, for more than anything else it is related to the loss of Phil: "A flood of feeling descended on Laurel. She let the papers slide from her hand and the books from her knees, and put her head down on the open lid of the desk and wept in grief for love and for the dead. She lay there with all that was adamant in her yielding to this night, yielding at last. Now all she had found had found her. The deepest spring in her heart had uncovered itself, and it began to flow again" (154).

The title of the book as we know it, *The Optimist's Daughter,* is not necessarily a better title than the two previous suggestions. The optimism of her father appears as rather marginal in the text and is understood to be a substitute for something else: an attitude adapted and used to endure the harshness of his wife in her long painful years of blindness and approaching death. Thinking back, Laurel sees it as "betrayal upon betrayal." Her father, being a man of great delicacy, abhors "any sort of private clash," and so he does not understand his wife's desperation or his own shortcomings. He had, we are told, "a horror of . . . divergence from the affectionate and the real and the explainable and recognizable" (146). His wife apparently has adjusted to his ways, although at a high price, because she had, in Laurel's late understanding, "known herself" (144). So one may ask what it really means being the daughter of this kind of optimist? It is plain enough that Laurel has inherited some of her father's delicacy, good manners, and respect for the established and proven ways, perhaps without the upper-class attitudes that accompanied her father's self-understanding. She is, however, also the daughter of the former mayor of Mount Salus, although she discovers that all the files and records he kept at home are unused and collecting dust, as obsolete and forgotten as something out of the past.

We could go on playing with the possible implications of the title or, more importantly, with the direction it gives to our reading of the text. The single most important clue we get from the title is that what follows is going to be Laurel's story, and it is. Everything is done to find room for her memories of childhood and of her mother's last years. This is before the emotional recollections of her husband that lead up to the final discussion with herself. Perhaps the novel ends with a new understanding, where Laurel's memory can again flow freely and where she, the living McKelva, is finally able to understand that her preoccupation with the dead parents is in fact a way to find *comfort for herself*: "What burdens we lay on the dying, Laurel thought, as she listened now to the accelerated rain on the roof: seeking to prove some little thing that we can keep to comfort us when they can no longer feel—something as incapable of being kept as of being proved: the lastingness of memory, vigilance against harm, self-reliance, good hope, trust in one another" (146). In a strange way Laurel also becomes her mother's daughter, using bits and scraps of memory from her mother's memory for comfort. The story of how Becky lost her father after having taken him to Baltimore returns to Laurel's memory and leads to this general understanding of the human predicament: "Neither of us saved our fathers, Laurel thought. But Becky was the brave one. I stood in the hall, too, but I did not any longer believe that anyone could be saved, anyone at all. Not from others" (144).

The Optimist's Daughter is about death and dying, about memories too sacred to be relinquished for the needs of the living and the present moment. In short, much, if not everything, in the text revolves around the question of the importance of the past in the present. In the final analysis, the basic difference between Fay and Laurel is that the former belongs to the future—she is allowed to say this herself in the breadboard confrontation— whereas Laurel is a slave to the past. If Laurel learns anything from class differences, from Fay's propensity for making scenes, from seeing that she would have as much trouble living in Mount Salus as Fay would have, it is that her version of the past may be a private and not very accurate one, and that memory should no longer be allowed to be the somnambulist, but rather something to learn from and grow on. The problem is that if Laurel learns a lesson, it is of little comfort. We may ask: the memory of father and mother lives on in her mind, but whose mind has she gotten into, to be remembered? No wonder that grief overcomes her, and that lamentation becomes more and more important in the text as we get closer to its conclusion.

The past is the major interest, the main theme of the novel. There is a lesson of the past formulated in the text on its final page. It comes after Laurel has shown real emotion for once and threatened to strike Fay with her cherished breadboard. She puts it away and is quoted as saying, "I think I can get along without that too" (179). That too? An impoverished life lies ahead for the textile designer in Chicago, when all Mount Salus ties are severed and the breadboard made by Phil's own hands is left behind for Fay McKelva, born Chisom, to throw away! The narrator's description reads as follows: "Memory lived not in initial possession but in the freed hands, pardoned and freed, and in the heart that can empty but fill again, in the patterns restored by dreams" (179). This is a text that read alone resists interpretation, vague and uncertain as it is. Read in the context of the whole narrative in *The Optimist's Daughter,* it clearly points to the burden of the dead which Laurel has thought about before, as well as to the message that we should free ourselves, be absolved, and not let the dead dominate the present. We should also stop feeling obliged to cherish the memory of the dead when it impedes our life among the living. The expression "the patterns restored by dreams" may mean many different things, but within the context of the narrative, it points to the new awareness of the dreamlike if not mythical and false nature of memories of the past. The patterns and the structures are necessary for our narratives of the past, which become *fictions* of our own lives but which are absolutely vital to our mental health.

Laurel seems to reach a better understanding of the *shortcomings* of past and of present, when it comes to the question of leading meaningful lives, but she has not changed much and she has given up nothing. While the text shows that she is still a strong believer in values that deserve to be carried on into the future, it also undercuts this. Readers must also see her as a slave of the past, a member of a lost breed of people. She is perhaps the last rose of Mount Salus, left blooming alone; but soon she will follow, wither, and go. This dual perspective may indicate that the novel is less monologic than I indicated earlier. Yet it only points to the ironies that arise when the reader is forced to question the values and judgments of the narrator. Simple images lead to this, e.g., in the novel's concluding paragraph: Passing the Courthouse, with all its powers of symbolic representation, on her way to the airport, the last thing Laurel can see of Mount Salus is "the twinkling of their hands," the hands of Miss Adele's first graders, the hands of the future of Mount Salus. Laurel and her companions leave it behind, whirling into speed.

So I insist, just as the text insists, on the single-mindedness of its narrative and its clear conviction that there are basic values threatened and even lost. They may be a nuisance even to Laurel McKelva Hand, and a new understanding of them may have come to her. I accept the interpretations that insist on Laurel's new understanding of the meaning of the past, but the important question of the text's meaning has to do with the conflicting understandings of the narrator and of the text's norm (its implied author). They are not necessarily very much apart, yet the discrepancy depends on the reader's acceptance or rejection of Laurel and her choices.

Do you remember Becky's climber? It is the rose Judge McKelva was pruning when he first discovered his eye trouble, and it was his wife's pride and joy, preferred to all other roses and perennials. It is so wonderful that Miss Tennyson thinks if Laurel could see the climber come out, she might change her mind and stay in Mount Salus. Laurel replies that she can *imagine* the rose, in Chicago, but stands corrected when Miss Tennyson argues, "But you can't smell it" (114). The more than one-hundred-year-old root came into strong growth and bloomed when it was given the room it asked for. If it did not bloom one year, it might bloom the next, was Becky's lesson, and Laurel's, or ours: "Memory returned like spring, Laurel thought. Memory had the character of spring. In some cases, it was the old wood that did the blooming" (115). I will not comment on this brief passage, revealing as it is both for our understanding of life in Mount Salus and for our understanding of a present rooted in the past, and of memory, returning like spring. Nor shall I take you through the exquisite literariness of parts of the book, i.e., the parts in which books are being discussed, read from, commented on. Laurel's reactions in her father's library are of course worth a separate discussion. Also, I will not comment on the strange and not too well handled chimney swift. If the implications of the bird episode are to show how Laurel must set her memory and her version of the past free, just as the ominous bird must be freed, it does not deserve much comment. There is, of course, more to it, and I can easily see an interpretation in which this episode (and the rose imagery, for that matter) functions as a kind of capsule story to retell in condensed form what the whole narrative tries to tell us.

I must admit that I have had to leave out elements that I find both beautiful, well written, and thematically important. The train ride from New Orleans to Mount Salus is one such scene. The remembered train ride overlooking Cairo and the confluence of the two big rivers is another. Here poetic language describes sorrow and despair and gives a quality to the text that you only find among the best of writers.

Laurel weeps time and again for what happened to life, not because it is being taken over by the Fay Chisoms of this world, but because what Fay represents has always been there, and has always threatened the decency and delicacy of emotional control. Laurel weeps for what happened to life, and the narrator not only understands this, but does everything to show its inevitability. Yet the narrative also tells us, in my interpretation, that she weeps unaware that what happens to life, and that which she dislikes, is *life itself,* from which only the dead and not the living should be protected.

Notes

1. Quoted from Michael Kreyling, *Author and Agent* (New York: Farrar, Straus & Giroux, 1991), p. 204.

2. Kreyling, *Author and Agent,* p. 204.

3. See, e.g., M. M. Bakhtin, *The Dialogic Imagination* (Austin: University of Texas Press, 1981).

4. Bakhtin (cf. note 3) describes the monologic narrative as a narrative characterized by a unifying voice superior to other voices in the text. The narrator's views and knowledge constitute the final authority as to our understanding of what happens in the text.

5. "Narrative desire" is here used in the sense that Peter Brooks establishes in his *Reading for the Plot* (Oxford: Oxford University Press, 1984).

6. See Jan Nordby Gretlund, *Eudora Welty's Aesthetics of Place* (Columbia: University of South Carolina Press, 1997), pp.189–207

Region, Time, and Memory

The Optimist's Daughter as
Southern Renascence Fiction
Mary Ann Wimsatt

Eudora Welty is perhaps the greatest author of the Southern Rena-scence—that remarkable flowering of twentieth-century writing which, precipitated by Ellen Glasgow, H. L. Mencken, and the Agrarians, produced such notable literary figures as Katherine Anne Porter, William Faulkner, Flannery O'Connor, and Thomas Wolfe. Critics have long agreed that among the central elements of Renascence literature are a strong sense of the South as a distinctive region, a correspondingly strong sense of place or locale, a belief in a hierarchical system of social classes, a feeling of shared community springing from a keen awareness of class and region, and an abiding recognition of the influence of the past upon the present—or of what is sometimes called the presence of the past in the present. Also important to Renascence literature is the role of memory in establishing an enlightened understanding of the past. These and other features of Renascence writing are well exemplified by what is perhaps Welty's finest novel, *The Optimist's Daughter*.

In Welty's classic manner, these elements in *The Optimist's Daughter* are deftly woven together; but to some extent they must be treated sepa-rately in order that we as readers may see how they function in the novel and especially how they affect its major character, Laurel McKelva Hand. As the novel opens, Laurel has taken a brief leave from her work in Chi-cago and returned to her birthplace in Mount Salus, Mississippi, to help her elderly father, Judge Clinton McKelva, who is about to undergo sur-gery on one of his eyes. In Mount Salus, Laurel must contend with her widowed father's second wife, Fay, a rural Texas woman who is in many respects the antithesis of his first wife, Becky. Shortly after his surgery, the Judge dies. At his wake and funeral, the problems that Fay and other characters cause for Laurel force her to confront several painful elements in her conflicted past. Through experiences associated with place and re-called through memory late in the book, Laurel slowly arrives at a new understanding of the life and death of her father and mother, of her own brief marriage and her widowhood, and, most importantly, of Fay and what Fay represents. These and other events in the book take place against the background of two vividly presented regions that validate the importance in Renascence literature of place while making evident Welty's genius for representing it. These regions are the Mount Salus community of Laurel's birth and upbringing, and the West Virginia mountains that had been her mother Becky's home.

Mount Salus, a small Mississippi town, could function as an exemplum for the elements of Renascence literature indicated above. Its inhabitants delight in their memories of the community's collective past and of the individual pasts of Laurel, Becky, and the Judge. It has clearly demarcated social classes, the most prominent of which is the genteel upper or upper middle class of Laurel's and her parents' upbringing represented by such notable Welty characters as Miss Adele Courtland, Miss Tennyson Bullock, and elderly Mrs. Pease. Townspeople belonging to this class exhibit strong community solidarity, which has both a fortunate and an unfortunate side, and a corresponding distrust of outsiders—particularly of Fay, the Judge's widow.

Fay, who constitutes the major obstacle for Laurel in the narrative, is a mystery, in large measure, to the Mount Salus community. Neither the townspeople nor Laurel can fully understand or accept her, in part because she represents a different region and social class from theirs. As a result, she repeatedly violates their standards of appropriate social conduct. Towheaded, bony, and possibly undernourished, Fay is often raw and callous in behavior. At her wedding she tells Laurel, who has flown in from Chicago, "It wasn't any use in you bothering to come so far"; she says of Judge McKelva, "If he hadn't spent so many years of his life poring over dusty old books, his eyes would have more strength saved up for now"; and as the Judge lies dying in the hospital, she tries to pull him out of bed while shouting, "I tell you enough is enough!" Repeatedly in the narrative, Fay voices shrill rejections of genteel Mount Salus's, and Laurel's, social rank and past and the town's shared recollection of these things. After she marries the Judge, for instance, one of his friends in Mount Salus offers to give her a tea. But Fay says, "Oh, please don't bother with a big wholesale reception. That kind of thing was for Becky" (*OD*, 126). When the townspeople, in a show of support for Laurel, gather at the Judge's wake, a middle-aged woman tells Fay, "The six of us right here, we were [Laurel's] bridesmaids." Fay retorts, "A lot of good her bridesmaids will ever do me." And when an older woman says that she and other friends at the wake are "the last, devoted remnants of [Becky's] old Garden Club," Fay snaps, "What's Becky's Garden Club got to do with me?" (53). These and similar remarks represent Fay's attempts, objectionable if understandable, to deny a past objectified by a closely knit community and class into which she cannot enter.

Early in the narrative Fay tells Laurel, in what proves to be a lie, that she has no living relatives. But after the Judge's death, Major Bullock, a longtime friend of the McKelvas, locates and contacts Fay's family, the Chisoms, who arrive *en masse* at the wake. Familiar rural-class Welty characters, the Chisoms are well-meaning, awkward, uneducated, and humorous. Welty effects delicious comedy through the contrast of this rough-hewn clan with the Mount Salus gentility while introducing serious elements that prepare the reader for major events to come. Shortly after arriving, Fay's mother, Mrs. Chisom, swoops down upon the grieving Laurel, pokes her in the side, laments that she "ain't got father, mother, brother, sister, husband, chick nor child," and then remarks: "Me and my brood believes in clustering just as close as we can get. . . . Bubba pulled his trailer right up in my yard when he married," while "Sis here got married and didn't even try to move away" (69, 70). Meanwhile, young Wendell Chisom—fair, delicate, unguarded, and very like "a young, undriven, unfalsifying, unvindictive Fay"—gazes at the Judge in his coffin and inquires, "How come he wanted to dress up?" (76, 70). Suddenly Fay, gleaming in black satin, darts into the room, glares at her relatives, asks "Who told *them* to come?," and cries to her dead husband, "Oh, Judge, how could you go off and leave me this way?" (84, 85). When Fay screams, "Why did he do me so *bad*?" Wendell says, "Don't cry! I'll shoot the bad man for you." . . . "You *can't* shoot him," says Sis (87).

In the meantime, the demonstration of community feeling in Mount Salus made possible by memory continues. Members of other social groups—the piano tuner Tom Farris and the sewing woman Mrs. Verna Longmeier—stop by to pay their respects. In honor of the dead, the bank closes, the courthouse flag is lowered, and school is let out early. At the church, people are standing around all the walls. "Black Mount Salus had come too," Welty observes, "and the black had dressed themselves in black." Fittingly, after the funeral the people file down the steps of the church together (89). The Judge's longtime private secretary aptly summarizes the solidarity apparent at the ceremonies when she says, "I saw everybody I know and everybody I used to know. It was old Mount Salus personified" (92). Unexpectedly, Fay—lonely, out of her element, and perhaps mollified by the presence of her relatives—decides to return briefly with them to Texas.

There ensues a brilliant series of scenes in which friends of Laurel's parents, gathered in the garden of the McKelva home, alternately condemn and attempt to account for Fay while urging Laurel to remain in Mississippi in order to help them cope with "Clinton's little minx" (115). In these scenes Welty combines an informed understanding of the Mount Salus community with implied, gently ironic criticism of its gossipy insularity; and she also combines the presentation of region, class, time, and memory with impressive subtlety and concision. Old Mrs. Pease, an acerbic commentator, remarks that while Judge McKelva was alive Fay did nothing all day but sit and eat while keeping "straight on looking like a sparrow"; Miss Tennyson Bullock, almost equally acerbic, says, "'Frying pan' was the one name she could give you of all the things" in Becky's kitchen (106, 107). Mrs. Pease proceeds to denounce Fay's relatives. "When the whole bunch of Chisoms got to going in concert," she says, "I thought the only safe way to get through the business alive was not say a word, just sit as still as a mouse" (109). But Miss Adele Courtland, the most perspicacious of the old Mount Salus group, insists that at the ceremonies "the Chisoms did every bit as well as we did"— and, defending Fay's melodramatic behavior during the wake, she observes, "I think that carrying-on was Fay's idea of giving a sad occasion its due. She was rising to it, splendidly.—By her lights!" (109). "'Are we all going to have to feel sorry for her?' inquires Miss Tennyson. Miss Adele, with one eye on Laurel, says, 'If there's nothing else to do, there's no help for it. . . . Is there, Laurel?' But Laurel—unable to understand or forgive her father's widow—replies, 'I hope I never see her again'" (112).

The talk turns to what Laurel should do in the future and what she might have done in the past. Miss Tennyson, gesturing toward her, observes, "That girl's had more now than she can say grace over. And she's going back to that life of labor when she could just as easily give it up. Clint's left her a grand hunk of money." Mrs. Pease, the most persistent voice of tradition in the group, warns Laurel, "Once you leave after this, you'll always come back as a visitor" (112). Somewhat later she tells Laurel she should have remained at home after her mother died because her father "needed him somebody *in* that house" (115). But Miss Adele, astute and mischievous, remarks, "Oh, Laurel can do anything. If it's been made hard enough for her. . . . Of *course* she can give up Mount Salus and say goodbye to this house and to us, and the past, and go on back to

Chicago day after tomorrow. . . . And take up one more time where she left off" (113).

What the McKelva friends, save Miss Adele, do not realize is that Laurel has long sustained an insider-outsider relationship with the Mount Salus community. Though reared in Mississippi, she had been educated in Chicago, where she had met and married a man from Ohio, Philip Hand, who a year later had been killed in World War II. When Laurel returns to Mount Salus, she appreciates the friendship and the participation in a shared past that her family's friends provide; but her residence in Chicago and her sudden widowhood have distanced her from her birthplace, and they have also given her a complex series of recollections that her Mount Salus friends cannot share. Her father's illness, coming shortly after his second marriage, impels her—in what are as indicated the most important actions in the book—to confront through memory her conflicting feelings about his life and death, her mother Becky's life and death, Phil's death, and the existence and meaning of Fay.

Part of Laurel's ordeal, though not the most trying part, derives from her idealized memory of Judge McKelva and what she thinks the community that he had cherished owes him. Her recollections naturally differ from what the townspeople recall. Wandering through the library, Laurel remembers her father's extensive work with flood control, realizes that it has become forgotten drudgery, and muses, "This town deserved him no more than Fay deserved him" (120). When Major Bullock boasts about how the Judge had once heroically faced down the Ku Klux Klan, Laurel complains to Miss Adele that the Major is inflating the facts. Miss Adele, trying to enlighten her, replies that Major Bullock and others are "trying to say for a man that his life is over"—and adds, "They're being clumsy. . . . because they [are] thinking of you" (82). Reminiscing over drinks, Laurel's bridesmaids merrily recall an impossibly heavy beaded dress the Judge had once bought for Becky. Laurel, wounded, inquires when her friends have started laughing at her parents. But Tish Bullock, Laurel's closest friend among the bridesmaids, explains, "We weren't laughing at them. . . . We're grieving *with* you" (127).

Laurel's most painful memories of her father are prompted by her inability to understand Fay, who she thinks has mistreated Judge McKelva. Fueling Laurel's beliefs are her anguished recollections. She remembers how her father had suffered with both Fay and Becky and how he had "died worn out with both wives—almost as if up to the last he had still had both of them." Then she remembers, in passages demonstrating the centrality of time and memory in the book, how as he had lain "without moving in the hospital he had concentrated utterly on time passing. . . . But which way had it been going for him? When he could no longer get up and encourage it, push it forward, had it turned on him, started moving back the other way?" (151–52). Alone at night in the McKelva home, Laurel—recalling how Fay had acted in the hospital—wants to cry out, "Abuse! Abuse!"—for "it is possible to say to the dying 'Enough is enough,' if the listener who overhears is his daughter with his memory to protect" (130). Brooding over the past, she realizes that unlike her father she cannot pity Fay. Only her dead mother, she thinks, would have had the ability to console her. "She had the proof, the damnable evidence ready for her mother, and was in anguish because she could not give it to her, and so be herself consoled." But then the "longing to tell her mother was brought about-face, and she saw the horror. Father, beginning to lose his sight, followed Mother, but who am I at the point of following but Fay? Laurel thought. The scene she had just imagined, herself confiding the abuse to her mother . . . was a more devastating one than all Fay had acted out in the hospital. What would I not do, perpetrate, she wondered, for consolation?" (132).

Armed with this new knowledge of herself, Laurel goes into her mother's sewing room, where family photographs and letters from the Judge propel her into recollections of both Mount Salus and West Virginia that precipitate further insights into her past. In particular, her memories of her childhood visits to Becky's mountain home make prominent the second important Southern region of the book while infusing important values associated with it into the narrative.

If Mount Salus reveals such significant aspects of settled Southern town life as community, gentility, and social class, West Virginia with its impressive physical landscape represents the isolation, autonomy, and freedom associated with mountain regions of the South. The solitude of West Virginia life has helped to foster the independence and determination that are the most pronounced traits of Becky's character. Laurel remembers her mother's tales of how she had ridden the family horse to school seven miles "over Nine Mile Mountain, seven miles home," reciting all the way to make time pass swiftly, and of how, somewhat later, she had made a blouse from homespun cloth, dyed it with pokeberry juice, and developed the photographs taken of her wearing it (137, 136). Becky's most strikingly independent act, one with reverberations in the present time of the narrative, had occurred when at age fifteen she had traveled with her ill father and a neighbor on a raft down an ice-filled river to Baltimore, where her father died. After his death, Becky had returned home by herself in the train's baggage car, "bearing the news and bringing the coffin, both together" (144).

Becky's remarkable self-sufficiency had not precluded—in fact, it had helped to nurture—the close family ties and the memories inevitably associated with them that had been as much a part of her upbringing as of Laurel's. Her six younger brothers had saddled the family pony and played the banjo for her; they had told her "so many stories . . . about people only she knew and they knew" that she had cried in order to be "able to stop laughing"; when she married, her youngest brother had gone out and wept on the ground (138, 139). Even her marriage and her life in Mount Salus had not disrupted her strong connections to her family bred by the mountains and nourished by her life-long recollections of her past. In *The Optimist's Daughter*, these various aspects of Becky's life come together in a poignant scene. When her mother dies unexpectedly and alone, Laurel hears Becky cry, "I wasn't there! I wasn't *there!*" (142).

By filtering elements from Becky's West Virginia upbringing through Laurel's recollections of Becky dying, sightless, Welty dramatizes the pain and the unresolved conflicts that Laurel through memory must confront. During Becky's long, difficult final illness, her adoring husband, helpless and bewildered, had not known how to assist her. Just as in the present time of the novel Laurel in her grief has temporarily turned against her Mount Salus friends, so in the past, young and newly widowed, she had turned against her father because she had felt he was not sufficiently grieved about the changes in his wife. When Becky accused him of letting people hurt her, "Laurel battled against them both, each for the other's sake. She loyally reproached her mother for yielding to the storms that began coming to her out of her darkness of vision. . . . As for her father, he apparently needed guidance in order to see the tragic" (145). Becky, meanwhile, had confronted her malady with the same spirited independence she had shown in the mountains. Asking Laurel for her "old McGuffey's Fifth Reader," she had recited from memory Robert Southey's "The Cataract of Lodore," a poem she had learned in childhood that had suited the river-threaded wilderness of her West Virginia home (146–47). But as her condition worsened and her mind began to wander, she had said sharply to her husband and daughter, "'All you do is hurt me. I wish I might know what it is I've done. Why is it necessary to punish me like this and not tell me why?' And still she held fast to their hands, to Laurel's too. Her cry was not complaint; it was anger at wanting to know and being denied knowledge; it was love's deep anger" (148).

After a stroke, Becky "had come to believe . . . that she had been taken somewhere that was neither home nor 'up home,' that she was left among strangers, for whom even anger meant nothing, on whom it would only be wasted. She had died without speaking a word, keeping everything to herself, in exile and humiliation." While she was still able to recognize her daughter, she had uttered a final, desperate remark: "You could have saved your mother's life. But you stood by and wouldn't intervene. I despair for you." Evoking the young Becky's raft journey and her father's subsequent death, Welty remarks, "Baltimore was as far a place as you could go with those you loved, and it was where they left you" (151). And Laurel, sadly recalling these scenes, wishes "her mother and father dragged back to any torment of living because that torment was something they had known together, through each other. She wanted them with her to share her grief as she had been the sharer of theirs" (151, 150).

What propels Laurel through this difficult recollection into one yet more difficult is her discovery of the letters her West Virginia grandmother—widowed, ill, and lonely—had written to her "young, venturesome, defiant, happily married daughter as to an exile." Laurel can scarcely believe the courage and tranquility her suffering grandmother "had put into these short letters, in the quickened pencil to catch the pocket of one of 'the boys' before he rode off again, dependent . . . upon his remembering to mail them from 'the courthouse.' She read on and met her own name on a page" (153). Unexpectedly overwhelmed by her feelings, Laurel "wept in grief for love and for the dead. She lay there with all that was adamant in her . . . yielding at last. Now all she had found had found her. The deepest spring in her heart had uncovered itself, and it began to flow again" (154).

It is apparently unrestricted love made possible by memories of her dead relatives that flows from the "deepest spring" in Laurel's heart. However it is interpreted, this impressive scene leads directly into an equally impressive one that centers on Laurel's new understanding of her husband Phil and of what their marriage might have become had he lived. Until the present time, she had kept the recollection of their love "sealed away in its perfection." But suddenly she sees Phil as an individual separate and distinct from herself; and she realizes that Phil's desires might have differed fundamentally from hers, even as their future might have differed materially from their past:

> By her own hands, the past had been raised up, and *he* looked at her, Phil himself—here waiting, all the time, Lazarus. He looked at her out of eyes wild with the craving for his unlived life, with mouth open like a funnel's.

What would have been their end, then? Suppose their marriage had ended like her father and mother's? Or like her mother's father and mother's? Like—

"Laurel! Laurel! Laurel!" Phil's voice cried.

She wept for what happened to life.

"I wanted it!" Phil cried. His voice rose with the wind in the night and. . . . became a roar. "I wanted it!" (154–55)

Laurel's new perception of Phil, which frees her from cherished but overly idealized beliefs about their marriage, begins her movement toward a future apart from Mount Salus and Fay. The next step in this process is her destruction of the tangible, painful evidence of the past represented by her mother's letters and papers. But as she is about to leave for Chicago, she sees a cupboard she has overlooked and in it an object "waiting for her to find": a breadboard Phil had carefully and lovingly made for Becky that, once whole and clean, has become, through Fay's carelessness, splintered and begrimed (172). At this moment, Fay enters the house; she and Laurel begin to argue; and matters between them worsen. For "all Laurel had felt and known in the night, all she'd remembered, and as much as she could understand this morning . . . could not tell her now how to stand and face the person whose own life had not taught her how to feel" (173).

Shortly after starting to quarrel with her stepmother, however, Laurel, reflecting on the relationship between time and memory, realizes that

> experience did, finally, get set into its right order, which is not always the order of other people's time. Her mother had suffered in life every symptom of having been betrayed, and it was not until she had died, and the protests of memory came due, that Fay had ever tripped in from Madrid, Texas. It was not until that later moment, perhaps, that her father himself had ever dreamed of a Fay. For Fay was Becky's own dread. What Becky had felt, and had been afraid of, might have existed right here in the house all the time, for her. Past and future might have changed places, in some convulsion of the mind, but that could do nothing to impugn the truth of the heart. Fay could have walked in early as well as late, she could have come at any time at all. She was coming. (174)

After blaming Fay for her handling of the breadboard, Laurel inquires about her treatment of the Judge: "What were you trying to scare Father into—when you struck him?" Fay explains, in statements that validate themselves, "I was trying to scare him into living. . . . I was going to make him live if I had to drag him! And I take good credit for what I did!" Laurel charges, "You hurt him," and Fay retorts, "I was being a wife to him! . . . Have you clean forgotten by this time what being a wife is?" "I haven't forgotten," Laurel tells Fay. To support what she has said, she gestures toward the breadboard and explains that it had been "a beautiful piece of work" because Phil, who had "the gift of his hands. . . . planed—fitted—glued—clamped," and in short made the board "on the true" (175).

As a living emblem of memory, a tribute to Phil and Becky, and a final repudiation of Fay, Laurel plans to take the board with her to Chicago. Lifting it out of Fay's reach, she contemplates striking her stepmother, who sneers, "Is that what you hit with? Is a moldy old breadboard the best you can find?" In a gesture of resignation, Laurel lowers the board and holds it level toward her opponent. Fay observes, "You were just before trying to hit me with that plank. But you couldn't have done it. You don't know the way to fight" (177, 178).

Then, in the climactic section of the book, Laurel realizes that "it was Fay who did not know how to fight. For Fay was without any powers of passion or imagination in herself and had no way to see it or reach it in the other person." Laurel admits to herself that she "had been ready to hurt Fay. . . . But such is the strangeness of the mind, it had been the memory of the child Wendell that had prevented her." When Fay asks what Laurel sees in the breadboard, Laurel replies, "The whole story, Fay. The whole solid past." Fay snaps, "Whose story? Whose past? Not mine. . . . I belong to the future"—a remark that simultaneously makes possible Laurel's ultimate experience of understanding and communicates much of what Welty has subtly expressed in the book. "I know you aren't anything to the past," Laurel tells Fay. "You can't do anything to it now." Then, in a passage contrasting the unchangeable, unassailable past with the shifting and vulnerable memory, she realizes, "The past is no more open to help or hurt than was Father in his coffin. The past is like him, impervious, and can never be awakened. It is memory that is the somnambulist. It will come back in its wounds from across the world, like Phil, calling us by our names and demanding its rightful tears" (179).

Having finally through memories born of time and region attained an understanding of the Judge, Becky, Phil, Fay, and, most importantly, herself, Laurel McKelva Hand can leave the family homestead more at peace than she has been before—at peace, finally, with the burden of the past, and its pain.

Notes

1. See, for example, C. Hugh Holman, *The Roots of Southern Writing: Essays on the Literature of the American South* (Athens: University of Georgia Press, 1972), passim, and Louis D. Rubin, Jr., *The Writer in the South: Studies in a Literary Community* (Athens: University of Georgia Press, 1972), passim.

2. See the well-known essay "Place in Fiction" in Eudora Welty, *The Eye of the Story: Selected Essays and Reviews* (New York: Random House, 1977), pp. 116–33.

3. OD, pp. 27, 25, 32.

4. For points similar to those in the text, see Marilyn Arnold, "Images of Memory in *The Optimist's Daughter*," *Southern Literary Journal* 14 (Spring 1982), especially pp. 30–36.

5. On critics' failure to interpret Fay and her behavior sympathetically, see Danielle Fuller, "Making a Scene: Some Thoughts on Female Sexuality and Marriage in Eudora Welty's *Delta Wedding* and *The Optimist's Daughter*," *Mississippi Quarterly* 48 (Spring 1995): 310–18, and Robert H. Brinkmeyer, Jr., "New Orleans, Mardi Gras, and Eudora Welty's *The Optimist's Daughter*," *Mississippi Quarterly* 44 (Fall 1991): 436.

The Swift Bird of Memory, the Breadboard of Art

Reflections on Eudora Welty and Her Storytelling
Marion Montgomery

What shall we say who have knowledge
Carried to the heart? Shall we take the act
To the grave? Shall we, more hopeful, set up the grave
In the house? The ravenous grave?
Allen Tate, "Ode to the Confederate Dead"

Considering the prominence of the theme of memory in Eudora Welty's *The Optimist's Daughter* and her dwelling on memory in her lectures, *One Writer's Beginnings,* one wonders whether she, as T. S. Eliot came to be, is well acquainted with Saint Augustine's "Philosophy of Memory" in his *Confessions.* Again, a "literary" influence is not our concern here, but rather correspondences between Saint Augustine's and Eliot's and Miss Welty's actual experiences of existing as persons, correspondences certified common to persons by signs. As persons they nevertheless differ essentially one from another. But in the witness of signs, whether those of such an open philosopher as Saint Augustine or so gifted a poet as Eudora Welty, we discover correspondences witnessing the self when it is self-conscious as it discovers a mysterious gift to that self, namely memory. Now Descartes long ago was concerned with consciousness as proof of existence, though it was difficult for him to break beyond the separation of thought from any *other* in a communion of consciousness and creation. He argued that the pineal gland was the locus to the intersection of thought with whatever existed separate from thought. Since then science has pursued consciousness almost relentlessly, but it centers more and more on consciousness as a sort of spume rising out of biological process

145

more diffusely intersecting in nerve synapse than in so simple a place as the pineal gland.

Just how far these researches and speculations about consciousness have advanced since Descartes is in doubt, I think, though there is an impressive library of researches aiding our collective memory on the question. Meanwhile, Saint Augustine's philosophical and theological address to the mystery of memory proves still a viable one. He accepted memory as a gift of capacity to consciousness itself, but in its nature hardly reducible to formulae, though metaphor might somewhat serve consciousness in reaching accommodation with its memory of itself. Metaphor qualified may prove visionary, as formulae reductive only distort the reality of memory in an attempt to deny mystery as a fundamental condition to existing at all. Thus we might say that memory is a holding *place* in one's continuous life, though it is no place such as the pineal gland. Limited to my consciousness, my memory is seemingly infinite in its holding capacity. It is an expandable container with no delineated margins, holding the self as continuously alive, unless that self attempt to freeze-dry consciousness by thought's action of arresting its own active continuity in this always continuous present moment.

Rather certainly, something like this is Saint Augustine's view, though the terms of our playful metaphor are not his. And rather certainly Eudora Welty sees memory in this perspective. This seeing is crucial, she says, to her making of stories. Hers is a "seeing" which comes early to her and very comfortably to her as she discovers her calling as poet, as story-maker—in contrast to Eliot, for instance, for whom an accommodation was most difficult, until he read Saint Augustine. For though early he cries out "Memory! / You have the key," Eliot has not used that key to open a door upon the mystery of existence in his present moment. Consequently at that point his memory can only throw up "high and dry / a crowd of twisted things" into consciousness. Miss Welty, however, attunes herself early to memory as continuous presence of past experiences, signifying by such presence that intellect is alive—however much memory may pulse in consciousness—now bright, now dim. Thus our past and our present are inescapably entangled, requiring that we address both our past as we may now know it and the contingent present that confronts us always here and now—in this place and at this moment.

What Miss Welty says of memory, deploying her concern for memory in an enveloping thematic order to her novel, sometimes bears striking echoes of what Saint Augustine says of that mystery in Book X of his *Confessions*. In a dramatic parallel also, Saint Augustine addresses the nature of memory in a present moment as he is remembering his mother, Saint Monica, only recently dead. The parallel is, of course, that of Laurel McKelva Hand, come home to attend her father, Judge McKelva, who dies soon after that return, leaving her burdened with the mystery of memory. Saint Augustine argues that it is through memory that we make fundamental recognitions concerning the truth of our own existence. By memory, we know that we possess knowledge, consequent perhaps upon an unremembered initiating openness to existence itself, which reason concludes precedent to self-awareness. There follows a gathering "in memory" of knowledge—knowledge which impinges upon this present action of *knowing* that we *know*. Thus out of a relation past to our own present, we respond to the world immediately contingent to our senses in this present moment. We do so out of a *past* which is *present* in a peculiar way, affecting our response to this contingent, immediate "real" world— this "existential reality" in which we find ourselves existing always in a present moment.

To put the point contingently: we either respond in a present moment by an opening of consciousness out of itself; or consciousness withers through will's refusal, through a closing of the self. The openness is possible through a paradoxical presentness of the past held in memory, which is the "key" Eliot's speaker cries out for in his "Rhapsody on a Windy Night." His has been a turning from openness, a locking of consciousness against its present outward life. That is what Laurel slowly begins to recognize as her failure. Her initial address to memory, summoned by the present circumstances of grief over her father's death, is to freeze this present misunderstanding of her obligation to the past, her obligation to the "memory" of her father. Her mother, Becky, at the point of her own death, proved just such an embittered, closed person as Laurel threatens to become. And so she died, as Laurel is prepared now to say, in "exile and humiliation." There has also been this same turning from life present by her father, Judge McKelva, on his deathbed. Dying, he clings to the second hand of his watch as it ticks him down to his own exile in death. (Suggestively, in relation to the lecture titles of Miss Welty's Harvard lectures, *One Writer's Beginnings,* both Becky and Judge McKelva descend into death through an encroaching physical blindness.)

There is a property in this Augustinian knowing of the self, a consciousness continuously alive through grace, which we would emphasize: our knowing is certified by memory, so that we *now* know that our *now* is also a new beginning, a *renewed* beginning. We describe this property to our knowing, in its present emotional effects upon us as we respond to existing: we are moved by *awe, wonder, curiosity, anticipation.* Such is a stirring in us made possible only because we both exist and know that we exist. And out of these emotional effects, there rises in consciousness *joy* or *sorrow* or *fear* or *desire.* Such is the complex conditions to a present intellectual life to which Miss Welty speaks in her Harvard lectures, as she remembers her own "beginnings" as writer. And to her Harvard audience she names as a continuing effect in her of these beginnings her open deportment to existence as a state of "anticipation." But anticipation of what?

In that first lecture, "Listening," she remembers herself as a child to have been "shy physically." She never rushed into things, "including relationships, headlong." Already by her nature, she is intent upon being "not effaced, but invisible," despite her "wild curiosity" about the world. In the security of her family she becomes comfortable as a "hidden observer," a "privileged observer," and so at last she becomes "the loving kind" of observer. Her circumstances are suited to her nature as she begins to write stories, and so she also begins to draw nearer to people, though slowly, "noting, guessing, apprehending, hoping." And she discovers of herself that her "wild curiosity was in large part suspense," the suspense of anticipation—not simply an anticipation of consequences of her actions in their surface spectacle, but their presence to us as historical event that may be recorded, and certified.

It is as if Miss Welty knows by intuition from very early in life that if we confuse spectacle with action, we shall end up reacting to spectacle only, as Laurel does at first in her response to Fay's spectacular presence in *The Optimist's Daughter.* Thus to the simpleminded nurse and the confused Laurel, Fay can only be seen as abusing Judge McKelva, when she intends instead to force him by her physical rudeness into holding life against the terror in his ticking watch. Certainly there is a self-centeredness in Fay, but if that were all, she would have easily surrendered her old husband to death so that she might be freed to live life at the simplistic level of spectacle, which she seems possessed by in Laurel's imagination. So convinced is Laurel that Fay in effect kills her father, thus confusing spectacle with depths of action out of human nature, that Laurel engages that conclusion with some fury. This occurs at that moment of terror to Laurel as she contends with the random chimney swift blown down into the empty McKelva house. As she follows the disoriented bird from room to room of her childhood home, she puts her charge against Fay legalistically: "Why, it would stand up in court! Laurel thought, as she heard the bird beating against the door, and felt the house itself shake in the rainy wind" (*OD*, 131). Here lies a mastery of art, a metaphysical conceit as it were, whereby Miss Welty implies inner weathers of the mind in the outer spectacle to that mind: Laurel is experiencing an afternoon thunderstorm, by herself in the empty house, engaging the panicked swift which has been blown down out of the chimney. The implied correspondences are to her confused consciousness, her house of memories buffeted by present weathers such as her father's death. She is unable to reconcile her terror in either haunted house at this present moment of loss.

As readers, we too find Fay's manner startling when she attempts to force Judge McKelva to hold onto life, to rise from his deathbed and walk into the carnival of the New Orleans Mardi Gras outside the hospital room. Fay acts out of a dark movement toward despair, for hers is also a response to the always closing shadow of death, hovering in *her* more profoundly if more secretly than in Laurel, though she lacks sophistication sufficient to confront her terror. Fay is unequal to an understanding of her own actions, and her disorder is emphasized by her speech and dress and the actions that so disturb Mount Salus society from beginning to end. But so too is Laurel unequal to ambiguous terror in her pursuit of the swift, lacking an understanding sufficient to prevent terror's growing residue in her—despair.

In this unfolding drama about memory, we are given a chorus of slowly ageing "bridesmaids," who provide ironic counterpoint to the profound implications in the current trivial events that are waiting Laurel's recognition as significant in their implications. For more is at risk than surface spectacle. The chorus puts Laurel off the mark at first because she does not realize this. They tempt a growing anger against Fay, whom they see as simply vulgar in manner and dress. She is not a person such as each bridesmaid supposes herself to be. They remark Fay a wild and random natural "life," in the most popular sense of "natural," as if she were limited to the merely biological plane of existence. The spectacle of Fay's presence to them suggests only that. But Fay, by a seeming cacophony to the settled Mount Salus society, plays against and so emphasizes to us the dying, almost dead nature of that closed society. From their dying center closing about the bridesmaids—such is the implicit reading they make of Fay's threatening presence—they find she will not put on the fig leaves of a deportment according to local customs. Human nature may indeed allow private titillations, but not such vulgar public display of emotions as Fay's. Of course, this chorus of bridesmaids is not averse to being titillated, so long as natural excesses, and pleasure in those excesses, are sufficiently clothed by a reserve of indirect language speaking "good taste."

Fay's dress and speech and public deportment demonstrate to the bridesmaids, as they say to Laurel in a variety of ways, just how right they are in maintaining their own manners, exercised in accord with their memories of their mamas' manners. Laurel proves susceptible, given that her most challenging problem is that of memory. For she is increasingly confused over responsibilities of a filial piety as buffeted by what she knows as the reality of her parents' lives, in contrast to the easy lies about them she hears spoken in their praise. She becomes especially disturbed when all are gathered in the McKelva house where the Judge lies in state, as Major Bullock and the local ladies summon memories of the Judge and his late wife, which Laurel knows to be simply lies about them, though spoken in their praise. Laurel begins to see that her bridesmaids in their own dress and chatter are most shallow. Their memory of the truth of things past is barely alive in this present, except remotely in the rote exercises of what they assume required of them in remembering their own past as touched by the dead man in the parlor. It is a species of the same deportment with which they respond to Fay, as if spectacle or memory of spectacle were substance itself. Their own present spectacle to Laurel begins to speak dying and sterile manners, dependent upon their own dying memory. And so what Laurel must contend with is the spectacle of social history arrested in this present moment of her grief.

There is a counterstrain within the choral unity in the person of Adele, the most sympathetic presence to Laurel among her old friends. It is she whom Laurel sees at novel's end with her first-graders waving good-bye, though the chorus leader, Tish, is allowed to speak the novel's last dialogue. Tish assures Laurel that she will make her plane for the flight to Chicago: "You'll make it by the skin of your teeth" (*OD*, 180)—again, shallow cliché, but with profoundly implicit "implications." Laurel is beginning to make many connections out of her memory as it begins to come alive. Meanwhile, Tish continues in her response to life at the level of whether one may catch a flight to Chicago or be inconvenienced by missing it; or have tea and cookies and gossip with the other bridesmaids in Laurel's garden, as they have so recently done.

No wonder in a world built on and dependent upon memory as ghostly spectacle, as is the general tendency holding the bridesmaids together, that Laurel will be shocked by Fay. Still, the bridesmaids appear to Laurel as growing old before her eyes with the ticking down of the social clock, a recognition promising some rescue by the recognition itself. And the outlander Fay insists with a passion shocking to Laurel that she was "trying to scare [the Judge] into living!" That was the intent of her violent actions in the hospital room, and it is this, in response to Laurel's own passion and confusion, out of which she charges Fay with having "desecrated" the McKelva house. Fay *knows,* at least intuitively, that life is good and to be held on to, though she cannot *understand* what she knows.

Life for a person is larger than its reductions to animal nature, despite the spectacles surrounding our age's culture suggesting the contrary, and to which Fay has proved susceptible. Even so, bad taste in dress and speech and manners may still be underlain by a nature more fundamental than appetitive limits, a recognition toward which Laurel herself is moving. Fay's response to existence seems shallow, judged by appearances. But Laurel begins to see in herself a shallowness as well, that recognition beginning to surface out of the embattled tastes of the bridesmaids and Fay's family. Increasingly, Laurel is hard-pressed to choose between them, becoming more standoffish from the social worlds buffeting her in her moment of grief. The Chisom clan's breaches of manners (as measured from Mount Salus) raise questions about the roots of manners feeding the continuum of persons, whatever the moment's clannish community. Laurel is caught in a disturbing confluence of manners, of the Chisom clan with the Mount Salus vestals of local propriety, the "bridesmaids," whose authority requires some ironic detachment. They are to be accepted with a grain if not a mountain of salt.

It would be our mistake to miss Fay's confusion in the midst of outrageous spectacle at the Judge's wake. Her actions, spectacularly gauche (as in her passionate embrace of the Judge's corpse) may well speak toward a desire in her we must value. For it may be that her deportment is out of a love for the Judge which Laurel has not recognized, mixed as it is in the spectacle of Fay's inevitably awkward attempt to fulfill what she supposes the proper gestures to be made out of her regret. At this point, at the wake, Laurel senses but does not yet see this possibility.

She is further confused by the open gesture of love by Fay's grandfather, who brings her the shelled pecans. There are additional implications in the wild curiosity of the outlaw child Wendell. For there is more than stage acting when Fay, glistening in "black satin," wails over the body, as there is more than a simplistic gesture by the grandfather handing Laurel his love-offering, pecans he has shelled on a park bench on his difficult journey to pay his respects and witness grief. Meanwhile Laurel, sensing but not recognizing such confusing aspects of the circus spectacle at her father's wake, is inclined to deliver a curse upon both the houses now so awkwardly gathered under what was once her roof, now Fay's.

Fay may prove to have been moved to desperations, out of which stir something of hope for her, though it be only a forlorn hope. It is with something of this recognition that Laurel parts from Fay at novel's end. Laurel's impassioned encounter with Fay over ownership of the bread-board modulates into Laurel's gentle withdrawal, as if she begins to understand at last that Fay in her grief is a pathetic creature, no less besieged by the Chisoms and by Mount Salus society than she. One of the anticipations with which we are left at the end is that Laurel will grow in understanding. What begins to stir in her in that fierceness over the seemingly trivial is *love*. She is already opening toward Fay. Tish would be horrified, of course. But we might thereby recover some hope of humanity as larger than random feral nature, even in a Fay—even, we may add, in a Tish.

In thus dramatizing a disparity of recognition, a disparity of awkward attempts to recover the openness called love in such unlike creatures as Fay and Laurel, Miss Welty reveals to us through her protagonist Laurel the beginnings of a maturity necessary to the artist. It occurs in a convergence between Laurel and her maker, Miss Welty, who already occupies that wise understanding as maker—as the poet Dante does in contrast to the pilgrim Dante as we meet that pilgrim in the opening lines of the *Divine Comedy*.

We are here exploring a surrogation of Miss Welty's own experiences of life as she has lived it, not in respect to any strict biographical detail, though *The Optimist's Daughter* as a history of the McKelva family carries a multitude of Welty biographical details adapted to the fiction. We need only compare extracted details from the novel to details from *One Writer's Beginnings*. What is at issue in both memoir and novel is not history, but a recovery of our personhood as common and to be valued beyond the limits of history. One instance of art adjusting history to that end, a fictional strategy using parallels between the two families, is the play in both these works with the terms *optimist* and *pessimist*.

In remembering her own parents, Miss Welty remarks that "the optimist [her father] was the one who was prepared for the worst, and she the pessimist [her mother] was the daredevil" (*OWB*, 45). The modification of these parallels we see in Laurel's gradual recognition of her parents' limited responses to life: "He, who had been declared optimist, had not once expressed hope" (*OD*, 29). He "scowlingly called" himself optimist, but Laurel must now acknowledge that his deportment was transparent to her mother, as it becomes to Laurel in her remembering. It leads to Laurel's frustrations at the wake when she must endure in a mannerly deportment the false eulogies pronounced by the Mount Salus townsfolk, friends who now tell lies in honoring the dead, lest they violate memory itself if they tell the truth. The radical violations of memory are almost more than Laurel can bear, drawing her toward an anarchy of honesty in that unmanageable child Wendell, to whom she is sympathetic.

Laurel can now value her mother's angry passion for the truth as she lay on her deathbed, the Judge attempting to soothe her with lies. For the Judge's "optimistic" deportment was a hoax out of his profound helplessness in the face of death. He promised Laurel's mother, Becky, on her deathbed that he would carry her back for a visit to her childhood West Virginia, which for her part she had clung to all along in her Mississippi exile, in her own species of arrest despite her daredevil spectacles of action. But dying, Becky McKelva responded in fury to the Judge's promise: "Lucifer! . . . *Liar!*" (*OD*, 150). And so she died, as Laurel can now see, "in exile and humiliation," not only from West Virginia but from her husband as well and from the falseness of Mount Salus as community. Here is a counterpointing to Laurel's slowly emerging reunion with her husband, Phil, who is alive to her at the end as never before.

What Laurel unfolds for us in her discoveries about memory is her own late opening to the holiness of existence, which Miss Welty very early became attuned to through *love*. And Laurel's opening toward the world out of love at novel's end is in accord with the necessities of good making, whether one be interior decorator or storyteller. In the novel, our storyteller controls and modulates this opening toward an inclusive epiphany, wherein Laurel recognizes a confluence of past and present, bringing her dead husband and his love into an active presence through memory rightly taken. For Laurel, memory comes alive in her present. Miss Welty herself seems to have been born with this knowing and accepts the obligation of understanding it as artist. She needs no shocking recognition of "desecrations" of memory, either by the Fays or bridesmaids of our world seen for a first time, or by her own mother and father remembered. And so as storyteller she can respond to the spectrum of persons with an equanimity suited to art. It has always been a lively pleasure to her to view this most various world with an anticipation hardly susceptible to shock, though on occasion she might be tempted by anger.

In addressing *anticipation* as we find it the rising action in Laurel, we may call anticipation a present hope in relation to a present desire. That hope is sustained by memory when memory is alive, as it so clearly is in Miss Welty herself. We discover anew through her art not only that hope and desire are companionable, but that we have known them to be so, intuitively, all along. And that is the point at which we accept reason as necessary complement to what we know intuitively, toward our under-standing the contingent—the possible or probable to our anticipations, whether we speak of life or of art. Whatever degree of reason we possess, short of pathological disorder, we find it sufficient to the ordering of hope in relation to circumstantial reality impinging upon consciousness. Even with a pathological complication, hope and desire seem manifest, a recog-nition we encounter again and again in Southern fiction, as in Faulkner's Benjy in *The Sound and the Fury* or Flannery O'Connor's Bishop in *The Violent Bear It Away*.

Such is the nature of anticipation to be dealt with, whether as Laurel's dead husband, Phil Hand, dealt with it or in less wise ways as Laurel at first attempts. Phil would make perfect houses, himself conditioned in that making by guidance of his reason, recognizing through reason that the perfect houses he would build are nevertheless houses of cards. He is not victim in a betrayal of himself through false optimism, as seems the unfortunate circumstances to Judge McKelva's decline into death. The Judge's optimism has proved only a disguise of his terror before death, making him (as Becky cries out) a liar in denying death. At his own death, he seems almost destroyed by despair.

Reason, then, is in anticipation of understanding beyond a mere know-ing. Reason thus sustains and values the *intuitively known*. By such anticipation of understanding, our hope and desire may be reconciled, lest despair overcome us in the last moment of our exile and humiliation at whatever place or time we find ourselves in the world at the point of our death. If Fay lacks a refined intuitive knowing such as Becky's, she yet recognizes in Judge McKelva very much what Becky recognized, and so attempts to shock him into life, as Becky attempts to shock him with the epithets *Lucifer* and *liar*. (One of the papers Laurel burns in purging her own memory is her mother's schoolgirl paper on Milton's *Paradise Lost*.)

These are high matters at issue in Miss Welty's fiction, despite the often comic spectacle attaching to character or situation in the novel. They are matters which a poet may engage in a high manner, as does T. S. Eliot—especially in his *Four Quartets*. In those poems Eliot dramatizes the movements of a sophisticated intellect within a sophisticated context of literary, philosophical, and theological traditions. Miss Welty's response to the virtues of a living memory engages the same high matters as Eliot's, in a quite different context. Her own childhood ventures in West Virginia country, her responses to birds, flowers, and folk songs, the comedy of family love, differ from Eliot's in respect to the spectacle of events which each has remembered from childhood. But in their differing responses, they prove to hold the same vision of *homo viator.* In his late poetry Eliot attempts to recover memory alive to his philosophical and theological inheritances from Plato and Saint Augustine down to Dante and Aquinas. What both Miss Welty and Eliot come to know in common is that these high concerns about human nature are always to be engaged in the immediacy of place, in this present moment, according to peculiar circumstances. Consciousness must enjoin the *human* nature of the self here and now, and most fundamentally. That is the concern of Eliot's *Little Gidding,* which concludes insistently on this point that "The end of all our exploring / Will be to arrive where we started / And know the place for the first time." That is an apt summary of Laurel's actions in Miss Welty's novel.

That is why we must inevitably discover in consequence a common vision independently earned, even between such seemingly disparate poets as Miss Welty and Eliot, correspondences between them of a high theme, however dissimilar the enveloping imagery which informs the art of such high theme. Nor should we be surprised to discover correspondences between their common theme and that of their kinsmen, remote in time and place but bearing a present common vision, whether that kinsman be Saint Augustine or Saint Thomas Aquinas. Eliot's art and essays carry deliberate and explicit acknowledgments of recognized kinship through literary allusions, as in his *Waste Land* and in "Ash-Wednesday." But we may anticipate as well discovering parallels between Miss Welty's understanding of nature and art and the understanding held by so unlikely a kinsman to her as Thomas Aquinas, in respect to which kinship ours is (once more) not a concern for historical influences. For both the philosopher and the poet (Miss Welty) are joined in a common deportment to truth, a piety toward the holiness of creation. Theirs is a common devotion to the truth of things, however differing their modes or manners in paying homage to that holiness.

Saint Thomas says of art, as Phil Hand might well say, that it requires reason in making. What we know intuitively about our own nature as person is that we are called to a perfection through our devotion to reasoned making, however various the modes of making as differentiated in discrete and peculiar gifts to each person. Reason devoted to making engages the known, in anticipation of understanding. And understanding is a condition of our individual nature fulfilled according to the degree of love in our actions in response to creation. Or so both Aquinas and Miss Welty believe. Through understanding, we accept as maker that we are responsible to the good of the thing we make. That is what Phil Hand in Miss Welty's novel understood most clearly. He would make perfect the thing, whether a house or a breadboard. But collaterally, by his act of making in which there is the intent to the good of the thing he makes, he fulfills his own nature, a nature made more or less perfect when in accord with the limits of his gifts as maker.

Within the limits of gift: That is the paradoxical witness Phil Hand bears in his makings, though Laurel comes late to see it. Thus, alone in her family's empty house in Mount Salus, she remembers Phil's hands at work. They were "double-jointed where they left the palms, nearly at right angles; their long, blunt tips curved strongly back. When she watched his right hand go about its work, it looked like the Hand of his name" (*OD*, 161). It is a recognition of convergence of person and world, more complex in its fictional correspondences than Miss Welty's earlier childhood experience of the word *moon* in her mouth like an Ohio grape, but essentially a like epiphany, made singular to remembrance. In such devices, we recognize an artistic wit at work as she explores in a fiction the mystery of making in relation to memory. The perfect house, Phil Hand argues, is made to a proximate but not eternal end. A house is a thing made in a place for people to live in, temporarily. Its perfection in proximate nature must be understood as a limit to any good that any hand makes through art. For in the light of eternity, as we used to say, any house can be understood only as a house of cards. That is the shocking recognition of the truth about worldly things to which Laurel comes, and in doing so she begins to approach the wisdom of our proper deportment in the world. As Eliot puts it, in the form of a prayer in "Ash-Wednesday," we must learn "to care and not to care." That is the recognition in Phil, when he at once perfects the house he would make, but knows it a house of cards nevertheless.

What is to be gained through understanding this paradox, whose proper virtue is piety, is a balance toward creation whereby a person at once cares for the proximate as its obligated steward, but does not care for it with such a growing obsession as transmutes stewardship into sheer ownership, as if by that ownership we are transmuted into creators of the thing possessed. Our artists make that point to us repeatedly in their abandoning the made thing, the poem or painting, to the world, in turning to a new making. We tend to make too much of history's irony in this sort of event. There is a public auction of a painting in London, perhaps. It is acquired for several million dollars, but our main recollection about it is that it fetched its maker only a few francs when he was finished with it. Such a confusion about *making* exacerbates our concerns as society for our poets and painters no doubt, as often as not with the effect of our corrupting them through a patronage divorced from a vision of art proper to patron no less than to artist. The vision of the artist, in his devotion to the good of the thing he makes, is always the central necessity to a spiritual state of the artist—the maker—whether a Phil Hand or a Laurel McKelva Hand, or Eudora Welty or T. S. Eliot. And properly speaking, so it must be to any intruding patron.

Even Judge McKelva as an old man, having lost Becky, responds intuitively to this truth, consequent to Becky's scathing anathema delivered upon him from her deathbed. He does so, though he lacks an understanding sufficient to the truth. And so he ends at last in a fixation upon the second hand of his watch as it mechanically measures him down to death. But he had made a right move toward recovery. He attempted to recover memory alive, pruning Becky's rosebush in the Mississippi garden, a plant brought long ago from West Virginia by Becky the pessimist into her exile, a gesture prompted by love larger than her love of her new husband. In the Judge's attempt at recovery, or so in her anger Fay argues, he hurt his eyes, initiating the decline into death. Fay rejects such attempts to rescue memory alive. After all, here is a present proof of its danger, her dead husband. And yet Fay also responds to that necessity, awkwardly and with a display scandalizing her Mount Salus neighbors—her deportment at the wake. She attempts a ceremonial expiation of grief which, culturally speaking—as we are so fond of speaking these days—embarrasses those maintaining any dying local culture. Fay is nevertheless, however gauche, vaguely attempting a ceremonial accommodation of memory to the present moment. With a comic relief within the cultural chaos, we see Major Bullock, the proximate cause of the Chisom invasion, saved embarrassment himself, and any sense of guilt, by the grace of good Southern bourbon ceremonially imbibed. (Given the disparity of encounters in this scene, one might recall the more orderly chaos of traditional wakes, especially that record of intellectual and spiritual disintegration so monumentally undertaken by Joyce in *Finnegans Wake* in his ironic detachment as maker.)

Thomas Aquinas, attuned to the ceremonies of grief and joy as of a special concern to the artist, remarks the artist's primary responsibility to be to the good of the thing he makes. The artist *as maker* has only a secondary concern for his own perfection through his making, however often the artists mistake themselves as the primary end in their worldly conduct. The self-love of artists is notorious, especially in our century, in sharp contrast to such witness as Miss Welty's. For her, the maker's special "calling" is to the good of the thing being made, in a self-sacrifice of gifts to the made thing. That is the proper stewardship of the artist's gifts, a moral responsibility to those gifts peculiar to this particular person. We are talking directly here of the making of stories, but the point is general and applies to pruning rosebushes, building houses, or decorating made houses. Thus Phil Hand bears a witness to Miss Welty's own vision, which she dramatizes through Laurel's actions in recovering memory alive. (As surrogate witness to Miss Welty's own position, Phil Hand's being dead is a convenience, in that she does not have to maintain him in a continuous perfection of that deportment, which might so easily make him more unconvincing.)

Laurel's recovery of Phil out of memory coming alive completes the unfolding action in the novel. Phil thus succeeds in bringing reason into consort with Laurel's intuitive recognition of the limits of her calling. That is, Phil had understood, as Laurel at last does, that one anticipates, through love, the perfection of the thing made. He was thereby enabled to move beyond the danger of despair over recognizing perfection doomed, limited by time or eternity, whether a despair threatening him as person or artist. And so the paradox: his is a surrender through love that enables him to make a "perfect" breadboard, even as he knows it vulnerable given the nature of worldly, made things. Almost in physical combat with Laurel over the breadboard, Fay demands of Laurel, "What do you see in that thing?" The question arrests the spectacle of action as Laurel is at last able to respond, "The whole story, Fay. The whole solid past" (*OD*, 178). She draws nearer to her own earlier anticipation that "Phil could still tell her of her life. For her life, any life, she had to believe, was nothing but the continuity of its love" (*OD*, 160).

If Laurel in this moment with the breadboard had immediate access to the tradition held by Eliot's speaker in *Little Gidding,* she might conclude her pilgrimage to Mount Salus by saying that "all shall be well, and all manner of thing shall be well," summoning Dame Julian of Norwich out of memory. Dame Julian, reaching Laurel's conclusion, holds a chestnut on her open palm in a quiet moment and discovers in that lowly thing of nature, as Miss Welty seems to discover in birds and flowers and people, the "continuity of love." Laurel, though her discovery is in a moment of spectacle when she is about to strike Fay with the breadboard, remembers at that point that Phil had made it out of love for her mother, Becky. Chestnut or breadboard? What we remark is that the *created* thing in nature or the thing *made* by art—chestnut or breadboard—depends from the actual nature of creation and by existing at all is limited to the conditions of its nature, whereby it is the thing it is. Existence is by limit.

This means that the made thing is especially limited by the actual and specific nature of the maker and by the material nature with which he makes. For he can in no wise create *ex nihilo*. One need not be surprised, therefore, should Fay as "maker," perhaps taking her mother's advice, turn the McKelva house into a boardinghouse, though that would prove a formidable undertaking given the opposition of the bridesmaids. A reader responding to the bridesmaids in irritation might even encourage Fay to make such a thing of the house, but out of malice and not love: It would serve them right! Whatever the present species of makings by a various community of persons, the thing made proves transient nevertheless, whether a boardinghouse or a breadboard—or petitions for the possession of the breadboard before a small claims court, or a zoning petition to a city council in order to turn an empty house into a boardinghouse.

Laurel, we may anticipate, returns to Chicago with a growing understanding of the mystery of confluent memory alive, yielding through her an active love in this always present moment. She, too, must cease in this world at last, as her mother and father have done and as Phil has done before them. The bridesmaids and Fay must as well. One need only remember the shifting nature of things as encountered in Mount Salus, Mississippi, to know this. Or one may note Miss Welty's remembering of Jackson in *One Writer's Beginnings*. There, for instance, we find her livening memory of her own father's insurance building now radically changed on its Jackson ground. So, too, the McKelva house must come to be changed. What Laurel carries with her, then, as Miss Welty has done for so long, is a growing recognition of love's rescue of the present moment, a rescue supported by memory when memory is rightly taken.

What Laurel rejects in doing so is her old dependence upon the shifting sands of memory growing sterile. By such a dependence, we may only be tempted to some variety of a program oriented to some species of "historical preservation," which if centering upon the old McKelva house would no doubt be made a common cause to the chorus of Laurel's bridesmaids trying to prevent its being made into a neighborhood boardinghouse. Miss Welty's own home on Pinehurst Street in Jackson likely has such a fate in store, though from what we know of her, we might suspect she would prefer a boardinghouse rather than a museum.

Though we share in a common nature as makers, if we confuse a sure arrest of memory in sterile sands with what Laurel calls memory as a "continuity of love," we shall prove false to our common nature. History so arrested is dead history. However artfully posted may be our historical house or district with maps and signs, we shall only certify memory dead if we do not discover how memory may recover us in our nature as makers, not creators. That requires humility and piety in response to our very nature as limited, specifically in relation to our intrinsic limits as *this* particular person.

That is the necessary recognition to us as makers that Thomas Aquinas addresses in the last year of his life, just before he sets his own pen aside and turns to silence, in his *Collationes Credo in Deum*. We have this work only in Latin, but Thomas speaks to an appreciative audience in his native vernacular, the Neapolitan dialect. He speaks with a directness to our point. He has come home at last. His dialect would have seemed no doubt quaint to his old intellectual familiars at the University of Paris, as perhaps Miss Welty's may have seemed to some of her Harvard audience. The truth in what he says may indeed seem quaint to some of us. Although human beings are not able to make anything without preexistent material, that is because "they are makers of the particular and are not able to draw forth this form without material determined and presupposed from another. The reason is that their own virtuosity is limited to the form alone, and therefore can be the cause only of this form. . . . To create differs from to make insofar as to create is to make something from nothing."

I myself have no doubt that Thomas Aquinas spoke to his hometown audience in a manner less formal and austere than his words seem to us at this remove, words that come down to us out of the memory of his attendant Reginald, who translated and so preserved these spoken things in "school" Latin. Even so, I am equally confident that the truth borne so formally to us is one shared by Eudora Welty. Her openness of love toward creation, including the disparateness of humanity itself, bears witness of the correspondence between her and Thomas. It is in the joyful humility and piety toward existence which she evidences in her makings through art, in perfections of things made out of recognition of her own most considerable gifts in making, which nevertheless—as Phil Hand or Eliot would say—are in response to limits within which we must both care and not care, lest we overlook that our own made things are always houses of cards. For we must care for perfection in making, but not care at last, knowing that the thing we make is in the light of slow-chapped time or the light of eternity already in decay. Even so, the truth living in such houses for so short a time is a permanent thing, namely love as an open surrender to the good, made always in this most local moment of making, whether a memoir or a novel—or this present paper in celebration of those things Eudora Welty makes out of her lively love of creation.

Concluding Essays

Component Parts

The Novelist as Autobiographer
Jan Nordby Gretlund

> It seems to me, writing of my parents now in my
> seventies, that I see continuities in their lives that
> weren't visible to me when they were living. . . . Could
> it be because I can better see their lives—or any lives I
> know—today because I'm a fiction writer? (*OWB*, 90)

All reading is the result of a desire to know a text. To know it fully is
to *have control* of it. We are curious about the author who wrote the text,
because we believe that knowledge of her will help us demystify her writings. More than sixty years of New Criticism, or for that matter decades
of structuralism, semiotics, hermeneutics, have not succeeded in killing
off our interest in the author.

Writers, teachers, and critics keep telling us that what we read is *fiction,* "a pure product of the imagination"—and "pure" means untainted
by the facts of our private lives. *Biography* has been officially banished,
but has anybody been convinced? Even critics read biographies. Maybe
because we still suspect that all literature is in essence autobiographical—
impervious to all abstract reasoning—our interest in biography endures.

Our reading of fiction is doubly oriented: we read it as a discourse
which invokes another. Our focus is often on the fiction *and* on the author's
involvement in her own fiction. We *want to know* more about the person
who wrote the fiction, and we are curious about the life that produced the
published thoughts. To what extent, we ask, does her life translate into
fiction? If we are honest, we must admit that we ask this question quite
frequently. What I ask is a related, but rarely voiced question: does fiction
translate into a life? In other words, instead of reading biography in the
fiction, I suggest that we see the fiction in biography, e.g., in Eudora Welty's
autobiography.

If we read, speak of, and teach fiction in terms of biography, is it because we sense, in the face of all opposition, that there is no difference in kind between fiction and biography? We are likely to get this notion when we read *contemporary fiction,* which is drifting toward biography, and also when we read *contemporary biography,* which looks more and more like fiction. We have been conditioned to think of the difference between fact and fiction as fundamental, and we come to autobiography with specific narrative expectations. But the dividing line between them is often obscured, and in some instances it is invisible. Should we not expect to find not only the life in the art, but also the use of the art in the life?

There is a pronounced out-of-life-into-fiction tendency in Welty's work. She realized early that by seeing the particulars of her native situation, she could successfully approach the universal. The permanent lesson she learned at the beginning of her career was that to write well, it is not enough to be fascinated with your subject, if you are really ignorant of it. She learned to write on subjects that grew naturally out of her own life, and she sums up her family with a realism worthy of Jane Austen. Nobody sees their limitations more clearly. In her fiction the view of mankind is not obscured by any crusading for a cause, nor has she in her autobiographical book become blinded by nostalgia for the family past.

Just as Welty's novel *Delta Wedding* was first received with many mistaken notions by established critics, *One Writer's Beginnings* met with misreadings, which were often based on a superficial acquaintance with Welty's work. One of the limited readings of the autobiography is by Carolyn G. Heilbrun in her influential *Writing a Woman's Life* (1988). She complains about the "real danger for women in books like Welty's in the nostalgia and romanticizing in which the author, and we in reading them, indulge."[1] I do not want to argue against the idea that nostalgia has "imprisoned women" for years; I am sure it has, and men too, I should think. But I would like to argue that *One Writer's Beginnings* is not an expression of "nostalgia and romanticizing"; it is a realistic account of what it was like to grow up in the Welty family. The Weltys are presented as the truly marvelous people they were on occasion, but we also see them as the limited human beings they sometimes proved to be. The portrait of the writer's mother is rich and rounded, but there is nothing romantic or nostalgic in the account of the years spent in the daily company of this awe-inspiring and demanding woman. In Eudora Welty's work the realism about family ties is nowhere more obvious than in her portrait of the Weltys at home. But to what extent have the Weltys we meet been fictionalized?

Welty has always considered the distinction between "private" and "personal" to be essential for the creative artist (C, 214). Good art is, of course, personal. If "art" is simply raw experience, it reveals the artist's lack of detachment. If the perspective remains private, it probably remains too subjective to offer universal significance, and therefore remains uninteresting to anybody but the artist. Good writing, like all good art, presupposes the work of the imagination on private experience. If detachment from the private experience can be achieved, it will still be the artist's experience. But with the gained distance to the experience, it is now *personal* rather than private. In *The Optimist's Daughter* Laurel and her creator belabor their private experience until they have distance enough to see it as personal memory and art. In *One Writer's Beginnings* Welty remembers through a finely honed narrative consciousness, belabors her private experience, and creates a great fictional memoir.

Autobiography is as thematic as any novel. The former is as heavily emplotted as the latter, i.e., the facts are "bent and shaped to specific ends" also in autobiography. Fiction and autobiography employ the same literary strategies to transform a chosen experience into art. Welty's autobiographical writing never becomes fiction, but it certainly stretches the boundaries of autobiography. She faithfully renders the social reality she experienced, and often her accurate rendition of stark reality reads as an indictment. The portrait of the happy mornings in the Welty home, when all sorts of whistling was going on, up and down the stairwell, is obviously idealized. We know that the Weltys were not whistling *every* morning, and that is perhaps the unstated subject of the passage.

The germ of the whole of *One Writer's Beginnings* is in the italicized opening note. It marks Eudora Welty's last step in a long journey toward independence from her mother. It is a text that brings out what it was the writer "feared realizing" about her mother (*OWB*, 102). It is about a child's earliest relationships, and it is about the successful writer "matching family faces" (58). As she feared, she finds that "the faces" of mother and daughter do not match in most respects. When Welty describes Ned Andrews's interests in detail, it is because there are several parallels to her own likes and dislikes—features in their mental make-up that Mrs. Welty, the "great keeper" of the family record, did not mind in her father, but could not possibly accept in her daughter (48–49).

The book contains a section of family photos. The family snapshots show Eudora at one year of age playing with her father's watch, and Eudora at four or five "with my father"; the mother is pictured alone under her full name, and, also by herself, coming down the stairs in the house on

North Congress Street in Jackson. In the photos where the mother appears with her children, her attention is focused on her youngest son, Walter. Even these selected photos reveal a certain disappointment as one childhood experience, and so do some passages of the text: "Events that weren't quite clear in meaning, things we children were shielded from, seemed to have their own routes, their own streets in town, and you might hear them coming near but then they never came, like the organ grinder with his monkey—surely you'd see him, but then the music went down the other street, and the monkey couldn't find you, though you waited with your penny" (37).

Welty has often talked of the "sheltered life" she lived as a child. But in case you wondered how the product of such an existence could grow up to know so much about us, the autobiographical book shows that the writer lived a sheltered life only in terms of the absence of dramatic physical events. In the realm of the psychological, young Eudora was exposed to a permanent drama. True to the strong matriarchal tradition of the South, the main character on the stage was "my mother," the "venturesome" woman who did everything expressively and with dramatic fervor, even *ferocity*. After the nature of "my mother" has been fully realized, the sentimental description of the happy mornings in the Welty home seems rather ironic.

If the tone of the book is far from the confessional, I do see Welty's *One Writer's Beginnings* as a necessary therapeutic exercise for her. The expression in print of her reexamination of her background is for her also its internalization. But is it autobiography or fiction? You could argue that in a first-person autobiographical narrative the outcome is known from the beginning, so that J. Hillis Miller's distinction between a first and a second reading could not apply to autobiography. But this is not true for most readers of Welty's autobiography. The majority of the readers of *One Writer's Beginnings* knew next to nothing of its author, her life and work, and they did not anticipate the contents of the book. For the people who kept it on the best-seller list there was a true first reading of it, as if it were fiction.

Both fiction and autobiography are the results of omission and selection, and both are more tidy than the diffuse reality actually lived—which is not likely to be a neatly patterned affair. But there is a difference between living a life and detaching yourself in order to view it as autobiography. In *writing* it you have to be able to create yourself and determine your own personality. Welty has to try to make her record of her life mean something. For that reason she sits down to select from memory, to tell what she remembers, to reject parts of her experience, to single out specific events, to skip long periods of her life for various reasons, and to focus on certain characters and events that seem all-important to her. This she does *deliberately,* and it is one of the ways in which she becomes her own inventor and the emplotter of her own past.

In an autobiography emphasis is expected to be given to the autobiographer herself. But Welty's autobiographical book is not about Eudora Welty. *One Writer's Beginnings* is not the traditional tale of a white girl growing up in the South and her search for self-discovery. It does not live up to V. S. Pritchett's "favored, if limited, definition of autobiography," which reads: "It is myself I portray."[2] And it is not a book in which the author sees herself as a member of a group, such as women or the middle classes. Nor does she write as a representative of a "minority," such as white Southern liberals—or Southern writers.

Welty is clearly anxious to discover the continuities of her own experiences and the legacies conferred on her. She tries to limit herself to the events of her life as a young woman that seem to have formed her as a writer. But that is, of course, an impossible limitation to observe in practice. Welty is definitely not the protagonist of her autobiography. But she is the central consciousness and has to re-create herself as such a literary device. The process of her autobiography is that of an explorative statement. And the exploration volunteers little about the emotional life of Eudora Alice Welty.

The subject of *One Writer's Beginnings* picked Welty, so to speak. It is obviously private concerns that surface and ask to be written. Telling it is her way of confronting the memories. The main characters of the book are her parents. It is their lives she makes narratable, and what Welty tells us about them are deliberate disclosures. There is no reason to assume that they are not exactly what Welty wanted them to be in this book. The artist re-creates them for a narrative purpose, and finally they are just as much literary characters as the characters in Welty's undisputed fiction.

Through her characters, primarily the character of her mother, Welty seeks to master a troubling past. The story she tells us of her mother is finally a type of psychoanalysis, but so is most storytelling. The uncharacteristic glimpses into her private life that Welty offers in this book are there for a reason. She is not trying to tell "the whole story," but rather only what is necessary—for her. The true narrative purpose seems only to have been revealed fully to her as she wrote down the private details. And used narratively they become instruments of explanation.

The autobiography appears as an instance of the fiction writer's traditional experience of a text *writing itself* and the characters escaping the regulating influence of the author. The published book probably says more than Welty planned to say, or even knew, about her parents, or about the characters in her narrative named for her parents. It could be argued that the book is a somewhat bemused journey toward an unexpected recognition of one writer's beginnings. The text cannot be read as an expression of "docile acceptance," as Carolyn Heilbrun describes it. If "anger" were the right term for the theme of *One Writer's Beginnings*—it is not—it would certainly be *recognized* anger. But the autobiography is also an acknowledgment of a shared responsibility for the crucial relationships in her life.

"The book," for lack of a more precise term, consists of three sections that were originally talks of about equal length. The tripart structure of initiation, realization, and expression is used in both autobiography, such as Richard Wright's *Black Boy,* and in fiction, such as Ralph Ellison's *Invisible Man.* According to Welty herself, the direction of the talks was *suggested* by Daniel Aaron, they were "firmly" *guided* by David Herbert Donald, and they were *prepared* for publication by Aida D. Donald—all of which removes the book from our romantic notions of a biography written, structured, and edited by the author herself.

Like fiction, the book is structured on certain moments. *If* it has a beating pulse, "it isn't steady" (9). It is true that "the events in our lives happen in a sequence in time, but in their significance to ourselves," Welty writes, "they find their own order, a timetable not necessarily—perhaps not possibly—chronological" (68–69). The autobiographer, or the novelist, may, of course, stumble upon an unexpected cause and effect sequence in her own life (90). The book shows clearly that what Eudora stumbled upon was the memory of Mrs. Welty. Her dominant presence in this memoir offers essential information for our understanding of the daughter.

I believe that Eudora Welty in everything she ever did and wrote has compared herself to her mother. The importance for the writer's development of the constant, but unvoiced, dialogue between them cannot be overestimated. She defined herself in relation to her mother. (The psychological battle between them has its parallel in Walker Percy's lifelong discussions with William Alexander Percy's thoughts and opinions.) This is the reason that, when she explains that "there has never been a line read that I didn't hear," she goes out of her way to announce that it is *not* her mother's voice she hears (11). Who claimed it was?

In his observation that *One Writer's Beginnings* is not your "generic tale of a white girl growing up in the South," James Olney does not consider the family conflicts in the book.[3] The conflicts are described in a rather poetic style, but they are there, and they are the generic conflicts between mother and father, and between mother and daughter. The latter relationship lasted much longer but only indirectly receives more attention in the book.

One Writer's Beginnings is like a musical composition unified by *motifs,* which are sounded at intervals throughout. When it comes to the fact and the fact reflected, the autobiographer has to structure her narrative as much as the writer of fiction. Welty describes *remembering* as an "inward journey that leads us through time—forward or back, seldom in a straight line, most often spiraling" (102). She cannot simply portray herself as a computerized memory dishing out the facts of her recollected world in chronological order. She deliberately disrupts her narrative and reorders the fragments. On one page (20) the character called Eudora is six or seven, although that information comes as a bit of a surprise (she sounds older), and a few pages later she is only five (22). Chronology is *not* Welty's primary concern, and the individual moment of experience, as recollected, is allowed time to crystallize.

Both autobiographer and fiction writer select, arrange a pattern, unify, and emplot certain significant moments *for effect,* and both use memory and imagination in an interplay of fact and fiction. In her biography Welty has to employ her knowledge of the artifices of fiction, so that the end product becomes a readable and lively narrative.

"The distinction between the genre of fiction and that of autobiography blurs," as Sally Wolff has said about *The Optimist's Daughter* and *One Writer's Beginnings.*[4] The recurrent formal features in these books are those of fiction. This is true whether we talk of narrative voice, control of the unstable narrator (with authorial intervention and suppression), characterization, choice of setting (and regional preoccupations), use of family history, imagery, plot delineation, scene-by-scene development, dramatization, use of dialogue, the revelation of theme, or the need for the fully participating narrator to come to an ending. Welty's literary technique and style in this book are as "postmodern" as Julian Barnes's *Flaubert's Parrot* and other so-called postmodern novels.

Welty's *themes* are love and separateness, independence gained through understanding, and final acceptance. The serious nature of her main topics makes some passages trying reading. The fiction writer has therefore inserted moments of comic relief, such as the humorous descriptions of her early schooling and first visits to the library (26, 29). Another way of breaking up the straining psychological story is by repeating family legends, such as the story of the Charles Dickens set that came up the river from Baltimore in a barrel and the mythical heroism of Ned Andrews, who built his farm "on the very top of the highest mountain he could find" (47).

Not only does the main character of the narrative have a "heroic descent," through Ned and the tall stories about him, but Chestina Andrews is also given a mythical and heroic childhood. As a girl she brought her suffering father across the icy Elk River on a raft and flagged down a train, in order to get him to a hospital in Baltimore, only to see him die there (at thirty-seven). But the story of the heroic daughter is brought to an absolute halt by the narrator with an anecdote about *not knowing anybody* in Baltimore (51). The purpose is clearly to reduce the heroics to human scale. After all, it is just an amusing anecdote, she seems to say.

Welty's narrative technique in this book is to enter the mind of a family. The family member named Christian Welty is portrayed as a kind man, full of boyish enthusiasm for science. He is described as a man without interest in ancient history, but with great interest in the future (63). He is characterized as a man who reads for information only and believes the newest edition of *Encyclopædia Britannica* is by definition superior to the previous one. The travels *he* longs for are not flights of the imagination, but real world tours. Sitting behind an assortment of scientific instruments he studies the limits of the universe, but he stays out of the confrontations between Eudora Alice and her mother, for he "could never bear pain very well" (18).

On the very first page of the book the importance of the father's instruments is undercut when we realize that what he is studying through his telescope is a constellation and a satellite easily seen with the naked eye. Later we learn that he "knew everything about train schedules," which does not rank high on most scales of valuable knowledge (18). The father's "almost childlike love of the ingenious" is demonstrated several times before it becomes a statement of observation (in the description of his kite building, p. 4). He is characterized as a man who had "the fondest beliefs" in progress, the narrator tells us. This also means *fond* in the sense of foolish. We see him on the train springing open his pocket watch, watching the signal lights change, and reading each individual milepost.

Mr. Welty is unfortunate that in his wife's mind he is always compared to his father-in-law—not objectively, of course, but to fantastic memories of him (53). When Christian Welty does something with a lasting effect, he still does it in the playful manner of a boy: he saves his wife's life with a bottle of champagne; and he builds a skyscraper in Jackson,

Mississippi, and adds gargoyles. But when Eudora Alice is sent to school early, it is her mother's decision. Later she will also decide what her daughter should read: the mother's set of Dickens is ready for her. Mr. Welty is contrasted to *the mother,* who is described as having "different gifts," and who is taken seriously. The father of the book enjoys several terms of endearment, but mostly he is "daddy." Excepting the references to her childhood in West Virginia, his contrast is only known as "my mother."

Let me stress that in enumerating characteristics of characters from *One Writer's Beginnings,* I am not at all interested in the real life of Mrs. Welty or that of any other character in the book. I never knew them, and my only impression of them comes from *One Writer's Beginnings.* I am interested only in the characteristics of the main characters as they are described in the text. I am fully convinced that Eudora Welty could have written a book full of wonderful episodes focusing on pleasant memories of her mother, but she chose not to. The main character of *One Writer's Beginnings* is named Chestina Andrews Welty; and the book's thematic drama is a coming to terms with the memory of the woman. As a first-time reader of the narrative, you cannot help wondering just when the mother will disappear out of the narrative or, at least, move out of the spotlight; but it does not happen. It proves impossible to keep the mother in abeyance while the father is being described. She manages to dominate even the account of her husband's death (93). Her failure to save his life and her pitying herself for that reason become more important than the man's death.

Toward the end of the book Welty writes:

> Writing a story or a novel is one way of discovering *sequence* in experience, of stumbling upon cause and effect in the happenings of a writer's own life. This has been the case with me. Connections slowly emerge. Like distant landmarks you are approaching, cause and effect begin to align themselves, draw closer together. Experiences too indefinite of outline in themselves to be recognized for themselves connect and are identified as a larger shape. And suddenly a light is thrown back, as when your train makes a curve, showing that there has been a mountain of meaning rising behind you on the way you've come, is rising there still, proven now through retrospect. (90)

The "larger shape" recognized in Eudora Welty's background is perhaps Mrs. Welty's decisive presence. Seen in retrospect, she is "a mountain of meaning" rising behind the writer, and her presence there is still felt. In this script the father and the daughter are only supporting actors. Their task is to keep the main character happy. To make *her* laugh would be a special triumph (98).

From the middle of page four, the mother is easily the most interesting character in this postmodern novel. She is shown to be a woman, who is mostly preoccupied with herself. She *will* be the main character and runs away with the narrative. We are told in no uncertain terms what to think of this character with her impatience and self-satisfaction. Technically this is done by leaving the mother standing apart "scoffing at caution as a character failing" (4). The presence of the mother is nevertheless what unifies the disjointed narrative. Many paragraphs have the word "mother" in the first sentence, and many focus entirely on this character.

"The mother" does not fit into the society in which she lives, for she has "little time for small talk." Although this may sound reasonable enough, the narrator makes sure that we know that the mother's attitude deprived her daughter of an important part of her heritage. One storyteller in Eudora's childhood was a neighbor who told stories in scenes (13–14). The point of that particular memory seems to be that "my mother could never have told me her stories." The girl does not share her mother's impatience with gossip; she identifies with the neighbor and her story of a doodlebug. The daughter blames her mother for not participating, for participation is a prerequisite for all successful storytelling.

The mother sees no humor in most things (12, 98). In general, we are told, "she suffered from a morbid streak which in all the life of the family reached out on occasions—the worst occasions—and touched us, clung around us, making it worse for her; her unbearable moments could find nowhere to go" (17). Her attitude to others is negative, and she has only "disdain" for the opinions of the majority (35, 25). She does not participate in the children's play except in an absentminded manner. She would accept the part of the wolf in playing "little red riding hood," but she would be reading *Time* magazine at the same time (30). She is by implication censored not only because she is preoccupied with the news, but also because she totally ignores the other participants in the game and displays no inclination to watch the children's performance. Her kisses are described as "business like." This is bad enough, but what is worse, she makes her children feel guilty because *she* was so deprived in her own youth.

The constant awareness of her mother's life prevents the daughter from enjoying herself fully. She could hardly bear her pleasure for guilt and "never managed to handle the guilt" (19, 20). It is not that the mother would lose her temper; on the contrary, she is proud that she does not lose her temper but rather just gets hurt. The narrator comments in a parenthesis: "But that was just it" (38). The implication is that "mother," instead of losing her temper, makes everybody around her suffer her displeasure (38). The narrator qualifies any potentially positive feature in the mental make-up of this character with phrases such as "as I knew she would" and "in the way she had" (24, 62). The author comes to realize that her first section has been almost exclusively devoted to this character, so in its last paragraph we find this ambiguous explanation: "Even as we grew up, my mother could not help imposing herself between her children and whatever it was they might take it in mind to reach out for in the world" (39).

Let me repeat that in enumerating these characteristics of a character from *One Writer's Beginnings,* I am not at all interested in the real life of Mrs. Welty or that of any other character in the book. My interest is not in whether *One Writer's Beginnings* is true to life. Statements such as "that is not the way it was" or "that is terribly unfair to Mrs. Welty" are totally irrelevant for my attempt to read the book as pure fiction. When we consider the number of times critics have read pure fiction as autobiography, I feel justified in ignoring Mrs. Welty's real story in my attempt to see her as the creation of the novelist's secondary imagination. I have no interest whatsoever in evaluating the ethics of anybody, but only in the characteristics of the main characters *as they are described* in the text.

The character of "my mother" in *One Writer's Beginnings* is always prepared "to challenge the world," not only for herself but also in defense of her children. Unfortunately, she sees the world as being in constant opposition to her, even to the point that the "road always became her adversary," as the narrator informs us. An instance of dialogue between husband and wife reveals how they see each other; the exchange becomes a characterization which sounds definitive:

"You're such an optimist, dear," she often said with a sigh, as she did now. . . .

"You're a good deal of a pessimist, sweetheart."

"I certainly *am*." (45)

One Writer's Beginnings is finally not so much an autobiography, but more of a postmodern narrative analyzing "my mother's component parts" (56). It is hard not to be fascinated by a character who is proud to be a pessimist, almost never gives in to her pleasure, finds it impossible to forgive, cannot be consoled, always blames herself, and "would remember" only the worst from her past (46–49). The explanations in the narrative for this extraordinary behavior are that she grew up in West Virginia, that mentally she always remained there, and that she lost her first baby boy (whom Eudora was supposed to replace) (53, 54, 17). There is no explanation why this character is allowed so much space. Even on the few pages, such as the opening of the third part, where she is not mentioned, she is there, as an absent presence.

The obvious difficulty for the fiction writer as biographer is to combine the literal transcription of her life with her accustomed creative freedom of the imagination—in short, how to write autobiography as fiction without actually making it fiction. "We just don't know all the elements that went into the brew that made us up, and consequently, when we start explaining," Madison Jones writes, "a good part of the explanation is likely to be supplied by imagination instead of by memory."[5] The art of autobiography can in this way be seen as a means for a writer to go back in time through memory *and* imagination in order to recover what has been lost. Welty's autobiography is fictional not only in form. When everything is seen from the present, the Welty remembering is, of course, different from the young Welty remembered. She writes of another person in another time, which leaves ample space for her imagination to fictionalize the memoir.

By remembering and through the act of writing it, call it fiction or autobiography, Welty hopes to be able to understand, alleviate, and perhaps preserve her memories against the diminishment of time. As Welty defines it on the last page of the book: "The memory is a living thing—it too is in transit. But during its moment, all that is remembered joins, and lives—the old and the young, the past and the present, the living and the dead" (104). For Welty memory is the very basis of identity. Her need is, of course, to understand, to be liberated from, and to be enriched by her family history and the origin of her identity. Toward this end she tells it, as she believes it was. Finally, *One Writer's Beginnings* is not a private biography; it is a fictionalized memoir that always remains personal. We have to accept that, like all autobiographers, Welty is mostly an unreliable informant about her life, and fully as imaginative in compensating and distorting as any other writer of postmodern fiction.

The autobiographer's intention of telling "the truth" may differ rather obviously from the intention of the fiction writer, but they are both engaged in asking questions of how we can invest our world with comprehensible life. The good autobiography is also an attempt to probe the depths of the human condition, which matters more than any historical accuracy. It is Eudora Welty's preoccupation with the human condition that gives *One Writer's Beginnings* a place in world literature.

Notes

1. Carolyn G. Heilbrun, *Writing a Woman's Life* (New York: Norton, 1988), p. 13.

2. V. S. Pritchett, "Autobiography," *Sewanee Review* 13 (January–March 1995): 15.

3. James Olney, "Autobiographical Traditions: Black and White," in *Located Lives: Place and Idea in Southern Autobiography,* ed. J. Bill Berry (Athens: University of Georgia Press, 1990), p. 72.

4. Sally Wollf, "Eudora Welty's Autobiographical Duet," in *Located Lives,* p. 80.

5. Madison Jones, "The Impulse to Fiction," *Southern Humanities Review* 14 (Summer 1980): 211.

The Construction of Confluence

The Female South and Eudora Welty's Art
Peggy Whitman Prenshaw

In the headnote that opens *One Writer's Beginnings* Eudora Welty describes her parents on a typical morning in her early childhood. Her father is shaving, preparing to leave the house for work, and her mother is frying bacon in the kitchen. Initiating what will shortly become a duet, her father begins to whistle a tune that Welty recognizes as "The Merry Widow," and her mother, who tries to whistle, responds by humming her part. Welty thus depicts her introduction to the world as an act of listening, an act of unmediated absorption of the sensual experience surrounding her. This experience is preeminently and intricately related to the domestic household, the world of her mother. Writing in her midseventies, Welty delineates a girl child who apprehends the worlds of father and mother. She takes delight in both worlds, acknowledging the powerful models these gave her, furnishing the imagination of the artist she would become. At the beginning of the autobiography, however, Welty explicitly links the father with what is culturally marked as "work," as well as with writing. He leaves the domestic hearth for his job as an insurance executive, and he originates tunes—a kind of paradigm for the writing career Welty will herself pursue. With her new walking shoes, she is a father's daughter, outsetting.

The inescapable association of authorship with male power in modern Western culture is a matter of continuing moment, a subject widely analyzed but hardly exhausted by numerous intellectual historians writing in recent years. Specific Southern manifestations of female authorial anxiety have also been subjected to wide-ranging study by such critics as Anne Goodwyn Jones, Lucinda MacKethan, Louise Hutchings Westling, and others, including many represented in this volume.[1] Ruth Weston, for example, discerningly analyzes the constraints acting upon Welty and other

Southern contemporaries, whom Weston shows as drawing upon a Gothic tradition to mediate anxieties and offer patterns of female agency and heroism.[2]

For Eudora Welty, who was clearly aware of the identification of "male" with "author," one sustaining strategy for allaying or slaying the monster of self-doubt seems to have been the familiar habit of mind of identifying ambition and separate selfhood as the emotional and intellectual inheritance from the father, an inheritance she depicts in *One Writer's Beginnings* as wholly legitimate and natural for her. Importantly for her own development, she associates the act of writing and of "journeying" with her father, whereas she always connects reading and the passionate love of books and storytelling with her mother. To the extent that her father did read, it was for information, to equip him to act upon the world. By contrast, her mother's reading of fiction is described as an act of passion, a show of love and independence, though the independence is voluntarily surrendered to the text: "she sank as a hedonist into novels. She read Dickens in the spirit in which she would have eloped with him" (*OWB*, 6–7).

Welty comments that it was her mother who always offered support for her ambition to be a writer; it was her father who bought her the typewriter she took with her to the University of Wisconsin. In the first section of the autobiography, Welty remembers, too, the trips she made in childhood with her brothers to her father's office, where he let them "peck at the typewriter." What they wrote on these occasions were letters to their mother, including one by the youngest, Walter, that Chestina Welty kept: "Dear Mrs. C. W. Welty. I think you know me. I think you like me." Throughout *One Writer's Beginnings* Welty explicitly associates the enterprise of journeying away from home and mother with the model of the father and with her own writing career. Time and again she would write to mother, who waited at home for her message. Welty observes, "I knew this was how she must have waited when my father had left on one of his business trips, and I thought I could guess how he, the train lover, the trip lover, must have felt too while he remained away." Welty records the "torment and guilt" she felt, "being the loved one gone," and yet, her joy, she knew, lay at a distance from home, lay in the land of publishers, editors, writers. Her "joy was connected with writing," and, despite her mother's enthusiasm for Welty's effort to become a writer, one unavoidably concludes that the actual enterprise of writing led to the most important and enduring instance in which Welty's bliss necessarily implied her "mother's deprivation or sacrifice" (*OWB*, 34, 94, 19).

In familiar patterns that many feminist critics have analyzed over the past several decades, Welty thus genders writing and art making as aligned importantly, though certainly not exclusively, with the masculine. The cost to the female writer of assuming such authority presents great risk, as Welty argues in the closing pages of *One Writer's Beginnings,* and courage is required if one is not to be undone by Medusa-like self-images that arise from a masculinist culture's perspective and transform the female artist into an unnatural monster. Danièle Pitavy-Souques's analysis of Medusa figures and Peter Schmidt's study of sibyls in Welty's fiction are helpful to an understanding of the ways such figures take shape and enact their damage in such a culture,[3] although Rebecca Mark's demurral on this point, i.e., the medusan and sibylline signification in Welty's fiction, provides a caution against such readings, which she sees as falsely demonizing the Medusa. Mark gives a persuasive interpretation of the interrelation and interdependence of the three phases of the female Gorgon figure in *The Golden Apples,* arguing that Welty not only writes a sweeping revision of "the Western myth of the literary hero in all his manifestations," but imaginatively does so by reinstating the integrity of the thrice-faced Gorgon and, indeed imaginatively reinstating thereby, the integrity and original energy of the cosmos.[4] I take Mark's point, but it seems to me that Schmidt and many other critics have in fact long been moving in the same general direction, finding and discussing various oppositions and dualities in Welty's fiction as a way of responding to her revisionary transformations of her culture's conventions.[5]

While acknowledging Welty's decentering of the culture's masculinist assumptions about authorship in her fiction, I nonetheless read in her nonfiction prose and interviews an explicit association of writing and maleness linked, as I have suggested, with her father. Furthermore, and especially interesting here, is the way in which this association also extends through the father to his native North. In Welty's cultural imagination, authorship is attached not only to gender but to region. Although Welty unhesitatingly recognizes the literary mastery of such fellow Southerners as William Faulkner, her reflections on her own psychic makeup in *One Writer's Beginnings* suggest that the singleness of mind and purposive action that she associates with her father and with the psychological makeup of the creative artist, she also associates with the North.[6] The characterization of the North as practical, progressive, and logical, and of the South as fanciful and imaginative reflects a long-running, even stereotypical, psychic drama of the American mind. When interviewer John Griffin Jones asked about her perceptions of Southern life, given "the fact that your mother and father weren't from the Deep South," she replied that her mother "considered herself a Southerner of the first water." She continued, "I think something to do with the Civil War and anti-slavery was why they moved to West Virginia. They set their slaves free—at least on one side; I don't know about the other—and went to West Virginia where there was no slavery. They were Methodist preachers, the men; one was a Baptist preacher. They went over there out of a sense of bringing up their family in West Virginia. My mother was a Southerner and a Democrat. My father was a Yankee and a Republican. They were very different in everything (C, 320–21).

In a 1986 BBC film documentary, Welty again makes a point of the confluent regional alliances that shaped her background. She narrates the story that brought her family to Mississippi, noting that her father offered his bride the choice of moving to upstate New York or Jackson, and that her mother made the choice of the South.[7] Significantly, in the John Griffin Jones interview, however, we see in Welty's portrait of her mother's Southern family an important revision of the plantation, slave-holding South; it is, rather, a South of preachers and teachers. For Welty, clearly, there are multiple Souths.

Although Welty repeatedly describes herself as psychically the daughter of both her mother and father, she was nonetheless a child of her time and place, and the experience that she knew most immediately growing up in Jackson, Mississippi, was the domestic life of the maternal world. Life at the roots, life known from the inside, life as emotion and feeling and intimate experience—this is experience chiefly associated with the home and hearth, with her mother, the Southerner. I suspect it was fortuitous for Welty that her family circumstance so closely matched the configuration of North-South relationships that were popularly, even stereotypically, imaged in the late nineteenth and early twentieth centuries. In the view of Northerners, at least, the public sphere of the white male had been submitted to the ultimate testing of physical might and courage in the Civil War, and the Northern male had proved the victor. Indeed, as Nina Silber has recently shown in *The Romance of Reunion,* a reiterated pattern in the popular culture of the later nineteenth century reveals a masculinized North and a feminized South frequently matched in romance plots that served a rather explicit and transparent cultural purpose: the amelioration of the bitter sectionalism of the war years. The opposition between North and South came increasingly to be figured as a family dispute, or a dispute between romantic partners, one that could be resolved by a wedding. "This gendered view of reunion and of the South,"

Silber writes, "offered a comfortable and familiar rubric, emphasizing as it did traditional notions of domestic harmony, through which northerners could reunite with former enemies."[8]

Although Welty's culture would confront her with a rigid gendering of male and female spheres—the South of her youth embodying an especially recalcitrant late-Victorianism in this regard—she would encounter no discordant tension between her "family romance"—to use Freud's phrase naming developmental relationships among father, mother, and child—and the regional romance. In the regional pattern the Northern patriarch operates powerfully in the public world; the Southern lady rules with verve and passion in the home and heart. What was required for Welty was to inherit male power sufficiently to energize and authorize her separation from the maternal place-bound world. As she indicates in the titles of the final two sections of *One Writer's Beginnings,* such separation was requisite to her "learning to see" and "getting her distance," that is, requisite to *writing* the truth of the multiplicitous world embodied by the maternal, writing the mother, one might say. The consequence for Welty's fiction is a fully engaged concentration upon the female and feminine, as I have discussed in an earlier essay, and as Louise Westling, Ruth D. Weston, and many other Welty critics have also noted.[9] I am not suggesting a reductionist reading of Welty's writing as limited to the feminine world her culture defined and stipulated for women; to the contrary, I think her work points the reader to a radically revised interpretation of what *that* world consisted in. In Welty's mind, it was much more expansive than that the culture typed. She pointedly notes in the BBC interview, for example, that she was the "first born" and the lone female and thereby was "awarded" the finest and largest room in the house.

Ann Romines offers a particularly suggestive reading of Welty's reminiscence about her childhood journeys to the "little store" to purchase bread for her mother, a reminiscence that shows an exposure to the world much beyond a sheltered "girl's view." Romines writes, "The necessity and delicious terror of this daughter's separation from her fruitful, housebound mother are combined with a heavy sense that her mother's myth, with the loaf of bread, is in her hands. If she fails in her mission, domestic ritual will be disrupted, and her mother will be displaced, forced to 'march' into the antidomestic world of journeys and transactions—a world that the daughter herself finds powerfully seductive." The trips enact a pattern of escapes and returns to the mother, a cyclical pattern of "daughterly birth, return, and rebirth" that becomes, Romines notes, a "powerful motif in Welty's fiction."[10]

It may be true, as one commentator has asserted, that Welty, along with other female Southern writers, has not placed the "region" at the center of her imaginative vision.[11] What is central to her work, no more or less than to a male writer's, is the direct life experience she absorbed and reflected upon. It is, of course, a capricious abstraction of thinkers to generalize the experience of one's own sex as exhaustively commensurate with and uniquely defining of the region that one inhabits, particularly in a culture that sees and inculcates vivid sex-role distinctions, but it seems that to do so is nearly inevitable (for scholars and writers). For Southern white males, the arena for discovering and enacting one's manhood has long been the public sphere of politics, a sphere undercut, however, by the Civil War defeat. Subsequently, the driving question for such men was not How could God have let us lose the war?, but rather How could the war have been lost if "real men" had been fighting it? The lessons drawn from the question-asking have been many, including an ironic, burdensome sense of man's limits, according to C. Vann Woodward.[12] But the experience of white men does not map the whole terrain of the South.

For Southern white females of Welty's era, the South was *female,* a world of matriarchs and children, a world of busy dailiness, teeming, unruly, but ruled by the mothers. It was a world of weddings and deaths and births, of gardening and feeding and preserving. It is the world of Ellen Fairchild in *Delta Wedding,* Edna Earle Ponder in *The Ponder Heart,* Becky McKelva in *The Optimist's Daughter,* and Beulah Beecham Renfro in *Losing Battles.* I have described it elsewhere as a woman's world in which males had a place, vital roles to play, but finally were peripheral to its daily enactments.[13] It is the South recorded in a long tradition of fiction and autobiography by women writers. Shirley Abbott, a generation younger than Welty, writes in *Womenfolks: Growing Up Down South* that she "grew up under the hegemony of a line of magnificent women—strong women, with an ancient pedigree, who adhered to a code of honor, who oversaw my conduct, who held (and still hold) me responsible for my actions." Like Welty, Abbott learned much of the wider world from her Yankee father, not from travel but from the books he shared with her. But her maternal ancestors in Arkansas reigned in her experience and imagination over corporeal, daily life, "representatives of a Southern feminine culture worth remembering." She continues: "They were independent almost from birth. They knew how to make do in harsh circumstances, and even in clement surroundings they maintained a stubborn equilibrium with their menfolks. To a degree that infuriated me and eventually drove me away from them, they gritted their teeth and were selfless, made sacrifices, and gave in. I am not like them. Yet I am of them, mindful of their legacy wherever I go."[14] A little later Abbott compares the extended family of women gathered around her aunt's table to members of a "corporate board," noting that "they could hardly display more intelligence and control."

It is not necessary to belabor evidence of the centrality of the domestic world in the lives of Southern girls and women of Welty's generation.[15] What I want to emphasize here is the way in which the direct impression of life that females in the South registered was affiliated with their concepts of the Southern region. No doubt it is true with Southern womanhood, as in all human societies, that idealized, unrealistic social roles and behavior have influenced the lives of the single individual, producing tensions and pain and internalized constraints for her. In the opening chapter of *Tomorrow Is Another Day,* Anne Goodwyn Jones gives a succinct and discerning discussion of the way in which Southern womanhood has been imaged in the service of a patriarchal culture and the way in which this complex image has "exerted through time tremendous power to define actual roles for Southern (perhaps all American) women of the white middle and upper classes." It is also true, of course, that Welty and many other Southern writers, the women especially, have well comprehended the diverse cultural business going on in the imaging of the Southern lady. They have also understood the complexity attending the creation of images and the inevitable duplicity enacted whenever one tries to "live" an image. Making a "marble statue live and move, and then to make it speak" is, after all, a "magician's trick," as Jones concludes.[16]

Still, I would argue that sculpting a marble statue is a considerable achievement, and to the extent that female writers have imaged women's experience to register their own direct knowledge of it and to make visible the powerful, passionate continuity of female lives, their literary efforts have seemed to me more nearly a celebration of women than a co-optation by the patriarchs.[17] Anne Jones makes the important point about the nineteenth- and early-twentieth-century women writers who are the subjects of her study (Augusta Jane Evans, Grace King, Kate Chopin, Mary Johnston, Ellen Glasgow, Frances Newman, and Margaret Mitchell) that the female authors' responses to the idea of Southern womanhood are an ambivalent meshing of idealized and realistic portrayals. One might observe that a mix of romance and realism also characterizes the fiction of the male writers of this period—Mark Twain, Stephen Crane, and William Faulkner, for example. The point may be self-evident and commonsensible, but it is one I think worth dwelling on, at least briefly.

The life refracted through the lens of fiction written by Southern women originates in their felt experience as women. It is no more, or less, derived from male-dominated images than is the culture at large. And for the woman writing, for the woman "inside" this experience, as for a man, there is, alas, no way to get outside one's own skin, albeit the imagination can assuage the limitation.

Welty links "regional" and "localized raw material of life" in her essay "Place in Fiction," sensing in the opprobrium attached to regional writing a condescension to the "regional." She writes, "'Regional' is an outsider's term; it has no meaning for the insider who is doing the writing, because as far as he knows he is simply writing about life" (*ES,* 132). It is far likelier that the opprobrium that Welty senses is a response to the world of female experience, a remote terrain for many male reviewers and critics and thereby thought deserving of the term "regional" to signify the exotic, the other, the inessential to one's own localized raw material of life.

"Place in Fiction" is one of Welty's early essays, initially offered as a lecture at Cambridge University and published in 1955. As she wrote it, she undoubtedly thought of Virginia Woolf's *A Room of One's Own* lectures. Welty approaches her subject in the opening paragraphs in an apologetic, defensive tone: "Place is one of the lesser angels that watch over the racing hand of fiction, perhaps the one that gazes benignly enough from off to one side, while others, like character, plot, symbolic meaning, and so on, are doing a good deal of wing-beating about her chair, and feeling, who in my eyes carries the crown, soars highest of them all and rightly relegates place into the shade" (*ES,* 116). The voice that presents "place" to us does so with teasing, ironic humor, personifying place as a heavenly female presence, though a "lesser angel," a comic one that might have been plucked from the environs of Pope's "The Rape of the Lock." With this modest disclaimer for her topic, she turns directly to the issue that interests her, namely, appropriate—and inappropriate—criteria for evaluating literary art.

Welty does not indict male traditions of socializing and intellectualizing as Woolf had. Rather, she makes an oblique and theoretical defense of her own work and circumstance as a Southern woman writer. She undertakes to deconstruct and then reconstruct "regionalism" as the term is applied to evaluations of fiction. What was and was not "regional" was a particularly lively issue in the early years of Welty's career. Both Ruth Vande Kieft and Michael Kreyling in early studies of her work address the onus of "regionalism" because they regard the term as a negative attribution.[18] In a recent study of Welty's "aesthetics of place," Jan Nordby Gretlund observes that Welty's "regionalism" is of a "subtle" nature, and he maintains that "she was never a social critic. . . ."[19]

Indeed, Welty's choice of the term "place" points up her intention from the outset to enlarge upon simplistic notions of "setting" or regional writing. What she ultimately means by "place" is the whole world of experience that a writer brings to her art—the "raw material of writing," "the achieved world of appearance," the full identity of the writer, that is, the writer's "worth." Substituting feminine for the masculine pronouns Welty employed in this 1950s essay, consider her explanation of a writer's "worth": "place is where [she] has [her] roots, place is where [she] stands; in [her] experience out of which [she] writes, it provides the base of reference; in [her] work, the point of view." Among writers who succeed in drawing upon what they directly know and realizing that experience in fiction are James, Chekhov, Emily Brontë, to begin her list. There are also stories "when the visibility is only partial or intermittent . . . as endangered as Eliza crossing the ice. Forty hounds of confusion are after it, the black waters of disbelief open up between its steps, and no matter which way it jumps it is bound to slip. Even if it has a little baby moral in its arms, it is more than likely a goner" (ES, 117, 120). Harriet Beecher Stowe does not fare so well with Welty, whose trope here builds upon an assumption of Stowe's inept knowledge and use of "place."

For Welty, the term "place" signifies home place, and a close reading of "Place in Fiction" reveals how closely she connects her own mother and her personality and sphere of power with both a generalized, literary conception of the term "place" and a more specific conception of "South." Welty writes that "fiction is all bound up in the local . . . *feelings* are bound up in place. The human mind is a mass of associations. . . ." One recalls that in *One Writer's Beginnings* Welty explicitly describes her mother as having a mind that was a "mass of associations" (OWB, 19). The art of writing, Welty continues, is "the one least likely to cut the cord that binds it to its source," whereas "music and dancing, while originating out of place—groves!—and perhaps invoking it still to minds pure or childlike, are no longer bound to dwell there" (ES, 118). Place furnishes an "abode" for the world of the novel, and place exerts "the most delicate control over character . . . by confining character, it defines it." "Place absorbs our earliest notice and attention, it bestows on us our original awareness. . . ." "Place heals the hurt, soothes the outrage, fills the terrible vacuum that . . . human beings make" (ES, 122, 128, 131). The explicit and buried metaphors in these descriptions of place (umbilical cord; sacred fertility groves; domestic habitation; nurturance that is constraining, sheltering, and directive; place as object of the child's earliest awareness, source of restorative life) all are directly associated with and invoke the image of the maternal.

The figure of artistic creation that Welty advances incorporates the great brimming world (place) and the unique imagination of the artist, which like a lamp casts interpreting light upon that world. This is, of course, the familiar paradigm of the Romantic artist, but for Welty there is a crucial difference. The artist is created by the world, linked lovingly to it, embraced, sheltered, not alienated, by it. The success of the artist is measured not by any sort of defiant struggle with the world but by her ability to create the world anew in her art and thereby to participate in the continuity of life. This conception is essentially imaged in the Psyche myth, in which the female psyche looks daringly upon the beloved so as to love more knowingly and deeply. In describing her world as "sheltered," Welty does no more than speak truly. But in directing her full imaginative vision upon this world, she is daring indeed.

How Welty manages to look upon her personal and regional experience as a Southern white woman with such candor and express her visioning with such equanimity raises interesting questions. In contrast to Carson McCullers and Flannery O'Connor, as Louise Westling observes, "she was able to be positive about the limited possibility for feminine life in the South."[20] An understanding of how and why she is so lies perhaps in Welty's identification of place just discussed. She was after bigger fish than swam in Southern waters, but fortuitously for her, her search was as suited to a specifically Southern species as to the ocean leviathan she pursued, e.g., the ancient mysteries of women, the continuity of mothers and daughters. When *Southern Review* editors Robert Penn Warren and Cleanth Brooks published her stories early in the 1940s, it is easy to imagine that they were responding not only to the literary artistry but to an invocation of the South that, with their Agrarian sympathies and affiliations, they honored. This was an elemental South, one that loomed larger and more anciently than the industrial New South. In it was manifest a mind or "temper," as Robert B. Heilman once wrote, that displayed a "sense of the concrete," "the elemental," "the ornamental," "the representative," and "the totality."[21] According to Richard Weaver in "Aspects of the Southern Philosophy," published in the 1953 *Southern Renascence,* "synthesis," the way of "religion and art," characterizes the Southern world view, whereas "analysis" and the way of "science and business" typify the North.[22] What the editors of the *Southern Review* may not have discerned, however, is how powerfully and essentially this "South" was a metaphor in Welty's imagination for "female."

One should emphasize that Welty's symbolization of the South is not one more version of the commodification of white womanhood as the South's Palladium, a flimsily romantic notion such as W. J. Cash attempted to expose in *The Mind of the South*. Hers is not a feminized South that is compensatory, arising from male anxiety such as Faulkner memorably embodies in *The Sound and the Fury*. The long-standing trope of South-as-woman, employed by generations of commentators, mostly male, doubtless gave Welty a rich word and image hoard to draw upon. The significant difference here is that Welty creates and uses the trope of the female South from a nativist point of view, the native land being "herland," the world of female experience.[23]

To return to the consideration of the equanimity that Welty brings to her artistic visioning, let me suggest that Welty was able to form from her own life experience a vision of herself as daughter and Southerner and creator-artist that was, both psychologically and aesthetically, satisfying, symmetrical, and confluent. We see the elements of the self she has invented with the tools of reflection and memory; these are revealed in her written texts. In these, many emblematic images help give an understanding of this "self," but an especially compelling and inclusive moment occurs in the final pages of *One Writer's Beginnings* in which Welty relates the incident of her father's death at age fifty-two of leukemia. The year was 1931; Welty was twenty-two. The passage occurs in a section in which Welty recalls her mother, explaining how "writing a story or novel is one way of discovering *sequence* in experience, or of stumbling upon cause and effect in the happenings of a writer's own life" (*OWB*, 90). What she tells then is how, in a transfusion meant to save his life, her mother's blood killed her father. Welty's account is reportorial, noncommittal: "How much was known about compatibility of blood types then, or about the procedure itself, I'm unable to say," she writes.

> I was present when it was done, my brothers were in school. Both my parents were lying on cots, my father had been brought in on one and my mother lay on the other. Then a tube was simply run from her arm to his. My father, I believe, was unconscious. My mother was looking at him. I could see her fervent face; there was no doubt as to what she was thinking. This time, *she* would save *his* life, as he'd saved hers so long ago, when she was dying of septicemia. What he'd done for her in giving her the champagne, she would be able to do for

him now in giving him her own blood. All at once his face turned dusky red all over. The doctor made a disparaging sound with his lips, the kind a woman knitting makes when she drops a stitch. What the doctor meant by it was that my father had died.

My mother never recovered emotionally. Though she lived for over thirty years more, and suffered other bitter losses, she never stopped blaming herself. She saw this as her failure to save his life. (*OWB*, 94–95)

The deeply etched memory that Welty reports, the attempt to transfuse blood from her mother to her father, is not a discovery of parents fused in sexual embrace but the witnessing of a life-destroying fusion. Like her mother, who tells the child Eudora not where babies come from, but of the death of her firstborn son, Welty tells the reader of death, not sexuality. But, of course, she is talking obliquely of sexuality, and, more broadly, of the desire and pain associated with materiality, the bodiness of life.

In this scene Welty occupies the position of observer, a position of "power," as she has discussed earlier in the autobiography. She looks upon a scene that we may infer would have been "unbearable" to her restrained father, the "optimist," who in this instance lies helplessly attached by cord to Welty's mother. In the mother's power lies the realm of death—and life. By means of her art, as protective as Perseus's shield, Welty is able to gaze upon this mortal scene, despite its nearly overwhelming intensity. Her gaze matches the power of the blood; both are equally "passionate," life filled. The daughter's gaze, recorded in the written text, indeed replicates the mother's power, continuing the cycle of generation. Like a new offspring, the daughter's seeing and telling the mother's story regenerates and transforms the mother. Making the story is a daring act, requiring the direct encounter with the mother, but it is finally an act of love, an internalization of the mother's legacy.

This drama forms the core of *The Optimist's Daughter*, in which the dying father causes the daughter at last to face the mother. At the conclusion of that novel it is not Becky's, the mother's, breadboard that Laurel Hand takes away from the encounter, but her sketchbook, as she heads north to Chicago to get on with her work as a designer. Emotionally anemic when she comes home to the South, Laurel has her passion for life restored through recourse to the mother. The wandering self, the spirit, the individualized daughter comes back to the mother place to feed and be fed. Her contribution to the reunion is *sight*, the ability to see and interpret the oracular wisdom of the mother. In "Place in Fiction" Welty personifies place as just such an oracle or sibyl: "From the dawn of man's imagination, place has enshrined the spirit; as soon as man stopped wandering and stood still and looked about him, he found a god in that place; and from then on that was where the god abided and spoke from if ever he spoke" (*ES*, 123).

Likewise, I read one of the centers of action in *Losing Battles* as Gloria's confrontation with the passionate, tragic intensity of Julia Mortimer (who reminds one of Becky McKelva) and a confronting of the fiercely communal, all-embracing family of Vaughn, Beechams, and Renfros, especially her mother-in-law, Beulah. Gloria is an orphan, probably a Sojourner, the daughter of Rachel. Like Fay and the Judge, Gloria claims she believes in the future—what is up ahead of us, she keeps insisting to Jack. But she also resembles Laurel as she listens, *hears,* internalizes Miss Julia's story— "It hurts," she says, as much in response to the account of Julia's anguished last days as to the needling she is getting from the repairing of her white organdy dress. Like Phil Hand, Jack instructs his wife in how to live and love, how to make things that work, and finally how to let go of the self.

In *Losing Battles* it is Vaughn, named for his maternal grandparents, as Laurel had been named in honor of her mother's beloved home, who holds to a vision of heroism, of separateness from the family. Vaughn sees the world as spectacle, to use Marion Montgomery's formulation, whereas it is Gloria who apprehends the limits of Julia Mortimer's pessimistic heroism and undergoes an initiation into the rites of self-sacrifice, of openness, and who begins to understand the risk and exposure of self that memory can enact.

When Welty turned from *Losing Battles* to write *The Optimist's Daughter,* I think it likely that she was working out the multiple aspects of the maternal in rather explicit ways in the figures of Becky and Fay, aspects that are figured in much greater complexity in *Losing Battles*. Peter Schmidt has elaborated the ways in which Welty suggests through her fiction the aspects of art that empower readers to "identify and change the cultural texts that confine them—to evolve from identifying with Medusa to identifying with a sibyl, from self-destructive rage and guilt to empowering acts of disguise and revision."[24] I would add that not only does Welty discern the duality of the Medusa and sibyl in the cultural raw material that furnishes the imagination; she discerns that she as well has a hand in creating them.

Certainly, one of the defining features of Eudora Welty's fiction is the iteration and reiteration of patterns of multivocality, as Rebecca Mark demonstrates in her study of *The Golden Apples*. Welty evinces an extraordinary degree of Keatsian negative capability, the capacity to resist an angry or irritable straining after resolution, the ability to understand and accept the conflicting, even contradictory nature of our own and others' being. Over the past fifty years of her writing career, many literary critics employing a variety of perspectives have addressed these patterns, which do clearly invite multiple and diverse interpretation. What I have been pursuing here is an understanding of Welty's equanimity, even delight, in the presence of an unstable signifier. And I have suggested that the synonymy, or synchronicity, of her inner experience and the outer world gave rise to a remarkable sense of self-definition for her, one might say a positionally continuous "fit" with the sexual, familial, and regional identities or subjectivities possible for her to imagine. These identities were expansive, comprising what has been culturally typed as masculinist (and modernist) attributes of separateness, "journeying," which she took to be her inheritance from her father, the Northerner who had chosen to make his life in the South. Even more multiplicitous was the identity available to her through her mother, the Southerner, an identity rendered through the symbolization of a maternal legacy that connects both mother and daughter with "place," terrestrial life, with the source of original energy.

Welty cherishes these tensions, recognizing them in her autobiographical writing as the constituents of her life. In her novels the imagined and formalized "confluence" of such tensions constitutes a central strain of her art, powerfully expressed in imagery that signifies a meeting point of separate parts of the self, that is, in images such as bridges, path crossings, and ferries, margins to be traversed, journeys from one realm of experience to another. There are also more-ominous and threatening markers of confluence, however, most notably in imagery associated with the site or sight of blood. In such imagery, she taps her deep roots of identity to imagine multiple transformations of reality.

In "A Memory," published in 1937, a work of short fiction that comes close to autobiography, the adult narrator describes a childhood memory of an appalling spectacle, a group of swimmers cavorting on the sandy beach of a public swimming lake in Jackson, Mississippi. The sight of the tanned and roughened group, some darting about, others lying in leggy confusion lumped in a pile, is as unsettling as another memory is sweetly comforting: her girlish love for one of her classmates, a boy whom she hardly knows but whom she has transformed through her dreaming into an object of love. Of direct encounters with him there have been two: a moment when her hand brushed his wrist on the stairway and a horrifying moment in the Latin class when her beloved "bent suddenly over and brought his handkerchief to his face." Then she saw "red—vermilion—blood flow over the handkerchief." It was, the narrator recalls, "a tremendous shock," "unforeseen, but at the same time dreaded" (CS, 76).

The narrator's childish notion of love was one of controlling, protecting order. She could not bear to think that her dream of love was subject to the vicissitudes of chance and messy mortality. What the child at the time does not fully comprehend, the mature narrator, however, does comprehend. The boy with the bleeding nose and the fleshy swimmers belong to the terrestrial world; they are beyond her protection, though they are subject to her discerning, interpreting eye. The memory that concludes the story is of the narrator's realization of her visioning power: "I remember continuing to lie there, squaring my vision with my hands, trying to think ahead to the time of my return to school in winter. I could imagine the boy I loved walking into a classroom, where I would watch him with this hour on the beach accompanying my recovered dream and added to my love. I could even foresee the way he would stare back, speechless and innocent, a medium-sized boy with blond hair, his unconscious eyes looking beyond me and out the window, solitary and unprotected" (CS, 80). In "A Memory" Welty writes of a significant threshold crossed by the narrator, a woman who recalls a childhood discovery of the irremediable but satisfying, revitalizing connectedness of love, blood, sexuality, hideous fleshy mortality and an onlooking, empathizing, participating artist—an artist whose stance and capacity for vision necessitate a separating distance.

Welty's metaphors of agency to express the process of creating a story are often derived from the domestic sphere of sewing or knitting. In "A Memory" the narrator recalls her beloved, and then, "like a needle going in and out" among her thoughts, she envisions the children running, the "upthrust oak trees," the adults lying prone and laughing on the water's edge—erotic images connecting her pubescent curiosity and desire with the rowdy, helter-skelter drama of procreation and death, a drama, one notes, that is vividly reminiscent of the feeding pigeons that are prominently associated with the maternal grandmother in The Optimist's Daughter and One Writer's Beginning. In those books, too, a revision and surer understanding of the pigeons, that is, of the vitality they represent and of the sympathetic, even grateful acceptance of the vitality, wait upon an adult narrator's sight. In stitching the fragments of memory together, the narrator creates sequence, plot, chronology. "I still would not care to say which was more real," the narrator reflects, "the dream I could make blossom at will, or the sight of the bathers. I am presenting them, you see, only as simultaneous" (*CS, 77*). The artist stitches her multiple fragments together to simulate simultaneity—domestic ritual is a central operating metaphor for artistic creativity here and elsewhere, as Ann Romines illustrates.[25] But as Danièle Pitavy-Souques argues in an earlier reading of "A Memory," the domestication of the world, the framing and ordering that is the modernist impulse designed to assuage the self's anxiety, forms only part of the girl's memory. There is also the image of death, signified by the swimmers, and there is the concluding spectacle of the devastated beach. Pitavy-Souques reads this conclusion as evidencing Welty's acknowledgment that the ordering/artist self can make only poor attempts at creating images. "It seems our lot in the end to accept the cleavage of the self, for what is the 'other' but the revelation of the non-identity of self to self."[26] Such a conclusion follows upon a reading of the artist's role as heroic, as an individual's unique confrontation with the world's resistance, but one may also find in this story an adult narrator who knows, even though the child remembered has not yet fully comprehended, that the beach will fill again and again. In "A Memory" the swimmers are equally images of life and death, as is the boy an embodiment of both beauty and horror. And all are simply and fully of the moment. One might say of "A Memory," as Rebecca Mark says of *The Golden Apples,* that the "degree of identification between artist and object collapses the duality of the subject/object split and allows for a much more fluid relationship between author and text."[27]

The tropes of stitching or of framing a scene expose the artifice of story-making and suggest the riskiness of it. Each stitch and each framed moment go forward in time, continuously susceptible to the "outside" world, the world of blood and bones, the sensible and material. The "big pattern" is forever contingent and in the process of being created by the stitcher-framer living within, part of and responsive to her world. Fusing these realities—the fields of time and blood—nearly overwhelms the child on the beach—the schoolgirl faints in response to the nosebleed, and she falls asleep in response to the disturbing, threatening swimmers. But she grows up to tell this story of an early prescience about the transformational, shape-shifting nature of her inner and outer worlds.

Like the narrator of "A Memory," Eudora Welty locates a pivotal moment of her own understanding of the complex relation between organic and word-made worlds at the site of her father's dying. In a nearly unbearable moment of seeing, she gazes upon the vitality and the limits of a powerful maternity. The sight/site marks the place of fiction for Welty, the location where she discovers a daughter's legacy and realizes the possibilities, through story-making, of continuing its generative power.

Notes

1. See Anne Goodwyn Jones, *Tomorrow Is Another Day* (Baton Rouge: Louisiana State University Press, 1981); Lucinda MacKethan, *Daughters of Time: Creating Woman's Voice in Southern Story* (Athens: University of Georgia Press, 1990); and Louise Hutchings Westling, *Sacred Groves and Ravaged Gardens: The Fiction of Eudora Welty, Carson McCullers, and Flannery O'Connor* (Athens: University of Georgia Press, 1985).

2. Ruth D. Weston, *Gothic Traditions and Narrative Techniques in the Fiction of Eudora Welty* (Baton Rouge: Louisiana State University Press, 1994), pp. 133–72.

3. See Danièle Pitavy-Souques, *La Mort de Meduse: L'Art de la Nouvelle chez Eudora Welty* (Lyon: Presses Universitaires de Lyon, 1992); and Peter Schmidt, *The Heart of the Story: Eudora Welty's Short Fiction* (Jackson: University Press of Mississippi, 1991).

4. Rebecca Mark, *The Dragon's Blood: Feminist Intertextuality in Eudora Welty's* The Golden Apples (Jackson: University Press of Mississippi, 1994), pp. 4ff.

5. On dualities and patterns of opposition in Welty's fiction, see, for example, Merrill Maguire Skaggs, "Morgana's Apples and Pears," in *Eudora Welty: Critical Essays,* ed. Peggy Whitman Prenshaw (Jackson: University Press of Mississippi, 1979), pp. 220–41; and Susan V. Donaldson, "'Contradictors, Interferers, and Prevaricators': Opposing Modes of Discourse in Eudora Welty's *Losing Battles,*" in *Eudora Welty: Eye of the Storyteller,* ed. Dawn Trouard (Kent, Ohio: Kent State University Press, 1989), pp. 32–43.

6. Lewis P. Simpson discusses a related and parallel instance of regional identities in "Why Quentin Compson Went to Harvard," his epilogue to *Mind and the American Civil War* (Baton Rouge: Louisiana State University Press, 1989), pp. 96–105.

7. *A Writer's Beginnings,* dir. Patricia Wheatley, Omnibus Series, British Broadcasting Company, July 1987; first aired in the United States, 1988.

8. Nina Silber, *The Romance of Reunion: Northerners and the South, 1865–1900* (Chapel Hill: University of North Carolina Press, 1993), p. 10.

9. See Peggy Whitman Prenshaw, "Woman's World, Man's Place: The Fiction of Eudora Welty," in *Eudora Welty: A Form of Thanks,* ed. Louis Dollarhide and Ann J. Abadie (Jackson: University Press of Mississippi, 1979), pp. 46–77.

10. Ann Romines, *The Home Plot: Women, Writing and Domestic Ritual* (Amherst: University of Massachusetts Press, 1992), p. 193. See also Thomas

McHaney's discussion of cyclical patterns in *The Golden Apples,* "Falling into Cycles: *The Golden Apples,*" in *Eudora Welty: Eye of the Storyteller,* pp. 173–89.

11. See Richard King, *A Southern Renaissance: The Cultural Awakening of the American South* (New York: Oxford University Press, 1980), pp. 8–9; see rebuttals by Carol Manning, *With Ears Opening Like Morning Glories: Eudora Welty and the Love of Storytelling* (Westport, Conn.: Greenwood Press, 1994), pp. 71–ff.; and Westling, *Sacred Groves and Ravaged Gardens,* pp. 16–ff.

12. C. Vann Woodward, *The Burden of Southern History,* rev. ed. (Baton Rouge: Louisiana State University Press, 1968).

13. See Prenshaw, "Woman's World," pp. 46–77; see also Westling, *Sacred Groves,* pp. 65–93.

14. Shirley Abbott, *Womenfolks: Growing Up Down South* (New York: Ticknor & Fields, 1983), pp. 3–4, 18.

15. See, for example, the autobiography of Virginia Foster Durr, born in 1903, who vividly describes her female-centered childhood and adolescence in Alabama, *Outside the Magic Circle: The Autobiography of Virginia Foster Durr,* ed. Hollinger F. Barnard (Tuscaloosa: University of Alabama Press, 1985; rpt. ed.: Touchstone, 1987) pp. 22–ff.

16. Jones, *Tomorrow Is Another Day,* pp. 9, 362.

17. In "Southern Ladies and the Southern Literary Renaissance," I have argued that Southern women writers have as much celebrated the strength as exposed the limitations of the "Southern lady" myth, in *The Female Tradition in Southern Literature,* ed. Carol Manning (Urbana: University of Illinois Press, 1993), pp. 73–88.

18. See Ruth M. Vande Kieft, *Eudora Welty* (New York: Twayne, 1962), pp. 19ff. and *Eudora Welty, Revised Edition* (Boston: Twayne, 1987); also see Michael Kreyling, *Eudora Welty's Achievement of Order* (Jackson: University Press of Mississippi, 1980), pp. xvff.

19. Jan Nordby Gretlund, *Eudora Welty's Aesthetics of Place* (Columbia: University of South Carolina Press, 1997), pp. 32ff.

20. Westling, *Sacred Groves,* p. 55.

21. Robert B. Heilman, "The Southern Temper," in *Southern Renascence: The Literature of the Modern South,* eds. Louis D. Rubin Jr. and Robert D. Jacobs (Baltimore: Johns Hopkins University Press, 1953; rpt., 1965), pp. 3–13.

22. Richard M. Weaver, "Aspects of the Southern Philosophy," in *Southern Renascence: The Literature of the Modern South,* p. 15.

23. One might profitably investigate the relationship between the female sphere that I am discussing here as maternal and Southern and Myra Jehlen's formulation regarding the interior life of the protagonist of the English novel, which she argues is metaphorically female. See Jehlen, "Archimedes and the Paradox of Feminist Criticism," *Signs* 6 (Summer 1981): 600.

24. Schmidt, *The Heart of the Story,* p. 263.

25. Romines, *The Home Plot,* pp. 192ff.

26. Danièle Pitavy-Souques, "A Blazing Butterfly: The Modernity of Eudora Welty," in *Welty: A Life in Literature,* ed. Albert J. Devlin (Jackson: University Press of Mississippi, 1987), p. 124.

27. Peter Schmidt in *The Heart of the Story,* pp. 3ff., Rebecca Mark in *The Dragon's Blood,* pp. 4ff., and Ruth Weston in *Gothic Traditions and Narrative Techniques,* pp. 133–72 all offer lengthy discussions of Welty's critique of the artist figured as "heroic."

Index